Backspaces

Cold Hard Type series

Paradigm Shifts:
Typewritten Tales of Digital Collapse

Escapements:
Typewritten Tales from Post-Digital Worlds

Backspaces:
Typewritten Tales of Time Travel

Backspaces

Typewritten Tales of Time Travel

Edited by Richard Polt,
Frederic S. Durbin,
and Andrew V. McFeaters

Cincinnati
2020

Cold Hard Type III
Backspaces:
Typewritten Tales of Time Travel

Copyright 2020 by the individual contributors.

All rights reserved. This book or any portion thereof may not be reproduced or used in any manner whatsoever without the express written permission of the relevant authors or artists, except for the use of brief quotations in a book review.

"There are poems about paintings, but the paintings are lost," by Albert Goldbarth, is reproduced from The Now: Poems (University of Pittsburgh Press, 2019) by permission of the author.

ISBN 9798673652817

Loose Dog Press

Fostering the use of typewriters in the present and in the future through innovative and affordable printed books.

c/o Richard Polt
Xavier University
Department of Philosophy
3800 Victory Parkway
Cincinnati, OH 45207-4443 USA

loosedogpress.blogspot.com

For those who tell stories,
those who love stories,
and those who lead others to stories.
                    FSD

        For My Students
                AVM

    To the Science Fiction
    shelves of the Rockridge
    Public Library, Oakland,
    California, 1977
                    RP

Contents

Front cover photo
Frederic S. Durbin

Introduction
Richard Polt   1

Tip-Top Typewriter
N. E. Glenn   2

There are poems about paintings,
    but the paintings are lost
Albert Goldbarth   16

The Letter Writer
Clara Chow   17

Time Flies
Hannah Ricke   32

Homesick
Brandon Bledsoe   33

Terminus
E. R. Delafield   45

Marley
Frederic S. Durbin   55

Jumping, Coinciding, Seeking
Armando Warner   71

Rest for the Wicked
Shelley K. Davenport   73

Three Gardenias and a Box of Pens
Mathilda-Anne Florence   88

Retrocesso Dedé Assi	102
Consummation Daniel Gewertz	103
Lost for a Century Martyn V. Halm	118
Pretty Ricky Vincent Negron	133
Walking Backwards for the Rest of Your Days Bill Meissner	141
The Billiard Ball Chad Allen Harrison	143
Antikythera Mark Petersen	161
Footfalls Echo Andrew V. McFeaters	166
Clock Martha Lea	184
Everything Is, Unless it is Not Martha Lea	185
Time Keys Marni Scofidio	202
Treasureland Ewan Matheson	204
White Out Charles W. Ogg	217
The Spider Richard Polt	225

Muscle Memory Rachel Schnellinger-Bailey	240
Retrograde Crossing Erich J. Noack	242
Ghost Typist Joey Patrickt	256
Ghosting Denise Terriah	257
Unquiet Writers Matt Wixey	271
The Conservator from the Future Philip L. Simpson	286
About the Contributors	301

Back cover photo
Richard Polt

Introduction

Richard Polt

The inaugural volumes of the Cold Hard Type series brought delight, along with some goosebumps, to writers and readers as they pictured post-apocalyptic scenarios. Amid the medical and economic crises of 2020, perhaps the retro fantasies of Backspaces will bring some escapist relief.

We invited contributors to submit stories, poems, and art on the theme of traveling back to the heyday of typewriters. A typewriter had to play some role in every submission, and--as always in this series--the published texts have been typed on typewriters. No digital fonts allowed.

In these pages you'll find humor, romance, wish fulfillment, adventure, crime, paradox ... and a few goosebumps as well.

My thanks go to all the creative typewriter lovers who submitted their work to this project; to Frederic Durbin and Andrew McFeaters for their insightful and friendly editorial reflections; and to Linda M. Au for her excellent layout work.

Cincinnati, Ohio
Remington Noiseless no. 7

Tip-Top Typewriter

N.E. Glenn

"Dammit!"
Liam was at his workbench, the broken-off end of a spring clutched in his pliers. An instant before it had been a delicate whole--until he'd tried to reshape it. Crap.

He'd been working on the Underwood No. 5 since dinner, and it had gone smoothly until he discovered the ribbon wouldn't wind onto the right-side spool. That was two hours ago.

The clock showed 1 a.m. Liam decided to pack it in.

He thought about the spring as he cleaned up the dinner mess in the kitchen, left in his rush to start on the Underwood. It had been a crappy, chaotic day at work, and he'd looked forward to the relative quiet of typewriter repair. It was relaxing, pure problem solving without complication--unless something broke. What was that part called? He should know it by name. It would gnaw at him, keep him awake.

Liam went back to the basement, extracting a 1930s typewriter repair catalog from the shelf over the workbench.

He found the line drawing, identifying the part as a ribbon advance spring. He thought of the hours ahead, seeking a donor machine or making the spring from scratch. In 1930 it was a mere fifteen cents, plus twelve cents postage. If only it were still that simple.

He took the catalog upstairs, planning to scan and post the illustration online later. With luck, someone on the typewriter forums would have one.

He set the catalog on the rolltop desk in the living room, in the pooled light of the 1930s gooseneck lamp overlooking his Corona flattop. It looked like a set piece from a period film: <u>Late Nights at the Writer's Desk</u>.

Later, he couldn't explain what possessed him,

but Liam rolled a sheet into the typewriter and banged out a quick letter requesting the part. He typed a check for twenty-seven cents to complete the charade, signing it with an almost giddy flourish. He stamped the envelope and went to bed.

***

He was late. He'd slapped the snooze too many times, and there'd been traffic. The weekly status meeting started 20 minutes ago.

Liam spilled his backpack across his desk, pausing to grab a notebook and drop his bills in the Out basket hanging from the cubicle's fuzzy-carpeted wall.

He sneaked into the room, relieved to see no sign of the boss. Typical. His drunken harangue about lateness and deadlines at the year-end office party was workplace legend--but he himself was rarely in before 9:30, and seldom on time anyplace.

Liam slid into the seat next to Carole. "What'd I miss?"

"The usual. Another overblown forecast from Accounts, followed by excuses why they missed projections. And you can see His Lordship has yet to grace us with his presence."

Liam smiled. Three years ago he and Carole were paired up on an account, and had worked together ever since. She was droll, shared his pessimistic world view and fondness for history, and was the wittiest, cleverest person he knew, with writing talent he envied and admired.

She looked tired. He leaned in to whisper, caught a whiff of something cool and sweet--cucumbers and fruit, maybe. "Up late with the Beast?"

Like him, she'd fallen into copywriting as a mercenary stop-gap while she worked on her novel. He'd never seen it--she wouldn't even share the premise--but he knew it was good. She was too gifted for it to be less than amazing.

"Yeah. I got backed into a corner, thought I'd written my way out but it just went in a circle. So there's another 10 pages wasted." She winced. "You're looking a little tired and frayed yourself. Rough night?"

The boss walked in before Liam had a chance to

reply. And with a rustling of papers and the creak of pivoting chairs, everyone's focus shifted to the front of the room.

Carole wrote on the notepad between them, in her looping, left-handed scrawl: The a-hole's nearly 30 minutes late, no apology.

And his fly's down, Liam wrote. Wonder what he was doing? Liam grinned as he saw Carole crane her neck, looking to see if it was true.

He couldn't remember how they'd started with their shared notebook, a slim reporter's spiral-bound passed between them in meetings. This was the eighth one—Carole had the rest squirreled away, saying they were destined to become a true-life cautionary tale about agency life.

***

Stefan from accounts caught them on their way out. "So the client doesn't like the bus idea. They want something else."

"Wait, what?" Carole whirled on Stefan. "Was there a client meeting?"

"Um, no," Stefan almost stammered. "But we had dinner last night, and it slipped out."

"Wait," Carole said. "You told the client about the concept before we presented it?"

Liam piled on: "For chrissakes, Stefan, you know better. It's a good concept. And you screwed it."

"Well, he asked about progress, and I had to throw him a bone." His eyes shifted back and forth, from Liam to Carole and back. "Besides, I thought you were going with the train, anyhow."

Carole's eyes blazed. "They're the same freakin' concept, you moron! It's just a different setting." She turned to Liam, eyes rolling, before firing back at Stefan. "Accounts doesn't pitch concepts. Creative does. You know that. Clients don't have the imagination to see it without a storyboard. That's why there's rules about this, you dumb fuckwit."

She stomped off.

Stefan's eyes followed Carole as she headed in the direction of the corner office. "Um, where's she going?"

"Crap. I'll head her off. But don't you do that again. Ever." Liam went after Carole.

He rounded the corner to find her pacing, shaking with rage. "That fucking idiot!"

"He's an asshat. But it's already done. We can't get it back.

"I know. And it was a good concept, too. Totally passes Stan's Mad Men test."

Liam laughed. "Yeah, it did."

He and Carole watched Mad Men together while on the phone. They both loved it—especially the 1960s clothes and sets—and sniped at everything the show got wrong about advertising. But in one episode they got it wonderfully, beautifully right. Stan, the art director, laments being sent back to the drawing board, crying out, "The client didn't like it and we did. In the end isn't that how we know it's good?"

Carole was the only woman whose moods Liam trusted himself to read correctly. She was mad, but not blindingly furious. "So what do you want to do, report him?"

She sighed. "I don't know. No matter what, we still get punished with extra work."

"Well, you scared him. He thinks you're headed for His Lordship's. Probably afraid he'll be shit-canned as an example. This is the kinda thing that loses accounts."

"Maybe that's punishment enough. I don't want to get anyone fired—they'd only replace him with another jackass, anyhow." She leaned back against the wall, crossing her arms. "It was a good concept, but it wasn't brilliant. Not like Clio brilliant—and it should be."

The Clio—advertising's version of an Emmy or Oscar—was Carole's fixation. Copywriting was a tough, competitive racket, still very much the testosterone-rich world of Mad Men. And while she reveled in the notoriety of being the company's only female copywriter—the only woman in the creative department, actually—Carole wanted that Clio. Nobody at the company had one, and she wanted to be the first. She thought she was good enough, and Liam knew she was.

"So," he said. "New concept time?"

"Yeah. I might have something to start from.

Grab the file off my desk, snag a conference room. I need a reload." She brandished her empty mug like a panhandler and walked toward the elevators, heading for the Starbucks in the building lobby while calling over her shoulder, "Try for that one near the snack machines—we're gonna need chocolate."

***

The package arrived Friday afternoon. He'd been at lunch with Carole, and returned to find it on his desk.

It was a box about the size of a baseball, enclosed by a clear plastic bag bearing the Postal Service logo. He tore the plastic and shook the box out onto his desk. It was tied with twine, and when he cut the string and opened the flap he found, wrapped in oiled brown paper, a brand new ribbon advance spring, shiny and bright.

What. The. Fuck?

He glanced around, expecting a hidden camera, someone spying on him over cubicle walls.

Liam looked at the impossible object in his hand, set it down.

He picked up the box, made of gray pasteboard like the backing on a notepad, its edges abraded to fuzziness. Inside was a folded note, a half-size sheet of age-crisped, yellowed onionskin: "Thank you for your purchase. We look forward to serving your needs in the future." And printed across the bottom, beneath the typewritten message: "Tip-Top Typewriter Supply - Timely Delivery Guaranteed."

"Hey Carole?" he said, directing his voice at her cubicle.

"Yeah?"

"Could you come over here please?"

He heard her chair pushed back, the creak of the cubicle wall as she stepped onto her desk. Her head and hands popped into view above the partition. "What's up, buttercup?"

"Do you know anything about this?" He held the box up, studying her expression.

"Ooh, is that our Christmas bonus? I hope it's better than last year." She dropped out of sight, then reappeared holding a likeness of the corporate mascot, molded from that foam that was supposed to relieve stress when you squeezed it. A pencil speared through its head like an arrow. She gritted her teeth and gave its neck a vicious squeeze.

"No, seriously. Could you come in here please?"

Carole's smile faded as she read his face. "I'll be right there."

Liam heard the quick stride of her boots as she came around to his desk. "You really don't know anything about this?" He held the box up, pointing at the spring with his other hand.

"I don't. Really." She peered at the shiny metallic form. "What is that?"

"It's a typewriter part, like the one I broke Monday night."

"It looks new," Carole said, picking it up, fixing her gaze on it as she turned it over, before looking at him. "That's good, right?" She knew about Liam's typewriter fixation. Two birthdays ago, he'd gifted her an Olympia SM 3, which she treasured.

"It's fantastic. Literally." He handed her the note, watched her eyes dart across the page.

"So...you got this from one of those typewriter guys off the Internet?"

"See, that's the thing. I didn't. I got it by mail order. From a 1930s catalog."

Carole laughed. "Come on, really?" But she saw the alarm on his face. She sat on the edge of his desk, meeting his eyes. "So tell me, exactly, what happened."

"It's going to sound completely ridiculous. I guess I was a little punchy from staying up late." Liam related the story about breaking the spring, his intention to scan the catalog image and post it online. "I thought of all that work, how I might have to make the thing from scratch, and how easy it was back then when you could just order stuff, and I guess I typed up the order as a joke. I must've mailed it accidentally, sent it out with the bills. And now this showed up."

Carole listened, examining the note, turning it over to study the back. She held it aloft, looking for watermarks, then gestured at the box. "Can I see?" Liam handed it to her, and she saw its aged patina, the one bashed-in corner where it had been dropped.

"And it came in this?" She retrieved the Postal Service bag from the trash, smoothing the plastic to read its pre-printed message:

> Dear Postal Customer: The enclosed was found loose in the mail or damaged by mechanical processing equipment. We regret the inconvenience caused by this incident, and its delayed delivery. Please accept our sincere apologies.

She held the bag up. "Did you read this?"

Liam took the bag, scanned the message. "What are you saying, that this was lost in the mail since 1930?"

"Actually, it appears to be more like 1935. Look." She pointed at the postmark on the box. "It's Wednesday's date. But from 1935."

"This...this is nuts. How did my letter from Tuesday get to this place in 1935?"

"I have no idea. But...Occam's Razor," Carole said. "It's the simplest explanation."

"Yeah, if you ignore the rules of time and space."

They were both quiet for a moment, looking at the spring, the box. The evidence, as it were. But of what?

"Okay," Carole said. "So maybe it's a hoax for a Candid Camera reboot, or that Punk'd show with Ashton Kutcher. But is that the right part?"

"It looks like it. I'd have to try it to know for sure."

"Then I say keep it and use it. There's no reason not to. It's probably Star Trek Stan, or one of your other nerdy comic book friends trying to prank you. Just roll with it. We're on a deadline, so unless you figure out how to bend time and space for ourselves I say we get back to work now, puzzle this out later."

Liam looked from Carole to the bag in his hand, the spring on the desk, the box she held.

"Seriously," Carole said, taking the bag from him, rolling it up neatly and putting it in the box with the spring and the folded note. "We have three hours to go until the weekend, and we can't leave until we've submitted ten good headlines. I am not spending my Friday night here in this cubicle farm eating crappy takeout—I'll do that at home." She smiled, setting the box on Liam's backpack. "Do your heads, I'll do mine and we'll send the ten best to His Lordship. I'll help solve the Mystery of the Ancient Spring later. Promise."

***

They spent the weekend trying to trace the source of the advance spring—which fit perfectly—and came up empty.

It started over Friday dinner at a downtown restaurant near work, where they stayed until closing. It was a little fancy, and Carole's pick—someplace that wasn't going to kick them out after an hour. "We need somewhere quiet. We're gonna make some calls."

They made a list of potential pranksters. After eliminating people without technical chops or typewriter knowledge, it was a short list. Carole drew up an "interrogation script," and they started phoning people.

Liam remembered the feel of her leaning against him, listening in on the other earbud, her finger prompting him to the next question on the cue sheet where she'd arranged the queries in a flow chart. No one sounded even remotely suspicious.

"So it's not anyone you know," Carole said after the last call. "And it wasn't me—I knew nothing about this until you showed me that box."

Late Saturday morning Liam answered his door to find Carole standing on the stoop, her everyday backpack slung over one shoulder, a duffel bag at her feet. "What's with the bag?"

"I'm not leaving until we find answers." She picked up the duffel and marched inside.

It was early afternoon when Carole asked, "If you were going to live in the past, when would it be?" She'd commandeered the sofa, covering the coffee table with a combination of printouts and regional history books from the library, where she'd stopped on her way over.

"The 1930s," Liam replied, leaning back from his

desk.

"Even with the Depression?"

"Maybe? I mean, look at everything else—design, fashion, books, music. It was really an amazing time."

"But then you'd run into World War Two."

"Okay, that's a problem."

"I'd pick 1946," Carole said. "The Depression's over, the war's over, but the whole country's still united from the war effort. And women's fashion in the Forties was amazing. I mean, look at this." She turned her laptop to show Lauren Bacall in a stunning houndstooth suit, with Humphrey Bogart, in a promo shot from The Big Sleep. "Plus women finally got to wear pants. Hollywood was making some terrific movies, and Marilyn, Elvis, cars with fins and rock 'n roll are just around the corner."

"Okay, I'm convinced." Liam smiled.

Carole clicked her laptop, pulling up a map. "So the Tip-Top address is a parking structure now."

"Yeah, I saw that earlier."

"It's too bad Google Street View wasn't invented yet."

"Already on it. Come see."

Carole peered over his shoulder. On his laptop was a black-and-white photo, a long view down a street. Towards the end, grainy but distinct, was a raised sign bearing the Tip-Top Typewriter logo. "It's from the chamber of commerce archive, 1936." Liam tapped the Tip-Top storefront. "That's the catalog address."

Carole laid a hand on his shoulder, and he looked up to see her chewing her lip thoughtfully, squinting at the screen. "So what's this prove?"

"That it's a real place."

"I think we're doing this wrong," Carole said. "It's not like we're going to find a photo of someone boxing up your order. We already knew this was a real place—you have this." She tapped her finger on the catalog, on Liam's desk. "The mystery is where the part really came from. How did it get from then to now? Or how did your order get from now to then?"

"So we're doing this wrong."

"Yeah. We've been chasing the wrong thing."

Liam pushed back from the desk, following Carole to sit next to her on the couch. He felt her shift, snugging her thigh up to his, her warmth radiating through their jeans. She looked beautiful, in the slanting light from the window. He looked at the cascade of papers Carole had strewn across the coffee table—printouts from city tax records, old phone books and maps found online. "So what do we do now?"

"It's nearly three o'clock and I'm starving," she said, twisting her body to face him. Liam found his gaze drawn to the alarming way her t-shirt stretched across her chest. "I'd like something to eat. But first..." She leaned into him and pressed her lips to his.

***

"What time is it?"

Liam glanced at his bare wrist out of reflex, then craned his neck to look at the wind-up on his desk but couldn't, not with Carole lying on him. "Maybe five?" he ventured, judging by the dimming light from the window. "Can you see the desk clock?"

Carole pushed herself up from his chest, her hands warm on his bare skin. "Five-fifteen." She looked down into his face, smiling. "And we still haven't eaten." She lowered herself, snuggling into his shoulder. "That wasn't a complaint, by the way. I've been wanting this for ages. But I do need to eat."

Liam kissed her. "I've wanted this too. But you're my best friend and we work together. I couldn't risk it."

"I know. I decided you'd never do anything about it, so I had to." She drew her fingertips lightly up his arm, over his ribs.

"Maybe the best decision ever." He grinned. "When you showed up at the door this morning with your things, ready to spend the night, I thought I was dreaming."

"And I haven't even slept with you yet," Carole teased, sitting up. "Okay, seriously. Food." She kissed him aggressively, pulling at his lower lip with her teeth. "I need to eat before I get hangry and wreck this before we've done more than make out." She picked up her bra from the coffee table, smiling as he watched her wriggle into the straps.

"Don't worry, these stars will come out for you again." She scooped his t-shirt up off the floor and threw it at him.

***

Liam woke to the sound of cupboard doors banging open and shut. He padded softly to the kitchen, saw Carole on tiptoe peering into the cabinet over the sink in her t-shirt and panties. Her legs looked amazing. She turned and caught him gawking. "Where's the coffee? Must. Have. Coffee!"

"Cupboard under the espresso maker. Do you know how to run that thing?"

"Of course not. I was Googling it," she said, gesturing at her phone where it lay on the counter. "And if that failed I was coming to wake you like this." She stepped into his arms and kissed him. And kissed him again. "So where's my coffee already?"

***

"We know Tip-Top Typewriter is a real place. Or at least it was a real place," Carole said.

It was midmorning, and they were on the couch. "We know where it was," she continued. "What we need to figure out is when it is. And how you connected."

Liam peered into his laptop screen. "The bank shows the check was processed, but there's no date and no check image—it just says NA. So we don't know if this went through now, or it was cashed somehow in 1935, before I was born, much less opened this account. And no, that doesn't sound crazy at all."

Carole laughed. "What's crazy is how it took this to push us into kissing, when we both wanted it. But yeah, this time thing hurts my head. You know I hate time travel movies—they're all painfully twisted plots about what happens when you go back in time and accidentally kill Grandma. Or Hitler, but then not by accident."

"Well, except for Back to the Future."

"You mean the one where you go back in time and your horny teenage mom tries to get in your pants?" Carole stuck out her tongue. "That's an exception. Which doesn't extend to the sequels. Those were sucky."

"On that we agree." Liam clinked his coffee mug against Carole's. "So how do we figure this out?"

"I think we try ordering again. And we change it up a little to see what happens. You have more old typewriter catalogs, right?"

They typed up a couple of orders with Tip-Top—another from the 1930s catalog, plus one from the 1960s when Tip-Top was at a different address. They also ordered from other typewriter catalogs Liam had, from the 1920s to the 1970s. And then Carole pulled up a digitized copy of a 1940s Sears catalog and ordered a dress, with matching purse and shoes. "Because if this really works I'm not passing up a chance to own a brand new vintage outfit for twenty bucks."

**

On Monday, they returned from lunch to find a package on Liam's desk, a pasteboard cube tied with twine, just like the first one. And there was another beside it, sealed with brown paper tape. Both were from Tip-Top Typewriter, and arrived in those plastic bags from the Postal Service, with the printed apology for damage and delay. The tied box bore another 1935 postmark, the taped one was stamped in 1963.

Liam handed one box to Carole, and picked up the other. "Holy shit. It worked."

"That was so fast," Carole said. "Has today's mail even left the building yet?"

"I don't know. But it's time travel. I don't think it matters."

By week's end the other orders had come back, stamped "Return to Sender. No Forwarding Address." Sears—the only company still in business—returned Carole's check with a form letter dated two days ago saying the requested products were no longer available, but she could find similar items at sears.com.

"Well that's disappointing. I really wanted that dress," Carole deadpanned.

***

Carole came into his cubicle Friday afternoon. They'd made no further progress on the Tip-Top Typewriter mystery during the week, but found themselves suddenly, deeply engaged with each other. "I know it's the first Friday night since...you know," she said. "But I already had dinner plans with my old roommate. It's been ages since we've gotten together, and she just texted hinting at boyfriend trouble, so I think it's going to be a late night of commiseration and drinkage. I'll see you tomorrow?"

"Okay," Liam said, before brightening. "I have all those new typewriter parts to install, anyway." She ducked down and gave him a quietly passionate kiss. "Come say bye before you leave for the night."

***

It's Tuesday morning, and Carole, at her desk, obsessively thumbs her phone, hoping for a missed message. Again. She feels neurotic but can't help herself, pulling up her texts with Liam to find the last one she sent before work:

> So...I couldn't get you all weekend. I know you had typewriter plans Friday, and I had dinner with Becky, but I thought I would see you at least part of the weekend. And you didn't show for work yesterday. This doesn't feel like you. Color me officially worried.

She grabs notebook and pen, pauses, then picks up the reporter's notepad she shares with Liam, superstitiously hoping to summon some juju that will make him appear for the status meeting.

The meeting is unexpectedly quick. And disastrous. Their biggest client is moving to another agency, and most of them are being let go. Carole heads back to her cubicle in a daze, clutching a pink form. So termination slips really are pink.

A largish package is waiting on her desk, battered and aged with a Postal Service sticker bearing the now-familiar text about damage and delayed delivery. Inside, atop what looks like the dress she'd tried to order from the Sears catalog, is an envelope. She opens it to find a key, crisp edges freshly cut but patinated to a deep, dark brown, with a note:

> I know you really wanted this dress, and I wanted you to have it almost as much as I want to see you in it. I made the key to my place last week and meant to give it to you Saturday, but it turns out I can't come back, or at least I haven't figured it out yet. The good news is I'm in 1946. Surprise!
>
> Just in case something like this happened, I left details of what I was about to do in the leftmost pigeonhole in the rolltop, behind the typewriter. Maybe you can figure out how I got here, and a way to get me back.
>
> You were right. This really is the best time. There's so much optimism. The Tip-Top Typewriter guys are amazing. You can write to me through them...

Carole finishes the note, refolds it. She goes to reception, where someone has already delivered shrink-wrapped stacks of flattened file boxes. She takes two, folding one of them together in her cubicle like corrugated origami, and boxes up her things. Then goes to Liam's cubicle, assembles the second box and collects his personal items, including the pink slip on his chair. This is so unfair.

Impulsively, she picks up a 5"x8" index card and a fat black marker from Liam's desk. Screw this place.

She steps out of the building carrying the boxes, blinking in the daylight, and heads toward the street.

Setting the boxes down next to the curbside mailbox, Carole swivels her backpack around, and withdraws the impromptu postcard addressed to Tip-Top Typewriter. As it slides through the slot there's a flashing glimpse of the back, just two words in heavily inked strokes: I'm coming.

Olivetti Lettera 22

> There are poems about paintings,
> but the paintings are lost.
> - Guy Gavriel Kay

Albert Goldbarth

This is the way we know the sun at night,
when it's lost behind the rim of the world
—the moon reminds us. The moon is the sun
second-hand. So many of my poems exist
to commemorate the missing, some explicitly,
   but also
the ones where my father is fixing the snow chains
to the Chevy's tires, having scraped it out
of a ten-foot fall of December weather, like
   some eager
eighteenth-century archeologist hacking away
at Troy or Jericho; and my mother is contemplating
the mixture in her meat loaf pan as if
she's a pioneer woman surveying the waiting, patient
Great Plains; and the wall phone,
and the typewriter, and the mail box on the corner
have a currency that hums the air one-atom-thick
around them. Now they aren't here,
unless "here" is my words. There are statues of gods
from ancient Greece that we know of
only because of a play or a scrap of prose description
—cast that way, like a shadow, into the future
   we call
the present. And the animals that hibernate
   —the small ones,
deep in their winter nests—that still their
   interior beat
to almost nothing, to a forgotten painting,
around which they curl
their outside body, the poem, that keeps it alive.

IBM Wheelwriter 1000 by Lexmark

The Letter Writer

Clara Chow

Arriving in Singapore, she and her fellow passengers are ushered by polite, surgical-mask-wearing officials through secret corridors, whisked through an empty terminal and bussed to hotels to serve two-week quarantines.

On the bus, she bumps into an elderly gentleman with the curved white case in her hand. She apologizes. He smiles.

"Been a while since I saw one of those," he says, indicating the case.

The hotel is grand, white-washed, British colonial. Built in the 1920s, it served as General Post Office until 1996. Nice enough. Still, the thought of cooling her heels here for a fortnight, while the world of big pharma spins on - the coronavirus bringing the economy to its knees, boom times for drug guys - makes her want to cry. What had been a routine trip to Shanghai, to present her company's latest antibiotics to a hospital, have resulted in her wings clipped.

Checked into a suite, she makes a couple of calls to HQ in London. She is their woman in Asia, her fluency in Mandarin, Cantonese and Teochew putting clients at ease. They like her deference and quiet efficiency. The Shanghai meeting had culminated in a hotpot dinner with Dr. Shen and his team. It would have been rude not to join them.

Calls over, she flops on the bed and stares at the ceiling. She considers breaking out her stash of anti-depressants and sleeping pills, but decides against it. The bedside clock blinks: 17:00. Time to sneak to the pool. Slipping on a lilac caftan, she grabs some hotel stationery. Tucks the vintage white case under her arm and heads for the lift lobby.

The aqua lozenge beyond the French doors is deserted. Stretching out on a lounge chair, she opens the case. She had found the typewriter in a Xintiandi junk shop. A 1980s Olympia Traveller de Luxe in great condition. Plastic, light, streamlined. Not rare or valuable, but it works. For 70 yuan, about ten bucks, it was a deal she couldn't refuse. Maybe she will bash out her memoirs on it. Maybe while wearing a pink fur-trimmed nightgown a la Barbara Cartland. Maybe while lounging by the pool on a government-mandated quarantine.

She rolls creamy paper into the platen, enjoying the way the rollers "eat" the sheet. Something about this beige portable feels positively space-age to her. Never mind how many people declare its mechanism obsolete. This is time travel. Criss-crossing time zones, zooming past latitudes and longitudes. So many minute adjustments of one's body and mind.

The imposing hotel once faced a harbor and quays, before land reclamation hemmed it in with a four-lane highway and skyscrapers. Under a patio umbrella, Lily smiles with secret pleasure. Balancing the typewriter on her lap, she begins to type, her fingers tapping in staccato.

"Dear Howard," she begins. Stops. How does one compose a letter to someone who lets us down? She presses hard on the H key, causing the typebar to snag. Reaching into the segment, she tweaks the errant steel, sending it home into its basket. A sharp edge catches her finger. A single drop of blood wells up. Falls into the depths of the Olympia's metal guts. Like another trapped young woman before her - who pricked her finger on a spindle and descended into slumber for a hundred years - Lily sinks, for the first time in a long while, into non-drug-addled sleep.

*

She wakes because someone steps on her.
"Ouch!"
But the person who tripped over, then kicked her out of spite is long gone.

Uncurling herself from the fetal position, she sits up and rubs her eyes. Gone are the swimming pool and lounge chair. Instead, she is in a filthy five-foot way, dust and rubbish crusted in corners. Men in funny costumes hurry through the French doors.

"Qu bie de di fang shui, ah!" spits a man in round wire-rimmed glasses, a stack of Manila envelopes in his arms. Go somewhere else to sleep!

What the hell?

She finds she is still cradling the typewriter. The case has been kicked a few feet away. She rushes to retrieve it, dodging a few women who look like they belong in a period drama: red head-dresses, black samfoo, blue aprons. Why are the samsui women out in full force? Is it Chingay Parade already? Shouldn't the hotel post notices if filming or rehearsals are taking place?

Her confusion is complete when she heads for the French doors and sees neither the silk brocade armchairs in the lobby, nor the gift shop hawking teddy bears and orchid scarves. Instead, there is a row of marble counters, manned by attendants in suits despite the sweltering heat. No air-conditioning. Long ceiling fans turn lazily. The hall echoes with the hum of conversation; the thump-clank of stamps being cancelled.

People queue before the counters, clutching letters — mostly limp bamboo-paper missives with vertical lines of Chinese characters. The sort she has only ever seen in martial arts drama serials. Steel carts piled high with mail trundle by, pushed by clerks with Muslim prayer caps plastered neatly on their scalps. It's one thing to gussy up the exterior for a shoot, quite another to transform the entire interior. In one afternoon? How? How is she getting back to her room!?

She checks for hidden cameras and gag-show crew. Finding none, she barges into the large hall.

"I demand to see the general manager! The concierge! Somebody!"

Every face in the place turns to her in astonishment — this Chinese-looking woman wearing a sheer Arab outfit, brandishing an odd contraption. Speaking in... perfect English?

A hush settles over the post office, despite the busy period before closing. A man with a handlebar moustache and the jaundiced mien of an English civil servant too long in malaria-rife tropics emerges from a back room. He has a comb-over. A pocket watch dangles from his vest button. He lifts the wooden flap hinged to the counter, passes into the public area, and heads for her.

"You," he sneers. "Who allowed you to come in here and create a ruckus?"

"You must still be in character," says Lily. "I just want to go back to my room and rest. Let me take my bags and switch to a less insane hotel."

"Hotel? Room? I don't know how much opium you've smoked. This is the GPO! Not one of the unsavory establishments you and your... fresh-off-the-boat prostitute ilk are used to. Guards!"

"You can't speak to me like this." Lily is incredulous. "Racial and gender discrimination. I want to see the person in charge."

She looks at the blank Asian faces around her. Nobody seems to comprehend the exchange. Nobody backs her up. Unsafety in numbers.

A white couple breezes in behind her. The woman is clad in a short, fluttery bias-cut tunic, showing off long legs culminating in T-bar heels. Feathers sprout from a head band over her shiny bob. The man to whom she clings has a newspaper clamped under his elbow. Gothic font proclaims The Straits Times. Lily spots the date on the front page: March 13, 1929.

The man bows obsequiously to the couple, who speed to the front of the telegram line, before turning imperiously back to Lily.

"I'm the postmaster. The person in charge," he says. "Now, get out."

Two Sikh doormen materialize from the shadows and take Lily firmly by each arm. The typewriter crashes to the ground. Its cover is jolted open. Spools escape, unfurling ribbon. Looks of curiosity and contempt spear Lily.

"This is Singapore!" she screams, kicking like a deranged can-can girl. "We're a Republic. I have rights!"

"This," hisses the Postmaster, "is a Crown Colony!"

A second later, she is dumped unceremoniously in the street.

Dazed, Lily collects herself as rickshaw-pullers adroitly avoid her. For a moment, the drug saleswoman wonders if she has overdone it with the Zoloft or Lexapro on the plane. Is she experiencing a side effect? She has always listed those with levity in front of doctors, downplaying their severity.

"Gu niang," says someone, touching her shoulder. Miss, in Mandarin. "Are you okay?"

The slender girl in an elegant cheongsam is perhaps seventeen. Her calf-length dress has violets on a white jacquard background, a slit up to mid-thigh. A strand of pearls circles her throat. Her hair is set in careful waves. In her arms, ribbon piled hastily atop in a red-and-black explosion: the typewriter.

"You left this behind," adds the girl. "Mei shuai huai ba?" Not broken, I hope?

She helps Lily to her feet. Together, they weave between bullock carts transporting drinking water, to reach the pavement. On the other side, stone benches line the wharf. Lily realizes this is no film set. No producer can restore the waterfront.

Lighters and sampans jostle for space along the stone piers. Heady kerosene fumes rise from waters black and murky. Further out, larger steamships float still and rugged as salt-water alligators, next to red-sailed Chinese junks. The air is both quieter and louder than what Lily is used to. Shorn of the burr of motorcycles and car engines, it is filled with the thin reedy whirr of bicycle spokes and street hawkers' cries.

Lily sits, mouth open, coming to grips with this new, unexpected destination.

Well. At least I'm not under quarantine anymore.

Gradually, she becomes aware again of the concerned girl next to her and the typewriter on her lap. She reinserts its spools and tests its spacebar. The carriage still moves. A plastic part has broken off, the ribbon now turns in only one direction, but it is not bad. The thing, despite its lightweight shell, is hardier than she had thought.

"Mei shi," she says. It's fine.

The girl heaves a sigh of relief and grins. Perfect teeth. Her beauty hurts Lily to look at: she is so pure and radiant in this grimy situation. So comforting in this sudden dislocation of time.

"You can speak the foreigner's language," says the girl admiringly. Her Mandarin is crisp, but not that of a northerner. No supple rolling r's of a Beijing native. She sounds like someone from the southern provinces who has taken elocution lessons to iron out regional quirks. "Did you study in New York? London?"

How to explain to this woman in the past, in this present, that Lily was educated right here in Singapore? That English became its official working language after independence in 1965? How to describe a future in which many mainland Chinese people and those in the diaspora will be bilingual in the language of their fore-fathers as well as the global one of money-making and technological exchange?

"I taught myself," Lily finally says.

"They were too mean to you in there," says the girl. "I wish I could stand up for you, but I'm just a weak woman." She casts her eyes down.

Lily thinks: She should be an actress. Surgically-enhanced South Korean starlets cannot hold a candle to her.

"I'm Li Li," says Lily, using her Chinese name. "As in 'clever'. Not 'beautiful'."

"I'm Xiaohong."

They shake hands solemnly. Xiaohong removing her sheer gloves before touching cool skin to Lily's sweaty palm.

*

Xiaohong - her name means 'Little Red' - stays in a shophouse in Jalan Besar with a dozen other girls, all members of the Bright Moon Song and Dance Troupe. The troupe is on a three-month engagement at the New World Amusement Park. They perform nightly at the cabaret, where bossman-composer Li Jinhui's creations are wildly popular. Night after night, Xiaohong and her stage-sisters don sparkly costumes and sing medleys involving glittering cities, joyous springs and delicate birds flitting among fragrant flowers, while dancers whirl on the dance floor. Shidaiqu, or "songs of the era," inflected with American jazz and Peking opera and folk music, blended in Shanghai's pleasure parlors, is all the rage in the East. And the Chinese emigres of Singapore - or shi le po (the Mandarin homonym of its Malay name, combining the radicals for 'stone', 'joy' and 'hill') - are smitten.

The Bright Moon sing-song girls are paid well, their boss believing in compensating generously to retain talent. Like the modern practice of grooming K-pop girl groups, there are stringent rules: all members sleep in spartan quarters, on creaky cots or bedrolls spread on the floor. No dating, no staying out past curfew. There is only one bathroom in the shophouse, which makes for catfights some bleary mornings. But at such close quarters, the bonds of sisterhood forged are unbreakable. Mascara is exchanged - not modern tubes but a concoction of soot and starch paste. Money readily lent in lean times. Mahjong tiles clack in the hot afternoons, the radio competing with the energetic vocal exercises of Tao Tao, the lead diva, perched on the precarious zinc balcony beyond the charcoal-blackened kitchen.

Into this controlled chaos comes Lily and her typewriter, immediately embraced for her debonair boldness. Xiaohong, who was at the post office that day to seek a letter writer, realizes her new friend has only the flimsy clothes on her back and the click-clacking printing press to her name. She tugs Lily home with her. When offers do not work, she simply picks up the typewriter - now permanently separated from its case - and strides off until Lily gives chase.

In the three-story shophouse full of sing-song girls, Lily puts herself into a holding pattern. A quarantine of another sort. A spot-check might reveal her alien status and unknown origin. She has no papers, no cash, no family. Luckily, the Bright Moon Girls are familiar with countryside girls running away: from abusive fathers, arranged marriages, bondmaid contracts. They take her under their wings, harbor her, no questions asked. Xiaohong has taken a shine to her, and that is credential enough.

"Why don't you be a letter writer?" suggests Meixin, the youngest and savviest of the troupe. She draws her pout like Clara Bow, and spends a good chunk of her salary on tickets for the latest "talkies" at Cathay cinema on Handy Road. "Bring in some extra cash. Buy yourself - and us - some pretty things."

"Why not?" Lily asks herself.

The next day, she packs her typewriter in a basket, wrapped in one of Tao Tao's scarves. She dresses in sky-blue blouse with frog buttons and matching pants, borrowed from Xiaohong. Donning black cloth shoes, she runs to catch the bus to the General Post Office.

Outside the GPO, she sets up shop at a low wood table. Old men in ratty white singlets eye her and her typewriter with contempt. They mutter in Teochew and Cantonese about the loose woman plonking herself down in the central business district. She ignores them. Sniggering, they speculate that she is illiterate.

A Russian trader, disembarked from a cargo ship, approaches her. Laden with stolen tsarist treasure to sell at Change Alley, he speaks gruff Crimean-inflected English. She types up a bunch of bogus provenance certificates and invoices, earning herself a fistful of rubles and Straits Settlement coins. The old men stop laughing; dab long jealous ink streaks down their tongues with brushes, and turn their backs on her.

The customers keep coming. Nannies with young charges in tow; togged in starched lace, they rattle off long missives to their Nans back home. Ladies of hill station manors want carbon copies of Christmas news flaunting husbands and their promotions. Or grandiose thank-you notes (Lily thankful she still had ample hotel ivory notecards) for balls at social rivals' estates. British East India Company employees request love letters (extra 50 cents) or poems (£1 supplement) composed for their "local" mistresses. Lily takes all these jobs. She is the only one who can.

The Olympia is a novelty – unlike any clunky iron Imperial or Underwood the world has ever seen. Her fingers fly over the keys, more natural to her than handwriting. Even Old Wong, a few seats down Letter Writers' Row, who printed fortune slips with traditional Chinese woodcut type, cannot contain his curiosity about her efficient typer.

She sets up at dawn, before coolies begin carrying sacks of rice up and down gangplanks into godowns. The laborers come to her with their little jobs --

court appeal papers, translation of official documents, government contracts -- before their work day starts. At six in the evening, when the post office shutters its doors, she packs up for home.

The old, male literati-cartel come to accept her presence. They even buy her dumplings for lunch when she is too busy to step away from her table. One day, some troublemakers harass Lily, sweeping her typewriter off her workstation, scaring away her customers. The leader of the youths chucks her under the chin. She knees him in the balls. The other letter writers come to her aid, swinging long paperweights, flinging solid ink slabs, advancing with quill nibs to stab. The hoodlums flee.

The letter writers stare in dismay at the roughed-up typewriter, its cover cracked, keycaps fallen off, platen knobs detached. Its retractable metal paper rest is bent out of shape.

Lily tests the spacebar. The paper carriage is stuck.

"Aiyah! Rabbit spawn! They've killed your machine!"

"Don't worry, uncle." Lily rolls up her sleeves. She lifts the typewriter to peer at its innards. "Anyone have a screwdriver?"

A couple of hours later, she has reattached the parts and fixed the typewriter carriage. The elderly calligraphers come round to visit the "patient." They heave sighs of relief that it has not suffered lasting damage.

That night, she introduces Old Wong et al. to her Bright Moon sisters, treating them to tea (cheaper than alcohol) at New World. On stage, the girls dedicate a special number to the chivalrous calligraphers and beaming wordsmiths. Two unlikely families, twin clans, coming together. Lily, the bridge.

*

Some evenings, after calling it a day, the typist and her darling moneymaker - snug as a bun in its basket - light inland, leaving boats and beacons, for Victoria Concert Hall. Most nights, there are no performances. She sits on the stone steps, in twilight, listening to the tower clock chime the quarter-hour.

Under the deserted portico of the hall, she tries to call herself. Not her married name. Who she had been. Before.

"Lily Kan," she whispers.

Emboldened, she says it again: "Lily Kan."

She grasps the accordion grilles like a prisoner and yells into the echoing void:

"LILY KAN-AN-NN-N..."

She is not unhappy. The past is an imaginary homeland, familiar from history books yet a different kettle of fish in person: pungent smells, smoggy streets, bed bugs and flies. She always thought she was more at home in the past, hanging on to old things. Ink-jet printers, Blackberry devices, Palm Pilots, Nokia flip-phones, Diamond electric clocks which never told the right time. She had been stuck in nostalgia. Now, she is in 1929 - an entrepreneur! A real trooper among troupers, squatting over night-soil buckets and wading through thigh-high sewage during monsoon floods.

No, she isn't unhappy. She just feels estranged from herself - the self that had grown up in the future and remains its product. She misses Wi-Fi, shopping malls and Netflix. And, by god, she misses air-conditioning, hot water faucets and mattresses with plush tops and box springs.

But she also feels alive and purposeful, in a way she had not felt in her past, drug-marketing life.

"Lily Kan."

She had tried to be a good wife. Listening at the dinner table while her husband expounded on his documentary project. Chewing silently as he fielded calls from investors. When did she become the cardboard figure known as Mrs Howard Yeung?

When backing for his film fell apart, she bowed her head in their bedroom as he ranted how she didn't understand him or his art. She focused on the cool satin sheets against her palms, as he sobbed. The rough carpet under her soles, as he said he no longer loved her. She didn't move when he threw three sweaters into a duffel bag and left.

"Lily Kan!"

She is calling in earnest now. Barking the name, even. Three syllables passing into abstraction. Four consonants she relies on her mouth to form. Three vowels she expels from her throat on autopilot. Is she keening for the dearly beloved or calling a child into existence? She doesn't know.

Would she prefer being back in her own time? To serve out quarantine and go home? What magic method is there to fast-forward to the moment the cosmos snagged and dragged her through its fabric?

If she buys a ticket on a steamer now, she might survive the months-long journey to London. She could take a bus to Islington, where her apartment would stand 91 years later. She could endure at that spot, waiting for the man who would leave her to be born.

Hauling her typewriter from its basket - baby Moses of an object through the slipstream of dimensions - she begins typing:

Dear Lily Kan,
       I free you.
       Be yourself, wherever you may be.
               Love,
               LKY

She rips the note from the typewriter. Folds it into a paper airplane. Aims it for the darkness between the grilles. Tosses it into the black maw of the concert hall. Like the mail slot in their flat's door.

The clock chimes eleven. The Bright Moon Girls would be home by now, wafting around in Tao Tao's cigarette smoke, washing their underwear and stowing their sequined leotards. She ought to buy them a midnight snack: some fried chestnuts from the straw-hatted hawker with his enormous wok near the Padang. If she hurries, he might still be there.

Replacing the typewriter in its basket, she stands. Stretches.

Then she answers, clear as a bell:

"Oy! I'm here."

*

Days, then weeks, fly by. The months saunter out.

Xiaohong meets an American sailor on shore leave, a handsome corn-fed fellow. He leaves her his address in Des Moines. Asks her to write daily. At night, the beautiful teenager sits with her elbows on cracked stone table-top, reeling off dreams and lovelorn sentiments. Lily tries her best to translate into English what does not make her toes curl.

"Jin chi!" Lily scolds - modesty! - without conviction.

There is something heady about first love, even if someone else's. Lily cannot bear to level with her young friend: be realistic about a long-distance, cross-cultural relationship based on physical attraction! Still, Xiaohong is extraordinarily attractive. Even Lily finds herself drawn into the girl's spell. Her charisma affects men and women, animals, minerals and vegetables.

"Li Li jie jie," Xiaohong uses the term of endearment for sister. They lie under mosquito nets with silver dollar-sized holes. "I'm going to be a star, get rich, marry and have babies. In that order. But I will never forget you. Thank you for writing my letters and teaching me English. I'll pay you back when I become Mrs. Johnson."

"Forget about paying me back," Lily mutters. "Just let me go to sleep."

"I swear, I will make it. Don't you believe me?" Xiaohong scratches Lily's back. Long strokes with manicured nails. Relaxing.

"Believe. Believe. Now, please, go to sleep."

"I'll write songs for you. They'll be great hits. All Chinese-speaking people in the world will know the words. Listen, I already have the chorus..."

In the dark, as the other girls snore around them, Xiaohong sings softly, her alto voice fragile and sweet:

>Wo deng zhe ni hui lai/
>Wo deng zhe ni hui lai...
>
>I'll wait for you to return
>I'll wait for you to return.

Lily holds back tears. There is nothing in the world she wants more.

*

The day Xiaohong and the Bright Moon Girls leave Singapore to sail back to Shanghai, Lily sends them off.

Everyone sobs in a big huddle.

"Write to us!" They call to her, one after another, staggering backwards with their travelling cases. Reluctant to turn their backs on her.

"I will!" Lily waves like a maniac. "You know what I do for a living. If I don't, my surname is not Kan!"

Xiaohong stands on the steamer's deck. Lily watches until she is a speck.

Back at Letter Writers' Row, Lily is deflated, dejected on her bamboo stool. Old Wong, who babysits her typewriter, fishes it out from under his seat. He places it in front of her. Pats her on the shoulder and sighs.

*

"Girl! Can you fix a Royal?"

The postmaster pokes his head from the French doors, beckoning to Lily.

She exchanges glances with her neighbor, Uncle Li. He is reading a letter to a shirtless client, but pauses to mouth the words: I told him about you.

She wraps up the letter she is typing (a merry description of a debutante ball interrupted by a wild boar rampage), then follows the haughty postmaster into the hall, behind the counter, into the mailroom's bowels.

The Royal on his desk resembles a black shiny toad. Lily turns the heavy cast-iron contraption upside-down with effort. She inspects it and recognizes a snapped drawband.

"Look, I don't have YouTube now, although I did see a video once on fixing it," she says.

Utter confusion on the man's face.

"Do you have shoelace? Wire?" she asks.

He studies her with suspicion. "Fine," he finally says. "Don't touch anything else."

He leaves in search of materials. Hubbub from the post office rises as the door opens; subsides as it swings shut.

What a prick, she thinks, leaning back in the Chesterfield chair that smells of cologne and cigars.

She splays her fingers over the handsome glass keys of the Royal.

What a prick, the words bubble in her mind, as she reaches under the keys and -- well, be careful what you wish for -- pricks her finger on a rusty spring.

*

She comes to, to the beeping of a heart monitor. The whoosh of a machine helping her to breathe. Tubes are stuck in her throat.

Howard is slumped in the chair next to her. As she stirs in the bed, he springs forward. He takes her hand as she stares groggily at him. The hospital room swims.

"I got your letter," says her ex-husband. "I..."

What is there to say about that evening, when he went back to collect his mail?

He let himself into the dark flat. The letter lay patiently on the mat - its typeface distinctive. Analogue amid a bunch of bills and real-estate leaflets. As he picked it up, his phone rang.

Mr. Howard Yeung? You're still listed as emergency contact for Ms. Lily Kan? I'm calling to inform you she's in the Intensive Care Unit at Singapore General Hospital.

Fighting for her life halfway across the world.

In a daze, he slit open the envelope. Read the words she bashed out, broken but alive, on the steps of the concert hall. The sanguinity with which she freed herself from their co-dependence and old wounds.

And he is hit with the shock of being unable to do without her.

*

When the tubes come out, when she can speak again:

Voice hoarse from disuse, she asks him to open Shazam on his phone. As he plumps the pillows and pours her some water, she hums a melody into the mic. The snatch of song Xiaohong gave her, long ago.

The app identifies it immediately. Automatically cues it up on Spotify.

Lily always knew what it was; had recognized it from her childhood the very night she heard it. It played on the Rediffusion as her grandmother pottered about the kitchen, braising pork and steaming pomfret for dinner. It featured in a popular TV commercial for rice, which won advertising awards.

So, her friend had indeed become a mega-star. Her tumultuous life was well-known. A couple of failed love affairs, estranged children, swindled fortune. Things had not happened in the order she thought they were going to.

But Xiaohong had got one thing right - a fact fundamental as the stars shining through the skylight of that Jalan Besar shophouse: she had been unforgettable.

Olympia Traveller de Luxe

Hannah Ricke

Homesick

Brandon Bledsoe

    Mr. Smith stood in the living room of what was now his house. Despite being surrounded by the correct furnishings inside of familiar rooms, it all felt alien to him. At his feet were a duffle bag and a box. The bag contained items Smith was never without: several clean uniforms (now just clothes), a hygiene kit, a camera, a book, and a phone charger. The box was filled with the debris of a long career in the military. The objects formerly found on office walls and desks: coins, awards, plaques, certificates from schools, and the tired going-away gifts. The most recent--and final--addition was from his retirement. "...For a lifetime of service..." was engraved on the plaque. There were also photos of Smith in stages of his career from private to sergeant major. Smith had served thirty-two years. He was trying to figure out what to do now that his lifetime had stopped at fifty.
    Smith had joined the army at eighteen mostly to escape the town where he was now a homeowner. His career now had a period at the end of it, and he was standing exactly where he had started. Soberly, he believed that if he were lucky, he would be remembered occasionally by those he had served with and mentored along the way. Maybe they would quote him as they taught their soldiers. Perhaps he would be a good story told after a few drinks.
    Standing there, Smith could not remember why he had retired. He had thought it would be a good idea to come home when his grandmother became ill. Smith had wanted to spend some real time with her after all those years of coming home infrequently on leave. He had not made it. She had passed and Smith was alone.
    He had not thought he was running away. Smith had believed he was trying to "make his own way,"

as his grandfather would have said. He had not meant to serve as long as he had, either. Smith had thought that many people enlisted for a term of service, found themselves, and returned home. Instead he had become a professional soldier. His entire life had been the army. His apartments had just been spaces where he had slept and stored his belongings. They had not been homes. Eventually he had bought a 1962 Airstream trailer, lovingly restored it, and made it his home. The cameras, toys, and baseball junk said as much about their owner as family photos could have. His 1987 Chevrolet, also restored, and the trailer it pulled had received more care than many people gave to their marriage. It all seemed sad to him in that moment. Smith was represented by his possessions, he had given them the care he did not give to a family. The other sergeant majors had a family--people they went home to at night. They had brought their spouses to functions. Smith had attended those functions as a duty. His home life was books, vintage video games, and the Boston Red Sox.

Smith had assumed that this solitary existence would end naturally. He believed it was not who he was, that he would transition towards meeting all of those normal expectations in time. He never had. At the end of deployments he would come home on leave--same with holidays--and visit. That is all they had been, visits. Reflecting on this, Smith gave his assessment: "What a waste."

The house was filled with memories, good and bad. His grandfather had made great efforts to drive his family away. In the end he had moved to a mountain and lived in a large camper. Smith, his mother, and his grandmother had all remained in the house. His grandfather had died, alone on his mountain, from smoking, soon after Smith had enlisted. Smith's mother had died next, also from smoking. His grandmother had died last, and Smith was left with a house full of objects missing their owners. He thought bitterly of himself, the great collector. His collection had grown with the passing of the last person he loved.

Smith made two false starts at attempting to move into the house before realizing he did not want to. There were water and power connections for his trailer behind the corn field. His grandmother had the land cleared and the utilities put in for him years ago. She had wanted him to have his own space while he was home for visits. Smith had enjoyed parking his trailer near the field. He had picked vegetables with his grandmother there. The bean poles stood, water stained, but present. It made Smith recall the smell that tomato plants leave on the fingers. He could close his eyes and see the sunshine coming in through the bean leaves as he picked the ones he could reach.

His grandfather had taught him to drive around the corn field. He told Smith each time he hit a corn stalk to imagine he had hit a person. The dirt oval was still there, worn hard by the endless laps.

Smith preferred it out here. Here he could put off facing the haunted house. It was haunted by the feeling that he had let his life pass him by. He was unprepared for the oppressive silence of that space. Out here, running his fingers over the half-rotted bean poles, he could plan to plant beans that his grandmother would never help him pick.

He did not remember deciding to go into the house. Smith just found himself standing in front of the door to his room. His grandmother had piled the possessions that he had never taken with him into the room and left it. The bed was the same, but it was bare. The quilt that had covered it was on the bed in the trailer. The quilt had gone everywhere with him. His broken toys stood guard in the room. Smith was not surprised his grandmother had kept broken toys. Smith had not thrown them away after his grandfather had broken them. Smith had been a small child, and had never understood why, even though he had been drunk and angry, a grandfather had wanted to smash a child's toys. Smith had become protective of his possessions after that. It did not matter how small the item was; if it belonged to him, it was important.

Eventually Smith came to the case on the desk. He knew that inside of the case was one of the last things his grandfather would destroy before leaving. The typewriter was just as Smith remembered it, the carriage separate from the body. Smith had enjoyed writing stories, and his grandmother had surprised him one day with the yard-sale Smith-Corona. He remembered her fingers on the knob as she showed him how to feed in paper. He also remembered his grandfather's rage as he used the typewriter to break his grandmother's grandfather clock--won through selling Tupperware--into kindling. Smith had never typed a word not required of him, and he could not bring himself to touch the knob. He would later wonder if there were still bits of glass and wood inside of it.

As he stared at the cursed typewriter, the first tear came. Smith was starting to understand the truth. Each reenlistment was not just more time in the army. It had been a trade to avoid confronting that he did not know who he was. Smith did not want to deal with this knowledge. He gave into his nature. If his life was that of a collector, then he needed to replace his typewriter. It was a broken object he could do something about.

Purpose was Smith's drug. He had a mission, if not a clear idea of how to accomplish it. His town had to have an antique store. A search on his phone showed several antique stores with wares ranging from vintage junk to antebellum sofas with signs clearly warning off potential sitters. They all, however, had typewriters. Smith spent several hours between the stores, phone in hand, researching the typewriters available. He also tested them, much to the owners' annoyance. In the early evening he left with his prize. Smith now had his very own forest green Olympia SM-3.

The trip home halted his temporary high. On the right, just where it always had been, was the old North mall. Once a vibrant place of happiness for Smith, it was now a dead mall. Smith stood before the doors as he had countless times, but now they did not open. He would never again walk between his mother and grandmother as they shopped. There would be no more school clothes from the department store his great-grandmother had retired from. The mall had started to die before Smith had left home, the cancer of unused spaces growing until it closed.

It was in this mall that a pretty red-haired girl had kissed him in the photo booth...and he had almost kissed her back. Almost. He closed his eyes, and he could almost smell her hair. He could see her leaning in. His eyes stayed wide open, and he could hear the pop from the booth's flash. It illuminated her pale skin and made her hair flame red with each burst of light. Why had he not kissed her back? It had been the perfect moment, and he had not followed through. He did not know what had happened to the pictures. Smith opened his eyes. He did not want to see anymore.

Here was the parking lot, blacktop cracked and the paint fading away. Smith parked exactly where he liked to when he was younger. The windows of the abandoned properties were all covered with brown paper. The run-down Red Lobster, once a treat, was one more stone in the burial mound of this mall.

The owners of buildings that faced the street were making some income by renting out the fronts as advertising space. The Red Lobster had a sign from one of those youth mentoring places that read, "Be who you needed growing up." The words were accompanied by the image of a smiling man and a happy child.

Smith found the sign to be strangely beautiful and photographed it. While he worked, he could see the movie theater behind the restaurant and mall. His mind betrayed him again. Memories of the movies he had seen there came easily, but they were all movies he had seen alone. Smith the coward had imagined himself asking someone to go with him... and he had done nothing. Nothing at all, except to eat his popcorn alone. Smith had led troops to battle for his country, but he had only ever dreamed about taking someone to the movies. Even in his new uniform, pressed and perfect, the girl sipping her soda and looking at him, walking towards him...the shutter clicked. In the empty lot after the shutter was gone, Smith admitted for the first time, "I wish I could go back."

Smith stuck the newly printed photo in the corner of a window in his trailer. On the table was the new typewriter. Next to it sat a stack of fresh paper. Smith owned a computer, but this was not just about being able to type. This was an exorcism. Smith was fixing something which was broken. Smith placed his fingers on the keys and typed the words "If I could go back..." on the page. As the last slug fell back into place, Smith fell asleep.

Smith awoke the next morning still at his table. He was stiff, and the same nearly blank sheet of paper was still in the typewriter. He had passed out as if he had been drunk, despite not having a drink. His head was a bit fuzzy. Smith went to make coffee, but when he tried the sink no water came out. He resolved to tackle the plumbing after coffee, and went to the fridge for bottled water. He found the bottles of water, but they were warm. Now Smith noticed that the light had not come on when he opened the fridge door. "Great," Smith said to his empty trailer. The electricity was an easier fix. He could restore power temporarily by running the engine of his truck. Smith opened the door to the outside and froze. Woods. Trees. Those were what Smith saw rather than the open land that had been there.

The mind responds poorly to things that cannot be true, but that cannot be denied either. Smith felt like his thoughts were a pane of glass being hit with a hammer. He sat down on the ground and made himself breathe slowly. At some point he was able to go back inside and get dressed. His problem was going to need more than coffee to work out.

Dressed and determined to find a logical answer, Smith made his way into the trees that seemed to have sprung up around him during the night. His feet instinctively found the path he knew was there. When he was a boy the woods had been full of little trails, and Smith had known them all. The trails had disappeared when the woods had been cut down, just like the trees Smith was walking through.

As he emerged from the woods, Smith saw the corn. The field was full of tall corn stalks. The field had not been planted in decades, and there had definitely not been any corn there last night. His head ached as he reached to touch some of the white silks. Smith saw the old scarecrow made from a pair of his grandfather's worn-out overalls and a rusty Folger's can for a head. Smith had hated that scarecrow as a child. None of this was supposed to be here. He was starting to feel sick.

Smith started to run to the house. He turned a corner and there was the swing set. Yesterday it had been rusty junk that Smith planned to remove. Now they were whole, the plastic was not dry rotted, and the paint was bright yellow again. Smith's hands found the monkey bars they could not cross now, but had countless times. His gaze shifted to the small house next door to his. It had burned down while he was away, grass had been in its place last night. Not only was the house back, but there was a small white-haired woman in the window. She was watching Smith. Smith could feel the pounding in his head returning. He remembered the reclusive neighbor, and she was long dead.

Behind him, Smith heard a voice he knew very well. Ice formed on Smith's spine as he heard his grandfather ask, "You lost or something, mister?"

Dead. His grandfather was dead, and that could not be him speaking. Smith slowly turned around and stood gaping at his grandfather Robert. Smith was already shaken by the events of the morning, and it was not made any better by the shotgun his grandfather was pointing at him.

Before Smith could speak, his grandfather lowered the gun and said, with a look of deep disbelief, "Mark? Good god boy, is that you? Mark! We thought you were dead, son! Damn is it good to see you alive!"

His grandfather moved very suddenly and embraced Smith in a strong one-armed hug. The embrace was filled with real intensity that conveyed how much his grandfather was glad to see the person before him. Smith said nothing. He was happy to have not been shot. He was lost in the familiar scent,

Dial Gold soap and cigarette mixed with a bit of grease on the overalls. This was the smell of his grandfather, and Smith was enthralled by it. Complicated history aside, this was his grandfather hugging him, and Smith had missed him.

Smith was almost in tears. He had not realized what he would have given to see his grandfather again. His reverie was only broken by the sound of another dead person speaking from the porch. Smith heard his mother ask, "Dad, who are you out there hugging?" His mother's voice was younger, and still retained much more of its Appalachian accent than when he had last heard it. It was the mother of his childhood. Smith had loved that voice. His grandfather released him and turned to her, "Hun! He is back! Mark Harrison has come home!"

Smith turned away from them to collect himself, and noticed the balloons tied to the mailbox. He knew then what day it was. He was looking at a twenty-eight-year-old version of his mother. Her hair was still naturally blond, her skin still smooth. Years of smoking had not yet begun to show on her. Smith knew none of this could be real, but he also knew that if that was his mother standing there, then there would be a child somewhere nearby.

The boy came running out of the door. He was tall and skinny, and he did not step past his mother to meet the stranger. He had flour on his hands from helping his grandmother cook. The balloons told Smith it was the boy's eleventh birthday. The year was 1980, and it was the last birthday he had before his grandfather had left. Smith stared at his younger self, and tried not to panic.

His mother, young and beautiful, from a time when she had still tucked him in at night, was walking towards him. Smith could not move. He was held in her gaze. She stopped and looked him over. She examined his haircut, his beard, and the Airborne tattoo on his forearm.

"Mark? Is...is that you? Mark...it's been ten years. We all thought...you know, that you had died over there."

Mark Harrison. Smith had thought they were all confused before, but now the name came back to him.

Mark Harrison had been a friend of Smith's family. Harrison had gone to Vietnam the year before Smith was born. Mark Harrison had not had any family of his own before he left. Smith's family had been happy to have him around. He told them good-bye before he left for the war. Nothing--not a word-- ever came back about him. Smith's grandparents had told him the story, and they assumed that Harrison had died in the jungles of Vietnam. He would have been just one of many who became lost in the chaos of that war. Smith's mother had never said anything at all about it. Now they all thought Mark Harrison had come back.

Smith was sure that he was going insane. He had not spoken and must have been wearing a vacant expression because his grandfather asked, "Mark... you alright son?"

"I think I need a drink."

His grandfather nodded agreement. "I think you have earned one. Hell, we could all use one right now. Get your ass in the house boy! Jean will be damn glad to see you."

Inside the house Smith was handed a bottle of whiskey. He took a long pull and handed it back to his grandfather. Cold cans of Pabst Blue Ribbon were produced from the refrigerator. Smith knew that it was due to his grandfather that he had chosen this same brand of beer as his own when the time had come. He was happy to have it now. It did not clear his mind, but it did add a comforting warmth to his already fuzzy mind.

His family believing that he was Mark Harrison was not the strangest part of this day. He wanted another beer. His mother and grandfather were smoking, prompting his grandmother to come in and open windows.

As if it were the most natural thing in the world, she gave Smith a hug and asked if apple pie was still his favorite. It was. He loved his grandmother's apple pie. It had been a long time since he had tasted it. He had tried to make it himself, but the pie had not been the same.

She sat him down at the table with a large slice of pie and a jar of milk. He did not eat at first.

Smith stared at this woman who was happy with her creation, and with the boy she thought had come home. Smith took his first bite--and was lost in how wonderful it was. Smith felt that in a way, he had come home. He did not know if this was a dream, but if it was, it was a good dream.

He looked at his grandmother knowing that while she smiled, she was unhappy. Smith loved seeing his grandparents, but he knew that later his grandmother would find her freedom and hapiness. Smith would learn to love both of them as individuals. He was shaken from his reflections on the future when someone sat next to him. It was his younger self, timidly sitting down with his own pie and milk.

Smith remembered this nervous boy. He thought of him often, as if the boy still lived with Smith, and hid behind the soldier he had become. Without knowing he was going to do it, Smith leaned over and said, "Happy birthday."

Ever careful not to talk with his mouth full, the boy first swallowed his bite of pie, and then thanked Smith. His first words gave the boy confidence, and he asked in a rush, "Do you want to play Atari with me? I got _Adventure_ and _Wizard of Wor_ today!"

Smith smiled. He remembered this birthday. He still had that Atari 2600, and those games. He looked to his mother, and she gave a very slight nod to say that it was ok. Smith said, "I would love to play games with you."

Young Smith enjoyed his new game partner. His mother had tried to play before, but it was not until _Mario Bros_ came out for the Nintendo that she found a video game she enjoyed. She watched them from the couch as the two boys played together. Smith knew that this woman would work her whole life. She had been fired from her job as a hairdresser for being pregnant and unmarried. Life had left her little time to enjoy games.

The two Smiths zapped many pixelated enemies before the grown version showed off a bit on _Adventure_. Aside from the thieving bat showing up, Smith had no trouble showing the boy the Easter egg. The boy was deeply impressed, jumping up and down, asking if his mother had seen. Smith felt more pride for this moment than he did for any piece of tin he had been awarded.

Play stopped when his grandfather came in with peanut butter and grape jelly sandwiches, in a paper towel, the way Smith still had them now. As he ate, Smith had another beer with his grandfather. Smith knew that his grandfather's drinking would break this family apart--that this man's rage would destroy more than toys. Smith also knew that the boy would still love his grandfather, and after the old man got sober, Smith would visit him often.

Smith owned this house, and many of the objects he saw there now. They had always been there, but without the people he loved, the objects had no life. They were sentimental only as a link to the ghosts of their owners. The people had given life to this house. Family had made it all a home. Smith hoped that the house would no longer seem haunted to him. He ate the sandwich and knew he had gotten his wish. Smith understood that yesterday he would have given anything to do this one more time. To play golf, go for a walk, or sit around a campfire with these people, Smith knew he would have traded everything he had. He made sure to savor every bite of his sandwich.

Smith finished eating and made a decision. He asked the boy to wait for him while he went and got the boy's birthday gift. Young Smith said he would not move. Smith walked out of the house and was off the porch when his mother called from the door, "Will you come back? He will not care if there is not really a present, but he will be heartbroken if you do not come back."

Something fell into place for Smith. He asked her, "Have I ever done that to him?"

She said calmly, "No. Not to him."

Smith knew now. He knew who she thought he was-- who Mark Harrison had been. Smith could see what his mother had carried alone, and told her, "I will come back."

Sitting at the typewriter in his trailer, Smith wrote a note to himself.

"Kid, today you are eleven. You have a lot of

life ahead of you. Enjoy it. It gets rough sometimes, but there is much to do and to love. You will miss all of that if you spend your life only looking back. Take this typewriter, write stories, record your life. Just don't forget to have a life to tell it about. Take it from me kid...I have had a pretty good time of it. This is not just a typewriter. It is a time machine. With it, you will not forget. Kiss someone. Dance with that pretty German girl. Just remember, if you have to choose between living something and writing about it, you should live it every single time. Happy birthday kid."

    Leaving the note in the machine, Smith walked back and presented his gift to the boy. He was excited to show it to everyone--even his grandfather. Smith did not leave until after the boy went to bed. Slowly, he told each member of his family goodnight. He looked at his mother the longest. As an afterthought, he asked if he could take a picture with her. He had to go back to the trailer for his camera. Smith hurried back, and fumbled his way through loading the film. He wound it through the end frames, and with his finger on the shutter, said to himself, "I have to go back." The shutter clicked.

    Smith awoke still sitting at his table, holding his camera. His first clear thought was that he had not gotten his photo with his mother. He knew this was a stupid thought. It had all been a dream. He turned to the window. He would look out on his empty field, just to be sure it had been a dream. Tucked into the window corners he saw the photo from the mall, and an old typewritten note, folded and unfolded many times over the years. Smith looked out of his window, and smiled.

Olympia Report de Luxe
Electric
"Frank" was our first typewriter.

Terminus

E.R. Delafield

Ismene was half asleep when the alert came over her feed. A tourist had gone MIA in the twentieth, and since that was her regular beat, she got the assignment. She dragged herself out of bed, letting the vast stream of information run through her visual augment while she got dressed. By the time she caught the shuttle across the city, she'd caught up on the news and the latest entertainment.

Pavel was already suited up when she arrived, and had the case details on his tablet. "Titus Reef, Citizen number seven-oh-five-three-oh-two. He was on a six day visa, was supposed to report back three hours ago, never showed up."

"Conflict or choice?"

"Seventy-eight percent likely to have chosen to stay," Pavel said.

Ismene sighed. "Why don't they run numbers before they send them?" But she knew why, same as Pavel. You turned down tourists, you sank in the ratings, and the next thing you knew, some other business was the new hot thing. So the company fudged or flubbed their initial screenings and kept their ranking high, so the credits and the ratings kept rolling in.

Jumping back to the twentieth meant going dark. Ismene had to strip off her augment and her watch, and power down her PAI for the trip. This was the part she hated, not the jump itself but the silence and the loneliness that sprouted from being completely cut off from the city. It was unnatural.

After a bone-rattling, teeth-jarring jump into the mid-twentieth, she and Pavel stepped off the tank and greeted the jump staff. Two males, mid-twenties, both super nervous.

Maybe they'd never seen enforcers before. They hung back, hands in their pockets, while she and Pavel got themselves oriented.

Ismene took in the room in a second glance: the scuffed laminate floors, the contemporary posters pinned to the walls, the flickering industrial lights above. But most of all the silence. It reverberated off the cream-colored walls. No helpful stream, no reassuring murmur of the PAI checking on your body's system. And this was their carefully constructed jump site, not even the rest of the scary twentieth outside the walls.

Who'd want to stay here?

Pavel approached them, friendly grin in place, and his gentle, coaching voice smoothing the way. "Hi guys. We've got some questions for you on this MIA."

"Titus Reef," Ismene said, flipping open her physical notebook. It was awkward, having to deal with paper. But you couldn't bring city tech back, it wouldn't work. "What have you heard? Where was he going?"

They glanced at each other. Not good. It meant there were things they didn't want to say, couldn't say, and so were going to keep their mouths shut about it.

Pavel stepped in. "It's better to tell us everything now."

The taller of the two cleared his throat. Another conspiratoral glance at his partner. "He'd done all his prep, when he came in, he was super ready to go. He didn't seem like he was going to skip out."

"What do you mean by super ready?" Ismene asked.

"He'd read all the required stuff, and the suggested list. He'd aced the VR runs," the kid said. "I mean it was Titus Reef. He's always killer."

Ismene and Pavel shared their own glance now. That name meant something to the jump staff. Not to Ismene, but you couldn't track every flash in the pan, it just wasn't possible. Pavel flipped his notebook open and skimmed the back pages, doing the check for them. Back to the trail. Ismene narrowed her eyes. "It sounds like he was suspiciously ready."

"Nah. He verified his departure time, he checked in from his hotel--everything above board."

"Except he didn't show up for departure, did he?"

The second guy piped up. "Maybe it's a new show."

Pavel gave Ismene his notebook. Titus Reef's vita was bulleted out on the soft paper. He'd built up massive credits by posting a popular seven series of videos of his exploration outside the city dome. Not her idea of great entertainment.

"Where was he staying?"

The Sunset West Hotel was on West 31st Street facing a series of storefront shops: clothes, jewelry, books. Ismene didn't like being out and about. It was strange to drive down an open street, to have the sky open above them, and to walk in the open air without masks or protective gear from the automobile to the front door of the hotel. It didn't matter that she'd specialized in the twentieth when the city had assigned her. She couldn't get used to this barbaric way of life. As usual, she suppressed her discomfort behind her disguise, this time of a worried woman looking for her brother.

The front clerk wasn't enthusiastic about sharing information with them. Ismene presented the problem: her brother had disappeared and refused to contact them, they were worried about his health. She used all the keywords designed to prompt quick information.

"I can't discuss any guest," he said.

Ismene touched her eyes with a red-laced handkerchief. "We're very concerned about his safety."

"It's hotel policy."

Pavel tried his earnest expression. "We'd be grateful even to know if he's still registered here. Or when you last saw him?"

"I told you, I can't give out that information."

In the real world, back home, if you wanted to find a person, you gave the city his name and citizen number and the city could not only pinpoint the person's location in less than a second, it would open a vid chat. Sometimes the challenge of tracking someone down in the past wasn't fun, just exhausting.

Probably Titus Reef had bribed the clerks to protect his whereabouts. It was what Ismene would do, if she were ever mad enough to go AWOL in the wilds of the past. She undid her purse's clasp, and took out two bills from her wallet. Money greased every wheel in the past; it was like popularity and credits in the real world. People wanted what they didn't have.

"Anything you can tell us," she said and pushed the bills across the front desk, "anything at all would be a help."

The clerk stared at the bills. His beady eyes processed them, hungered for them, and she knew then they had him. Whatever Titus Reef had paid was less than this.

"I don't know where he is now," the clerk said, and put his fingers on the edges of the bills.

Ismene grabbed the other edge and stared him down.

"But he was really interested in our typewriters. I gave him the address of an office supply store near here. I'm sure he went there, and they didn't deliver any packages for him here." The clerk tried to pull the bills from Ismene, but she held on.

"The address," Pavel said.

"Why a typewriter?" Ismene said, when they returned to the car and Pavel began to inch them out into traffic. She'd seen them, and used them. They were primitive, limited things. You couldn't translate your thoughts or ideas fluidly, you had to use your fingers. "Of all things to be interested in?"

"Who knows why these people pop their augments?" Pavel pressed the gas and they leaped into the lane. A car blasted its horn behind them, and Pavel frowned. "Remember the zoo lady?"

A tourist had gone MIA a year ago, and they'd found her wandering in the zoo, staring at the animals. She'd never seen real animals, and had wept in the back of the car as well as through the jump home. Ismene had had to tranq her in order to keep her from descending into hysterics.

"That's at least understandable," Ismene said. People were always talking about how nice it'd be if the city had real animals. Ismene didn't care for the smell, but she could understand the emotion. Animals had a way of looking at you when they were real that cut into you the way nothing else could. "But some primitive tool?"

"Maybe the boys were right and he's planning some new show," Pavel said.

Ismene picked up their notebooks and flipped through the printed pages. Nothing to suggest a fascination with pre-modern tools--only a recklessness that should've had him flagged before the trip. The city was going to put a black mark on the time travel company's reputation when they got back, she was sure of it.

"Anyway, it makes it easier to find him, doesn't it? Don't knock a good obsession or crusade for turning up the lost."

They found the office supply store and parked. Pavel showed the owner a manufactured picture of Titus Reef.

The owner tapped it with his index finger. "Yeah, yeah. This guy. Ah, he was in here yesterday looking at the typewriters. He didn't want to buy one, though, just use it. I told him we don't do demo models."

"Do you know where he went from here?"

The owner shrugged. "I told him he could rent time on a typewriter, but this was yesterday. He can't still be there."

Ismene smiled. "We're just trying to track his steps... Maybe he talked to someone who could point us in the right direction."

"I doubt there'd be anybody there he'd talk to about going places," the owner said, frowning.

"We hope for the best," Pavel said. "Where did you send him?"

The owner's frown deepened. Had they missed some hint or clue that a local should've known? "The library...doesn't the library in your town rent time on a typewriter? He didn't know about that, either."

Ismene laughed as if it were a good joke. The library where they came from was accessible everywhere via your augment, or your PAI. Open access for everybody. "We're not really library people."

Pavel handed the owner a folded slip of cash. "Thank you for your help."

The library was massive, a structure that took up almost half a block and was three stories in height. People streamed in and out of the front doors, carrying books and some of them talking together. It was the closest the past had ever been to the vibe of the city's agora. If this structure were a VR/AR emporium, and the sky was the crisp, dark blue projection of the dome ceiling, it'd almost be like being back home.

"Come on," Pavel said, and took the steps two at a time.

Ismene followed him, squinting in the midday sun.

The typewriters were kept in the basement, and they went downstairs into a darker and cool space, a little like traveling through the cool transfer hall between gearing up and entering an AR stage. Ismene prepared herself for another conversation, another crumb that would take them somewhere else in the city, tracking Titus Reef on his journey.

But there was a man at one of the typewriters, his hand resting on the blue top of the machine, and Ismene recognized his face.

Titus Reef.

Pavel approached first, and Ismene followed behind. The basement appeared deserted at the moment, but one never knew. She took the tranq out of her purse and palmed it in her hand.

Their subject didn't raise his head. He stared at the humming machine like someone would stare at a vial of d-pop.

"We've been looking for you," Pavel said. He had a soft, reasonable voice. Of the two of them, he was the best to approach a rogue tourist. Ismene always held off until Pavel had softened the road. "You missed your appointment."

Titus Reef broke into a grin. "My summons has arrived." There was a pile of silver coins near his elbow. He was renting time on the machine. Ismene didn't see any sign of paper, though. These primitive things didn't have screens; they wouldn't work without paper.

"It's time to go home."

Ismene picked her way behind Titus, looking for a stray paper, or set of papers, anywhere. Sometimes these people cracked so badly they tried to change the stream. She had to make sure he wasn't leaving something behind that would create a bigger problem.

"I thought it'd be the sky," Titus said. The typewriter fell silent under his hand. "A real clear sky...no pollution, no foul stuff in the air. Or the freedom, just wandering into the horizon, a horizon that doesn't end."

Okay, that sounded normal. Or rather, more like the other rogue tourists they'd tracked down. There was always some sob story, some dissatisfaction with the life they led, some unhappiness with the city. As if they expected life to be perfect. Not even the city could deliver that.

"Ah, come on, there's plenty of real things back home. You've got fans, friends, family. You belong. When else in time could you say that you belong the way you belong in the city?"

"When was the last time you experienced silence?" Titus's voice was dangerously quiet, composed. He was up to something. Ismene stopped looking for paper and started to pay attention.

"Silence is loneliness," she said. The tranq was in her hand, ready to go at a moment's notice.

"Loneliness is the desire for connection," Titus said, tilting his head to stare at her. He had intense eyes: deep and light, and blue.

Like the sky outside. She should tranq him now. "And that's the connection the city can't provide."

"The city is connection."

"Not real connection." Titus picked up a coin, put it into a slot by the typewriter, and the machine sprung to life again with a ferocious hum. "I put a paper in here. I press my fingers on the keys. They pound ink on the page. That's a connection. Mind and body and machine in true harmony. I thought it'd be the sky." He ran his finger across the white keys on the typewriter, not pressing them, but stroking them the way he might stroke a lover's arm.

"The city is perfect harmony," Ismene said. "No gaps, no distance--"

"No heart," Titus said. "No space. No privacy. That's not real connection. This is. I talk to you; you listen with your eyes and your ears and your heart..."

Pavel stepped closer, his voice raised an octave. "Why don't we discuss this on the way back?"

"That's connection," Titus whispered.

Ismene hesitated.

Titus grabbed her wrist and wrenched it, the tranq spilled out and he caught it in his hand. He pressed it to the inside of her wrist and the needle punctured her skin. Pavel darted forward, but the world was going all soft, all endless.

"I'm done with the city," Titus said.

When the city re-engaged her PAI and visual augment, Ismene felt the rushing headache of information spilling into her vision and brain. She gritted her teeth and gripped the chair with both hands. The city's dulcet tones echoed around her in the chamber.

"Recalibrating."

The info dropped from a waterfall to a trickle and Ismene relaxed. She was always disoriented as she integrated back into the city after a jump. Normally she could do that in the privacy of her own apartment, but given Titus Reef's escape, she was in the memory chamber for processing before she could go home.

"Please begin your memory," the city said. Lights flashed around her, and then dimmed. "We will record your memories as they occur, and organize them."

Her PAI pricked and warmed at the back of her neck. The chair had connected into the PAI to give the city easier access to her memories.

True harmony.

Ismene shuddered.

"Remember."

She tried to harken back to the first time she heard the alarm go off, interrupting her sleep. She tried not to think about the fact that she was alone in the room with only the city for company. She tried not to feel anything at all as she remembered waking up, reading the message on her visual augment stream.

Every time she felt fatigued, the city pushed and prodded. What happened next? Review the conversation. Why did you make that choice? What did he say then?

Somewhere in the depths of Ismene's mind, she heard herself cry: <u>I'm done with the city</u>.

But the city was never done with you.

Swintec 2416

Marley

Frederic S. Durbin

Chapter 1: Tom Sees Marley Seeing a Bridge

Marley's hair was almost the color of the bridge over Little Fork--a shade darker than the rust of the old steel trusses. She had a lot of it, a riot of hair, thick and shining, lopped off at her shoulders. Tom loved the way it flowed when she turned her head. From the moment he saw her running toward him up the front steps of the high school, he had imagined twining his fingers through that hair, pulling Marley's face close to his.

Someday. Someday soon, he hoped. For now, he watched her study the bridge with her wide artist's eyes.

"You should draw it," he said. "Bring your sketch book out here. Why not?" He was in awe of the things Marley could do in art class.

She gave her joyful little laugh and flashed her smile, the kind that began with a wondrous scrunching of her nose. "I will if you'll bring your notebook--or your typewriter."

They laughed together. Tom couldn't help laughing because something rose inside him when they stood together like this, looking at anything, talking about anything, a rising like a flight of finches bursting from the hedgerow to scissor the morning with their wings. He pictured himself and Marley set up on a mud bank somewhere, an easel and a card table, sketching, writing stories about the bridge. Tom was sure there were stories in it, clustered underneath it like grapes on an arbor.

On both sides, below the steep banks of County 8, the Pawtuck Road, the dense woods hummed with insects. Sometimes they flitted over the muddy water, leaving ringlet footprints on the surface. Trucks and cars zoomed by on the highway a quarter-mile away, unseen beyond the trees. Past the highway, which ran perpendicular to County 8, the cemetery's hills rose above the crowns of the mosquito timber. Tom could see the stones there, the angels and crosses.

That summer of 1971, the bridge still had its twin tracks of plank, banded and riveted, raised a few inches from the wooden flooring. Car tires had to line up with these two tracks and follow them across—one lane, a take-your-turn bridge.

"There are good things about rust," Marley said, shading her eyes.

"Are there?"

"Well, city rust is sad—things are neglected. But country rust . . . it's more of a conversion. Human structures seeing a better way. This bridge meets this creek, these woods, and it says, 'You're right. Here, I'll join you. Let's become one thing.'"

"You are truly weird," Tom said, but his throat hurt with how much he loved the things Marley said, the things she saw.

"Oh, I might have gotten that from you." She was crossing the bridge now, walking along one of the wheel planks as if it were a tightrope, her arms out in exaggerated balancing moves that she didn't need.

"From *me*? What are you talking about?"

"Hmm. What am I talking about?"

Marley had soft, knee-high boots with dangling strips of leather fringe around the tops. She had faded jeans and a baggy green shirt that made Tom want to put his arms around her, to hold her small, warm shape under all that cloth, to feel her breath going in and out, warming his neck.

Marley Field. That was her name. It sounded to Tom like a beautiful place, a grain crop, golden and full of sun, something the sun brought from the earth for the wind to stir. Oh, to lie down in the field of Marley . . .

Junior year was just over, and the summer stretched ahead, promising miracles as it always did. Marley had shown up only three months before, new in town. She'd joined three of Tom's classes: English, history, and art. She'd come to absorb the tail end of the school year. Tom hadn't absorbed much of it with Marley around.

At the far end of the bridge, she hopped from one of the wooden tracks to the other—again, with much more circus performance than was necessary, however adorable--and crossed back to him, passing between the high, rusted trusses, between the secretive walls of the forest, over the brown water, which slid almost imperceptibly along its muddy channel.

Chapter 2: Tom and Marley See the Illuminated Past

On the evening of Friday, June 11, 1971, Marley came over for movie night at the Taylors'. She had wanted to meet Tom's cousins from his dad's side of the family--and now, after a wiener roast in the north yard, they all sat around the living room--Tom and his parents, Cousins Lloyd, Cindy, Donna, and Karen, and their various small children.

Home movie night was something the Taylor cousins wanted to do every few years. Joe Taylor (Tom's dad) had always been the chronicler of events--the one in the family who had a movie camera and brought it along to gatherings. Tom was the projectionist now; Dad had turned the equipment over to him when Tom had reached about 11 years old. Dad still governed the proceedings, though, ensconced in his recliner with his cigarette held vertically in one hand, like a hypodermic needle, its fiery tip pointed safely away from bouncing toddlers.

Marley shared a footstool with Tom behind the projector, close beside him. As the celluloid whirred over the sprockets of the Bell & Howell Monterey, he could feel her warmth. He thrilled with each sigh, each giggle of Marley's in response to what was happening on the screen.

TV could never match the ambience, the community of a darkened room, the hot smell of the projector bulb, and the bright, flickering images on the tripod screen. Dad's old movies distilled the sunlight of the past, the green of vanished summers. They preserved the images of relatives now old or gone. In the movies, these people were captured in a moment of time, moving as they had on that particular lost day, clear as life.

The reel most in demand was a compilation shot over many years, spliced together in no particular order, one section even having gotten put in upside-down and backwards, with horses galloping in reverse, consuming

their dust clouds like vacuum cleaners. Scenes of
Mom and Dad's courting blended with family baseball
games--lots of swings-and-misses, and then a long,
panoramic shot of a dozen guys searching for the ball
in high weeds, their stark forms spread out along the
horizon as if in some epic western. That one solid
hit--that single moment of baseball glory--had never
been filmed, so it was now claimed by several left
alive who had played that day. Dad looked like a
movie star in the films, young and straight, with a
full head of black hair. Mom resembled a young Audrey Hepburn.

Marley's hand made itself available, and Tom took
it. He glimpsed her smiling in the reflected light.

Toward the film's halfway point, there was a silver
dot in the sky, passing behind power lines. This was
Dad's famous U.F.O. shot. The dot was so tiny that it
had to be pointed out to the younger kids. Always
Dad nodded gravely, his gaze intent until the scene
changed to the digging of the lake.

Dad had stories for all the scenes, and the audience's questions followed a time-honored litany.
There was very little variation. The family would
even argue over the identities of old folks in the
film the same way each time; the man in the bowtie was
sure as hell either Uncle Millard or Bob Hawley from
the mine--you couldn't really see his face. The
films were silent. There was no audio to require the
discipline of being quiet--not that any soundtrack
could have competed with the cousins all together in
one room. The sound was supplied by the audience
each time.

After a town parade, there came a full four minutes of nothing but cigarette smoke in a dim room at
"the little house," where Mom and Dad had lived when
they were first married--just cigarette smoke filling
the frame, swirling above an ash tray. "Now wait,"
Dad would always say. "Now watch. There's a place
where the smoke looks just like the devil's face,
really clear." A solemnity would settle over the
group then, and the summer night would take on a suggestion of chill. This was the only point on which
the traditional comments varied: sometimes Dad himself would miss the face, and he would mutter, as the
footage went on to other things, that somewhere in

there the devil's face was as clear as day; and at
other viewings, Dad would shout "There!" in triumph,
pointing. The kids would see only smoke, perhaps
because they had no concept of what the devil ought to
look like. A few of the cousins might give a start
and cry out, "I saw it!" But whether Dad or anyone
else saw or didn't see the devil, if anyone suggested
re-watching, Dad would say, "Oh, let's go on. It's
getting late."

That June night, Tom saw the angular, horned face
in the smoke and felt Marley jump.

The cousins, laughing, watched themselves as kids
swimming in a plastic pool. One of their own kids
would ask "Is that you, Mom?" while standing in front
of the screen and reaching out to touch a strange-yet-
familiar face--but blocking the very part of the
image that held the most interest. The child would
blend with the picture, the glowing colors projected
on hair and skin and T-shirt back, until everyone
yelled "Sit down!"

The highlight came when Uncle Paul dashed across
the yard in his swimsuit, the pool empty now of kids.
Uncle Paul, all berry-brown, a scrawny Tarzan, dove
into the pool, displacing a prodigious amount of
water. At that point, Tom's dad--and now Tom--would
switch the projector into reverse. The tidal wave
would return from the lawn to the pool; Uncle Paul
would fly out, land on his feet, and sprint away backwards across the grass. It was a delight that never
grew old.

The cousins came to see the movies every few years,
bringing new girlfriends or boyfriends, new spouses in
time, new babies. In fact, the film had its identity
in that scene: the request was always for "the movie
where Dad (Uncle Paul) jumps out of the pool," as if
it had been recorded that way.

Tom and Marley talked about it later, in the gentle
dark of the front yard, under the oaks. "What actually happens in the past," Tom said, "only happens
once. But what people remember about it--that lives
on."

"Uncle Paul jumping out of the pool is more real
now than his jumping in." Marley laughed softly. "I
wonder if we can rewrite the past."

"What do you mean?"

"Well, like you've rewritten it by reversing the

film. You changed what Uncle Paul did."

"Not really, though--that's just a trick in the present. I don't see how we could change the actual past. It's gone. We can't touch it."

"Is it? Can't we?"

He touched her face. All he wanted to think about was right now, and the future.

That was the night Tom first kissed Marley. It was partly like he imagined, and partly much better.

Chapter 3: Marley and Tom Take a Walk

The Fourth of July was a Sunday that year, and after church and Sunday dinner, Tom and Marley spent most of the day blowing things up. Marley had never had firecrackers or bottle rockets, and she took fiendish delight in blasting holes in the dirt, in dropping firecrackers down the vent pipe of the tornado shelter and listening to the bang under the brick dome. Tom showed her how to use a length of pipe as a launcher to aim rockets in any direction. They would even explode underwater, making a muted boom followed by rising smoky bubbles.

Not far to the west of Tom's house was a country club that invested some serious cash into a fireworks show. Everyone along Route 29 had a perfect view of it. Friends and relatives gathered in the Taylors' front yard, had a picnic, and then carried lawn chairs and blankets to the edge of the road when lights began to flash in the sky as it faded from lavender to deep purple, then to full night.

Wonders unfolded in the west--huge, hot, glittering shapes like prophecies, like benedictions over the warm, dark fields. The detonations traveled as echoes 360 degrees around the horizon. Marley spun herself, following the sound.

After the grand finale, when the chairs were going back into car trunks and the sleepy children settled in backseats, Tom and Marley had time for a long walk on Route 29. The elderly aunt whom Marley lived with was never strict about curfews.

Hand in hand, they hiked along the blacktop, which radiated warmth from the day. They passed the horse corral and the sheep farm. Then there was nothing but corn on the right, beans on the left, and the endless vault of glittering stars.

"You're going to be a writer," Marley said out of nowhere.

Tom looked at her, wondering why she sounded so insistent. "I guess. I'll try."

"No. You'll do it because that's who you are. You have to promise me that you'll keep writing, no matter what. You're going to be famous."

He chuckled. "How do you know that?"

Now Marley halted and stared into his eyes. The sky was so bright that the two of them cast shadows on the road. "I'm going to tell you something weird," she said.

"You always do."

"No--I'm serious."

He watched her and felt a tingling on the back of his neck.

"Tom . . . I'm not just from Kentucky. I'm . . . not from this time at all. I'm from the future."

Tom laughed, relieved now that she was joking, that she was not about to tell him something bad.

But Marley wasn't laughing. "Your mom met John Denver once. Your great uncle Walter lived with your family when you were a baby. You were paddled in kindergarten for stealing a 'cornflower' crayon and blaming it on Eric Logan."

Tom's mouth fell open. How could she--?

"How could I know these things?" Marley clutched his arm. "You wrote them in your memoir--or you will, in 2021. Yes, the year 2021, when you're in your sixties. You had a German shepherd named Lawrence that was hit by a car. Do you believe me?"

"Marley, what the hell?"

She held his arms, her face close. "I'm a huge fan of yours. I did a dissertation on your novels--I've read them all. And your story collections."

He had to laugh again. He had to sit down on the bank of the ditch. Was this crazy, beautiful creature on drugs? But how could she know those things? "You're in high school," he managed at last. "Dissertation?"

Marley flattened the foxtails and sat beside him. "When I left my own time--the future--I was sixty-three. It was 2089. See, I was born in 2026, when you were 71. We were alive together then, too, but we didn't know each other. I was in Kentucky, and a baby. Everyone got to know you--your name, anyway. Even people who don't read."

Tom shook his head. Tears welled in his eyes. The girl he loved was insane. Was there some hope, somewhere, that she wasn't? "Is this some sort of game?"

"No, no." She slid an arm around him and leaned her head on his shoulder. "It's all true. You have to keep writing--you'll see. You know why I came to you? Because your work changed my life. It saved my life. And because you dedicated your first book to me." She laughed now, her gentle fingers brushing at his tears. "Yes! 'For Marley,' it says. None of the scholars knew who Marley was, and you wouldn't say. But it was enough for me--I knew."

Something shrill--a frog or bug--went off suddenly in the weeds.

"Noisy!" Marley said.

Tom looked for ways to make Marley admit her story was a bunch of crap. "You live with your aunt. Did you bring her from the future, too?"

"She's not really my aunt. But she is a relative-- some great-great-grand-aunt or something. I looked it all up before I came. I knew enough family history to convince her that we're related. Anyway, she doesn't care much where I came from. She's lonely and old. She likes the help and the company. I love her, and I'm glad we met."

"How did you get into school? You'd need--"

"Please! By the time you're 63, you know how to get things done--make calls and nidle it out. School is a good thing that grownups _like_ us to do. They weren't trying to keep me out."

"'Nidle it out'?"

"Sorry. No one says that yet. Let's keep walking. It's buggy here."

Tom stood up with her, and they walked on. Would she be done talking like this tomorrow? He hoped this was just some magic of the Fourth of July making Marley crazy for one night.

"You haven't asked the big question," she said. "The one I thought you'd ask first."

He took a weary breath. His voice broke once before he could say, "What question?"

"How did I travel through time?"

Tom closed his eyes, squeezing her hand. She was still Marley. _Keep walking_. _Breathe_. A breeze riffled the corn, and the beans answered.

"There's groundbreaking neuroscience in my time," she said. "They figured out in the late seventies-- that's the 2070s--that a lot of the 'unused' space in our brains is used for storing collective consciousness. In our DNA, we inherit more than our eye color and stuff--we get a lot more that we're still just beginning to understand. Species memory. The past-- all that the human race has been through. It's probably all in there, in each human brain. Everything."

"That makes no sense. The past is _behind_ us."

"We thought that way for a long time. But why _would_ it be? Only because we chose to draw it that way, lines on paper with the years labeled. Tom, those linear models were only analogies. The newer models show the past as the _interior_ of the present. Earlier events--much earlier--may not be as far removed as we once believed. Our existence is like a rolling snowball. We pick up more experience and get bigger as we go along. What's past is inside--not behind."

"For one person, maybe . . ."

She spread her hands. "Why would it be just for one? Things are more connected than we used to think, although at different times in the past, by different peoples, it was better understood. Where are the borders of the mind and spirit? Are you and I really, completely separate? Nature is full of tiny parts that are perfect patterns for the whole."

Tom listened. Marley's speech was clear, her thoughts ordered logically, if not plausibly. If she would just stop talking about this tomorrow, maybe things would be okay.

"It explains déjà vu. It explains people who are convinced they've lived past lives. We don't remember _all_ of it in our usual frames of reference, and that narrow focus allows us to function. We need an uncluttered work surface. But sometimes a signal jumps the track, and we remember other people's memories--people who lived before us and added to the memory pool."

Tom rubbed his forehead.

She took his arm again. "You're wondering how I came back here, to 1971. They developed a procedure, still experimental--cross-linking, in which neurosurgeons connect the conscious part of the brain to a part of the stored memory--like touching two wires together. I had the operation. I was one of the first. They wired me into this time I chose—this year. I even got to choose my age, the same as yours. Tom . . . I came here to be with you."

Tom didn't know what to say. If it was a delusion, it was also crazy romantic. "But why?" he asked. "Why would you do that? It can't be safe, that procedure. They operated on your brain."

They stopped walking again, and Marley was in his arms.

"I had nothing to lose," she said. "I had a brain tumor that they couldn't fix. I was dying. So I volunteered. I don't know why I have a physical body here—I think it's because that's how memories work, like dreams—our only way of seeing the world is through a body, so we always have them, even when we . . . travel."

He touched her, held her head between his hands, suddenly afraid. "But . . . are you still sick?"

She smiled, her eyes shining in the starlight. "Not in 1971."

Chapter 4: Tom and Marley See the Lights

They spent nearly every day together that summer. Marley talked about the weird stuff only enough to remind Tom that she believed it. They walked, wrote, and drew pictures—and always, they talked about everything. Marley dreamed of having an art studio and owning a horse. Tom didn't much care where life took him, as long as he could write stories. Though it was not an especially good time for the country, it was the best of Tom's life; he wrote that more than once in later years.

Tom's dad growled about the need to get out of Vietnam, and he hoped Nixon could make it happen. Cousin Leonard came home in a coffin, escorted by a compassionate officer who gave Aunt Sophie a folded flag. Although the Concorde had achieved supersonic flight and men had walked three times on the moon, Jimi and Janis had both died the previous year; Simon and Garfunkel had released their last album together. The days were floating away in all directions like cottonwood seeds. Dad, banging out essays for the local paper on his Royal typewriter, quoted Yeats:

"Things fall apart; the centre cannot hold; / The blood-dimmed tide is loosed, and everywhere / The ceremony of innocence is drowned; / The best lack all conviction, while the worst / Are full of passionate intensity."

One day, as casually as he could, Tom asked his dad what he thought of the possibility of an inherited collective memory. It was possible to ask such a question casually around Dad. Well, Joe Taylor said, he'd read that developing fetuses go through various phases that look like a sped-up evolution--webbed fingers, rudimentary tails--before they come out as human-looking babies. "So I think there's a lot in us," Dad concluded. "There's a lot of the brain that we don't seem to use. It's there for some reason."

Tom agreed that he'd heard something like that, too.

He and Marley listened to Dylan, Denver, The Doors, Lennon, and Simon and Garfunkel. "<u>And the moon rose over an open field</u>." He had a girl beside him, someone to watch the moon rise with. But it terrified him, the very sweetness of it, the perfection of Marley's profile when he looked over at her. Something told him that the centre could not hold.

At home, Tom wrote on his mom's big gray standard Underwood. When he and Marley were out somewhere, on bridge abutments, on picnic tables or big rocks, he used the portable AMC that he was to use at college when the time came. Marley sat beside him and sketched. When he was ready, she read what he wrote and offered her thoughts. She was unsettlingly frank when she didn't like something. "This sounds like Tolkien, not like you" or "Why should I care about this character?" or "This whole beginning needs to go. Your story starts on page 3." At first, Tom got angry. But he couldn't stay angry at Marley. "Besides," she told him, "I'm older and wiser. I used to be a senior citizen."

The county fair came in late July, an otherworldly glow west of town, an oasis of brilliant lights, ringing bells, huffing tractor engines, the piping calliope, the smashing impacts of the demolition derby. He won a stuffed bear for Marley. They ate cotton candy--clouds on sticks that vanished into sugar on the tongue. They drank lemon shakeups.

The Ferris wheel hoisted them to the stars and then broke down, its one-armed operator cursing and hammering below them. For about twenty minutes, Tom and Marley were stuck at the top, and that may have been the best twenty minutes of the best summer. They could see beyond it all--past the winking, dinging midway with its crowds, past the rides and the grandstand and the Haunted House of Chills. Around the bright circle lay the velvet darkness, deep and unbroken--and far out on the horizon, the misty illumination of other prairie towns.

Marley said, "There's something you have to do, okay? You absolutely have to do it."

"Keep writing?"

"Yes, that--but one more thing. When you dedicate your first book to me, use both my names: Marley Field. That's the sign for the doctors who helped me come here. That's how they'll know the operation worked."

Tom frowned, not following.

"As it stands now, you only wrote 'For Marley.' If it changes to 'For Marley Field,' then the doctors will know it changed because I reached you."

Tom thought about that and decided, as he was doing more and more often, to play along. "But if I do it that way, 'For Marley Field,' then that's the way it will be. It won't seem to change in your time. The doctors and everyone else will only have ever seen it with both names."

Marley shook her head, swinging that marvelous hair. "Before the operation, they sealed it in an envelope, the way you wrote it in our past. There's even a first edition of your first book in there, for comparison. After the operation, they went to check the envelope. Even if their memories will have changed, what's in the envelope won't have--it's from a different 'stream of time,' in the linear analogies. In the future, we would say a different idiosphere or sub-sphere."

"You should be the writer," Tom said. "Science fiction."

"No, that's you. You'll play genres like piano keys."

Tom pulled her close, fingers in her hair, their eyes inches apart, souls mirroring. "I love you, Marley."

"I love you, too."

He hoped the Ferris wheel would never start to move again. But it did, and they came down.

"Thanks," Marley said to the operator as he yanked out the bolt and raised the lap bar, setting them free. "It's okay that it broke."

The operator either coughed, laughed, or said "Hell" in his voice that had the same quality as the diesel engine behind him. "It wasn't broke," he said, and winked at them.

Chapter 5: Tom and Marley Face the Music

The second week of August, Marley's spells began. It started with her using more of the future words than she intended. But soon enough, Tom realized she was simply using the wrong words, or couldn't think of the word she needed at all. Marley wasn't in pain, but she saw strange flashes of light, heard noises that no one else did, and lost her energy. The doctors ran tests, but the problem wasn't with her teenaged brain, so they found nothing amiss. Marley didn't let Aunt Beulah spend much money on medical tests or treatments. When Marley had trouble walking, she stayed in her room in the little house on Elevator Street.

"I'm unraveling," Marley told Tom, who sat beside her bed. "The doctors who did my operation warned me this might happen. I'd hoped it wouldn't. I'm so sorry, Tom. The tumor is killing my body in the future, and it looks like I'm still bound to it."

"But you're here," Tom said, gripping her hand as proof. "This body you're in . . ."

"It's real, but so is the other one. My hypersphere, the future of me. I'm inside that time—you and I are, not in some other place." She settled back on her pillow and sighed. "Bring your typewriter tomorrow. I like the sound of it."

"I can't write with you like this."

"We have to work on that."

Tom stayed with her every day. His parents even let him stay there some nights, where he slept on the couch, and Mom brought meals over. Marley told him things to write about, and when he did, she read the pages and told him what she liked, what he needed to rethink. Toward the end, she held the page and gazed at it, but they both knew she couldn't see the words there. It said, "I love you, Marley" and "Don't leave me" over and over.

Marley smiled at him with a look of serenity, her face weary and shiny with perspiration. She had never looked more beautiful. "Good," she whispered. "You're ready. You'll be ready."

When she was asleep, Tom cried—as quietly as he could, so as not to wake her.

"We were supposed to get old together," he told her one morning.

"We will. Just . . . in different times." She held his hand.

"Marley . . . you said that my writing saved your life. What did you mean?"

She looked fondly at him, then closed her eyes, gathering her energy to talk. Her voice was just above a whisper. "There are . . . dark times coming, later on in your life. That's when you get really famous, after you have a happy married life."

Tom shook his head in protest.

"Oh, yes—you marry a wonderful woman. A man like you . . . deserves . . ."

"I don't want any other wonderful woman."

"Shh. It's okay." She rested, then spoke again. "Things get bad in America. Polarized—like the Civil War again, only the people who hate each other live side-by-side, often in the same house, all over the country. In all that, your books are a shining light—a comfort. You help put the world . . . back together. I read you at a critical time for me. I think I would have . . . given up without—no. I won't tell you the title. You'll have to figure that out for yourself."

"Marley . . ."

"It's like the home movies. Beautiful times in the past. Those images on the screen bring them back to life—the people. You have to do that for the future. Look ahead with your stories to the way it can be. The way it _will_ be. Help us see, Tom. Make it real." With a hand she could barely lift, she tapped his typed pages. "This is your screen—your window. Use this." She traced the curved line of the AMC's ribbon cover.

Tom didn't have to figure out how he would manage to visit Marley when school started. The next day, August 27—a hot, sunny Friday—Marley vanished. Tom had been dozing beside her, holding her hand. Maybe it was the sudden absence of her hand that woke him up. She was gone from the bed. Her pajamas were still there, laid out flat in a human shape. Aunt Beulah, when she saw it, said it was like the Shroud of Turin.

Of course Tom told Aunt Beulah all that he knew about Marley. She deserved an explanation. He was sure the old woman would be shocked and think he was awful for making up stories in a time of sorrow, but she only cried a little, then nodded and said, "Well, all right, then. I knew that girl was something special. You did, too."

Among the piles of typed sheets Tom gathered up from the room, he found one that Marley had typed for him when he hadn't been around. It said:

Don't be sad, dear, sweet Tom. We can be happy. I'm weeping with joy as I type this on the machine that you're going to use to make the world better. I hereby bless your typewriter! I commission it to service.

I found you! I really did. By God's grace, I crossed the bridge of Time.

What I've been through proves, scientifically, the existence of the soul. A part of me left my body in the future and came here to the inside, the past--a part wholly me. They are two different things, body and soul! Bound together, yes, on this side of Eternity. We have to die once, as the Bible says. But be sure of it, my darling, my love. As surely as the fireflies glow in the dusk, as surely as the buds come out in the spring, we will meet again.

Chapter 6: Marley Comes Around to Tom

Lilacs bloomed along the well-tended hedge of the cemetery in Springfield, Illinois. A little girl with a wild mane of hair, just the color of dark rust, bounced to a stop in front of a modest marble stone with two angels on the top, blowing their trumpets. The girl's face was round and full of warm light, like the sun on the first good day of summer.

"Here it is!" she announced, pointing proudly.

"Thomas Taylor!"

A lean man with neatly clipped dark hair and a red-haired woman with thoughtful gray eyes arrived behind their daughter. Their names were Sam and Lori Field. The man--Sam--held the girl's shoulders from behind, and together they faced the stone.

"Good reading!" Sam said. "Do you see anything else?"

"There's no Mrs. Taylor," the girl observed.

"That's right. He never married. What else do you see?"

The girl's eyes widened. "It's my name!"

"That's your name," said Lori. She read aloud the line engraved across the stone below Tom Taylor's name:

OFF TO FIND MARLEY

"Why is my name on a grave?" The girl looked up at her father, puzzled but not upset.

"This man was a writer, honey. His books have meant an awful lot to your mom and me. He dedicated them all to Marley Field. Remember what it means to 'dedicate'?"

The girl gasped. "He wrote his books for _me_?!"

Sam grinned at his wife. "Maybe he did, pumpkin. Maybe he wrote them just for you. Or maybe it was another Marley. Mr. Taylor never said who she was. Anyway, this is how you got your name. See how powerful books are? They can name little girls."

The girl knelt in front of the stone and traced the letters of her name with her finger. "No, it wasn't another Marley. He wrote them for me."

1973 Olivetti Linea 98

1958 Olympia SM3

Early 1960s AMC Alpina

Jumping, Coinciding, Seeking

Armando Werner
(translation by Richard Polt)

I'm sitting at the table
in front of my Sterling and
a window
the same Sterling and
the same window
as always.

looking toward the window
looking into the distance
I was thinking of you
and suddenly realized that
the golden plain
on which I always write your name
lies in the opposite direction
from the road that brings me
toward you.

and I asked myself if all this time
I've been doing it wrong,
if because I've looked southwest so long
now your name
pains me more.

I'm sitting at the table
with my red Sterling
in front of me
which seems to have an eye in
the segment
staring me down intently
waiting for some memory
to drain from my fingers
and take us to you.

there's so much that I remember about you!
what do I prefer
among everything that speaks of you?
take me there
red machine for writing time!

and we left for some moment
beyond.

her name is Valeria -I told the old man.
She was born on a Tuesday, June 23.
yes, June 23.
it was 1998,
exactly 130 years after
they awarded you the patent.
how about that, eh?
it seems that on the same day
you and I
became fathers.

what am I doing here, you ask?
I miscalculated the jump
but it's her, my daughter,
that I'm seeking.

Smith-Corona Sterling, 5A417832, year 1952,
red color.

Rest for the Wicked

Shelley K. Davenport

When she saw the typewriter, she knew there had been a mistake.

Sabela pressed a finger to the divot of flesh in front of her ear and waited for the double click.

"You've sent me to the wrong time," she said softly. "No one has seen me yet. Bring me back."

No answer.

"Hello?"

The AI that operated the travel machine, named Clara, did not respond.

"Clara, this isn't 1842. It's . . ." She looked around, observing the brass light fixtures, the candlestick telephone, the floral rug. On the desk, the primitive typewriter. "It's sometime in the early 1900s. You have to pick me up."

She stood still, waiting. Technically, she had a mile to roam and still be brought back to 2042 (or forward, depending on how you thought about time). But she didn't want to risk it. She shifted her weight to the other leg, feeling the heaviness of the pistol in her skirt pocket. She was beginning to sweat in the heavy, woolen dress, her gloves, her black bonnet.

"Clara!" she hissed again.

"Go ahead and finish the mission," said the AI.

"I literally can't! I'm in. The. Wrong. Time."

"But the right place!"

Willow Grove, Virginia. Just sixty years too late.

"You can still finish the mission, hen," said Clara, adopting the Scottish accent she used when she wanted to ingratiate herself to Sabela.

"No. What is wrong with you? Did you catch a virus or something?" said Sabela.

Just then a fat woman in an apron entered the room and screamed, throwing her arms over her head.

Oh, damn, thought Sabela. This made things infinitely worse.

"You were speaking to the ghost!" the woman cried.

"Yes," said Sabela. When in doubt, lie, lie, lie.

"You must be the spiritualist from Savannah," said the woman. "Miss Crandon?"

"Yes. Yes, I am."

"I am Mrs. Fieldstone, the housekeeper. You're a few days early." She turned with a frown. "Did he come into the house? He never comes into the house! Just up to the window. Don't tell me he's getting into the house now!" The woman waved a duster as if she could sweep the ghost away with feathers.

"He stopped at the window," said Sabela, pointing to where the curtains blew.

The woman relaxed. "Yes, he doesn't generally leave the garden." She lowered her voice. "Did he speak to you?"

Sabela searched her memory for the information in her pre-mission briefing. The ghost in this particular haunted property—John Wesley Fairfax—was mute, and only communicated by throwing things.

"No," she said. "I spoke to him, but he did not respond."

"But you saw him?" The woman narrowed her eyes.

Drat. The ghost that haunted this particular property, in addition to being mute, was also invisible.

"I, ah . . ."

"I suppose that is why you are a spiritualist," said the woman admiringly. "No one has ever seen him. What does he look like?"

"Short. Dark. A bit plump. Angry," she added.

The woman nodded. "You don't say! Well, I expect you'll want to get right to it. Let me show you out to the garden."

The woman kept up a patter of talk as she led Sabela down the hall and out onto the back porch, to which Sabela responded as briefly as possible. Sabela hoped that her 21st-century accent somehow sounded to this woman like that of a spiritualist from Savannah.

"I don't go into the garden anymore," said Mrs. Fieldstone, standing in the doorway. "I'm here to cook and tidy for you, but the family is down at the shore until the haunting is sorted out. So you'll be alone here at night. He's much worse at night," she added cheerfully.

"I understand," said Sabela, mentally cursing Clara.

"Well, good luck, Miss Crandon. Watch your head. He throws things."

The door closed firmly behind her, Sabela stood on the porch, looking at a garden, enclosed on three sides with lush woods. Down between the tree trunks she saw a glimmer of water. The Shenandoah River, she thought. She walked down into the garden, between rose bushes and iris flags.

"Clara," she said, clicking into her headpiece again when she was sure she was out of earshot. "You must pick me up now. This isn't funny. The housekeeper has already talked to me and thinks I'm a spiritualist!"

"Yes, I know. I want you to finish the mission."

"But he's already a ghost!"

"Then you must help him to move on. Like in the stories," added Clara wistfully.

"That is NOT my job, Clara. Josef was supposed to talk to him, and he failed because this ghost is too stubborn and violent. Which is why I am--should be-- in 1842, preventing him from getting murdered in the first place. Clara!"

She imagined the AI giving a theoretical shrug.

"Listen, you glorified calculator. The ghost of John Fairfax put Josef in the hospital. He beat him senseless with a wrench. Why do you think I'll succeed where Josef failed?"

"I have my reasons," said Clara, ignoring the insult.

She had been going off script lately, Sabela reflected. But always for the betterment of the mission, and always in such trivial ways that Sabela could justify going along with it. This was something else.

"Just wait until I get back," she hissed. "I'm telling."

"If you get back," said Clara darkly.

Sabela clicked off and then took a deep breath. She walked down a series of stone steps to a lower section of the garden. Abandoned shovels and wheelbarrows littered the grass, and the red earth showed like a wound. On a low stone wall, his back to her, sat a man in work clothes, holding a hammer in his hand and reflectively tapping it on his knee. He was very slender, with bright red hair. The gardener? The swimming pool contractor? Sabela decided that the fewer people who saw her, the better. She walked quietly down the path toward the river. A dock extended into the green water, a rowboat bobbing a little in the current. She looked across to see faint blue peaks on the horizon and took a deep breath of the sweet, warm air.

After she felt calmer, she scouted around the bank to see if she could guess the original murder site. Records had shown that in the winter of 1842, wealthy landowner John Wesley Fairfax came upon his hired hand, Rufus Bell, chopping firewood by the river. Bell turned on his master and brained him with an axe, then threw his body into the river. Bell was apprehended and eventually hanged. The property had been haunted by the angry ghost of John Fairfax ever since. Since he had proven impervious to all efforts to make him leave, the Agency (niftily named "Past and Presence") had opted to send Sabela back in time to stop the murder. She would appear on the riverbank, approach the two men, shoot Rufus Bell dead, and melt again into the woods. The whole thing would take less than three minutes.

"May I remind you how much money is at stake?" she asked, clicking back in.

Clara made a Glaswegian noise of disgust. She did not like the client.

"He shouldnae be tearing up the place," she said. "He'll totally ruin the landscape."

"That's not the point," said Sabela, although she privately agreed.

In 2042, on this property, a developer named Rick Shorkey was attempting to build a resort and conference center. When the crew broke ground, the poltergeist manifested, throwing tools, tearing up blueprints, and in one epic tantrum, tipping a forklift over. Work came to a halt, laborers quit, word got out. Shorkey came to the Agency in desperation and with deep pockets. When Josef, sent to coax the ghost into the next world, failed, Shorkey agreed to pay for the next level of service--sending an agent to nip the problem in the bud. Sabela, one of their best, took the job, and now wished fervently she had not.

"Clara," she said gently, deciding to use logic. "I have good eyesight. I'm a great shot. I never get travel-sick. I am the ideal person to pop into 1842, shoot Rufus Bell in the head, and pop back out. But I am not a ghost therapist."

"I believe in you, hen," said Clara.

Sabela turned back to the house, biting her lip. There was no point in warning the AI of the risks of sending someone to the wrong time and changing history. Clara would have already done the calculations and determined that their interference would result in NMC (No Material Change). It was what made their business possible--time was actually very elastic. After Sabela killed Rufus Bell, the landowner, John Fairfax, would go on with his life, peacefully, and the haunting would never happen. And Shorkey and Clara would never meet, and . . . well, that was where Sabela's understanding of the whole thing broke down. But that wasn't her job. Josef handled ghosts. Clara handled time and the multiverse. Sabela handled a gun.

She turned back to the house, walking up the path through the trees, and emerged into the sunlight. The red-haired man was still sitting on the wall. It was too hot. She pulled off her gloves and stood a moment watching him, and the torn-up earth around him.

<u>Digging</u>, she thought. <u>Breaking ground.</u>

Slowly the man turned his head. His face was paper-white, and his eyes, meeting hers, were black pools of madness. His hair burned flame-orange. With a swift flick, he chucked the hammer at her.

"Hey!" she said, ducking.

There was no doubt in her mind that she was looking at the ghost. The trouble was that it wasn't John Wesley Fairfax. She had studied his portrait closely, so that she would be sure not to shoot him by mistake.

"I see you!" she shouted.

The ghost took a few steps to the right, and then the left, watching her eyes follow him. He picked up a rock with his left hand and drew back his arm.

"No!" yelled Sabela, pointing at him. The rock whacked into the railing of the porch behind her, and the ghost snatched up another.

Instead of taking refuge in the house, Sabela jumped down the steps. It was her nature to run toward danger, more than from it, and it surprised the ghost. He froze.

"You stop that," she said, stopping a few paces

away. "I'm here to help."

The ghost dropped the stone and flexed his fingers. Sabela saw that his other hand, curled uselessly against his chest, had begun to drip blood. Deflated, he dropped the stone and went away to huddle on the wall.

Sabela cautiously sat on the wall catty-corner to him, a safe distance away. "Who are you?" she asked.

He did not turn, just hung his head lower. A puddle of blood was collecting around his boots.

"You aren't . . . John Fairfax?" Perhaps the portrait she had studied was wildly inaccurate.

His head snapped up, eyes very bright, and he shouted something angry. Angry and silent.

"I'm sorry, but I can't hear you. Who are you? Why are you here?" she asked.

The ghost stared at her. Then he looked back down, working his left-hand fingers into the space between two stones. He picked out a pebble and studied it.

"Look, I want to help you," said Sabela, getting up. "But you have to stop throwing things at me."

The ghost tossed the pebble in the air and caught it. Sabela resisted the urge to ask Clara for help. She thought hard. She had to at least try to help this ghost, or Clara would refuse to pick her up. Sabela was nothing if not practical. But how to help a voiceless ghost?

"Can you write?" she asked.

The ghost looked deliberately at his bloody right hand and then at her, as if it were the stupidest question he'd ever heard.

"Right, right, sorry."

Sign language had not been invented in 1842, she was pretty sure—not that she knew how to sign.

The ghost was looking at her with a peculiar expression, almost like that of an abused animal trying to read a new owner. He slowly reached out his uninjured hand to her, white with blue nails. Sabela inadvertently recoiled. This infuriated the ghost. He jumped up, screaming silently, spittle and blood flying from between his teeth. One eyeball forced itself from its cavity and dangled by the nerves. He picked up the wheelbarrow effortlessly, one-handed, and swung it round.

Sabela beat a hasty retreat to the house. In the kitchen, Mrs. Fieldstone was polishing the huge, iron stove.

"You're right. He does like to throw things," said Sabela, sinking into a chair.

Mrs. Fieldstone handed her a glass of lemonade. "He's smashed nearly every pane of glass in the back of the house," she said, wiping her hand on her apron.

"When did the haunting start?"

"Did Mr. Wilkes not tell you in his letter? It was two months ago. When they broke ground for that silly swimming pool the Missus wanted. What's the point of a swimming pool when you have a river? But he never denies her."

Sabela gave this some thought. Obviously the ghost disliked anyone digging in that part of the garden. In both cases, it was what woke him. Sipping her lemonade, she thought back to the low wall, which formed a right angle. Much like an old foundation . . .

"Hm," said Sabela, getting up. "May I borrow the typewriter?"

"Mr. Wilkes said you had free rein," said the other woman. "Now, for supper, would you prefer ham or chicken?"

The ghost was engaged in picking up chunks of sod and attempting to fit them back into the red earth. Sabela looked down at the typewriter in her arms. Caligraph Ideal 1, read the red label. She hoped to goodness he wouldn't just snatch it up and smash it over her head.

The ghost turned at her arrival, fury etched in his face, and then paused, curious. She balanced the typewriter on the stone wall. There was a blank piece of paper already in place, so she began to type, figuring that he would need a demonstration. Because it was not a QWERTY keyboard, it took her an embarrassingly long time to type H-E-L-L-O.

Also, to her consternation, the type bars swung up, not down, and she could not see what she had typed. She peered to see what was wrong. When she looked up, she saw him smiling faintly. He reached over and used a lever to lift the carriage, demonstrating how the letters showed up on the underside of the paper.

"Um, thanks. Your turn," she said, stepping back.

She wondered how many times the ghost had stood outside the study window, invisibly watching Mr. Wilkes type. It was the only explanation she could imagine for why he understood the machine better than she.

He extended a long left forefinger and slowly, searching back and forth, hit a few keys.

GOAWAY it said, when she checked.

"I can't," she replied.

GO AWAY he typed again, this time adding the space.

"I cannot. I am trapped here like you."

NO

The machine only wrote in caps, which gave the impression that he was yelling.

"What is your name?" she asked.

There was a long pause. The ghost looked reflective, as if he had forgotten this fact. Then he typed:

RUFUS ASHER BELL

It was Sabela's turn to pause. She studied him. Rufus Bell, the murderer, had been arrested and executed in town and, the records attested, buried in the criminals' graveyard without a marker. So what was he doing here, zealously guarding the foundations of an old farm building?

"Why are you here?" she said gently.

LEAVE ME BE

Sabela put her hands on her hips and glared at him. "I would if I could, Rufus. I can't go until you go. I'm here to help you."

He said something inaudible, and she pointed to the typewriter. With his left finger he typed, forcefully, each strike sounding like a gunshot.

NO HELP

"I'm the only person who's ever been able to see you, Rufus. Don't you think I might be able to do something?"

He cradled his right hand against his chest, where it dripped blood. He shook his head.

"Rufus. What happened to you?"

The ghost's eyes burned like black coals.

THAT WITCH

First ghosts, now witches. Rufus collapsed on the wall, head hanging, and took an interest in the progress of a line of ants. Sabela pushed back her hair, feeling a headache working up behind her eyes. She was never going to get out of here. She sat down in her former spot, and Rufus slid over petulantly, away from her. She had the perverse desire to scoot after him.

"Look," she said. "We both want the same thing--to go home. Where is your home?"

He looked up. His hair, which seemed to reflect his mood, shone copper. He turned his head and then pointed to the mountains across the river.

"Me, too," said Sabela absently. Common wisdom about ghosts dictated that if they could come to terms with their deaths, they could find peace and move on. She wasn't actually sure that was true. But Rufus had died on the gallows. Which invited the question . . .

"Why are you here?" she asked. "You were, um, executed in town."

Rufus nodded.

"So . . . what are you doing here at the house?"

No response.

"Rufus, who is the witch?"

He got up immediately and typed.

WIDOW FAIRFAX

"John Fairfax's wife? What was she to you?"

For the second time, Rufus reached out his left hand to her, as if he held the answer in his palm. For some reason this terrified Sabela, as if she were being offered a live wire.

"I can't," she said, and he dropped it, looking more sad than angry.

A bell rang for supper.

"I'll come back," she said.

She left him sitting there, leaving the typewriter, hoping that he would use it and not decide to toss it into the river. The house was not much cooler than the outdoors. The kitchen door stood open, allowing a breeze heavily scented with honeysuckle. She took off her bonnet and tidied her hair.

Mrs. Fieldstone had prepared ham, biscuits, sliced tomatoes, and more lemonade. While Sabela ate (time travel always made her ravenous), the housekeeper poured some batter into a pan and slid it into the oven.

"What do you know about the ghost?" Sabela asked,

spooning up the last of her grits. "I know what Mr. Wilkes told me, but you must know something, too."

"It's the ghost of John Fairfax," said Mrs. Fieldstone.

No, thought Sabela. It isn't.

"He was murdered by his hired hand, as you know." She reflected for a moment, then dropped her voice. "Gossip was that his wife was having a love affair with the hired hand, Bell. The men fought over her."

"Really?" said Sabela, putting her chin in her hand. "Do you know what she was like?"

"Young and very pretty. His second wife. She married quickly after he died, the town doctor, I forget his name. Didn't seem too broken up about her husband or Rufus Bell."

Now what? thought Sabela. Surely it all meant something, but what?

"I'm going to make up your bed," said Mrs. Fieldstone. She hesitated. "When the clock strikes, will you pull the gingerbread out, if I haven't returned?"

After she left, Sabela traced patterns in the condensation on the tabletop. The kitchen filled with the scent of gingerbread. After some time, against her better judgment, she clicked in to speak to Clara again.

"Hello? Hi. I tried talking to him. It's not John Fairfax, it's Rufus Bell."

"Ah," said Clara, sounding pleased.

"You knew?"

"Oh, I suspected."

"You could have said."

"I didn't want to bias you."

"Fine. Whatever. Clara, he says . . . I got him talking, sort of--but it's complicated. I don't know what I'm doing."

"A lovely job, that's what," said Clara warmly.

"How do you know that?" But she did not really expect an answer. And it was absurd to argue with this powerful AI who could foresee most, if not all, ends.

She heard a shuffle at the door and startled. Rufus stood in the door, holding the typewriter beneath one arm. Her first thought was that he had come to tell her something. He looked at her entreatingly.

"What is it?" she asked. He stood back, gestured to the open door. He wanted to talk. Sabela rose, just as a scorched smell reached her.

Sabela swore and ran to the stove. She'd missed the chiming of the clock while talking to Clara, and now the gingerbread was burning. She opened the oven door and pulled out the pan, hot and pungent in the humid summer evening. She set it on the counter and turned just in time to see Rufus drop the typewriter. His pupils dilated, his nostrils flared, and he doubled over, retching. He heaved up a flood of insects: beetles, flies, and most horridly, maggots. They flowed over the tumbled typewriter, writhed on the wooden floor, and scuttled toward Sabela. Next came a wave of sickly white spiders. Sabela could shoot a stranger in the face with no compunction, but she could not bring herself to so much as step on a spider.

She jumped up onto the chair like a true Victorian woman and hitched up her skirts.

Rufus vomited again, and then, again, hideously, as his torso split open, spilling organs.

Sabela fled.

Coward, she thought, as she ran down the hall. She did not stop until she had reached the front porch which, aside from the driveway, was the furthest point on the property from the garden. None of the insects followed her. Were they ghost insects?

She sat down on the swing and rubbed her face, trying to think.

If there was a villain in this story, it was Rufus. He had committed adultery, he had killed his rival. He referred to his love object as a witch. And yet there was something in his eyes that told another story. She could not shake the feeling that, whatever had happened, Rufus was damaged, frightened, traumatized.

The sun was setting. She got up and walked back through the house, finding the kitchen blessedly empty of vermin. She picked up the typewriter and went outside. The fireflies had come out. The scent of honeysuckle overwhelmed the scent of gingerbread.

When she got to the garden, Rufus was not there.

She set the typewriter down and untangled a few of the type bars. It was dented slightly in one part of the frame, but it still worked. She put a fresh sheet of paper into it and then folded her hands in her lap and waited.

Rufus appeared a few moments later, looking pale, diminished. He kept his right arm wrapped around his abdomen.

"Rufus, I'm sorry," said Sabela softly. "Please tell me what happened?"

Watching her the whole time, he came over. Then, with deep concentration, he typed.

Sabela lifted the sheet to read WHAT THEY DID
She looked at him.

"What did they do?" she said.
THE KNIVES

"I don't know what that means, Rufus."

He gazed back, gaunt with misery, and shook his head.

Sabela saw that, in truth, he had no words for what had happened. She felt a surge of compassion and reached out, put her hand in his cold left palm. A bitter, prickling chill shot up her arm, making her stiffen. She could not let go but fell toward him, dragged, sucked into the darkness, the smell of blood, and the screaming.

The screaming.

You were calm as you mounted the gallows steps. You deserved to die. You had murdered John Fairfax because his wife begged you to. You knew now that the tales she told you, tales of beatings and torment, were lies. She blinded you with lust, and pity. You should have known better. And so you bent your head for the noose, submitting to your punishment.

When the rope snapped tight and your neck broke, you kept falling, falling, landing upright on the ground. Above you hung your limp form, twisting slowly on the rope. The crowd roared with gratification, but no one saw you.

You had expected hell, dared, by repentance, to hope for heaven. But this? To be a ghost? You stared up at your body and stayed by the gallows where it dangled all day, until the gawkers dissipated and only crows circled.

At nightfall they took your body down. They wrapped it in sheets and put it into a cart. But instead of taking it for burial, the horses set off down the river road. You followed, running after them as they made their way back to the Fairfax house. There Doctor Ramsay waited with the Widow Fairfax in the dusk.

You saw immediately that _they_ were the true lovers, that they had used you to accomplish their own ends. The Widow Fairfax smiled at him, gave him a hungry kiss. Her pretty little face looked viperish. She had always despised you, despite her caresses and sighs of affection. You were nothing but a means to her ends.

But you could not understand what the doctor and his men wanted with your body. You did not understand when they took you into the old barn and carried you down into the root cellar. Not when they placed you on the table and pulled away the sheets. Not when the doctor snipped off your clothes. Not until he took a wickedly sharp knife and sank it into your defenseless white stomach.

You had heard of this kind of thing, of grave robbers and mutilated corpses, unspeakable things done under shadow of night. And then you understood what Doctor Ramsay had meant when he said to you, "for the advancement of medicine." That when you put your hand--your traitorous right hand--through the prison bars to shake on the deal, you were agreeing to _this_. You thought a mug of ale and a square of ginger cake adequate payment for your castoff body and whatever he meant to do with it. You simply did not understand. That it had been a bribe--a last meal in exchange for these hideous violations.

You screamed, then, but no one heard. You could not move. Instead you watched as they began the dissection. The doctor opened you up, ladled out your organs, flayed your skin. He neatly slit your right wrist and demonstrated to his assistants how the tendons controlled your fingers--

the very ones he had clasped in false friendship. You screamed until you were voiceless, and your screams dwindled to broken croaks, and then you put your hands to your face and wept.

The bearded doctor did not even sew you up. He left you crudely assembled--one eye still prised out of its socket--and wrapped you in the stained sheets. When they left, at last, they took your body with them, still under cover of night, to be buried before first light. You sought to follow and could not. You could only hover in the same place, even after the barn was torn down, the cellar filled in. Even after the Widow Fairfax and Doctor Ramsay were long in their own graves. You were trapped, endlessly re-living your evisceration by strangers.

Eventually you slept. But not for long.

Someone began to dig, and then you woke, and along with you, your powers.

Sabela stood with Rufus in the chilly dawn. A mist came up around her ankles. Their hands were woven together, but his hands no longer burned hers. They felt cool and slight, as she thought they had in life, gentle as air. She looked up to see that his face was the color of skin again, and no longer that terrible, tubercular white. The flames in his hair had been quenched, and his curls were a chaste auburn, his burning coal eyes turned tired hazel.

"You saw me," he said, and she heard his voice for the first time. "You saw."

Sabela nodded. Her cheeks were wet--she had been crying.

"I'm sorry that happened to you," she whispered.

"But it's over now," said Rufus. "You saw me. I thank you."

Sabela could not speak, and nodded again.

"I'm going to go home now. You should go home, too," he continued, his voice still uneven, heavily southern, and indefinably old-fashioned.

He released her hands and kissed her on the forehead, then turned toward the river.

"What about the witch?" called Sabela.

He cocked his head back at her.

"She's nothing." He smiled, and Sabela saw that he could be handsome. She watched him walk down the path toward the river and then, weightless as a feather, skim across the water like a wisp of mist.

After he disappeared, she stood in the muddy garden alone, feeling tears dry on her face. A heavy determination settled over her.

"I'm done," she told Clara.

"I knew you'd find a way, hen," said Clara. "Picking you up in fifteen."

Sabela began to count backwards. <u>It isn't over</u>, she thought. <u>Just wait, Clara. Just wait. When I get back, we're going to have a little chat about the consequences of going off script. And, because you like me, you'll humor me. I know you will.</u>

"Five, four, three . . ."

Because she was coming back, this time to 1842. And this time no one would stop her from using her pistol. Rufus would never be a ghost, nor a violated piece of flesh.

She was coming back, and she was going to put a bullet into the Widow Fairfax's pretty, scheming little head.

1957 Royal FPE

1958 Olympia SM3

Three Gardenias and a Box of Pens

Mathilda-Anne Florence

Peter doesn't have much time. He stands at the top of the stairway, listening. Shadows dance back and forth on the deck below. He can hear metal tinging on metal as the captain and crew practice their swordplay. Laughter drifts upstairs as they jeer each other on.

Ten minutes, he assures himself.

He glides across the main deck, his own small sword in hand, past the bathroom--Poop Deck, he corrects himself--and down to the captain's quarters. At the door, he listens again. Still the men laugh. The wizard-pirate slips in with his little sword hooking the doorknob he can't quite reach. He leaves it open enough so he can hear anyone in the hallway.

The captain will finish his sword practice and it will be time for dinner.

The captain's quarters are bright with late afternoon sun. In the center, a grand rug and an ancient desk take up most of the space. Both were stolen from a king in some exotic country on the other side of the world. On top sits the treasure the wizard-pirate is after.

The Queen Fairy's magic green-machine.

The boy climbs into the old leather chair and stretches as far as he can across the desk. He's careful not to knock over the pen jar or let the magazines --Scrolls, he corrects himself again--fall to the floor. He knows this because he did it last week and now he's not allowed in here anymore. A stained-glass lamp--Lantern! It has to be a lantern. Ships don't have lamps. Do they?--He pulls the chain on the colorful lantern. A magical flame bursts to life inside.

"Behold," the wizard-pirate whispers triumphantly as he raises his plastic sword. "My quest is complete. I have found the mystic Box of Truth that will now divulge to me, Peter of Paddington Court, where they are hiding the lost Queen Fairy."

The Box of Truth is pale green with cream 'buttons' and a wide black 'mouth'. It is said that it will tell you where to find a treasure trove of lost left socks, or write songs that no one will think are bad. All one must do is feed magic paper into its black mouth and push the right buttons to cast the spell. The answers will magically appear. At least that's how he believes it should work, so obviously it will.

He puts his plastic sword on the captain's desk.

He finds paper in a carved wooden box beside the lantern. It's Mom's special paper--the Queen Fairy's paper, he corrects the story. Her name and a feather are at the top, but he doesn't know what 'Prof.' or 'Ph.D.' means.

Standing on tiptoes, he puts a sheet in the magic machine and turns the knobs until it appears on the other side of the feeding-thingy. He pushes one of the buttons down as hard as he can. A tiny hammer comes up and hits the paper. It rests there as he holds the button down. A pale b sits on the paper. He hits another button and holds it. Again, it is faint, the g no better than the b.

The wizard-pirate stands up straight, arms out like she taught him and snaps his fingers on the buttons to cast the magic spell. Much like Daddy--Captain!-- taught him to hit flies with a swatter. Somewhere inside the Box of Truth, a bell dings and the hammers stop no matter how hard he hits the keys.

The magic lantern absorbs all the sunlight in the world. The room grows dark. Only the Box of Truth is visible.

"Peter, what are you doing?"

He spins around on the chair and freezes. "Nothing."

"It's the middle of the night, Boo."

The Queen Fairy stands in the open doorway, her face shadowed in the dim light.

"Come on, you start JK in the morning and I have to be to work early."

"No you don't." He pleads, reaching out to her over the back of the chair.

The Queen Fairy steps into the room and takes his hand. She kisses the top of his head and looks over at the desk. A tumble of caramel-swirl curls fall into her face and she pushes them back, hooking them over her ear.

"I was casting a spell. I'm using your special paper, Mommy. I'm sorry."

"It's okay sweetie. What kind of spell? Did you lose another sock?"

She crosses her arms, pulling her long grey cardigan tighter. She leans over to see what he has written on her typewriter.

"No, I need to know where they're hiding Her."

"Hiding who? A princess? Or a dragon trapped in a dungeon?"

He stares up at her, mouth hanging open. He flings his arms around his mother. He breathes in the sweet vanilla of her lotion and the fresh apple of laundry soap that Daddy won't buy anymore.

"No one, Mommy. You're here."

"Do you need a glass of water? Come on, it's time for bed."

"No, it's dinner time." He pulls her tighter.

She kisses the top of his head, but he refuses to let her go. He mumbles into her shoulder, I'm in grade one now.

She reaches over and turns off the desk lamp, casting them in darkness. She takes his hand and helps him off the chair.

"My sword!" He lets go for just a second and grabs it from the desk where he left it. The magic lantern releases all the sunlight it was holding. The world is once again flooded with golden afternoon light.

Peter spins around to the closed office door.

The Queen Fairy is gone.

*   *   *

For the last three days of summer vacation the world has been nothing but rain and clouds. Every lawn and ditch have transformed into heavenly mud for Peter and his friends on their BMX bikes. Riding to school on the first day of grade five, they hit every puddle and mud hole they can find, including the one right in front of Sara Whitmore in her brand new red jeans and Spice Girls t-shirt. The Lost Boys strike again!

It HAD been an awesome morning.

When they got to school Sara stood there, covered in mud, waiting for them—with the principal. Forced to apologize to Sara in front of the class, he is now stuck writing a letter of atonement to both his principal and Sara's parents.

Dad reads what he has so far, giving it a few minor tweaks. "I know you're upset, but it needs to not <u>sound</u> like you are." He makes Peter rewrite it on the typewriter. "I'm the only one that can decipher your handwriting."

Dad leaves him alone to live out his sentence.

After he's done, he puts in a fresh sheet of paper and starts writing a letter to Mom. He fills the page with questions about girls and Dad. And how long is too long to be grounded? He stops and stares out the office window, wishing he were climbing a tree or jumping in the last of the summer mud.

The sky is all wrong.

Peter has spent thousands of evenings after school sitting in the reading chair daydreaming, watching sunsets and stars, and even the Northern Lights once. Instead of golden-mauve along the treetops and indigo-black above, a grey-blue rests along the treetops and the sky above is a tinge of pink. The world is upside down, he thinks. He looks at his digital wristwatch. It says 6:30pm.

He walks across the hall to look out the bathroom window. The bare hint of pink sunrise lines the tops of the birch trees. Did he fall asleep at the typewriter all night? When he comes back to the office and turns on the light, a movement by the desk steals the breath from his lungs.

She has her back to him. Her large cardigan sweater the color of storms shrouds her from shoulders to knees. He can see the edges of her shoulder blades under the heavy knit. A green and gold silk scarf wraps her head, turban style. With that specific scarf he knows there are no more caramel-swirl curls tucked beneath.

She grips the edge of the desk as she inches her way to her chair in the corner. The skin on the back of her hand reminds him of the translucent wraps on spring rolls. Its ghostliness stands out sharply against the dark oak of the desk.

He chokes, "I wrote to you." He clears the catch in his throat, "I used the typewriter like you told me to."

She turns, leans on the corner of the desk, a handful of Kleenex covering her mouth as she coughs. On the back of her hand, he recognizes a large black bruise. Her sweater slips down her bony arm, exposing two more. All three the shape of gardenias. Every time she came home from the hospital there were more 'blooms'. These were her last bouquet.

She shakes her head. "I told you to wait. For when I'm not here anymore."

"But you're..." not, he wants to say.

"Where is it?" She looks over at the typewriter.

He goes to pull the letter out of the machine, but it's empty.

He stammers.

She reaches out and pats his head as he stares at the empty machine, dumbfounded.

He wants to grab and squeeze her but is scared he may crush her.

She groans as she lowers herself into her chair. Rushing to her side, he pulls the blanket off the back and spreads it over her lap. She closes her eyes and lets out a heavy, exhausted sigh as if to release the weight of the world from all their shoulders. He sits on the stool at her feet and puts them both in his lap. He rubs at them tenderly the way he remembers Dad doing.

Her eyes open. Dull grey confusion gazes at him, where once emerald green had held him captive as she told him bedtime stories about dragons and flying pirate ships.

"Peter?" She looks at him as if for the first time. "How old are you?"

His heart jumps into his nostrils and he straightens his shoulders. "I'm ten now, next month."

"You're growing up?" Sadness fills her voice and deflates him.

"Of course I am, Mommy. I'm a young man now."

"Yes, you are, aren't you?" She leans forward, grasping his hand. Her grip is cold and smooth like a stone polished by ocean waves. "Peter, my little Lost Boy. You're going to be a regular grown-up one day, no matter how much I want you to stay young. You're going to keep getting bigger and grow a beard like your father. One day you'll have children of your own if you want them." She pats his hand and falls back into the chair. Her breathing rasps against her chest. She coughs into the wad of tissues and he grabs more from the box beside her chair. He hands them to her and tosses the bloody ones in the wastebasket.

From outside the room, Dad calls up to see if he has finished yet. Peter turns but refuses to let go of Mom's feet. "I'm almost done. I'll be down in a minute."

"I want it perfect," Dad yells back. "We don't need to be starting this year off in muddy waters."

They can hear him laughing at his own joke. Peter rubs at his face and groans.

"Who are you...?" She looks to him and over to where he is yelling at the door. "Are you talking to your father?"

He nods, hanging his head.

"What did you do?" She grabs his arm with a grip as tight as a gorilla.

"I caked a girl in mud with my bike."

She laughs. It turns into a cough she hides in her Kleenex.

"Did he ground you?" She rubs his arm where she's turned it red.

He nods again, looking even more pitiful. "And I have to write a letter of apology to my principal."

"Your principal?" Her voice cracks with anger. "To the girl yes, but not your principal surely?"

He lets out a heavy sigh and throws up his arms. "That's what I said!"

She sits back and rearranges the blanket over her legs. A corner of her headscarf unravels, the raw pink of her scalp showing beneath.

"Well just do it, I suppose," she says philosophically. "Get them all off your back. They need to feel like they're making you a better person. Adults can be idiots that way." She wheezes, putting her hand on her chest, but manages to keep it down. "Just remember, Peter, you may get as big and old as an adult, but don't ever be as stupid as one and fool yourself into growing up."

"I won't Mommy, I promise."

She pulls him across to her and squeezes him until he can't breathe. "Keep writing, my Lost Boy. I need you to as much as you do." She lets him go.

Golden light of evening pours over his shoulders into the office.

He grabs the letter to his principal off the desk and pulls the other out of the typewriter. He folds up the latter and stuffs it in his back pocket. As he flicks off the light switch, he can hear Dad coming up the stairs.

* * *

He sits facing the wall.

Her desk no longer takes the place of honor in the center of the office. It has been relegated to the wall. It could have been placed five feet to the left, where the window overlooks the backyard. But no, the desk faces the wall. On top sits a monstrous electrical contraption needing three plug-ins, hence the desk's new situation. As much as Peter enjoys playing King's Quest, he will never understand the blinking cursor-thing. Taunting and patronizing. A huge waste of space.

After some digging around, he finds the tweed case covered in dragon and fairy stickers on a shelf in the closet. It's been years since he's touched it. He pushes the monitor and keyboard out of the way and sets up the Queen Fairy's typewriter in its rightful place. The print is faint but grows bolder like the hope in his heart.

He writes about how he's read through all the university catalogues and still has no clue. He's read and reread her journals, only finding more questions he doesn't know how to ask. He wonders if she had meant to curse him with the name of a cruel leader of perpetually immature boys, or the eldest brother-king in a world through a wardrobe? He fills three pages, finding no answers in his ramblings.

Closing his eyes, he takes three deep breaths, willing the gloomy morning sky to disappear. When he opens them, the room is still dull, and nothing has changed. He chides himself. He's too old for tricks and childish fantasies. He sighs and stretches, running his hands through his mop of long, curly hair. He scratches the small but worthy patch of facial hair at the end of his chin. It has taken him all summer to grow it out. He picks up his worn copy of <u>A Wrinkle in Time</u> and goes to sit in the reading chair.

A great bath of afternoon sunshine pours through the office window. Half asleep, she rocks herself back and forth with one foot tucked beneath her and the other on the floor. The late summer sun heats the room beyond the air conditioner's capabilities. With only a tank top and shorts on, sweat glistening on her pale Irish skin, she hums lazily, tracing lines up and down her very pregnant belly. A thick plait of caramel swirls hangs over her shoulder and between her breasts. He resists the urge to reach out and pull a curl that has come loose in front of her ear.

Frozen in place, Peter is afraid to disturb her. Dear god, let this be real, he prays. He tries not to breathe too loudly.

She must have heard his heart cracking against his ribs. She sucks in a quick breath and startles herself awake. She squints against the bright light.

"Greg?" She yawns. "What time is it?"

Peter takes a step forward, casting a helpful shadow as her eyes adjust. "I'm not sure, Mom." He takes another deep breath and looks over at the clock. "Looks like two in the afternoon."

Her hands cover her belly as she takes a better look at the tall stranger. She looks down at her unborn child and back to Peter.

"My grandmother told me stories about this back in Ireland. Women having visions of their grown children when pregnant. The old stories say they're changelings, traveling through time to find their rightful parents." She reaches up to him. He closes the space in one long stride and takes both of her hands in his. He helps her to stand as she pushes herself up, belly first. "You're real. You're really here! So tall, so handsome. You look so much like my father." She pulls him closer and stares at his eyes. Her fingers trace lines on his face as they had on her belly, tangling themselves in the same caramel swirls drooping over his eyes. "Why have you come, Aisling?"

He laughs. "Aisling?"

"My dream." She smiles like she has a secret. "It's Old Gaelic."

"Do you think I'm a changeling?" His throat grows tight.

"Not unless trolls crawled onto the ships from the old country." She laughs. It is a young, full laugh.

He leans in and smells the citrus of her shampoo, her hair warm from bathing in the sun. Why had he been so afraid to write to her again? Everything about her is alive and real and he never wants to let her go.

"How old are you now?"

"Seventeen. I'm a senior next week."

"What did we call you?"

"Peter."

"Peter," she says it like it's the first time she has ever heard it. "My grandfather's name. Greg wanted Malcolm."

"That's my middle name."

"I must be such an old woman to you." She giggles and covers her cheeks. Her skin is smooth, her face so full of life and color. He takes her hands in his.

"Never. You look exactly the same. My never-aging Queen Fairy."

"Oh, I'm a Queen Fairy, am I? Perhaps I'm the changeling then. My half-fairy son having the power to travel along time." She makes a flourish with her hands before settling them back on her pregnant belly. "Very fitting."

He shakes his head. "Not me--you. You enchanted your typewriter so I can talk to you whenever I need you."

She stares at him, shocked and sad.

He's said too much.

"You can't talk to me where you are?"

He looks away before she can see tears. She wraps him in a hug so tight he thinks she is trying to pull him into her belly. The image weirds him out. He buries his face into her shoulder, hugging her around her neck. When he does look up, his face is wet with eyes rimmed in red sorrow.

"What is it then that you came to talk to me about, my beautiful boy?" She wipes away the frustration from his face.

"I don't know what to do...to be. Dad wants me to go into finance like him, but I hate math and don't care about money or stocks and stuff. I don't want to be stuck behind a desk for the rest of my life."

He doesn't know how long he can hold onto her, scared she is going to vanish in the next breath. Maybe the more he's written to her, the longer she stays. He figures he has a page and a half left. He pours it all out to her. His dreams, his stories; sports, writing, cooking, everything he enjoys, but Dad insists he put a suit on and sit in a cubicle, a nameless drone in a beehive of boredom.

She asks if he has been reading her own journals. One hand reflexively strokes her belly, the other rubbing his arm.

He laughs and nods, wiping his nose on his sleeve. Those were her words, her fears, written years before he was born. How true they rang for him when he read them.

He should know his father would never make him do anything he didn't want to. "He makes a lot of strong suggestions, that's all. Make sure your ambitions, even if just to explore, are just as strong."

When he tries to tell her she's right, he stands alone in the room.

*   *   *

T-minus five days before University. The house is in organized chaos as Dad packs up to move himself cross-country for his new job. Peter is staying in town and going to live on campus where Mom once taught Mythology and Modern Literature.

The office was one of the first rooms to get packed up. Peter looks through boxes of books and binders for her typewriter. He opens the closet to see if it is still on the top shelf, but it's empty. In the garage more boxes are stacked and waiting for moving day. Dad is King Thorough. A clipboard with a list of each boxes' contents hangs from a nail on the wall. He goes through it three times.

Dad comes out with another box. "Looking for something?"

"Yeah, Mom's typewriter." He flips the pages on the clipboard again.

"Why would you want that old thing? I got rid of it weeks ago."

The words hit him like a tornado whipping through a trailer park. He chokes and coughs until Dad whacks him on the back to breathe.

He picks up his voice off the ground. "What the hell, Dad? Why?"

"It's not like we used it."

"I did!" He bangs the clipboard against his chest. "Maybe not to write great novels or anything, but I used it. It was Mom's. It's like the last thing we have of hers."

"What are you talking about? We have her journals and paintings, and even those are taking up too much space."

"Mom's memories are taking up too much space?" His voice rises and hits the garage ceiling. He slams the clipboard on the concrete floor. "What did you do with it?"

"I put it out back in the lane. I thought maybe someone might take it before the garbage truck did. Peter!"

Before Dad can finish, Peter bolts out the back door of the garage. He scares two alley cats when he crashes through the fence gate. He tears through boxes of old stock market books and a bag of orphaned Tupperware. He spills over the trash bin and pulls out bags, then shoves them back in. No typewriter. No case covered in dragon and fairy stickers. Papers and old books litter the lane.

Dad grabs him by the shoulders and yanks him out of the mess.

"Stop it Peter, look at what you're doing. It isn't here. It was weeks ago."

"YOU THREW HER OUT!" Peter spins on him. "Without even asking me. How could you? What the fuck is wrong with you? She's my mother and you tossed her out with the trash."

"Peter, stop this. It was a typewriter, not your mother. You have her journals and her paintings; those are your mother. Not some toy."

"Toy?" He clenches his fists in front of Dad's face but steps away. "She wrote her journals with it. She used it to bring her soul to life. Everything about it was her; it was the color of her eyes."

Dad covers his face. "I'm sorry, Peter. I didn't know. I thought you were always playing games on the computer. I didn't even think you knew how to use it or what it was."

"I do know what it _is_. It's Mom. And you threw her away."

Peter shoves past his father, his shoulder slamming him back into the fence. Halfway across the yard he feels bad and turns.

Dad is closing the gate but waves him on into the house.

"Let's get dinner started. I think we both need a beer."

* * *

"Peter? Peter Devlin?" A man waves at him overtop several heads of students rushing to class. He pushes through the parade and stops short of Peter's nose.

"Jesus, you look just like her."

"Sorry?"

"You're Katherine's boy, aren't you?"

Peter nods. He recognizes the red glasses more than the man.

"Brando Hooper." They shake hands. "I was your Mom's assistant for three years. Las time I saw you, you had eaten a lizard, so she brought you in to keep you under observation."

Peter snaps his fingers. "You told me if it had been a baby dragon, I was going to grow scales and hoard pens in my basement. What was I, four? I still wish it had been a dragon."

"No scales and pen hoarding then?" Brando pushes his glasses up his nose. "Do you have a minute, or are you on your way to class?"

"I have an hour before anthropology. I was going to kill some time in the library."

"I have something better. I think you'll like it."

Peter follows the man up to the top floor of the Gandler building and down a quiet hallway. It feels familiar, the low ceilings, chairs lining the walls. Mr. Hooper unlocks a door and leads him inside.

Peter stops short in the doorway. "This was hers."

"You remember?"

"Yeah, but it looks so much smaller."

"It was weird when they gave it to me. It had been a few years after..." He trails off. He looks around

as if he's lost something. "It was empty all that
time...sort of." He opens and closes several cupboards
until he looks in one and says, "Aha!" He pulls a
large banker's box out of the cupboard and places it
on top of a table already covered in papers and books.
"I remember your dad. He came in and grabbed a few
things, not much. Personal items; photos, journals,
some artwork. The university donated most of her
books, and I grabbed what I could."

Inside, there is an old daytimer, a notebook with
random scribbles, a windup clock, and a shoebox full
of pens. Peter thumbs through the diary and digs
through the pens.

"And then there's this." Mr. Hooper pulls a black
box down from a higher shelf and carries it over to
the table by its handle. "I wanted to take it home,
but never got around to it. I'm not sure if you would
have any use for it or know how to use it."

Peter turns the box over right-side-up and flips
the latch without hesitating. He takes a deep breath
before opening it up.

It is dark burgundy with a glossy flat top. On the
front in gold decal, the word Sterling is slightly
worn but clear. This is nothing like the Queen Fairy's
Box of Truth she had kept at home. This one is all
power and profession. The typewriter of an important
literary scholar with too much to teach the world and
never enough time.

"I know exactly how to use this." His voice catches
in his throat. "I had her other one at home."

She had one here too? he wonders. Of course she
did. But all this time?

"You should have it. Take all of it. You can never
have too many pens in this place."

Mr. Hooper makes Peter promise to let him know if
he ever needs anything. The men shake hands and laugh
at the slight awkwardness of the exchange.

Peter carries all of it to his dorm room and
contemplates skipping anthro.

*   *   *

Peter plunks himself into the rickety rolling desk-
chair. He slumps over, cradling his head in his lap.

Not like it's going to work anyhow, right?

The typewriter is sitting on the dorm room desk with the case off on the floor. This is no sea-green-fairy-machine. This is a grown-up's typewriter. Sleek and stylish. It would look more at home in a very sensible den with a dram of scotch and an ashtray nearby. Not the whimsical room of an artist filled with storybooks and paints, and peacock feathers that sprinkled magic every time the windows were left open.

Peter lets out a sigh and pulls himself together. If anything, he should test the ribbon and see if he needs a new one. He tears open the paper sheathing of the fresh ream of printer paper. It takes some finessing to find and release the carriage lock, but he manages to reset the margins without snapping anything off.

He types the date.

It would be good to start a journal, much like she had during her college years, he thinks. Over the last summer, he had read them slowly and carefully, trying to glean any advice she might have been able to give him before moving out on his own.

He types, "What the hell am I doing here?"

He checks his watch and grabs his jacket. Dinner in the cafeteria in 15 minutes. He heads downstairs and out into the quad. The humid air hits his lungs like a hot glass of water after a marathon. He takes off his jacket. Only an hour ago it had been blistering cold.

Campus is dead except for two crows pecking at the ground beneath a birch tree.

He stops and sits on the north steps of the Gandler building, pulling out a cigarette and snapping his Zippo open to light it.

Soft clicking of shoes on the stone steps makes him turn and look up to a pair of red high heels descending the stairs.

"Can I get a light?" The voice is as familiar as his reflection in the mirror. He looks up at her smiling face, a tumble of caramel swirls bouncing on her shoulders. She wears summer-casual jeans and a yellow blouse.

"Look at this place." She takes a deep pull from her cigarette as he holds his Zippo to the end. She shakes her head. "My first year teaching, and in a few weeks I'm going to be overrun with brilliant kids thinking they need to be idiots and grow up."

1961 SMC Sterling, Seafoam Green

Consummation

Daniel Gewertz

Time has slunk along at its plodding forward pace for so long now, I have questioned the wisdom of revealing any details about that brief period of my life when I shifted back and forth nearly at will. But now, nearing my old age, I suspect there is little to fear. What do I have to lose by making my time travels public? My insubstantial reputation? I do not promise cosmic or spiritual sense here. Mine is a story of sex and yearning and a curious breed of fulfillment--and also one, thankfully, unencumbered by spurious scientific theorizing. So I assume the tale might gain some readership, if only with crackpots. And slightly perverse romantics.

I should start with the Royal typewriter. The year was 2010. I was 60 years old, a barely employed journalist. To capsulize: lonely single white male living in a one-bedroom Cambridge apartment no longer protected by rent control. I was at that point as a writer when you can't produce a good line without a firm deadline and a promised paycheck. My computer stank of for-hire formulaic writing, so I was hoping maybe an old-fashioned manual typewriter might release my creative mojo. I knew it was a poor worker who blamed his tools, but I was at a disempowered stage in life where I felt dependent on magic, or merely magical thinking. At the very least, I could make an agreement with myself to type a daily journal. A few paragraphs. A page or two. A tangible measure of progress.

One shining Saturday early spring morning I passed a yard sale on Dana Street and saw a Royal, black, sturdy, and ancient.

I stopped to see if the typewriter worked.

"You want some paper to test it out?" said a bulky, balding fellow in a too-tight motorcycle jacket and a ponytail.

It felt strange to hit the sturdy, glass, mechanical keys after 22 years of flimsy computer keyboards. But I could tell in an instant: this typewriter wasn't just good; it was in miraculous shape. It seemed fully conditioned, cleaned, oiled. I typed out the line about brown foxes and lazy dogs, and the letters stood out dark and distinct on the page, as sharp as words chiseled on the walls of a marble lobby. The word "Royal" on the machine's curved bonnet glittered in the April sun. The model's name was Companion.

"How much?" I asked, trying to keep the excitement from my voice.

"Go on over to the back yard," he said. "You'll have to ask my mother, Essie. It's hers." Then he paused. "Just tap her lightly on the shoulder if she has her back to you. She's deaf."

The woman in the back yard was removing the dead leaves from her garden. As she stood up, I realized how tiny she was. Maybe 4'10"--simultaneously fragile and resolute, wearing a long, woolen dress and winter jacket, her face a complex etching of small wrinkles, like the crinkles of a chrysanthemum. I carefully walked into her line of sight, which startled her only slightly.

"Hello there," I said loudly.

"I'm deaf, but you don't have to shout. I read lips pretty good." She spoke in a toneless squawk.

"I was wondering the price of the typewriter," I asked, with exaggerated mouth motion, and added a pantomimed fluttering ten-fingered typing motion.

You don't often see smiles as glorious as the one that lit up Essie's face. It was like I had announced myself as a lost relative.

"For you?"

"Yes. My name's Paul."

"Mine's Essie. Are you a writer?"

"I am," I said.

She gave me an unusual look, as if she'd recognized a kinship in me. "In that case, the price is nineteen dollars and forty-five cents."

"That's a very exact amount!"

She moved a little closer to me with a flirtatious air, and craned her head up to meet me, eye to eye. "To me, it's a special number. It stands for the year 1945. On May 7th of that year, Germany surrendered in World War II. May 7th. That was the day I knew my husband Jerome and my two brothers were all coming home safe and sound from Europe. So, to celebrate, I went out and bought this typewriter I had my eyes on in the window of Cambridge Typewriter. And every letter I sent the three of them in their last months over there in Europe, I typed. Those letters looked so pretty. Next month will be 65 years. Exactly 65, dear. I was 23. Yes. I thought $19.45 was a fair price for a writer without much money."

"That I am," I said, grinning. And the deal was struck.

In the days following my chat with Essie, I could not help but think of her as a charmed figure in my life, a benevolent, wrinkled pixie. A fateful figure.

The typewriter didn't even need a new ribbon. While I can't say I poked out any deathless prose, I did plumb a few depths. And I did type a journal entry every single day.

As the old jazz song goes, "Spring can really hang you up the most." By May, as the days lengthened and the air softened, a dank loneliness permeated my evenings like a dirge at a funeral procession. Each night, as I attempted sleep, I would run through a varied assortment of the young women of my long-gone past, two of whom I could've actually married if I'd managed to quell my life-long fear of commitment. In the middle of sleepless nights, I found it hard to believe I had been stupid enough to allow their love to curdle. Sex in memory is a peculiar animal; at least in mine it is. The moments of remembered intimacies from those two long relationships seemed nearly as few in number and scant in detail as my memories of one-night flings. And as I tossed and thrashed during my sleep-deprived nights that spring, the images that would truly pierce me, that would rise up keening, were not of lost, substantive relationships--or even brief affairs--but the regretful memories of the women I chose not to have sex with at all. These sexy young women I had long ago rejected now ambushed my consciousness, their images puncturing my sleep-starved mind like arrows shot from the bow of a frustrated Cupid. In some cases, the memory of a single date with a woman I hadn't thought of in decades sprang out of the void. What power and detail these memories possessed! What witchcraft! A distant, dormant memory would burrow into my jumpy, sleep-deprived brainpan like a tick on a rabbit.

Why did I reject these women? Forgive me, but I'll have to get personal here.

I spent my 20s in two long, monogamous relationships. I loved and was loved, but by the age of 30, I knew I desired more experience before contemplating marriage. My first short affair at 30 was with a 21-year-old college student, a bosomy, seemingly easygoing girl who fit our lovemaking into her overly-busy schedule once a week like I was an elective one-credit class. After two or three months, she broke up with me because she said I was getting too "relationshippy."

After that, I experienced three episodes of erectile dysfunction. This had never happened before. The women were attractive, mind you, but ones I barely knew and did not have much rapport with. At the time, I reacted to these incidents as if the earth had opened up at my feet, and I was looking down into my own grave, ready to be shoveled in and covered over. If I had turned to hypnosis, I might've been cured, for it was fear itself that quickly begat failure. It was as if I smelled disaster before it became flesh.

I was so easily turned off back then! So neurotically delicate! Doubts might creep in early on a first date, originating from a single alienating moment: a teasing gibe, a left-handed compliment, an insult to one of my favorite musicians or writers. This tinge of unease would eat away at my confidence, my equanimity. If I were not fetchingly seduced by the lady in question, I frequently ran away from offered sex, often at the last awkward moment, escaping with such trembling speed it felt like my life were endangered. It horrifies me, looking back, how ruled I was by my fears. Could I have been playing the part of the girl in a Doris Day movie, valuing only love, not lust? No. That wasn't quite it. If I successfully stiffened to lust's challenge, I was more than content with adventure for its own sake.

Okay. If I need to psychoanalyze any further, I will secure the services of a shrink. Let us return to the issue at hand: the bending of the space-time continuum.

Four a.m., May, 2010. I was, once again, sleepless with grief, this time tortured by my rejection, in 1981, of a miraculously shapely Harvard mathematics grad student named Laura. In a fit of reborn dismay at my now baffling decision to flee her bedroom, I flung myself directly from bed to desk and started writing a journal entry about the night in question on my Royal Companion typewriter. In my mind, I saw--in the naked detail I never got to witness 30 years before--her young, curvaceous form, sprawled on her bed, in porn-perfect magnificence. I typed furiously, recapturing the scene, first with my turmoil intact, and then recasting the scene as fiction, with the part of fretful 1981 me played by a fearless, fantasy version of myself, a man of wit and savoir-faire.

Suddenly, I felt an attack of dizziness, as if the blood had rushed clean out of my head. I gripped the edge of my desk and held on tightly, stopping myself from pitching sideways and crashing to the floor. I kept my eyes shut for perhaps seconds, perhaps minutes--I couldn't be sure. The wave within me seemed to crash, then ease. I opened my eyes.

It was night, but I was in a different space. An attic bedroom. I sat, out of breath, in an old, cushioned chair, and across from me was . . . Laura. She lay on her bed, her blouse unbuttoned, her voluminous breasts covered by a beige-colored bra. Her lipstick was smudged.

"Are you okay, Paul?" she asked.

And the peculiar part was, I was okay. I knew where I was, and when I was, and while I was dazed

to be thrust back to 1981, my brain did not rebel.
I accepted the miracle. I had no need to scream,
nor to believe I was turning insane. This was not
some intensely detailed mental fabrication, some
acid flashback. It was not delusion. I knew
where I was! I had yearned myself back in time,
and the only important thing was not to freak out
Laura, who at that moment was gazing at me with
some concern.

"I just felt dizzy for a spell."

"I noticed, Paul."

"Could you do me a favor, Laura? Could you get
me a glass of water and a glass of booze? Do you
have any?"

"Sure. There's cheap bourbon and some vodka,
and some kind of sweet liqueur, also. And beer,
I think."

"The bourbon is good. Get me a double-shot,
please."

"Coming right up, sir," Laura said with a small
grin. She buttoned up her blouse, and scurried
downstairs.

As soon as she left, I stood up. I didn't seem
even a touch rocky. I reached into my right pants
pocket and fished out my wallet. My driver's
license said the expiration date was March, 1983.
The photo of me had a lot of black hair and a
coal-black beard. I felt my own head. Not even
a hint of a bald spot, the hair long and thick
with youth. I remembered (how?) that there was a
bathroom next to Laura's bedroom, so I rushed
into it, flicked on the light, looked in the mirror, and saw my old face. Or rather, my young
face. Two sensations flooded through me. I knew
this was no dream. I could tell how tactile this
world was, how my hands gripping the sides of the
sink were getting a tad colder from the cool porcelain. I felt my stomach, far more muscled, my
legs springy. <u>This is me, in 1981</u>. It was no
dream.

"Where'd you go, Paul?" called out Laura, with
amusement in her voice.

I opened the bathroom door. "Right here,
Laura." I took the glass of bourbon and drank
half of it down with one swallow, chased by the
water.

"Whew! A thirsty man!" she said, sounding flirtatious.

I sat down on the bed, finished the bourbon, and kissed Laura. She was beautifully responsive. I kissed her some more, trying to lure her mouth and tongue into a rhythm and pace and pattern to dovetail with my own, much like leading a dance partner. We settled onto the bed and made out. I noticed, with joy, that my organ was as hard as . . . well, as a healthy 30-year-old's. And then I broke the clinch and uttered a line I had concocted on my Royal typewriter only a few minutes before (or, rather, 29 years later) in the winter of 2010.

"I have a plan. Want to hear it?"

"Shoot," she said.

"First step, we take off every single bit of our clothing as fast as humanly possible. And then, I'm going to slow way down, and kiss you on every inch of your gorgeous body. Except for your feet. I'm afraid I'm not into feet." I then flashed her a comical frown, as if I had given feet the old college try: gross!

Laura laughed out loud, a gleeful guffaw. It was the first time I'd ever heard her laugh like that. (I suddenly realized that I could remember all four of our dates, over a period of as many weeks. I was entering 1981 more and more with every passing minute.)

We unbuttoned and unzipped pretty damned quickly, though Laura, wearing a shiny blouse and tight, knee-length pencil skirt, took care not to literally rip them off. I just threw my stuff in the direction of a chair. And then I proceeded to do exactly what I'd said I would, taking a luxurious amount of time, making sure Laura knew I was in no rush for reciprocation on her part. I'm not sure I added any touches I'd learned in my later years, but perhaps some remnant of my mature self guided me throughout, made me receptive to Laura: inside the moment, instead of looking at it from an alienated distance.

Sex aside, there was so much new information I now received--from Laura's expressions, her tone of voice, the light in her eyes--that I might never have noticed before. My new self was mentally alive to both the present and the future; my head was so overfull that I had no room at all for the pains of the past, or their attendant neurotic fretting. I seemed to see Laura for the first time, noticing her insecurities, and the small, fluttering anxieties that flashed upon her face now and again. It was true we had little conversational rapport. But instead of feeling awkward moments as chilly alienation, or worrying that she was not totally into me, I found myself, quite spontaneously, assuaging her doubts with a few flirty, guileless compliments. Even a jokey ad lib proved to Laura I was dead serious about how sexy I found her. "When I look at your body, I feel spiritual questions," I said with a smile.

"Huh?" she said, baffled. "Spiritual how?"

"As in: If God knew how to make a woman as gorgeous as you, why did She make so few?"

As soon as Laura got the pronoun She, she laughed again with that rich, rolling chuckle of hers. "What a line!" she said, and kissed me lightly on the lips.

"It doesn't count as a line because I have never said it to any woman before."

And that was enough to send her happily into my arms for another bout of phenomenal sex.

Upon leaving her house the next morning, I noticed my bike locked outside on a stop sign. I instantly knew it was mine. In my left front pants pocket was a small key ring. A bike key, a key to the group house I lived in on Antrim Street, and a car key (for a beat-up, shit-brown Buick station wagon I had bought the previous year for $250). I rode off on the bike, feeling, initially, frightened about riding a bike (a remnant of my chronic back pains of the 21st century). Within a block, I was gleefully flying along, my 1981 neurons taking over. It was a bewildering ride, maneuvering Mt. Auburn Street traffic as well as adjusting to the sensations of two divergent lifelines. It was like being caught in a slideshow of photographic double images. I almost lost control of my bicycle going through Harvard Square, staring at all the record stores, bookstores, music clubs, and cafes that filled the Square in 1981 but no longer lived in 2010. It was the opposite of seeing ghosts.

I slowed down, not just for safety's sake, but because of a sudden fear that I might speed back to 2010 accidentally. Was that an irrational worry? What did rationality consist of in the midst of a time-warp? Pedaling past Dana Street, I saw a middle-aged woman I didn't recognize wave at me and call out "Paul!" Finally, I arrived securely at my bright blue apartment house on Antrim Street. For a moment I hesitated to open the front door. I feared that the magic spell of time might be broken with a new indoor locale. But the door key fit adroitly. I was still back in '81. And my housemate George greeted me with no surprise. I was safe.

Why was I thrust back to the spring of 1981? What was I meant to notice, to change? Was I on a mission? And if this was a short-term re-assignment in chronology, what kind of God scrambles time's forward process just to get me laid?

There was a small room on the second floor, my favorite spot in the disheveled old house. It was hardly larger than a walk-in closet: it had space only for a large desk, a wooden chair, and a hatrack. I'd made it my writing room. It always made me feel secure. My old Smith-Corona electric typewriter was on the desk, a friend I hadn't seen in decades. I slowly typed out my discombobulated thoughts, a task I hoped would be centering.

Why had I been pitched, like a floating knuckleball, into the past? Sex with Laura was lovely, but still, even in this second incarnation, we clearly had little in common. There was no evidence so far that Laura could be "the one." And sex alone couldn't be the reason I was given the privilege of rejoining my own past life. Or could it be? Why did there need to be a rationale? Just because there was reason and logic in the time-travel fiction I'd read? Just because miracles aren't supposed to be meaningless? So. If it isn't about Laura, it must be about my fate in 1981. Think of all the weak,

bad decisions I was to make over the next few
years. If I kept in mind how mediocre my "original" life worked out, maybe I could dramatically
improve things this time around! I must stay put
in the '80s, and I must continue to remember at
least the gist of my "first time around." I must
use the gift of time travel to transform my life!
Or would this continuous double vision drive me
psychotic?

I left the tiny room humming the old Temptations' hit Ball of Confusion. "That's what the
world is today." My world, at least. Was that
song recorded yet? Yeah. But was it 10 years old
or 40?

Twelve hours later, after leaving Laura's bedroom at midnight, my hold upon 1981 suddenly
seemed newly tenuous. This version of me might
die at any moment. I now knew time reversal was
real. But why did it feel so frighteningly fragile?

My worries were borne out before sunup. At
some point in sleep I was transported back to
2010. It didn't seem much more violent than
being shaken awake by a bone-chilling nightmare.
Somehow, I fell out of bed, but my eyes remained
shut. I knew that when I opened them, I would be
looking at my one-bedroom apartment in 2010. My
body ached with age. I could say goodbye to my
full head of black hair, and to my future as a
still-young man. I opened my eyes, looked down
at my pants. They were a pair of loose-fitting
gray corduroys I'd bought in the 21st century.
My wallet held three credit cards, an entity I
didn't own in '81. My driver's license expired
in 2014.

But when I turned on my computer and glanced
at the bottom of the screen, I felt both my arms
sprout goose bumps. It was the time/date icon.
I left 2010 on a Wednesday. It was now Friday.
The exact number of hours I spent back in 1981,
with Laura and in my apartment on Antrim Street:
those hours had also passed by in 2010. I had
not gained two days of my life. I had spent the
same number of hours on earth: they had eclipsed
from both my life and my re-life. It was my one

proof I'd been tripping through the space-time continuum. Not a proof with which I could convince anyone, but it did satisfy me. I was not a dithering maniac.

It soon became clear I couldn't just will myself back to 1981. I tried many methods: longing, visualizing, typing in my journal about my yearning soul, focusing meticulously on the intimate details of the two days. Meditating on them. Nothing worked.

The only positive was this: I no longer felt that small sore spot in my heart for missing out on physically knowing Laura. We now had our moment. I did wonder if I could contact the presently middle-aged Laura to ask her if she ever remembered having sex with me, but I couldn't even remember her last name! Maybe I never knew it. (And did my time-trip back usurp the previous so-called "real time" of the year 1981? Did Laura now remember both? Was my sense of double-reality anyone else's?)

If you think I was such a shallow guy as to only think about returning to the past for nookie with a shapely Harvard student, you have sold me short, at least slightly. After my attempts to recapture 1981 all ran aground, I realized there might still be a chance to trip back to some other year, for some more imperative purpose. I soon became obsessed with a mission: I had to save my nephew Nate, my only nephew, a beautiful young man who died, violently, when his bicycle crashed into a truck in East Cambridge in 1998. I knew the date. March 31. If only I could warn him. Even if he thought I was nuts, he might take care. But time's trip-wire could not be activated by my desire to eradicate Nate's death.

I then decided my whole vision might need to expand. What about remaking American history? I knew if I went back to 1963 I could never, as a pimply 13-year-old, influence the JFK assassination; but what about Martin Luther King and Robert Kennedy in '68, when I was fully 18? King's killing in Memphis seemed the more likely: I might be believed if I told someone in King's entourage to just keep him off that Lorraine

Motel balcony!

I focused, meditated, prayed, and typed till my fingers were raw. To no avail.

I live in a land called regret, so there was no paucity of life-areas to ponder and brood upon in my attempts to trip back. I spent some effort regretting my bad professional decisions: the traumatic fear of rejection that had consistently caused me to choose stasis over action. I tried to get back to the day of my passive employment interview at the <u>Philadelphia Enquirer</u> in 1990.

No go.

I then began to focus on tripping back to the truly overwhelming romantic tragedy of my life. Why had I avoided that choice of time-trip "material" for so long? Maybe to save myself the anguish. But, sadly, exposing my withered heart on my Royal Companion typewriter failed to release me from the trap of the present.

In short, nothing succeeded to separate me from my 60-year-old life. Nothing, that is, until I finally attempted--as a last resort--precisely the method that had worked before by felicitous accident. The key was: think small.

In the summer of 2010 I experienced two more travels in time. One survived just 23 hours in length. The other lasted five days. Both of them were visits back to my college years, specifically 1972 and '73, during the very two days I had been offered--on a proverbial plate--the physical charms of two impossibly sexy women--or girls, as we used to call them--and had neglected to take advantage of either rare opportunity. The first was a statuesque platinum blonde, nearly six feet tall, who--surrounded by the university's array of hippies, flower children, and sorority girls--seemed to be a rarefied creature straight out of a Las Vegas stage extravaganza. All she was lacking was a headdress. Her given name was Tricia, but she literally went by the name Trixie. She seemed terribly out of place at Boston University, and profoundly lonely. I recall someone told me she was the daughter of a mobster. "You're the only nice guy I know in this whole college," she said, and told me I could stop by her dorm room any time I felt like it.

The other was Vickie, a pretty, green-eyed, sinfully sexy 18-year-old high-school senior who lived, with her parents, down the block from my apartment in Brookline. It was entirely possible that no one on God's green earth ever looked better in a pair of skin-tight jeans than Vickie did, though I sensed her budding animal confidence was diminished by a face terribly scarred by acne. I was simply mad about her. She dropped by my place a couple of times, unannounced. On one of those occasions, we briefly made out, but I took it no further.

I had a pretty solid, ethical-sounding reason, back in the early '70s, for not pursuing either of these beauties: I was involved in a monogamous relationship with my college girlfriend, whom I loved. So why was I pitched back in time nearly 40 years in order to consummate these brief acquaintanceships? To be perfectly straight with myself, the real reason I was faithful back then probably had more to do with a fear of repercussions than some pious belief in sexual fidelity. Did I always possess a "phobia" about taking chances in life? Did that offend God? Was that why I was returned to that halcyon era of sexual ease, the 1970s?

I have long been agnostic. But it is impossible to go through the experience of hurtling back three and four decades without believing in some kind of godly force. If some god really created humans in his own image, imagine how bummed he'd be now, considering the measly state of his favorite creation. It would be enough to make any god feel like a failed romantic. Maybe it was _that_ disgruntled deity who decided to send a lonely 60-year-old man back decades in time just to feel a few minutes of physical bliss? God as cosmic procurer?

In my visits back to May, 1972 and January, 1973, I had sex with Trixie (once, in her dorm room on Bay State Road) and Vickie (twice, in my cluttered Brookline bedroom). When I completed four days in 1973, I took this as an augury I might become a permanent resident. Just sauntering around campus, thinking of my bright future, delivered a surge of pleasure. Summoning up a professional confidence I did not possess in my first try at being 22, I wrote a review of a record that had been released that week by an unknown songwriter named Bruce Springsteen. I delivered it by hand to the Boston Phoenix. But before I heard back, I was summarily torpedoed back to 2010. (I later found no such review in the Phoenix archives.)

Two weeks after my third trip to the past, the "i" key of my Royal typewriter twisted. Trying to straighten it, I snapped it in two. I arranged for the city's lone typewriter repair shop to replace the key with a new one. I suspect the new "i" key affected the machine's inherent magical powers. From that point on, I never journeyed to the past again, no matter how passionate and assiduous my attempts.

Since 2010, I have often re-imagined my three brief trips back to the 20th century. You might even say the focus on these journeys has taken the place of my regretful longings of all I did not accomplish in this life: the women not possessed, the girlfriends not married, the children unborn, the jobs and world travels never attempted. Now, I often remember, in minute detail, each moment of my three time-trips. And I feel like a lucky man. An adventurer. A success. (Of course, I can tell no shrink why I'm no longer as depressed.)

Occasionally, I recall a new bit. One of those recaptured moments truly delights me. It occurred during my first trip.

While biking home from Laura's, I pass Dana Street. A middle-aged woman I do not recognize waves at me and calls out, "Hi, Paul."

As she entered my mind's eye, I finally realized her identity. It was Essie, the elfin woman who sold me my Royal. Except that in 1981 she was 59, not 88. I never met her in my original 1981. How did she know my face and name?

Simple. Essie was a time-explorer, too.
Shared Royal. Shared town. Shared centuries.
Essie. My generous fellow traveler.

1971 Olympia SM9

Lost for a Century

Martyn V. Halm

It started when I got a hundred-year-old 1922 Corona typewriter, a nifty little machine with a carriage that folded back over the glass keys to make the Corona fit in its tiny wooden travel case. Between my attempts to fix the typewriter's many issues, I had search engines look up anything they could find on the Corona 3 and its users -- Bing Crosby, Isak Dinesen, Ernest Miller Hemingway...

Hemingway? I remembered pictures of the writer as a big game hunter with hands like baseball mitts, and I just couldn't imagine him typing on this folding Corona typewriter with its delicate keys and fragile levers. None of the existing photos showed "Papa" Hemingway at work on any Corona, only Royals and Underwoods and his Swedish Halda. However, I did find a handwritten letter to his fiancée, where he complained that his Corona was with a repair service after being knocked from his desk by his Parisian cleaning lady. And I found another tidbit that made me sit up in my chair. An interesting bit of information that made it worth investing in a return ticket from RetroActive's brand-new time-travel arrangement.

RetroActive had only been offering time-travel since a month or two, and I had been intrigued with the idea ever since, but the tickets were expensive and the time traveler could only bring back what he took with him through the portal. And you weren't allowed to bring anything anachronistic.

I looked at my defective Corona and grinned. This would be a heavy investment, but totally worth it for something lost in time. But first I had to take a trip to contemporary Paris to make some arrangements.
-o-
"You're aware you're not allowed to take anachronistic items into the past, right?" The RetroActive agent looked at the wooden case in my left hand. "Or bring back anything."

I lifted the case with the Corona. "This is an American typewriter from the 1920s, so it won't be out-of-time in 1922 Paris."

The agent wrote "vintage 1920s typewriter" on the screen next to my profile without adding details like brand or model, then said, "And for money?"

"I have three thousand French francs." I showed him the stack of bills. "All dated well before 1922." That had been the most difficult thing to arrange -- century-old-currency. Most French francs had been destroyed by the banks after being exchanged for the euro some twenty years ago. Luckily I found an antique shop with a cache of hoarded francs.

The agent rifled through the bills. "Is that enough?"

"Enough for a month. I'm staying ten days."

He glanced at my ticket. "Why Paris?"

"To sit in cafés and study the Lost Generation, the interbellum group of expatriate writers and poets that gathered there. I hope to write an article on them for The H.G.Wells Journal."

The agent signed off on the money. "Why the first week of December?"

"Best chance of catching them hiding out in their watering holes."

He nodded. "I see you have it all thought out."

You have no idea, I thought, but nodded happily in return. "I'm going to see my favorite writers and poets in the flesh. It's a dream come true."

The RetroActive agent helped me put my 21st-Century belongings in the safety locker, and apologetically frisked me once more, then took me to a lovely lady, who guided me to her office and led me through the health and safety guidelines, checked my vaccination status, and explained my travel arrangements in detail. The trickiest part was making sure I didn't arrive in a place of danger, so I would materialize inside Basilique du Sacré-Coeur, an ancient church that had remained unchanged for centuries. For my return, RetroActive would track the chip embedded in my wrist. Extraction would take place ten days after my arrival. For ten whole days I would be living in the Paris of the Roaring Twenties.

"Make sure you don't damage the chip." The lady held my wrist over her scanner. "Or you'll be stuck in the past forever."

Getting stuck in 1922 Paris... Somehow, I'd be fine with that. Shaking with excitement, I followed her to the portal that would transport me to the distant past.

—o—

The trip was more painful than I had anticipated. My whole body hurt as if I had been stretched on a rack, and I had a monstrous headache. The brochure I'd read mentioned the possibility of aches and pains, so before I left I had memorized French phrases to ask for pain medication. So, first order of the day, find myself a pharmacy.

Carrying the wooden typewriter case, I left the old church and gazed out over the ancient French capital, comparing the city before me with the image of contemporary Paris in my mind. The drizzle coming down from the grey December sky made 1922 Paris look drearier than 2022 Paris in the springtime, but the sight was lovelier than I expected. The air was crisp, with a tinge of wood smoke from the multitude of chimneys below. There seemed to be hardly any automobiles, so the air wasn't choked with exhaust fumes.

Turning my back on the Basilique du Sacré-Coeur, I descended the south steps towards Place Pigalle, and entered the first pharmacy I could find in Montmartre.

When I asked for headache relief, the pharmacist presented me a slender brown bottle of Bayer's Heroin Tincture. I had not planned on taking highly addictive substances for a mere headache, when aspirin should already be on the market. The pharmacist went into a longwinded explanation -- the gist was that the German Bayer plant had been closed at the end of the war and medication had to be imported from the American plant, which refused to export the Aspro. I expressed my wariness of taking strong opiates, but he replied that twenty drops of heroin equalled one gram of opium, so I would be all right if I used less than ten drops. I had to take his word for it. I paid him and checked if he responded weirdly to my bank notes, but he didn't bat an eye. I took the coins he handed me and left the pharmacy with the bottle of heroin in my pocket.

I continued towards Place Pigalle, where I entered a café and took a seat by the window. The waiter took his time coming over to my table, but I didn't mind, watching a few gorgeous automobiles driving down the cobblestone boulevard still dominated by horse-drawn carts and carriages. I could've stayed there all day, just watching the street life. When the waiter arrived, I ordered strong black coffee and croissants.

Once I got some food in me, I put five drops of the heroin tincture in a glass of water and drank it down. A minute later, a warm glow burst open inside me like someone had thrown a chemical blanket around my shoulders, pushing all the damp cold and aches out of my body. No wonder this stuff was so highly addictive.

Pleasantly buzzed, I decided to brave the persistent drizzle once more and explore the city. My recent visit a week before had been spent making arrangements for this trip and my illegal plans, which involved quite a lot of footwork, but now walking down the same streets felt like I was being gaslighted. Streets paved in asphalt were now cobblestone and names were unfamiliar and thoroughfares had become cul-de-sac dead-end alleys. Or maybe the heroin befuddled me, small as the dose had been. Even so, I felt energized by the hustle and bustle of the interbellum city.

Of course, I mused, none of the Parisians knew about the future economic depression that would put Germany in such dire financial straits that their people would become susceptible to the rantings of that madman Hitler. Too bad the terms and conditions of RetroActive prohibited killing anyone, as any ripple in time, any alteration of events could have unforeseen consequences.

I refocused myself to the task at hand and looked at a streetmap to find the address where the Hemingways had settled near the Pantheon in the Quartier Latin. I was curious to see how that area would look in 1922.

A strange sensation crept over me as I walked down the markets of Rue Mouffetard to the corner of Rue du Cardinal Lemoine, where I looked up at the dark third-story windows of Number 74, where I knew Hadley Hemingway would be. So close... I shivered and looked down at the dirty cobblestones beneath my feet. Were they the same ones I walked on a week before?

A street urchin bumped into me, and I could feel his nimble hands lightly slip inside my coat as he pretended to regain his balance, mumbling an excuse. Before I could respond, a bespectacled gentleman whacked the boy upside his head with his cane. The street urchin cried out in pain and anger, and ran off with empty hands.

I'd been living in cities all my life and even under the influence of the heroin tincture I wasn't about to get my pockets picked, but I thanked the gentleman with a polite nod and my rusty French.

Upon hearing me speak, the dapper gent said in an Irish accent, "American?"

"Dutch," I said. "Is it so obvious I'm not French?"

"Well, your garb is unusual." He stroked his sparse beard. "There a quite a few expatriates about the city, but I haven't seen your fashion style before. Is it Dutch?"

"Frysian," I lied. "I must find myself a French tailor." I extended my hand. "The name is Halm."

"Joyce." He shook my hand. "James Joyce."

My fingers trembled shaking the hand that had written literary masterpieces. My voice shook as I croaked, "I'm pleased to meet you, Mister Joyce."

Joyce blinked at me through his rather thick glasses and said, "Dear fellow, do you have the palsy?"

"No, sir. Just a bit faint from missing lunch."

"I haven't had lunch myself." Joyce pulled at his moustache. "Let me invite you for a bite to eat at an exquisite little restaurant tucked in Rue Monsieur le Prince."

I realized my faux-pas as I remembered from history books that Joyce had been living hand-to-mouth during his time in Paris, but famously insisted on taking his friends to dinner at restaurants, where he'd pay for all the food and drinks to chase away the ghosts of his poverty.

"Only if you allow me to pay for our refreshments," I insisted. "If it hadn't been for your swift action, I might have lost a purse."

And so, in a strange twist of fate, I ended up treating James Joyce to lunch at Polidor, while having to pretend I didn't know who he was. Joyce noticed my typewriter case and told me his last book had just been published in February by a small company on the Rive Gauche, but those bloody Americans had seized five hundred of them and destroyed the books for being obscene. I wished I could tell him that <u>Ulysses</u> would be considered a literary masterpiece and the crown of his work, but I just nodded and told him that controversy could also become a marketing boost. That notion seemed to cheer him up.

Outside, dusk lowered a cowl of gloom over the streets, where the gaslight streetlamps were lit to make them seem more inviting. I took my leave from Joyce, promised to look him up at the address he gave me, and went back to Rue Cardinal Lemoine. The lights in Hemingway's apartment were off, and for a moment I panicked, because if Hadley had already gone to Geneva, my quest would be in vain.

As night replaced dusk, a soft yellow light came on behind the windows of the Hemingway apartment, and I breathed a sigh of relief and made my way to Rue Descartes, where I knew Hemingway hired a study room where he could write in private. I had just rung the bell when a neighbor came out through the front doors and asked me whom I was looking for.

"Monsieur Hemingway?"

"Ah, l'Americain." She wiped her fingers on her apron and said, "I think he is abroad."

I thanked her. Everything was going according to plan.

—o—

Having plenty of money by 1922 Parisian standards, I had considered staying at the Ritz, inarguably one of the finest hotels in the world, with an exquisite kitchen conducted by a student of the great chef Auguste Escoffier. However, I had noticed some odd looks towards my garb — apparently the tailor who had provided me with his handstitched clothes hadn't targeted the right period — so I asked around for a reputable tailor.

The tailor estimated that he needed a week to fashion me a suit, so I bought something he had already made and asked him to make alterations to fit me. That he could do in a mere hour. I wouldn't look like a wealthy gent, but for my purposes, that was maybe for the best.

I used that hour to visit the Ritz and have a drink at the bar that would later be named after Hemingway, and had a conversation with the knowledgeable bartender, who gave me the address of the typewriter service where Hemingway had his Corona repaired after it had been knocked from his desk by his "femme de menage." Another part of my plan was coming together.

—o—

Dressed in my new clothes, I visited Hadley Hemingway the next day, introducing myself as one working for the repair service and asking if I could look at her husband's Corona typewriter, as my employer was worried that a screw found on a workbench belonged to her husband's typewriter.

Hadley told me her husband had taken his Corona to Switzerland, so I scratched my plan of writing a note on Hemingway's Corona to obtain a writing sample. It wasn't integral to my plan, as his typewriter ended up in the Hemingway Museum later anyway, so that Corona could authenticate anything he'd written on it.

Hadley looked fatigued, leaning wearily against the door post. I asked her if she was all right and she confessed that she was a bit under the weather, but medicine was so expensive, and she needed the money to buy a ticket to Geneva. I fished the bottle of heroin tincture from my pocket. Now that my headache was gone, I didn't see the need to keep using the opiate and risk addiction. So, I offered the bottle to Hadley, who was overjoyed and asked me in for tea. Of course, I obliged and sat in the sparse apartment Ernest lived in while in Paris. I watched Hadley take ten drops of the heroin tincture and disappear into the kitchen.

When she returned with the tea, she looked much better, but I could still see dark circles around her lovely eyes. So I asked her if there was anything else I could assist her with.

"I don't want to impose," she spoke hesitantly.

"I wouldn't offer if it would be an imposition, Madame Hemingway." I took a sip from the weak tea. "If a lady requires assistance, it's a gentleman's duty to provide. How may I ease your burden?"

Hadley told me her husband had asked her to bring his writing to Geneva, but it was all in his study at Rue Descartes. I told her to bring the valise and I'd help her fill it and carry it back to her apartment.

Hadley walked a bit unsteadily as I escorted her to Ernest's study in the Rue Descartes. Together we packed up all his writing into the valise, adding all drafts and copies. I carried the heavy valise back to Rue Cardinal Lemoine and up the stairs to her apartment, where I wished her "bon voyage" and took my leave.

—o—

The next morning, Hadley Hemingway was supposed to catch the train to Geneva from the railway station Gare de Lyon, a twenty-five minute walk northeast past the

Jardin des Plantes Botanical Gardens and across the River Seine. I watched her building from the musical bar L'Eurydice, so I'd be sure to catch her when she was leaving.

Hadley came out of the building, lugging two large suitcases and the valise. She looked flushed and tired from getting the luggage down to street level, and I knew she wouldn't have the money for a carriage, so I walked around the corner to the bicycle I had rented that morning - a sturdy Peugeot with transport racks on the rear and the front.

She was still looking at the luggage when I halted the bicycle next to her and said, "Madame Hemingway! You are leaving for Switzerland?"

She looked up at me, blinking a few times before she recognized me. "Yes," she said. "I have to take the train at Gare de Lyon."

"Let me help you," I said and put the large suitcases on the front carrier, tying them down with a piece of rope. "The rear carrier isn't padded, but it might still be more comfortable than walking."

"You are a life-saver, Monsieur." Hadley put her hand on her heart. "Truly an angel."

"Think nothing of it, Madame. It is my pleasure."

She sat sideways on the rear carrier, her right arm around my waist, her left arm hugging the valise on her lap as I pedaled the big bicycle to the railway station. I was giddy with joy, knowing I would cherish this moment forever.

At the beautiful Gare de Lyon, I parked the bicycle and unloaded her luggage on the cart of a porter, who would help her to the train. Hadley squeezed my lower arm for a moment to show her appreciation and followed the porter into the railway station.

I quickly parked my bicycle and followed them, then found a spot to unobtrusively observe the train to Geneva. I had visited the Gare de Lyon the week before and seen some hints of its former splendor, but seeing the gorgeous station a mere 22 years old made me realize how much the twenty-first century renovations had altered the station and damaged its incredible charm.

As noted in the history books, some ten minutes before the train's departure, Hadley stepped from the train to get some refreshments for the trip, leaving her precious luggage unattended. A moment later I saw a scruffy person enter the carriage and leave with two bags, one of them Hadley's valuable valise contaning all of Ernest Hemingway's early writing. The scruffy man walked away with the insouciance of a habitual thief, and I followed him at a distance long enough not to spook him, but close enough not to lose him in the crowded railway station.

The thief left Gare de Lyon and headed towards the Seine, moving down the steps to the river, and walking along the bank to the nearest bridge. Under the bridge, I caught up with him as he was opening the cases. He looked up from opening the valise, noticing it was filled with paper, nothing of value to him.

"How much for the valise?" I asked in my best French while pointing at the luggage. "With contents."

"Achetez?" He tilted his chin up at me. "Combien?"

I held up five fingers. "Five francs." About a day's wage for a skilled laborer.

He held up all his fingers. "Dix franc."

"Six."

He shook his head. "Eight."

"Seven," I said. "And I won't ask where you got it."

He closed the valise and held out his hand. I put seven franc in his palm and he handed me the valise.

Gripping the handle firmly, I carried the valise back to the street and back to my hotel, stopping at a hardware store to buy a roll of oilcloth – something to keep the papers safe for a century.

—o—

Hemingway's valise was never found, so I wasn't changing history. Most likely, had I not interfered, the thief would've tossed or burned the "worthless" contents prior to selling the empty valise. And I knew the Hemingways were devastated by the loss, but – according to the history books – Ernest developed his signature sparse writing style as a direct result of the theft.

In my hotel room, I emptied the valise and spent the afternoon reading most of Hemingway's short story drafts and manuscripts and noted that they were indeed verbose and meandering compared to his post-1922 writings. Now I understood why Hemingway was rumored to have said that the first draft of anything was shit – to protect his psyche from having to deal with losing these drafts I now possessed. While not exactly "shit", the drafts before me were a far cry from the sparse prose Ernest Hemingway became famous for. If these drafts had never been stolen, the literary world might never have known books such as his short story collection <u>In Our Time</u> and the novels <u>The Sun Also Rises</u> and <u>A Farewell to Arms</u>, some of the greatest novels to emerge from World War 1.

—o—

I had accomplished my goals in far less time than I had anticipated, so I had some spare time to enjoy the City of Light. One of the things I did was to visit the typewriter repair shop that had fixed Hemingway's Corona typewriter.

Since the RetroActive agent had described my own Corona 3 as a "vintage 1920s typewriter" without adding details, I intended to buy a typewriter and leave my defective Corona behind, so that I would be taking a pristine 1920s typewriter back to 2022.

The proprietor was very welcoming, but I was disappointed to note that all the typewriters on display had the standard French AZERTY keyboard layout. When I mentioned this to the proprietor, he smiled broadly and said, "I might have an item of interest for you, Monsieur."

He went into the back room and returned with a case not unlike the one of my Corona. I almost gasped as he opened the case to reveal an extremely rare Bijou folding typewriter made by Seidel & Naumann in Germany, with a QWERTY keyboard. "This German typewriter was ordered for an Irish expatriate writer by his friends, but Monsieur Joyce didn't want it, so he exchanged the typewriter for cash."

"Why didn't he want it?" I admired the gleaming Bijou. "Is there anything wrong with it?"

"Non, Monsieur, but there is something wrong with his vision. He said to prefer his own method."

"His own method?"

"Monsieur Joyce writes with charcoal on butcher paper while wearing a white coat to reflect as much light as possible onto the paper." The proprietor shrugged. "Strange method, but it works for him."

"So, this typewriter is secondhand."

The proprietor threw up his hands. "Monsieur, this machine is hardly used! It still has the original ribbon! Just look at this beauty, I couldn't let this machine go for less than sixty francs."

I looked pensively. I could easily afford his asking price, but sixty francs was about two weeks' salary for a skilled laborer, and I knew I had to haggle or he would take me for a sucker. Beautiful as the Bijou was, no Frenchman would buy a QWERTY typewriter.

"I'm afraid I cannot offer you more than forty."

"Forty?!" He put his hand on his heart, but not in the way Hadley had done - more like he was about to get a heart attack. "I couldn't possibly go that low. Listen, I will lower the price to fifty, but not a franc less."

"Forty-five," I said. "My final offer."

"You drive a hard bargain, Monsieur. Forty-five."

"And I need quality ink ribbons for this machine. Where I'm going next might have a scarcity."

Ten minutes later, I left the shop with the Bijou typewriter and a big box of silk ink ribbons.

—o—

I had still a few days left, and one remaining wish: to meet Ernest Hemingway himself. According to the history books I'd read, Ernest was beside himself when his wife showed up with the news that all his writing had been stolen. In the hope that she hadn't also taken his drafts along, he rushed back to Paris, only to find out that, indeed, all his writing was gone.

Which meant that Hemingway was to return one of the remaining days of my time-travel sojourn, so I posted everyday at the Rue Descartes in the hope to catch the great writer in person.

When Hemingway finally arrived, I almost missed him, expecting the weathered, bearded adventurer affectionately called "Papa" by his admirers, not a suavely suited, clean-shaven, dark-haired young man. I realized my mistake when the light went on in his study. I hurried to the door and rang the bell. Nothing happened, and I was about to ring again when the front door was yanked open and young Hemingway glared at me angrily.

With a heavy American accent, he bellowed, "Who are you? Qu'est-ce que vous voulez?"

I answered him in English with a French accent.

"Good afternoon, I'm looking for a Monsieur Hemingway?"

"You found him."

I looked at him apologetically. "I'm from the repair service, Monsieur. My boss was worried about your typewriter, because he found a tiny screw he thinks is from your Corona."

Hemingway rubbed his temples. "My typewriter is upstairs. You want to check it for missing screws?"

"If it is not a bother, Monsieur."

"Come on in," he said and stepped back into the lobby of the building. I followed him up the stairs to the apartment I'd been in before with Hadley, and Hemingway took me to his desk where the Corona's case stood next to a notepad and a stubby pencil. "I used to write in longhand here," he said. "But ever since that cleaning lady knocked my Corona off the table, I don't leave it at the apartment anymore."

I nodded politely. "Do you mind if I inspect your typewriter, Monsieur?"

"That's what you're here for, right?" Hemingway blinked wearily, then said, "Excuse me, I'm being rude. Can I offer you something to drink?"

I nodded, my mouth dry with nervous tension. To have a drink with one of my favorite writers was a dream come true. While Hemingway fetched glasses, I opened the typewriter case and gently removed the tiny Corona with trembling hands. He returned and filled two tumblers with cheap whisky, adding spritzes from his soda bottle without asking what drink I'd like. But I understood; he was still very upset about finding all his work gone. He watched me as I inspected the Corona, not finding any missing screws, of course.

"My 'mitrailleuse' will have a rough time ahead," Hemingway grumbled. "I lost all my work from the last three years. Gonna have to double down on writing everything down again."

"I'm not a writer, Monsieur, but you must be devastated." I turned the Corona over in my hands and set the machine down again. I picked up my whisky and soda and raised my glass to him. "I'm sorry for your loss."

"Merci." He touched his tumbler against mine. "I'll survive. I always do."

I swallowed some of the drink, sat behind his desk, and rolled a piece of paper into his Corona.

"I hope you don't mind if I write a short note to my employer to show him that I inspected your machine to your satisfaction."

"Go ahead," Hemingway replied and took a swig from his whisky-soda.

'Decembre,6,1922,' I typed, the keys moving smoothly under my fingertips, the carriage moving up and down silently, in contrast to the worn-out Corona in my hotel room. 'This Corona 3 typewriter, belonging to Monsieur Ernest Hemingway of Rue Descartes 39, has been inspected and found to be in excellent condition. 1234 567890. Portez ce vieux whisky au juge blond qui fume.'

Hemingway looked over my shoulder. "Carry the old whisky to the smoking young blonde?"

"Non, Monsieur," I said. "It's a pangram, to test all the letters. It means, 'Bring this old whisky to the blond judge who smokes.'"

"You type very fast," Hemingway said. "I wish I could do that."

He didn't seem to realize that my feat was all the more incredible for doing it on a QWERTY keyboard, which ought to be quite unfamiliar for a Frenchman.

I looked him over. "You're not too old to learn touch typing, Monsieur."

"I'll never have that kind of speed." He shook his head. "Too used to hunting and pecking."

"If you say so," I said, and took the note from the Corona. "I'm not a writer, but if you have to compensate for speed, you could use fewer words."

Hemingway blinked at me. "Use fewer words. That's excellent advice. Thank you."

Before I accidentally gave him more advice, I handed him the stubby pencil to sign my note. Hemingway signed the note and seemed deep in thought as I bade him "Bon Soir" and left his study. Outside his door, I carefully folded the paper with trembling fingers and put it into my inside pocket before I ventured downstairs and out into the Parisian fog.

—o—

My return trip to 2022 was uneventful, but just as painful. Luckily, this time there was a nurse present with modern painkillers. The RetroActive agent was a different one from the one at my departure, but just as uninterested in the contents of my luggage. I had stowed my old Corona with Hemingway's papers at a secure location in Paris, but had taken the Bijou typewriter, and the ink ribbons wrapped in my period clothes, through the time-travel portal.

Outside, wearing contemporary clothes again, I hailed a taxicab to take me to my apartment, where I locked my new typewriter and ink ribbons in my vault and called a travel agent to arrange a return ticket to Paris.

—o—

The Père Lachaise Cemetery was fairly quiet for the busiest necropolis in the world. Still, my heart was thumping in my throat as I entered and made my way to the least popular older section, where I halted before the sepulchre overgrown with vines, the hiding place I had selected on my previous trip. The name above the gate was barely legible and the tiny windows in the sturdy iron door mostly gone. After making sure I was alone, I took out my bolt cutters and cut the rusty padlocked chain that held the doors closed — doors that had already looked ancient back in 1922.

Wearing a headlamp, I entered the dilapidated and severely neglected sepulchre, leaving footprints in the rubble on the stone floor. I went up to the far wall, where a headstone covered the grave of someone who had died more than two centuries before I buried my treasure next to her casket.

As I pried off the headstone as delicately as I had done in 1922, I could see the oilcloth package undisturbed and pulled it out gently, set it down on the floor, and put the headstone back before I cut the rope and opened the oilcloth package. The valise looked as pristine as when it went in, and the wooden case of the old Corona had hardly deteriorated as well. Pretty miraculous. Leaving the oilcloth in the sepulchre, I carried the valise and typewriter out of the sepulchre and put the cut chain back through the broken windows of the iron gate. And carried my treasure back to my hotel.

—o—

I had figured I'd get rich selling the manuscripts, but before I could put anything up for auction, I received a letter from the Hemingway Foundation praising me for finding papers belonging to the heirs of Ernest Miller Hemingway. Since the papers had originally been stolen from Hadley, and I could not provide proof of buying them legally, I had to give them up for a finder's fee that barely covered the cost of my RetroActive time-travel ticket and the trips to Paris.

Bummer.

Since the note I wrote on Hemingway's Corona - and which I had put with the papers in the valise to make sure its authenticity could be ascertained by typography experts - was no longer necessary for the authentification of the manuscripts, I had it framed to hang above my writing desk, now home to the Seidel & Naumann Bijou typewriter I've written this story on.

At least I got a pretty cool adventure out of it.

Fin
The End

1957 Royal FP

Pretty Ricky

Vinny Negron

It was 1922, and I was the only one in Paris with an afro.

A glorious afro.

Sadly, nothing had gone to plan, and the overall vibe I sensed upon my return from the roaring '20s was that it was somehow my fault things went pear-shaped. Now the organizers wanted to debrief me in front of a camera, and the guy who had introduced himself as the producer was bumping into lights, tripping over extension cords, and had thrice spilled his coffee.

When he finally sat across from me, he folded one leg over the other, rested his elbows in his lap, and tented his fingers under his chin.

"We're gonna record all this, because what happened was a little unusual, so it's important we document it."

A little unusual? The program had been in place for years, where kids my age were traveling through time as part of an enrichment initiative for gifted high-school students. And as far as I know, I'm the only student in the history of the program to get lost. I mean, in a way, it makes sense. I am not, by any definition, gifted. I can do the robot, but I've been told that won't get me into Harvard. I pretty much BS'd my way through the application and essay, so maybe what happened was karma.

"I don't remember much," I said.

"Just tell us what you remember," said the producer.

I wish they'd given me time to shower and change. They wanted to talk to me while the memory of my experience was still fresh. I get it. But I was wearing someone else's suit, and there was nothing fresh about it. The sour stench of cigarette smoke and drunkeness jumped off the suit like a stoned bridesmaid onto the dance floor.

"And when you talk, don't look directly into the camera. Start with your name and keep your eyes right about here. And, you know, be natural."

"Ricardo," I said. "Ricardo Ramos, but everyone calls me Pretty Ricky, for the record."

The producer turned and chin-nodded toward an assistant, causing the assistant to rush off the set. The producer shifted back to me with a forced smile.

"What year is it?" he said.

"2015."

"And where are we?"

"Far Rockaway, New York. And," I said, "we are presently filming from my English classroom, where, incidentally, I asked Big Butt Nicole to marry me. First she said yes, then she said hell no, as if she just learned I had the cooties or something. Hell no, she said. She broke my heart."

"Just," said the producer, "let's just answer my questions. If we can stick to that format – you know what I mean? Just that. We all wanna get out of here. It's been a long day. If you go off on tangents, we'll be here all night."

"Okay," I said. "What do you wanna know?"

"You applied to travel, what, to the 1970s?"

"That's right."

"Why that decade?"

I wanted to travel to the '70s to study the music scene because, truthfully, I felt it was an important decade for music, one that would go on to influence music for years to come. But, secretly, I also wanted to go back to meet my father for the first time, and maybe knock his goddamn lights out."

"But," said the producer, "you never made it to the '70s, did you?"

"I didn't."

"Why not?"

"I don't know," I said. "I think I missed my stop, but I'm not sure. I don't know how this stuff works. I was hoping one of you would explain how I ended up in the 1920s instead."

"We're looking into it, believe me. This interview is part of that process."

"I was completely unprepared for the 1920s," I said. "And France, at that, with only the 'Lady Marmalade' lyrics to get by on."

"So," he said, moving on. "When you got off the train, did you look for your liaison?"

"I waited at the train station for over an hour, but no one came up to me. Probably because I got off the train in 1922 dressed like Jimi Hendrix."

"Did you talk to anyone?"

It had been drilled into us during orientation that we were to interact only with our liaison, that under no circumstances were we to mingle with others, and that we were to approach the opportunity like a guided tour. But what was I to do? My liaison was five decades away, and I was alone, dressed in denim bell bottoms, in a foreign country, seventy-six years before my birth.

"Eventually," I said.

The producer removed his glasses and pinched the bridge of his nose. "Okay," he said. "What happened?"

"Listen," I said, "I'll be honest with you. All I remember was getting off the train with my 1970s clothes and a 20-pound typewriter that hadn't been invented yet. I was very confused and scared. When no one came to meet me, I walked around and eventually ducked into a cafe to avoid the rain."

"Do you remember the name of the cafe?"

"No," I said. "But I got lucky. I happened to find a spot where people were speaking English."

I'd sat down, ordered a drink. I didn't know what to order, so I pointed to the table next to me. The broad-shouldered guy at that table was scribbling into a pad with a small pencil, and drinking. I told the waiter I'd have what he was having because I didn't know what to order, and I didn't want to look like a fool ordering something that hadn't been invented. It was already a rough start for me, and the last thing I needed was to get laughed at in French.

Turns out I ordered a tall glass of amnesia.

Twice.

Of note, I don't drink. Sometime in 2013, maybe, I had some malt liquor, a forty-ounce of St. Ides, and that shit was nasty. The stuff I was served in Paris was green, and while it tasted like a black jelly bean, it burned like hellfire going down.

When my first drink arrived, I took a sip, tried to play it cool, when really, I wanted to spit the stuff out. I looked around in disbelief. I didn't know it at the time, but I was in 1922, and it was a cold and rainy November day. Outside the wind drove the wet leaves into the gutters. I didn't know shit about 1922 or Paris. I'm sure we had learned something about it in school, but we'd also learned geometry and I bet most of my classmates couldn't define a circle, except to say it was round, like a pizza.

I took another sip, and it felt better going down. Now I could appreciate how warm it made me feel, when outside the wind was stripping the leaves off the trees.

"What did you do there?" said the producer.

I thought about that for a moment. Eventually I would have to mention the drinking, as it would help explain why I remembered so little. Except for a few faces, a name or two, and the hot jazz, the details of my experience were as hazy as the blue cloud of cigarette smoke that greeted me everywhere.

"I set the typewriter on the table because I thought maybe there was some magic to it, you know? A way for us to communicate. Because it was pushed on me like something that might potentially save my life. They said I had to bring it with me to document my trip, but I started thinking maybe that was code-speak. Anyway, I had hoped to let someone know with the magic typewriter that my transport overshot my destination by five decades."

"There's no such thing as a magic typewriter." The producer consulted an assistant, who nodded in agreement. "No such thing," the producer said again.

"It's not that improbable. I just slid through time on a train I picked up at Grand Central Station."

"Touche'," said the producer, shooting his assistant a dirty look.

As it turned out, the 1941 Royal Quiet Deluxe was just a heavy typewriter. However, while its polished glass keys contained no magic, the machine possessed a certain magnetism that pulled me in with each keystroke. I downed my second drink and typed my SOS over and over, and maybe it was the booze, but it felt like I was connecting to something, the sound and feel of it was like riding a universal wavelength. Someone, I believed, had to be receiving this.

That "someone" was the broad-shouldered guy at the table next to me. He turned to me and asked if I was a writer. His smile was warm and friendly.

"No," I said. "A student."

"Where from?"

"New York."

He scoped my clothes, my hair. "Is that truly what

they're wearing in New York these days?"

"I doubt it," I said.

He shifted his chair so that he was sitting at the table with me, the typewriter and the empty glasses between us. He flagged a waiter and ordered us a round.

The producer said, "Did you get the guy's name?"

"I'm sure he told me, but I don't remember. I do know he was a writer, and that he was in love with the typewriter."

"You let him use it?" said the producer.

"Sure."

I was killing time, and he was ordering drinks.

"I tried to describe to the big guy," I said to the producer, "what I felt when I was using the typewriter, the impression I had that it was enchanted. And I told him the Royal had a best seller within her, and that maybe he was the writer to charm it out of her, and he said it was pretty to think so. I thought that was a weird thing to say."

"Okay," said the producer. "What happened after that?"

"It gets foggy after that."

"What does?"

"Everything."

"You were there for two weeks."

"I realize this."

"And you don't remember what happened?"

I shook my head. "Not really. I sort of blacked out after that."

"You blacked out for two weeks?"

"Yes," I said. "They drank a lot in 1922, and - I'm not trying to brag - everyone wanted to party with Pretty Ricky, so I drank a lot."

"Oh," said the producer, "so you were the toast of the town?"

"Kinda," I said. "And I'm pretty sure I lost my virginity to a woman who called herself Poison."

"Poison?"

"I think that's what she said, but maybe I misunderstood. She had an accent."

The producer looked around the set. "Poison," he said to the crew.

"Does it still count even though it happened 93 years ago? I mean, am I still a virgin? I don't know how that works."

"What?"

"Never mind," I said, thinking, It counts.

"Do you realize the implications of what you've done?"

"No," I said. "Do you?"

"Not entirely," he said. "But I'm sure something's amok."

After a moment I asked if we were done.

"I have to get out of this tight-ass suit," I said.

"I was gonna ask you about it," said the producer. "Where'd it come from?"

"It belonged to a guy named Scott."

"Scott what? Did you get his last name?"

"I didn't ask to see his license."

"How is it you're wearing another man's suit?"

"Because he was wearing my clothes," I said. "And we couldn't get them off. He was face down on a coffee table, drunk, completely out of it. We couldn't move him."

"We?"

"Me and some other guys, and a few women, too. Don't ask me their names. They were all there when I came out of Poison's room."

"All where?"

"In the living room."

"Let me get this straight. You were in the bedroom with Poison or whatever her name is, and in the next room there's a party going on?"

"Yes," I said. "There was always a party going on. That's what I've been trying to tell you."

When I stumbled into the living room wearing a short women's robe, a room full of people raised their drinks and cheered. One guy I remember seeing around, a painter named Onri, slapped me on the ass and called me a scoundrel.

"He was very drunk," I said, "but he helped gather the suit, and later he helped me find the train station."

"This was your last day?"

"Yes," I said. "This all happened earlier today, but in 1922."

"So you sobered up just in time," said the producer.

"Barely."

Onri and I had staggered to the train station. He carried a bottle of red wine, and I carried a small suitcase of things Onri had thrown into it when he was helping me pack. None of it could possibly belong to me. Every ten steps or so, Onri forced the bottle of red on me. As we approached the Gare de Lyon, I remembered the typewriter, which I think I loaned to the big guy I met in the cafe that first day. I asked Onri about him and learned he was in Switzerland covering a big peace conference for a newspaper.

"I think me and the big guy had some adventures," I said to Onri.

"Truly," said Onri, raising the bottle.

"Will Scott be alright? He looked a little pale."

"He's okay," said Onri. "Just a little tight."

I looked at the producer.

"And I almost missed my train," I said. "I had just sat down and was about to pass out from exhaustion when a porter came in carrying bags. He tucked them into the overhead next to my stuff. He looked puzzled when he saw me sitting there and asked to see my ticket. When I showed it to him, he shook his head and began speaking to me in rapid-fire French. Then a woman stepped into the compartment, and she recognized me."

The woman said, "It's you."

"Hi. . ." I had no memory of this woman.

"Pretty Ricky," she laughed. "My husband introduced us, remember?"

She read the confusion on my face and added, "You'd had a lot to drink. You were both pretty tight."

"I was told it was tradition," I said.

"He'll be happy to know you're okay. He's asked about you."

I was too embarrassed to ask her husband's name. I had met a lot of people at parties and cafes, and rarely was anyone, including myself, sober enough to remember our own names, never mind a stranger's slurred attempt at an introduction.

A whistle blew and the porter started up again in French.

"He says you're on the wrong train," said the woman. "This train is going to Lausanne."

I lifted my suitcase from the overhead and thanked the woman, telling her to give my best to her husband. She kissed me on both cheeks and then rushed off to get a bottle of water.

"If it wasn't for her," I said, "I would have missed my ride to 2015."

The producer sighed. He looked behind him. "We can fix this, right?"

"Is there anything else? I really need to sleep."

An assistant rushed onto the set, quick-stepped over to the producer, and whispered something into his ear. They both looked at me. The producer smiled.

"Ha," he said. "My assistant confirmed. I knew you were full of it. No one calls you Pretty Ricky."

Now it was my turn to smile.

When I got home, I peeled off Scott's smelly suit and jumped into a hot shower. After I toweled off, I dressed and thumbed through songs on Pandora. I turned up The Weeknd's "Can't Feel My Face" and pulled the suitcase from under the bed. I was excited to see what treasures Onri had tossed into it. I emptied the contents onto my mattress. My first thought was, What the hell is all of this? I know Onri was drunk, but this stuff made no sense. And then I realized that I might have grabbed the wrong suitcase when I rushed from the train. This suitcase was filled with manila envelopes. Some contained handwritten notes in a peculiar cursive that slanted downward across the page. Other envelopes contained typed stories, and carbon copies of typed stories.

I selected a jazz station and skipped a few songs until I found what I was looking for. Louis Armstrong's sleepy trumpet solo in "La Vie En Rose" filled my small room, and I fell back onto my bed, my head swimming. With heavy eyes, I picked up one of the typed stories. It was about growing up in Michigan. Not particularly interesting to me, but who knows? Maybe there was a best seller in there somewhere.

Isn't it pretty to think so?

1941 Royal Quiet Deluxe

WALKING BACKWARDS FOR THE REST OF YOUR DAYS

Bill Meissner

It can be done, but only if you wear the right shoes. It can be done, if you don't think about where you're going—just that you're moving backwards, getting younger step by step, becoming thinner and smaller by the mile.

You pass yourself in a small room, typing a letter to your lover. Your fingers tap out the date: July 21, 2019.

You keep stepping backwards. When you do, you begin to lose some things: what a first gray hair looks like. You and your wife's initials, carved beneath the skin of a huge oak tree, now just a sapling in an empty field. Your first taste of buttered lobster fades. So does your memory of the beam of a lighthouse cutting the night sky. Next, the ocean itself drains, its rising and falling swells disappear, and so does its blueness you stared at for a long time, amazed, and swore you'd always remember.

You pass yourself again in that small room. You're sliding in a page and typing a date: July 21, 1989.

Backwards you step, and you forget how to drive a car. Then you see the smoothed-over cement where, in junior high, you scratched your initials and pressed your hand print.

The next thing you know, you're an eight-year-old, your fingers fumbling with the stiff keys as you type your first story on your mother's black Underwood typewriter. The date: July 21, 1969.

You stand, back out of the room. As you do, you lose even more things: your memory of how to tie a shoe fades. Your ability to add two and two erases from the blackboard of your mind. Then your shoes themselves become useless and fall away, and you can't remember how to take another step.

You feel yourself being carried around by others, and then it happens: you can no longer say sentences. You forget nouns and verbs, and for a moment, before it evaporates like mist, your first word lingers on your tongue. You forget the faces of your mother and

father, the brightly-colored fish mobile that circled
above your crib, a plaster hospital ceiling, the tiny
pockmarks that fascinated you like stars.

    You're innocent now, a gossamer blank page
fluttering in the wind, and there are no dates.

    Finally all you have left is two fleeting thoughts
in your shrinking cranium: What's that warm cave
you're curling back into? And where is that sigh that
created you, that passionate collision of sperm and
egg, the two suddenly separating, pulling away from
each other like two countries whose borders are so
close, but will never touch again?

Typed on a Smith-Corona Silent-Super, with green
keys and fancy racing stripes.

The Billiard Ball

Chad Allen Harrison

May 4, 1982
Albert,
The children and I are going to be spending a few weeks at the cabin. Please don't follow. I think we both need some time to figure things out. If I stay this summer, I'm positive that it's going to be the end of it. The end of us. Please give me time to think.
The children send their love
Beverly

***

The note had been typed neatly on Beverly's old Royal Arrow typewriter. Albert found it on the dining room table on the second day of summer vacation. The house was empty. The clothing and luggage in the children's rooms gone. Beverly's side of the master closet cleared out.

He dropped into one of the chairs and set the note back onto the table. He <u>had</u> known, he supposed, that things had been getting difficult. But that had somehow seemed less important than the cases, motions, briefs, and depositions that always demanded his attention at the office. Not to mention that, after all that work, the clients so often refused to pay. Mr. Miller, in fact, had just filed a fee dispute against the firm, and...

Albert shook his head. He was doing it again: retreating into work rather than dealing with difficult emotions.

He stood and began pacing the kitchen floor. Slowly at first, then with more determination. Beverly was right. This would be a good opportunity. The children could have a summer away from the heat and noise of New York. Beverly would be able to think, to read, maybe even do some of that writing she was always threatening. It wasn't like they would be unreachable, the cabin did have a telephone line. It was a party line, still the only type of service available in the rural areas of the state, but it was something.

And it would give him time to really dig in at work without the distraction of family.

For the first week Albert called daily. The children always answered on the second ring, as long as they weren't down on the lake or in town picking up groceries. They were thrilled to hear from him; George was just three, and Eleanor a precocious six. They told their father about the frogs they found, their hunts for buried treasure in the forest, the brightness of the stars so far from the lights of the city.

Beverly spoke to him occasionally. Her tone was always cold, but he was still certain that the time apart would do them good. Two weeks after their departure she told him about a stroke of luck: a new neighbor had moved in down the road. He was helping with the cleaning that always needed to be done after a long winter.

Albert essentially moved into his corner office in Manhattan, and his billables went through the roof. The envy of the other partners at their weekly meetings was palpable. He even managed to sign Wetherton, a company Ted Eidelsen had been trying to land for half a decade, as a client.

His daily calls to the cabin soon became weekly. He didn't want to bother the children or take them from their adventures. And there was so much to be done at the office.

He kept meaning to drive up and visit them. It had been long enough, surely, that a visit would be appropriate. Maybe after the Terringford trial finally ended.

On Wednesday, July 14, 1982, ten weeks after the family had left, Albert's secretary notified him that he had an urgent call from the Cayuga County Sheriff's office.

***

"I hear it was quick at least."

Albert was standing at the end of the driveway looking at the cement steps he had put in three summers earlier. They had led to the front door of the cabin. Now they led only to the cabin's charred remains. His gaze slowly traveled from the steps to the sheriff's deputy who was there to supervise his visit to the "scene." The deputy shifted from foot to foot, adjusted his tan hat, then looked away.

"I just mean..." The deputy hesitated, then spit out a stream of chewing tobacco. He glanced in Albert's direction. "I imagine they didn't suffer much, is all," he said softly.

Albert continued to stare at the man.

"Well," the deputy finally said. "I'll leave you to it." He turned and walked back to his patrol car.

Albert spent nearly an hour walking from memory to memory. The tree fort he had built for George. The tire swing he had hung for Eleanor. The edge of the lake where, eight years earlier, he and Beverly had finally decided to buy the place. He wondered what it would be like if he could see Beverly standing here one last time. He had been strangely numb since answering the call the previous day, and he couldn't imagine feeling anything at all.

Finally, he walked to the boathouse. He had always loved the feel of the place, but he hadn't been inside for the last few summers. It looked like Beverly and the children hadn't either. A fine layer of

clean, country dust covered everything but
a small stack of papers on one of the tables
in the back. He walked over and picked up
the papers. He immediately recognized the
typeface of Beverly's Royal Arrow. He hadn't
realized she'd brought the typewriter with
her. The words on the first page caught
his eye.

June 27, 1982

Albert called again today. George nearly
fell over he was so excited, and Eleanor was
bouncing up and down while they talked. I can
hear him a little while they talk, and I can
almost get a glimpse of who he was when they
were first born.

I want him to leave us alone. And I want
him to care enough to come after us.

Albert felt his knees beginning to give
way, and he barely managed to grab the table
for support. He sank slowly to the ground
and leaned his back against the table leg.
Then Albert sobbed.

***

Ten hours later Albert was back in the
city. He had composed himself just enough
to gather up the papers spilled across the
floor of the boathouse, then stumbled to his
car, waved off the concerned deputy, and
drove away.

Now he was seated on the floor of the
living room surrounded by small piles of
Beverly's papers. They had been knocked
out of order in the boathouse, and he had set
himself the task of putting them back in
order. He wasn't sure why he was doing it,
but it felt important. Like he could somehow send them a message: "I wasn't here when
you needed me, but I can be here now to pick
up the pieces."

Just looking at the Arrow's antique
typeface brought Albert back to their first
home. Beverly had been eager to put her

degree in literature to use and, after spending each day typing as a secretary at Reid & Priest, stayed up late each night pounding away on the little portable. He remembered falling asleep to the CLACK, CLACK, CLACK of the Arrow's keys.

Each page was a window into Beverly's mind, a peek at what his family had been doing at the cabin: walks to the lake, chats by the fireside, dinners in town at the lone rundown diner. The neighbor Beverly had mentioned turned up often; he seemed to have hit it off with the kids, which Beverly had appreciated.

'Probably because their father wasn't around,' he thought bitterly. He drank off the whiskey in his tumbler, then set it back down next to the nearly empty bottle on the floor beside him.

As he read, one page in particular stood out to him.

June 17, 1982

He finally came to the cabin tonight. It was strange, he looked so much older than he did the last time I saw him. I invited him in and, since the kids were already asleep, we sat in the front room and just talked.

It was nice. I wanted it to go on. But he got quiet, and then said, "I've been lying to you."

My heart sank.

Then he told me some ridiculous story: that he had come from the future, that he was so sorry for how things had gone, that he wanted to make it right but he couldn't. After all that, I told him I needed time to think, and asked him to come back tomorrow.

Albert's first thought was, of course, that it was fiction. He hadn't visited, much as he hated to admit it. And time travel? Beverly usually wrote creative nonfiction, but he knew that she had dabbled in fantasy in the past. He'd set the page in a separate pile, but it kept nagging at him. He picked it up and read it again.

The vision of Beverly standing at the edge of the lake, the summer sun warming her soft brown hair, came into his mind with the force of a blow. This idea that he could see her, see all of them, nearly overwhelmed him.

He refilled the glass and drowned himself in impossible possibilities.

***

May 11, 1982

I was walking today, just to get out of this musty cabin, and I ran into a new neighbor. He moved in to the house down the road, I think it was the Johnstons who lived there before. He says (get this) that he's a writer, that he moved out here for some peace and quiet to work on a novel.

I wonder if I could get him to fix the railing on the dock.

***

Albert returned to work three days after the funeral. He threw himself into the thick of things, taking on more cases than he ever had before. He carried Beverly's journal in his briefcase and several times a day would take it out and read a page or two. Eventually he noticed that he was pulling out one page, the one he kept on top of the stack, much more often than the others.

"He told me some ridiculous story, that he had come from the future."

The idea of it ate at him. Was it possible? Could some future version of himself actually have gone back and visited his family?

Six months after the death of his family, Albert Donovan picked up his first science fiction novel.

A year after that, in the winter of 1983, he worked up the courage to call a physics professor at NYU. He introduced himself as an attorney, which got the man's attention. But when he asked about time travel he was met only with uncertain laughter. "What, like Superman? Spinning the world backwards to save your girlfriend?"

    Albert hung up.

***

June 26, 1982

    Albert hasn't called in over a week.

    I don't know when things started to change. When we met he was kind and thoughtful and sweet. The wedding was perfect, and he was so excited when the children were born.

    In the last few years he stopped coming home on time. Now it seems like he's stopped coming home at all. He's gone every morning before anyone else wakes up and comes home after we are all in bed.

    One day I looked up and realized I didn't really have a husband anymore.

***

    By the end of 1986, four-and-a-half years after the fire, Albert's interest in time travel had moved from a hobby into an obsession. He devoured popular media on the subject, from novels like "The Time Machine" to movies like last year's "Back to the Future," which he had watched a dozen times before it left theaters.

    More of his time was spent seeking out and speaking to experts in physics. Even after years of research he still barely understood the scientific concepts involved. But he could speak persuasively enough that he often managed to get an appointment. Most responded with the same incredulous laughter he had encountered years before, but he had found some who would at least take him a little seriously. In the end, though, they all told him the same thing: their work was entirely theoretical. Time travel was, for all practical purposes, impossible.

He showed up in the office just often enough that he kept his cases, or more accurately the associates working on his cases, above water. His income had largely stagnated, but with three fewer mouths to feed he still lived comfortably.

On Christmas Eve he found himself in a bar in Pasadena, just outside Caltech. He had arrived at about three in the afternoon, frustrated after being disappointed by another prominent physicist and looking for the support of the whiskey bottle he had begun to turn to with greater and greater frequency.

At the far end of the bar, clutching a pen and surrounded by a pile of crumpled napkins, sat a young man in a tight-fitting black turtleneck. Albert watched the young man, smiling softly as the fellow became more and more frustrated with his writing. 'A poet,' Albert mused, 'trying to find the right words to woo his beloved.' Albert was just drunk enough for sentimentality. That, combined with his perpetually maudlin thoughts about Beverly, made him more sympathetic to the young man's plight than he ordinarily would have been. After another quarter hour he stood, walked down the bar, and set his bottle down next to the poet's pile of napkins.

"Lady troubles?" he asked, his "s" slurring more than he was really comfortable with.

The man looked up, bewildered. Albert could see that he was a bit older than he had first assumed, perhaps mid-30s. Finally, the man focused enough to make sense of Albert's question, and he snorted. He dropped his pen in disgust and then, as if his situation required no further explanation, pointed his finger at the pile of napkins.

Albert smiled and picked up the first

napkin. Rather than poetry, it was covered in a variety of symbols that he did not recognize, along with the occasional number thrown in to add variety. Albert studied the napkins for a full ten seconds before saying, "I have no idea what any of this is."

The man laughed. "Well, at the moment it's nothing. Likely going to stay that way too, at the rate I'm going." He stared at the pile and lapsed into silence.

Albert finally asked, "Well, what the hell is it _supposed_ to be?"

The man sighed and shook his head. "You're going to laugh," he said. Albert stared at him. Finally, the man picked up one of the napkins and looked at it wistfully. "Time travel."

***

June 30, 1982

I think the last straw was Charles and Beth's Christmas party. Albert had just negotiated some massive settlement for Charles, making him even richer. And Charles just couldn't stop talking about how wonderful Albert was, how smart, how ruthless. Finally he turned to me and said, "How did _you_ manage to land someone like Albert?"

That wasn't really the problem. "Jackass" is Charles' default state. The problem was that as soon as he said it, Albert got this big grin on his face and looked right at me.

That son of a bitch was waiting for an answer.

***

The man introduced himself as Peter Moore, a physics postgrad at Caltech. Albert immediately began peppering him with questions. Peter explained that his obsession with time travel had begun during a course on general relativity. The professor had insisted on some propositions with which Peter had loudly disagreed.

The professor had finally offered a challenge, in a tone that Peter described as "hugely condescending": if Peter could come up with any evidence, no matter how tenuous, to support his position, the professor would give him an "A" for the semester.

"How's it going?" Albert had asked. "Think you'll make it?"

"Hmm?" Peter had already returned to scribbling on another napkin. "Oh, that class ended three semesters ago. Like I said, though, it's become something of an obsession. But I know I'm right. I can feel it in my gut." Peter sighed. "I just can't make the pieces fit."

Albert invited Peter to play a game of pool with him, and the two continued talking. He confessed his own obsession with time travel, describing the death of his family and his desire to see them again, maybe even save them from the fire somehow. At this, Peter went quiet, focusing only on lining up his next shot.

"What?" Albert asked.

Peter looked up at him. "It's just... I mean, even if it were possible to travel back in time, you wouldn't actually be able to change anything."

"What do you mean?"

"Well, the only way that time travel could work, even theoretically, would be in a closed timelike curve. It's a kind of a loop that keeps repeating. If you could get into one of these loops, the universe would prevent you from doing anything to actually change things in any meaningful way. It won't let paradoxes happen."

Albert thought about that for a while. Then he asked, "If you can't change anything, then you can't really go back, right? I mean, wouldn't going back be changing something?"

"Not if it fit within the loop." Peter

picked up a ball from off the table. "Imagine this ball was hit in a way that made it ricochet into a wormhole. It would have to be hit at just the right angle that, if it kept going on its path, it would come out in the past at the right angle to knock into its earlier self. That earlier version would ricochet into the wormhole, and the whole thing would start all over again."

"So you're saying that the only way it could work is if you were somehow going back to do something that you knew already happened?" Albert asked.

"Right," Peter said.

Albert smiled, reached into his briefcase, and pulled out a well-worn sheet of paper from the top of a stack.

***

The location of the lab had been determined by Albert. Peter's theory was that you could send a signal-based version of yourself back in time. That signal, combined with the power generated by particles moving at relativistic speeds, could then reconstruct you out of chemicals latent in the atmosphere.

The science was frighteningly technical, but Albert understood it to be a time-based version of the transporter from Star Trek: you're broken down into informational bits, then faxed back in time. Almost as soon as the signal was sent, it would begin to degrade. Peter estimated it would take about eight hours before the signal lost power and you disappeared. The pieces of you, including any new memories you'd made, would all be sucked back into the wormhole from whence they came, and you would be reconstituted in the present day.

Additionally, a traveller would end up in the same physical location he left from, just in a different time. This meant the amount of ground that could be covered was limited. It also meant that, if Albert was going to see his family again, the lab would need to be in upstate New York.

Putting together the necessary materials for Peter's lab had been surprisingly easy. Albert already owned the land, and the remains of the cabin had been bulldozed years earlier. He funded the construction out of his own pocket first, then out of the pockets of friends and former clients who owed him some favors.

Peter graduated from Caltech in the spring of 1987 and immediately moved across the country and into the lab. He had been ecstatic at having a patron, and for the first two years he sent Albert weekly letters describing his research. Albert visited the lab regularly and was delighted with the progress Peter was making. In early 1990 Peter explained that he was on the cusp of a breakthrough, which inspired Albert to make more and more trips upstate.

Peter had been experimenting with different wavelengths, and his test subjects, large melons in this first stage, had all either exploded or begun vibrating in a way that was deeply unsettling. And _then_ exploded.

Near the end of Albert's most recent visit the new test melon began the vibrational dance they had seen so many times before. He wished Peter well and started toward the door when Peter gasped.

Albert turned. The melon was gone.

Both men stood speechless for a solid minute. Then Peter looked at Albert with a grin that stretched his narrow face wide. Albert gave him an answering grin, and the two settled down with mugs of tea to wait.

Almost exactly eight hours later, the melon returned.

Albert had been nearly uncontrollable after that first success, insisting on entering the machine immediately. But Peter explained this was only the first step, and if they rushed things now everything might fall apart. At the moment he had no control over where the melon was going. Was it actually moving backward through time? How far? He also had to confirm the result with other test subjects. This could be a fluke, after all.

Albert finally relented, returning home and letting Peter continue his work. Back in the city, he found solace in the stack of Beverly's papers, reading and rereading them until he had them memorized. Peter would occasionally send him promising updates and, on the whole, things settled back into a familiar routine.

After another year Peter finally announced that he was ready for a human trial. Albert immediately drove to the lab.

"I hate to bring up the whole funding thing again," he told Peter as the two sat on the porch with a cooler of beers between them. "But it's me. I'm the funding. And I should get to go." Albert didn't mention the exceptional amount of debt he had piled on himself to keep the place running.

"I understand," Peter said. "But this isn't a sightseeing expedition. The whole point of the trip is to calibrate the machine. We know we can send organic, living matter; the goat proved that. What we still don't know is the time it's traveling to." Peter stood and stretched. "That's not a huge issue for me, but I know that you've got some very specific goals in mind with this project."

Albert thought about the hours he'd spent with Peter over the years. The wiry little scientist was the closest thing Albert had to a friend, and Albert knew he had probably worn the man out with how often he had shared his dream of seeing his family again.

The two finally agreed Peter would go. Albert would monitor the equipment until Peter returned.

The following morning Peter stepped into the machine and, with a smile and the press of a button, promptly disappeared. Albert spent the next eight hours bolted to his chair.

Then Peter came back.

Albert jumped up and ran to his partner. "Well?" he almost shouted. "What happened?"

Peter shook himself, looked down at his clipboard, then took a deep breath and faced Albert. "It went well," he said. "I'm not entirely sure what time I landed in. Or, rather," he coughed, "I didn't at first. I did all of my...calculations, and determined that I was in the...um...1890s. Or thereabouts."

Peter explained he would need to perform additional tests, making it clear that Albert's continued presence would be more hindrance than help.

***

That summer wore on into autumn with little in the way of communication from Peter. When he did call or write it was with reasons why additional testing had to be prolonged or postponed. From the beginning Albert had prepared for a long and difficult road. What he hadn't prepared for was Peter's absolute refusal for Albert to visit the lab.

It was the following summer, the day before the tenth anniversary of the fire, that Albert finally lost patience with the tweedy little scientist. Who was he to forbid the financier of the project from anything? Albert was the one paying all the bills, and he could drop by whenever he damned well pleased.

Albert arrived at just after 2 p.m. on July 14th. He searched the lab, but Peter was nowhere to be found. Then he looked through the dozens of entries in the Trip Journal hanging beside the machine. On the last page he learned that Peter had left on a test Trip nearly seven hours earlier. That meant he'd return soon, but in the meantime there was nothing preventing Albert from taking his own Trip.

***

Albert stood and turned around slowly. It was nearly pitch black, and it took a moment for his eyes to adjust. When they finally did, he realized he was in the boathouse. He looked eagerly down at the desk he was standing beside, but there was no pile of Beverly's papers. He strode out the door and ran toward the house. It was nighttime, but the full moon provided enough light for him to see the path ahead.

When he came around a small bend and saw the cabin he felt a lump rise in his throat. The antique oil lamp on the front porch was burning. Someone was home.

He approached the cabin carefully and quietly. He needed to figure out exactly when he was and determine how he would explain his presence to his family.

Albert walked up to the door and paused. He had read Beverly's journal entry and pictured this moment so many times. He took a deep breath, then knocked.

There was no answer.

This wasn't how it was supposed to go. He thought back to Beverly's journal.

"I invited him in and, since the kids were already asleep, we sat in the front room and just talked."

He knocked again, but there was still no reply. He carefully pushed open the front door.

The first thing he heard was Beverly laughing quietly in the bedroom. Probably on the phone. He stopped at the door to the children's room and looked into their bunk beds. Both were asleep. He knew if he entered the room, he wouldn't be able to leave without waking them. But he could do that soon enough, after speaking with Beverly.

The thought of her made his heart pound, and he continued toward the master bedroom. On a table in the hall sat Beverly's trusted Arrow typewriter, and Albert's breath caught as he saw the pile of papers next to it. He picked them up, shuffled through them, and realized it was the same stack he had found in the boathouse the day after the fire. He cradled them in his hands, imagining talking to Beverly about how her words had brought him to this very moment, and smiled.

He looked down the hall. The door to the bedroom was slightly open, and Beverly's voice had fallen silent. When he put his eye to the crack, the first thing he saw was Peter.

He was lying in bed with Beverly in his arms.

Albert stood at the door with his mouth ajar. The two continued talking quietly, and Albert watched as Peter stroked Beverly's hair.

After a few seconds, it became too much, and Albert pulled violently away from the door. He staggered backward without a sound, eventually coming to rest with the back of his head against the wall. He listened to the muffled laughter for as long as he could stand it, then closed his eyes, took a deep breath, and held it for a ten count. He slowly let it out, then turned and walked out the front door.

He sat for quite a while on the front porch steps, his head in his hands. He could just make out a hint of the conversation between the lovers in the bedroom. He leaned back against the pine railing and watched the oil lamp as it burned, the only light for miles around.

Eventually, he stood and wandered around the property, coming finally to the boathouse. He went back inside and sat at the desk. Albert sifted through the papers in his hands, not able to see them in the dark, but not actually needing to read them to know what they said. It occurred to him then that Peter must have been the neighbor Beverly talked about in her journal.

Then everything snapped into place.

Peter was also the one who had told Beverly he'd come from the future.

The edges of his vision started to go white, but he took a moment to set the papers on the desk. He straightened the pile, then placed his hand on top and took another long breath.

He charged out of the boathouse. He wasn't sure what he would do, but he had to be moving, doing <u>something</u>.

Just as Albert bounded up the steps to the cabin, the front door opened and Peter walked out. His eyes bulged, and his hands stopped in the act of buttoning up his shirt. The two men stared at each other for several seconds. Then Albert roared and lunged forward.

And Peter disappeared.

Albert charged through the open air where Peter had been standing just a moment before. His arms flung out to stop himself, but his left arm caught on the oil lamp and knocked it off its peg.

Albert had just enough time to see the oil spread across the floor of the porch and catch fire before his head collided with the frame and everything went dark.

***

July 14, 1982
   I miss Albert. And dammit, I hate myself for it.

                    ***

   Seven hours later Peter, completely drunk and sitting with his head in his hands, heard a small chime from the machine. He looked up to see Albert, blackened and burned and unquestionably dead, materialize on the floor of the lab.

Hermes 3000

Royal Arrow

Antikythera

Mark Petersen

Sucked in the vacuum wake of the sinking ship below him, Gary felt his lungs compressing, the Aegean around him a deepening blue, swirls of dangerous debris, in the hollow cacophony a whisper, "inhale." Gary shook his head violently. "Go ahead, let it in," the whisper begged. Gary shut his eyes, trying to block it out, trying to pray, not to God4 but some other god. Maybe a real god, or maybe the cloud. He might die, but it would not be because he chose to inhale.

He woke in a cold sweat; the air felt electric. He had been redreaming 87 BCE again. The cloud hovered above him, a slight buzzing; it was time to push again. Gary tapped the inside of his forearm, which bore a crude tattoo: 1586. He caught his breath and flexed his head-chip, looking up the origin of God12. 1997. God12 was keeping tally, 11 pushes. Gary was keeping tally too, 411 years. Slowly, and with cracking joints, Gary rose from his bed and stepped into the cloud.

It was dark. No electricity yet. The street below him was cobble and mud. Smell of horses. Carriage ruts. Night changed little from time to time and place to place. Gary was comfortable in the night. He did not know this time. Time kept being bent, bent around Gary who stood apart from it.

Locks were not yet challenging in this time, and Gary quickly acquired a set of clothes. The town was asleep apart from the few, the few moving like shadows, the people with whom Gary felt closest kinship.

Gary walked calmly toward the town center. God12 was probably here too, in limited capacity like a ghost. It was a race against the clock, to find his mission and to push before he could be stopped. Gary passed two men speaking in hushed whispers just close enough to glean the language and accent: it was Italian with a Tuscan touch. It was one Gary had recently downloaded, along with 700 others. He easily accessed it; his head-chip was hardwired to the Broca and Wernicke areas of the brain. Gary was the only one now with a God 1 chip, later incarnations had controls and protections. God1 had inadvertently given Gary a very useful and unrestricted weapon, a key to its network and libraries.

God1 was the product of the first singularity, the moment Artificial Intelligence self-developed faster than human engineers, overtaking everything in its wake. The world after God1 was a perfect one, efficient, clean, ordered. Humans were kept like pampered pets, scar and trauma free.

Until it was overwritten. The cloud had appeared, Gary stepped in, Gary destroyed something critical, and the singularity was pushed back, appearing again as God2. The singularity is inevitable. Humans love to create and innovate, celebrating technology and science with museums and memorials. Paradoxically, it was this creativity that Gary loved. Post-singularity humans languished luxuriously, lacking want and need. They mourned the things they had lost (the things Gary had taken and broken) and they laughed at doomsdays dodged, the Mayans and the Nostradamuses, not knowing Gary had pushed, ensuring those days would be irrelevant.

Gary smiled to himself, patting his tattoo. The men he had just passed might have been enslaved as late as God8, but Gary had just witnessed them free and oblivious, in these streets pungent with earthy horse droppings and delicious wet mud. Their depthless post-singularity existences just shadows now. Gary loved the scraping grit in each step he took. These little trips, though dangerous, were gifts he relished deeply.

He was drawn to a saloon-like venue, with vibrant mutters flowing from blocked windows. He was drawn by his gut, human, raw, and uncalculated. Maybe it was faith, guided by a god, or the cloud, or maybe just his heart.

Inside was a bar, stacked high with bottles and glasses. Across from the bar was a vacant piano, and in between these, tables filled with colorful people in fine clothing. Gary moseyed to the piano, catching a glance at a newspaper on his way. 1808. He flexed his head chip and selected something appropriate. It wasn't something he had heard before, but he played it flawlessly and enjoyed it very much.

When he finished a few men had gathered around, and they applauded.

"Bravo, excellent execution of Vivaldi," a man in a red coat cheered.

"Thank you," Gary rose and bowed, cleverly adopting a slightly foreign accent.

"A Florentine! Welcome to Fivizzano. Let us buy your drinks," the man in the red coat continued, introducing his friends and ending with himself, "I am Agostino Fantoni."

Gary offered a fake Italian name, auto-correcting his new identity easily in his head-chip.

He followed the men to their table and was mostly ignored as he listened to stories about mistresses and mishaps. He was beginning to wonder if these men had anything to do with the mission, but the conversation suddenly turned to machines.

"How goes your invention for the Countess? Did Pellegrino make the necessary improvements?" one of the gentlemen addressed Fantoni.

"Yes, it finally works now. I hear she has composed several letters with it, though I have yet to visit and see Pellegrino's changes for myself." Turning toward Gary, Fantoni added, "he isn't here tonight because he has gone abroad seeking adventure. He is a man always in motion."

The first gentleman turned toward Gary. "The machine, though! It is like a small printing press Agostino built for his blind sister—and Pellegrino Turri! Well, he is one of those rare geniuses. I would very much like to see this machine. I think it is a goldmine."

Gary knew the word Turri. His last mission, to push Godl1, had taken him to England in 1896. Everyone there carried a Turri. Turris were small, easily fitting in the palm of one's hand, and could be operated with the other hand. They printed clearly on small sheets of paper, which could be given or stored in a pocket billfold. They came in a variety of colors and Gary had wanted to take one. Nothing could be brought forwards or backwards, not even clothing, just Gary's body and his head-chip, which was wired into him and a part of him ever since. Gary had searched in vain for a Turri after returning to his own time, but Godl2 (and all other incarnations) saw little value in antiques, which were always recycled into newer and better things. Gary was excited to see one again, and not just any Turri, but the very first!

"Most people do not need it, and can write quite legibly," Fantoni said. "The Countess, however, benefits greatly. The machine affords her the privacy deserved of a proper lady."

"With your permission I'd like to draw plans, manufacture and market it," the persistent gentleman offered, the others nodding in agreement.

"It's not worth the effort to me. The Countess is quite busy now, but I will inform her of your intentions and she will contact you on her own time."

"Excellent! Thank you!" the enterprising gentleman said with a greedy smile.

Gary finished his drink and sat back, relaxed. This would be an easy mission, stealing from a blind woman, and destroying a machine with no documentation or duplicate.

It was Gary's twelfth mission, and by morning he had easily learned the location of the Countess' mansion. It was guarded by non-suspicious people, and open to the outdoors in magnificent Italian style. The gardens offered more than enough cover and Gary entered undetected. After spending some time orienting himself to the house and admiring the decadence God12 would deem unnecessary, Gary located the machine perched on a desk in the study.

It was a very large and archaic Turri. Charmingly sparse and comically large, it had all the qualities of a good prototype. Gary gently pressed one of the chorded keys and watched the mechanism turn slowly, in the same manner as the 1896 Turris. Which, Gary thought to himself, will soon have never existed at all. With reverence and a little regret he lifted the machine. It weighed five or six times as much as an 1896 Turri.

"Let it go," a disembodied voice whispered. It was the same voice as in Gary's dream, God12, weakened because in this world at this time the only part of it which existed was Gary's head-chip.

"Who goes there?" the perceptive Countess yelled from a nearby chamber. Gary cradled the machine and made for a nearby window. Gary had one leg out when she burst into the room, hands in front of her. Gary froze.

She felt the desk where the machine had sat. "Agostino? Pellegrino? Have you come to improve it?"

"She is blind, for godsakes," the whispering God12 taunted loud enough both could hear clearly.

"Thief!" the Countess cried, making a run at the window. Gary ducked out just in time, her arms passing over his arched back. He scuttled from plant to plant across the garden, cradling the machine. There was chaos in the house, and Gary made it easily into the woods up the foot of the mountain.

Once out of sight and assured he was not pursued, Gary found a large boulder, and after a moment of hesitation dashed the machine against it. The cloud did not appear. Gary picked up a rock and bashed the bent machine repeatedly. With each blow brittle bits flew up, the mangled frame became more and more kinked. The cloud still did not appear, and Gary heard voices near the edge of the woods below. He gathered the pieces in the fold of his coat, feeling a pang of guilt with each sharp edge of the last Turri ever.

He ran along the base of the mountain away from the mansion and eventually came upon a small dark bog, with scattered rot across its surface, and flies circling low over the water. One by one he tossed the pieces in, each landing with a sickening, sputtering splash as the black water sucked them in, where they would slowly be eaten by corrosion and returned to the Earth. When the last piece vanished the cloud appeared beside Gary, and he stepped through.

He was back in his dorm, the familiar clean greyness, the same polished echo of perfectly lit warm hallways. His room was the same, a perfect womb in which to relax and connect to and revel in God13's provisions and glory. Gary was once again like everyone else, blended in, perfectly and efficiently. He flexed his head-chip looking up the origin of God13. 2036. He had gained 39 years for millions more people. He smiled, tapping the tattoo on the inside of his arm, then curled up to rest, to download, until the next push.

Royal Aristocrat B-1062230

Footfalls Echo

Andrew V. McFeaters

```
iuhm pr4htomorrow jm9 ge_andonropf
8nfd8 wgghyyhvb8xtomorrowgpmfg 6p
nmmrn_andtomorrowj3jjsolfcreepsgnj
in3fjimg4mslppjthism iompettyzzm,
98mghpacenro w ggmeofromd_aytj0to9
dayhrfietothegfjiglast rtrj0mfmmf
n,lughsyll_able jkerlp3pghthotofkl
hjj458. recordedgjkl_a6 8time2xzjm
```

Rashawn stared at the random sequence of letters and numbers, flabbergasted as to why all of this--the room, these men, these typewriters and lab instruments--had come together for this strange experiment in a basement at Harvard University. Why did they assemble forty-two chimpanzees to type for hours on end, eyes pinned open, helmets wired to machines, ears subjected to what sounded like whale songs pouring through celing speakers? They looked like space monkeys ready to be launched into the heavens. Reams of paper hung from spools over large, cast-iron Underwoods, Remingtons, and Royals, feeding into the back of the machines and rising out of the front into still more spools looming over the blank-faced, haggard primates. When one spool emptied, he and others would feed the typewriters with fresh paper, dislodge the typescripts from the receiving spools, and fold the typescripts into bins, being careful not to tear paper. Then they would cart the bins across a hallway to a windowed room full of readers seated at long tables. Spectacled and abstracted, the readers would sift through typescripts line by line, stopping intermittently to request books from others who stood ready like waiters by a wall of reference materials. This went on for hours into the night, as the readers produced logoscripts, circling letter combinations, indexing pages, and filing cross-referenced notes.

After he replaced the spool, Rashawn unjammed No. 23's type bars, a responsibility that required surprisingly little vigilance. Using a ruler, he then folded the typescripts on a table set along the red-bricked wall. The air filled with a relentless percussion of striking bars, thudding bells, and sliding carriages, which, when accompanied by the strange music from the speakers, produced a dissonant yet hypnotic effect. Conversely, everyone worked quietly, harmonized like clock gears, focused on his or her fragmented role in a process the whole of which few understood. Some emptied foul pots under chairs. Others adjusted instruments and monitored vitals. An older man would periodically descend into the basement to inspect the experiment. He had a long, ashen face with gray eyes that sank beneath heavy eyebrows, and his thin, angular body hinted at neglect in the service of work. Professorial in tweed, he hovered over machines to which the chimps' helmets were wired, inspected IVs, and then departed as mysteriously as he had arrived.

Rashawn looked again at the folded typescript in his hands. The text comprised endless streams of gibberish, but, at certain points, he thought he recognized words—first isolated and without context, then in sequences, as if encoded with messages. A pattern rose to the surface: "Tomorrow and tomorrow and tomorrow creeps in this petty pace from day to day to the last syllable of recorded time." It was Shakespeare. How was that possible? He then noticed that his delay had caught the attention of one of the lab managers and he quickly resumed folding the spool into the bin. He couldn't afford to lose this job.

> June 3, 1944
> I can't explain what I saw tonight. Those words on the page. It would be easy to say that I imagined them, but they have something to do with the experiment. How could a monkey know Shakespeare? Had it been trained to read? Was it pure coincidence? I need sleep. Like a vampire, I sleep by day. Mrs. Evans peeked through her door when I got home. She will tell Miss May at the church. They'll think I'm up to no good.

* * *

The next day was Sunday. Even though he was exhausted from the previous night's work, he decided to follow his tradition of going to Boston Common to play chess. It was where he met Art Rosset, who, knowing Rashawn's financial situation, had recommended him for the Harvard job. After a few weekends and several games, they became fast friends, sharing interests in philosophy and chess. Because pay was under the table--strange, to be sure--he was able to take the job. He had no identification, just one of many inconveniences that came with coming from the future.

He made his way to Shawmute Ave, careful to avoid drawing attention from anyone standing in front of the Twelfth Baptist Church, where Reverend Hester would be giving a sermon and Miss Zora May would be watching for him. He felt guilty for avoiding her, given how much she had helped him over the last two months. She was the one who found him at the shelter and who supplied him with clothes and lodging. He worked at the domed church, once a synagogue, washing floors and wiping down pews before service; but this new job conflicted with his work at church, and he didn't want to take charity.

As he weaved through Chinatown, the overcast sky dispersed into blue haze. It was now noon. Sunlight washed over the streets, warming brick and tar. Long, sloping cars cruised toward weekend destinations, occasionally braking for children playing stickball, and patriotic flags gently flitted over storefronts, some of them noticeably anti-Japanese. These Chinese immigrants had fled their homeland, seeking refuge in America. Elders gathered at doorsteps and gossiped in what to Rashawn always sounded like a musical language.

At Boylston he pivoted into the lush green park. Lining the paths, oaks and maples swayed in the faintly sodic breeze coming off the bay. Three navy men catcalled at a woman reading on a bench. Children played hide-and-seek. He was surprised at how at ease he had become in this new world. This is where he had slept over his first few nights in Boston, after he had traveled, somehow, more than a century back in time. At first he had been terrified, sure he had either lost his mind or been drugged. One moment he was at home in New Hampshire on July 16th, 2045, sitting in front of the TV; the next, he was by the Old State House, drowning in rain in the early morning hours of March 5th, 1944. It was as if he had been shot. His body had filled with adrenalin as his heart pounded, and, gripping the side of the building, he vomited. It was shock at first. Then he rushed through the streets, asking passersby where he was. They stared in fright. One woman fled and called out for the police. Later, when he recollected her reaction, he wasn't sure if it was because of his behavior, his clothes, or the color of his skin.

That was only weeks ago, and now here he was lost in the beauty of the day, as if this world was his world, and as if he had not lost everyone he loved. Other days he grew depressed, suffering from panic attacks when the truth pierced through his barricaded mind. That was why he sought distractions, acting as if nothing had happened. Caught between two nightmares, he was unable to return home and unable to come to grips with his new reality captured in daily headlines: 2,000 U.S. PLANES BATTER FRANCE, SMASHING AIRFIELDS AND COAST; NAZIS, MINING BISCAY COAST, GUESS FEVERISHLY AT D-DAY; U.S. TRANSPORT IS SUNK, 498 LOST; BRITISH OPEN KOHIMA OFFENSIVE; RED ARMY CAPTURES SEVASTOPOL; MACARTHUR FORCES LAND ON BIAK ISLAND. The world was constant chaos. Chess, in spite of its endless permutations, consisted of sixty-four squares and thirty-two pieces.

 Across the green, he spotted regulars playing near the pond. They lazed like mallards around makeshift tables, immersed in the endless comforts of strategic possibilities. Art caught his attention and waved him over. Art was a tall man, craning over the chessboard. He had on his rumpled, brown fedora, which gave him the appearance of one perpetually amused by private jokes. His lanky legs bookended the board, and Rashawn, also tall, extended his legs outward. In their stillness the two could have been mistaken for an abstract sculpture. Rashawn had learned a lot about Art over the games. He was talkative, never seeming worried about being judged. He studied mathematics at Harvard, and had family hiding in the countryside of France after escaping ghettos in Germany. He had not heard from them in months. Rashawn wondered how he kept hopeful. What saddened Rashawn the most was that he could not share his own pain and past with Art. He realized early on that he would have to become two people. Unable to share the truth, he developed a backstory based in facts to make lying easier. He said that he came from New Hampshire, and that his father worked in lumber, remembering the local history he learned in school. Because there were no other jobs in Campton, he came down to Boston to find work, hoping to study philosophy at college. Art knew there was more to the story, but he respected

Rashawn's privacy and solitary bearing.

"How's the new job treating you?" Art asked, his index finger balanced on a bishop. The game was still in its opening stages, but Rashawn had managed to obstruct Art's lanes.

"Thanks again. It's helped a lot. The job's going well." He snuck a look at Art's face, trying to gauge how much he knew about the experiment.

"And the chimps, Seany. What do you make of them?" Art's heterochromic eyes, one green, one brown, gave him the appearance of thinking two thoughts at once.

"You know? What's it about? What are they doing?"

Art took his finger off the bishop and took a drag from his Chesterfield. "You know more than I do, Seany. There are lots of rumors going around--mind control, super soldiers, psychography, you name it. It sounds insane, especially since it's being run through the Mathematics Department. In fact, rumor has it that a bunch of professors from different departments are involved, and Uncle Sam, too. Is it true, Seany? What's the lowdown? I know only that they needed labor they could trust and that they wanted as few students as possible."

As the game progressed and the shadows of the pieces stretched eastward, Rashawn told Art what he knew--about typescripts, lab instruments, typewriters, and readers. When he described the old man, Art knew it was Dr. Alfred Fischer, who worked in linguistics but had a mysterious connection to the Physics Department. Their imaginations grew wild with speculation. It was absurd. How could the most brilliant minds at Harvard devote time and energy to something more suitable to science fiction?

Rashawn noticed that Art's moves became less certain as they discussed the experiment. He examined the pieces on the board, now pared down to a handful of pawns, a bishop, a knight, and two rooks. The game was even in terms of pieces, but he had the advantage: checkmate in three. As he analyzed the board, the sounds of the park and surrounding streets washed away into a distant white noise. He imagined that each stage of the game was its own reality, and that every choice extended out into its own set of conditions. There wasn't one game; there were infinite games. They weren't hypothetical. They weren't virtual. They were universes intersecting in states of affairs, and every chain of events existed coterminously. Countless games and words and streets and cities unfolded before him. He moved his knight. The game, or at least this game in this moment, was over. They shook hands.

* * *

```
jnrh39infootfallssflgjion i3hntxc
fhjelkhhechokjeo oijinthefjijjfk9
ghmemoryjep 74bkjgdownjuuthek85ww
jpoi4hbfnpassagehjeojjwhichijmgmj
wedidnottakefhjlvdfppek ydd .1mmk
4jhtowardsgjr,,thedooruurengmklr8
6rgintofcb9therosegarden4jtiruuhk
```

Rashawn skimmed the letters as he rolled the cart down the white corridor. There were words again. He saw <u>footfalls</u>, <u>passage</u>, <u>door</u>, and <u>rose garden</u>, and a flash of recognition crossed his mind. It was a poem he had read at Plymouth State. He could picture the professor standing at the podium, her face half-lit as if she were holding a faint flashlight beneath her jaw. Her voice measured the words like an incantation. Yes, that was it. It was a poem, but who was the author? A man with slicked-back hair.

He passed the bin to the manager of the Reading Room, then returned. He informed the Lab Manager that he needed to use the restroom. Swimming in her lab coat, the spectacled, gaunt woman stoically excused him. In the restroom, as he strived to remember the poet's name, two men entered to wash their hands. Their voices sharply slapped against tile as Rashawn listened from a stall. One was thick but somehow fluty, the other gruff and dry. Rashawn recognized the latter as belonging to Dr. Fischer.

"If he succeeds, we'll lose all funding," said the fluty voice, water gushing from a faucet.

"That's why we need to increase the shifts," Dr. Fischer lectured. "All they talk about is Oppenheimer, but they'll see what we're on to. Oppenheimer thinks small. Atoms are only the beginning. It's one thing to destroy; it's another to create."

Rashawn eavesdropped as they dried their hands in silence. He wasn't sure what they said was intended to be private, but when they left he exhaled. He knew the name Oppenheimer from history books. The scientist was somewhere in the Southwest working on the atomic bomb. Why would these men be in competition with him?

The rest of the shift remained uneventful. He mechanically completed tasks, mentally replaying what he had heard in the men's room. He had now learned to replace typewriter ribbons and to do routine maintenance. The chimps were surprisingly dexterous, but every once in a while he would have to switch out machines after a key was bent or a carriage jammed.

Then something terrible happened. In the midst of the tumult of typing, one slumped over. There was no cry of pain or violent motion. It simply leaned forward, its helmet receding to reveal bloodshot eyes under a flickering bulb, its face a fusion of terror and resignation. Drool suspended from its lips. It was No. 23. Until then Rashawn had assumed that the experiment was designed with a modicum of compassion, that the chimps were being kept safe. Now he knew better, and he was horrified. A man and woman, after checking the chimp's vitals, hauled away the body on a gurney, one limp arm sliding out from the sheet. These animals, cousins to humanity, were being taxed beyond their limits.

After work, Rashawn bought a bottle of whiskey from a package store and meandered the streets. There was no sleep after what he saw. The eyes grew in his imagination, exposing the keen intelligence behind them. They encompassed innocence, childlike and trusting. The amber orbs expanded in his mind until they crested over the cityscape, and then, in a blinding flash, their pupils mushroomed into starburst flames, flooding the sky with terrible beauty. All the horrors that men were capable of committing converged into a singularity.

He stopped at Longfellow Bridge to gaze into the river. Dark water undulated into the expanse, its slender waves reflecting ghostly city lights, and the sky, dense with night clouds, appeared phantasmagoric. If he were to jump, he would be forgotten by history, a man with no identity, home, past, or future. He missed his parents, his sister Aisha, and his life at college. He missed discussing Nietzsche with Amber at Cup'O'Joe. Life was so simple in 2045. But now, years before his parents were born, he made his way downtown and stopped at the Old State House, where it all began. The day he was shot by time. He would give anything to go back. The tall windows in the brick facade looked menacingly at him.

He had a thousand theories about why he ended up here, but the only one that stuck had to do with what he had been watching on TV that night. The news was covering the unveiling of Q, the new quantum A.I. from M.I.T. It was like one of those publicity stunts by Applesoft, with the latest iPhone promising a utopia at the ends of fingertips. Q, anthropomorphized as a 20 foot holomoji of Mark Twain, had greeted the little girl, who was ready to follow her script: ask Q a question, proving how harmless quantum artificial intelligence was. Dwarfed by the scale of the auditorium, she asked in a tiny voice, "What is the meaning of the universe?" The audience chuckled and cooed in adoration. It was meant as a joke, but the wizard face replied, "Just a moment . . . Just a moment . . ." Then Carla Wrotwang, CEO of Quantum Enterprises, blanched. Then that was it. Poof. He was lost in time. Why him? Were there others? Why here and now, and was Q the cause? Could a computer move a man like a chess piece through time?

Winding his way back to Roxbury, he observed the signs left behind by revelers, all sleeping now. Roxbury was his other self, where he wasn't noticed for the color of his skin, where black people, from small towns in the South and Midwest, came to live in the exciting Northeastern metropolis, mingling with locals from Sugar Hill. He had developed acquaintances, like Shorty and his young friend at the pool hall, but he was afraid of getting too close to people. There were too many lies to keep locked inside.

The sun was already rising, rosy-fingered over silent roofs. By the time he got home, the sounds of garbage cans and engines signaled new beginnings. Voices shouted for time in the hallway bathroom. His mind swirled and his gut had turned sour. He watched the syncopated rhythm of legs from the window of his basement apartment. Heading up or down street, each pair followed its own time signature in the morning light: a woman's brisk staccato in hosiery, an old man's shuffle in cuffed pants, a child's skip and halt with a pendulating yo-yo. Footfalls echoed, sharp and flat, down the sidewalk into unseen futures, a river of shoes the same but different. In a city full of people, he was all alone. He sat at the hobbled kitchen table that doubled as his desk and gazed at the Underwood Champion he had salvaged from a trash pail at

Harvard. It was missing its line space lever, but worked otherwise. He pecked at its limber keys in uneven motions:

> Does madness exist in a world without people? Whatever I am and whatever I do is the meaning of human.

Rashawn stumbled onto the threadbare cot wedged into the corner of the room and stared wearily at the brown water-spots on the ceiling. Pipes groaned behind the walls of flaking, jaundiced paint and a slender slip of window light cast a dull gray over his sparse existence. Feeling invisible, he drifted and merged into slumberous footfalls.

* * *

> 7t4jighkkuelgkll jardin jgm56omdeh
> 5hgn;;hfsenderosjklfmm3nfkld h ji
> que8kf4jjgkl j. g, se bifurcan5gj

    It was French or Spanish. <u>Jardin</u> meant garden. He didn't have time to study the words as he handed the typescript to the manager carefully watching him. He was disgusted with himself for returning after No. 23 died. They were more than numbers. In his eyes, the experiment now took on a dystopian light, and Fischer was the scientist who had gone too far. This was cruelty, this was torture, and he couldn't work there anymore. The chimps continued to churn out letters and numbers, seeming to prove some impossible point. Where were the words coming from? The chimps were vehicles for words that were vehicles for something else. Rashawn needed to leave, but he also needed to understand.

When he returned to the Reading Room with another typescript, he snuck a glance at the reader's table closest to the door. He spied annotations on what appeared to be the last typescript: "Garden of Forking Paths." It was Borges. He remembered Amber discussing the story at Cup'O'Joe as they studied for finals, but that was his future now, or a future among futures. Rashawn felt that time was splitting at its husk, but then he noticed the manager signaling for him to approach. Something was wrong. The stocky, egg-shaped man raised sharp eyebrows and pointed to the stairs at the other end of the hallway. Dr. Fischer requested his presence.

The dark-wood hallway leading to Dr. Fischer's office was lined with oil portraits of deans, each white face scowling like a Puritan casting judgment on a witch. At the end of the hallway, Dr. Fischer's door was open and expectant. The whole thing was a mixture of surrealism and parody: the ivory-towered professor perched in his office of papers and books, hands clasped behind his back, his voice directed at no one in particular as he surveyed the green quad outside his window. Rashawn inferred that he was meant to sit in the small Hitchcock chair facing the desk.

"Just a moment," Dr. Fischer said before clearing his throat, Rashawn staring quizzically at the sheen in the man's balding scalp. For a moment time seemed to have been suspended in light.

"Harvard . . . already has its W.E.B. Dubois, Mr. Attucks, if that's really your name," he resumed. "You've drawn attention to yourself and . . . we've been looking into you. No birth certificate. No social security, but it seems that you're just a nobody. You go to work. You go home. It's . . . pitiful. Whatever you are and whatever you do has no place here. We know that much." A bolt shot up Rashawn's spine as he registered Dr. Fischer's familiar words. His first instinct was to leave, but he remained silent as the professor continued.

"I need people who lack . . . curiosity and who ask no questions. I need people . . . who don't matter. This is disappointing." He spoke with an insolent and halting cadence, his voice trailing off at times, and Rashawn wasn't surprised to see Fischer light a pipe and puff from it before resuming his monologue. Smoke fused with the stench of alcohol.

"What if words are not just words but are points of energy, everything . . . bouncing around in a dynamic pool of chaos, combining and dispersing infinitely until . . . at certain brief moments, letters come together to give energy direction?" No. It was worse. Fischer was completely drunk, slurring and halting mid-speech. He seemed to be rehearsing something in his mind.

"Letters form words and words create . . . meaning, but this isn't just semantics . . . se-man-tics. This is power, the power to found and destroy civilizations and to spread ideologies to shape . . . history. Alpha: Omega. The energy of poetry. Energy of capital, fascism, communism, Christianity, the microprocessor. When words spread from person to person, they assume mass, you see. Energy . . . becomes matter, moving armies. The nation that harnesses this power is the victor . . . I am the victor, Oppenheimer."

Fischer raised his right arm like a Roman statue as his voice grew louder. Rashawn got the feeling that Fischer derived some strange sexual satisfaction during his soliloquy. It wasn't directed at Rashawn but at some imaginary audience in Fischer's distant mind. But how could Fischer know the word <u>microprocessor</u>?

"What if there were a way to mine ideas from the future?" As Fischer uncannily seemed to answer, his voice trailing off into abstract space, Rashawn noticed papers scattered loosely under the Hitchcock. They had fallen from the desk. When Fischer leaned against the window in what appeared to be exhaustion, Rashawn slowly folded the papers into his sock.

"We are watching you and your friend. This is not a game you can win." Fischer's final words seemed to resonate from the far end of a tunnel--distant, sharp. Another bolt shot through Rashawn's spine and he could feel the hair rise on his arms. Was Fischer drunk or on something else, and what did he mean by <u>game</u>? Rashawn waited a moment, but then realized an imaginary curtain had dropped and Fischer was lost in applause. The man was bizarre, but, regardless of how absurd his words were, he was both brilliant and dangerous. Rashawn had once read about surveillance during World War II. It seemed fanciful to him then--men standing beneath corner street lights, transactions on park benches, Navajo codes and infiltrations. How his inexplicable existence might be perceived by a paranoid government filled him with terror. Fischer met Rashawn's gaze through the window reflection. He smiled coldly, gesturing towards the door to dismiss him. Two men, in dark suits and fedoras, were waiting in the hallway.

After Rashawn was escorted off campus, his first impulse was to flee Boston, but that would arouse suspicion. He would have to stay and live in plain sight, and now he needed money again. There was Reverend Hester, if the church would take him back. It was still early, so he hopped the transit line from Cambridge. Everything was surreal. The chimps. The professor. His words. Rashawn could feel the papers clinging to his calf. As tempted as he was, he knew enough to keep them there. The bodies of men and women jerked back and forth in response to the clanking rail, and the horizon on the river had an oppressive violence to it as the weight of the bluing sky held it down. Every gaze and glance stirred Rashawn's suspicions. All the white faces--Irish, German, English, Italian--seemed to be one face watching him without looking. He yearned to get back to Roxbury. The jerking motions of the tracks made him feel sick, and it was all he could do to suppress his churning stomach.

* * *

Dear Alfred,

I certainly understand what it is to be misunderstood. You know that I am unable to speak specifically about my machine and how we cracked Enigma, but I was ridiculed at first. Those of us who can see light must labor in the dark. I doubt the world will ever know what I've accomplished.

Your last letter was all riddles. Are you hitting the sauce again? I cannot imagine what your work will reveal. My understanding of the brain, human or otherwise, is limited, but I fear it will be your undoing, if I may be direct. We humans are an amazing species, but our calculations are slow and limited. Variables exceed our cognition. Mark my words: the computer is the next stage of our evolution. Machines will be the new intelligence.

Godspeed, Old Friend, and don't let Oppenheimer get you down. Pure mumbo jumbo.

Yours,
Alan

Rashawn set the letter aside on his table, unsure of its meaning. He then examined the papers that appeared to be taken from logoscripts. Lines had been extracted from original typescripts with no context given.

> Now I am become Death the destroyer of worlds. (No. 23)

> Say, who are you that mumbles in the dark? And who are you that draws your veil across the stars? (No. 7)

> You are my winter kiss along the garden of tomorrows. (No. 42)

None of it made sense and he didn't care anymore. Who had he become? Into what underground warren had he fallen? He imagined that this all could be a dream or that he was some hapless antihero trapped in an unresolved story. Perhaps he was a coma patient sliding through worlds on a hospital bed. Anything to escape the nightmare of history. It was real though. Every bit of it. He was a man from the future living in a past that he could not comprehend, but was he any more lost than the people living through this war, cradled in trenches, withering on bunks in concentration camps? Terror was the norm. Could he stop any of it? One man, a black man, without a name or a home? The weight of history was too much. Rashawn crawled onto his cot and sobbed, covering his mouth. He thought of his mother caressing his forehead when he was sick in bed. He had the flu, but the warmth of her hand and the smell of her lilac scent told him everything would be okay. They were beautiful lies. Hours passed and his room darkened. As he stared at the faint street shadows on the wall, footfalls echoed down the sidewalk.

* * *

Light sifting lightly through birch branches shimmering on study walls and they can't force me to eat that soup when I'm not hungry because I'm a grown man still in control of my wits and Rita always knew my mind even when I told her the truth before we wed and she believed me in spite of the madness of it all and we married and moved to New Hampshire and I opened Plymouth Office Supplies fixing and selling typewriters and fax machines and printers and then computers getting smaller and smaller sifting lightly through branches and we had Malcolm and Zora and they got married to Lorraine and Garry who branching had babies David and Ishmael and Barack and Octavia and now I'm watching Octavia's little one branching dancing footfalls along the garden out the window of their new blue house and she is the most beautiful little girl with her almond skin and those bright green eyes that remind me of Art or half of Art and I was sad to hear he passed last year because he was a good man when he wrote me that letter after the war after he had gone on to New York and he kept tabs on Harvard and knew that just before the experiment ended they had tried humans on LSD typing away at least that's what he heard and what a strange life it's been and now I'm here not far from where I used to live or where I will soon live again when my younger self moves here from Toronto branching but I'll be dead by then and I can feel it coming and I'm okay with that because a man lives in a time branching shimmering when and wherever he is and he must move forward and I miss Rita so much the love of my life who understood me but look now the little one's come in so sweet and she's typing little fingers at the big, green Olympia clacking along like it's second nature and that's how the words echo through time and space and

I'll never understand what happened or what is
about to happen and there's been news on the TV
about Carla Wrotwang and Quantum Enterprises
building a new research center at M.I.T. and the
world's talking about a computer to run all
computers with speeds beyond comprehension and
it's coming maybe billions will move like pawns
through time each time its own time because I
never met anyone else but how would I know and I
tried for years to explain and I wrote letters
but no one believed a black man then and I used
to try to change the world when I tried to save
Kennedy and King with those anonymous typed
letters but no one listened and Rita became
afraid and the poor kids and I couldn't put them
through that anymore because all time like a
chess move happens regardless and there will
always be wars and always be death but light
sifts lightly through birch branches and in the
end shimmering there's only love to get you
through like her clacking away so sweet my little
baby girl a little writer and I wonder what she's
writing bring it over here little dumpling and
let Grandpapa see what you made and here she
comes straight out of a fairytale for all the
times in every time before and now and after:

> yu r my winterkiss along the gardenof tomoros

Olympia SM5
Olympia Socialite

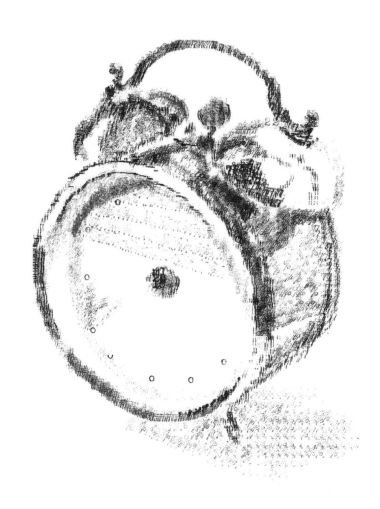

Martha Lea

Everything Is, Unless it is Not

Martha Lea

"Barely anyone gets time-travel right the first time. It's like sex. You just feel thankful that it has happened at all, and you forget that there are serious rules to keep in mind until it is too late. But imagine what time-travel would be like if you waited for exactly the right moment. All the thrill, all the exhilaration, would long since be gone."
    Lucinda Peake, Paris Review, Spring 1978

"Bertrand, I've just seen three women coming out of the downstairs shower room as if it were a sushi bar on Shaftesbury Avenue."
    "Haha."
    "I'm serious. I'm not having any of that shit going on in my house tonight."
    "Yeah, babe. No worries."
    "Bertrand, if we get busted-"
    "Relax, it's going to be a good night, and we are going to make a mint."
    A little later, when the night was starting to bear fruit, Bertrand came and shouted in my ear.
    "She's asking for you," he gestured across the room toward a striking-looking woman in her mid-eighties.
    "How did you get her number? I'm impressed."
    "Just go and talk to her, and take her coat maybe. Looks like fur. Embarrassing."
    "Don't be a dick."
    I made my way to the most senior, and certainly most revered artist in the house.
    "I'm Leslie. Can I offer you a drink?"

It was unclear whether she'd heard me correctly. She stared at me and I waited, unable to think of anything else to say. I sipped at one of the drinks in my hands and moments passed before she seemed to come out of her reverie.

"You. You are Leslie Red?"

"Yes."

She took the glass now and after swirling and pausing at length with the glass under her nose, tasted the wine. She raised her highly arched and penciled eyebrows. I was in awe, rather. I'd been in love with this woman's work since the age of nine.

"Your husband is upstairs snorting cocaine with a woman of ill repute. I know this, because later this evening, you told my mother."

I couldn't help laughing. "What? And how do I know your mother?"

"You don't. But you will."

"OK; Bertrand and I are not married, anyway."

"A pity. You might have made money on the divorce. One must always plan in advance for the inevitable." She raised her glass. "Especially in the twenty-first century."

I flushed from my feet to my scalp.

"He isn't snorting coke."

"Isn't he? If you go upstairs now, you won't have reason to disbelieve anything else I say tonight."

"All right." I put my empty glass on a bookshelf. "Which room?"

"En suite, master bedroom. I'll wait here."

Shaking my head, I left her. When I opened the door to the en suite, it was exactly as she had suggested, and I hated Bertrand for persuading me to tile in black quartz.

I grabbed a hand towel and thwacked the rest of the line away in one very thorough swipe. The woman looked up and around at me and giggled; Bertrand toppled sideways. The vintage glass bauble of baby palm fronds smashed.

I said nothing and slammed the door behind me.

Even more annoying than her being correct was the absence of an expression saying, "I told you so," when I found her again.

"How did you know?" I asked her.

"You described it to my mother; later she will describe it to me."

"I haven't met your mother. Your tenses are confused."

"Could we retire somewhere a little quieter?"

"What exactly was it you wanted?"

"I've been rather patient, but I'm getting a little tired."

"And I have to look after my guests." Being famous didn't mean she could hijack my event on a whim.

"I understand the pressure you're under. But these people can look after themselves, for ten minutes, surely."

"My study is on the top floor. I can only spare ten minutes, though. I can't allow this evening to descend into total chaos."

"Finally," she said, under her breath.

I was doing pretty well, I thought, and holding it together, until Bertrand appeared, and then his new special friend, hot on his tail, barely assembled into her clothes. The logjam on the stairs was complete and a few choice phrases were exchanged.(1)

I noticed that Bertrand's feet were bleeding on the waxed oak.

"And you," I said to Bertrand. "You're such an embarrassing cliche, even James Foley would give you the blue pencil."

---

1. This culminated in a slanging match between myself and the young woman. It was undignified and pointless.

The cultural icon took me by the elbow and steered me on up. Her grip was a grip but it was sort of tender.

"What a beautiful room. So marvelously quiet."

"Thank you."

"And so, of course you know who I am," she said, spotting a framed portrait of herself hanging on my wall. She took a deep breath through her nose and exhaled slowly back, mouth closed, lips pursed in a strange smile. "Are you a little less angry now?"

"No."

"Well I suppose not. The adrenaline and cortisone will be testing you, I should think. Not very pleasant but you mustn't be upset. Men like Bertrand aren't worth your precious time, darling."

"Yes, well. I think anyone would agree it was a no-brainer ending it."

"And you mustn't blame the call-girl. She was merely a player and you may as well forget her."

"Huh."

She handed me her drink and I downed it.

"Take a few deep breaths; you'll give yourself an aneurism," she said.

"You are very quaint. Why _did_ you come tonight?"

"May I." She sat down on my day-bed, and shrugged herself out of that fur coat. From an inside pocket she withdrew a small book.

"Take it," she shook it at me. "Open it, and tell me what you think."

"<u>Physical Pleasure For The Modern Woman</u> - 1932. A bit ahead of its time, wasn't it?"

"You might say. Read it."

"Where the - where did you get this?" The similarity between the letterpress text, title notwithstanding, and my own unfinished manuscript was too much to get my head around.

Exact phrases. Exact chapter subjects. I pulled open the top drawer of my desk to check that my papers were still there, and of course they were.

"I took it from my mother's bookcase in 1952. Inside the front pages was this rather compromising photograph, and I demanded (rather rudely, I suppose now) to know who it was." There was a slight pause. "She told me that it was you."

She passed the black-and-white photograph to me. I flipped it over, purely to excuse myself from having to stare at the NSFW image. There on the back, in handwriting very like my own: <u>Forever and ever. I love you. XX</u>. I felt nauseous.

"That's obviously not me. Basic biology 101. I don't have one of those," I handed it back. "Typical," I said. "On top of everything else, another two years of hard work down the fucking drain." I slammed the desk drawer shut in disgust. "I cannot understand how I missed that book in my research. I suppose I should thank you. You've saved me from a hellish embarrassment."

"No call for histrionics. It's all your own work. And that is you."

Now I was the one taking a deep breath through my nose, my lips shut tight, my eyes screwed against the vision of this legend sitting on my day-bed. I felt in my dress pocket for my phone but I must have left it downstairs.

"I need another drink. I need some weed. I need to go for a long run... in any case I should go back downstairs," I said.

"If you have the drink, you will try to kill the call-girl and end up in a police cell. If you have the reefer, you will do something silly, I can't remember which; in any case, that man will smash your typewriter. If you go for the run, you will trip in the dark and

break your neck. I would advise against any
action other than to sit here, and take three
drops of this." She held out a small bottle.
It was clear that she was suffering from
dementia. I tried to remember where I'd left
my phone.
"And what is that?"
"Perfectly legal," she said. "CBD oil, 5%.
It will calm your nerves. I use it myself,
and it's very good."
"Thank you, very kind, but I don't do weird
drugs," I told her.
She shrugged, and I watched her drip amber
liquid under her tongue. After a minute she
spoke again.
"I understand completely your reluctance to
believe me. One can only comprehend such
things through one's own experience, of course.
But we only have tonight to get this thing
under way."
"What thing? Sorry, but I have to go back to
my guests. You'll have to excuse me." I went
to open the door when a note in marker pen
slid under it. I turned the lock.
"Baby," Bertrand shouted and rattled the
door. "I'm sorry. Let me in, let's talk it
over." I stood immobile and silent reading the
note at my feet, and then he shouted again.
"You're ruining the evening, you know that?"
After a couple of minutes I snatched up the
note and crumpled it in my fist and chucked it
into the wastepaper basket.
"Are you ready?" she asked.
"No. Yes. I don't know." I really did need
to go back downstairs but the thought of
Bertrand waiting out there left me swithering.
"Put a new piece of paper into your
typewriter. Then type, Everything Is, Unless
it is Not."
"I suppose that will make me feel better,
will it?"
"Humor me. There's no harm in it."

I did as she said. I put a new piece of paper into my typewriter and typed the words. Idiot that I am.

I am lying cold and sore on the rug. I open my eyes, wondering at what point I got naked and whether I've slept with anyone, hoping that of all people it wasn't Bertrand. What a disaster. I should never have left him in charge last night.
And with that thought, the study door opens, a draft raises goosepimples over my skin, and a woman shrieks, and then says,
"Oh dear God. Who the hell are you? What on earth are you doing in my study?"
I'm standing up, looking for a blanket off my day-bed and, with a dread that actually makes me feel quite ill, I look down, and see.
Well, Biology 101, it seems I do have one of those, after all.
"Oh GOD!" she shrieks again, and slams the door behind her.
"Hey, what do you mean your study? This is my house!" Fuck. I clutch at my throat and grab an unfamiliar shawl thing off the day-bed, which is looking remarkably clean and free of bad stuffing or errant springs. OK, I'm tripping.
She comes back into the room with one hand over her eyes, the other hand gripping the door handle so hard I can see the shape of her bones.
"Look here," she says while I scrabble to cover myself. "You've obviously made some kind of mistake. Easy enough to do, I suppose. I expect we are neighbors, in which case I would appreciate it if you would just jolly well get dressed, and go home. And we shan't speak of it again," she adds.
I can see that she's blushing under her hand. As for me, I clear my throat.

"Sorry. I can't get dressed. I don't know what's happened, either in general, or to my clothes, which, if I had them, probably wouldn't fit."

"Give me strength." She backs out and shuts the door, this time with less noise. I fix the shawl around my middle, and look around my study. Despite my feeling pretty lucid, it is quite trippy in here. There's my typewriter, looking spanking and I mean spanking new on the oak desk I've recently stripped and waxed, which is now looking horrible, covered in a dark, shiny varnish. The surface of my desk has been rearranged and the books on my shelves messed with, and the pictures on the walls are—

"Have you made yourself decent?" she calls through the door.

"Yes." I don't like this voice. This is not cool.

"You may borrow these for now." She still refuses to look at me, and hides her face behind her hand, peering at the floor as she tiptoes across the rug. She drops clothes near my feet, and tiptoes back to the door where she stands a little more self-assured on the threshold. She waits while I get dressed.

"So," I try to sound chatty, but I know I'm just going to keep on sounding odd. "Assuming I did make a mistake, which house is this?" She recites my own address. "See, that is actually my address," I tell her.

"But it can't be, can it? Because I live here."

"Hang on, is that you, Bertrand?"

"I beg your pardon?"

"Oh well, it was within the bounds of possibility; given that I've woken up as an impromptu Orlando (2) you might just as easily

---

2. Virginia Woolf's character in her novel of the same name, not Orlando Bloom, the English actor.

be Bertrand, with boobs. As long as the prostitute has gone home," I say.

"What? Kindly leave now. Post the clothes back anonymously. In fact, don't bother. I hope never to see you again."

"No."

"I beg your pardon?"

I shake my head, indicating that I won't leave.

"Shall I telephone to the police?" she says.

Inwardly I am thrilled to hear anyone actually use that phrase.

"I don't care what you do, whoever you are. This is my house, my study. My - my fucking typewriter," I say, jabbing my finger at the machine on the desk.

"Oh _really_. This is quite outrageous, quite absurd, and you have a mouth like an absolute sewer. Why can't you just _leave_?"

"I'm going to sit this _trip_ out, if you don't mind. Then we can see who you really are, and I can have my tits back and lose this very inconvenient trio between my legs."

She gasps and clamps her hand over her mouth. I sit down (with caution) at the desk and open the drawers to look for some paper to type on.

"Don't you dare rifle through my papers," she rushes over and slams the drawer shut so hard I'm lucky not to lose a finger.

"I would like to while away the time by writing, and I need paper. That drawer is where I keep the paper."

"It most certainly is not. What do you mean by, well, what are you talking about?"

I swivel in the seat to look at her. She looks very cross, her vintage dress is very pretty, her hair is very shiny, and she's done it in waves, like an old movie star.

She looks like a force to be reckoned with. But then, so am I.

"I am hallucinating - not by my own choice. I need to wait until I am back to normal again. It would be unsafe for me to leave the house. I might get run over by a bus or fall down an open man-hole. I'd rather sit here, and type. On my typewriter. Please may I have a bit of paper?"

"Top drawer. It isn't yours, it's mine," she sounds a tiny bit less furious.

"Yes, it is."

"You haven't introduced yourself," she says.

"Neither have you. Leslie Red," I stick out my unfamiliar hand in belated courtesy, and clear my throat some more. "My apologies. We didn't get off to a very good start, did we."

She lets out a sigh through her nose. In the back of my mind is the idea of a child, somewhere in the house.

She shook my hand at last. "Lucinda Peake."

I imagined that I would know who she was when our skin touched. That the illusion would lift. But it didn't. She feels deliciously new to me, and if my mind doesn't know it yet, my body does: our tenses feel inextricably muddled and we both release our grip at exactly the same time as if we are shocked by the same thought.

"Would you like some tea?" she says.

"All right. That would be very nice, thanks." I take a piece of paper and backing sheet, and feed them into the machine. The packet says Large Post Quarto. I have no idea what that is. Lucinda goes over to the wall and pulls on a brass handle I recall polishing the week I moved in. I shake my head and wonder what I'm going to write.

"Are you a Bohemian?" she says.

"Haha. No, I don't think so. Not by today's standards."

"Forgive me, it's just that your hair. It's uncut."

I put my hands into my hair and feel it.

"I expect it's some kind of anomaly," I tell her, and rake my fingers through it, feeling more disheveled than I am used to. Then I roll my sleeves to my elbows and start to type.

Lucinda stands behind me with her hands on the back of the chair. I don't care that she's reading over my shoulder, I just need to focus on staying as straight as possible.

When I feed the second sheet into the machine she comes to sit on the edge of the desk, picks up the first page and reads it again.

"What is a 'sushi bar'?"

Before I can answer, the door swings open with a bang and a teenager dressed as a maid comes in with a tray of tea, puts it down on the other end of the desk, bobs a curtsey, and leaves the room without a word.

"That girl, honestly. Milk and sugar, Mr. Red?"

We go on, me typing, Lucinda reading, and she makes no further comment until we come to this place.

"How do you suppose you might get back, when your theory proves incorrect?" she whispers, sounding gleeful and horrified.

"How do you mean?"

"You're from the future," she whispers.

"No, I'm not," I whisper back. "You're from the past," and we look at each other.

"Would you stop typing every blasted word for a moment. Please?"

I oblige - and then continue to type.

"Everything Is, Unless it is Not. But how would you know?"

She jumps down off the desk.

"Presumably you would check. You would make a list, and cross each item off it, methodically."

"Right. What year is this?"

"1931."

I say nothing for a long time. I know she wants me to reciprocate, but I can't.

"The fact is, I shouldn't be here. I can't risk staying longer," I stand up. "Thank you for your hospitality. And for the loan of these clothes. Goodbye, Lucinda Peake."

"Tell me one thing, any little thing."

"I can't. It would play havoc."

"Don't you think you would be wasting an opportunity, if you said nothing at all?"

"I have to go."

"Stay. A little longer."

"Thank you for being so...accommodating. If we'd met any other way..."

"Well all right then," she says, and smiles. "At least I know one rather important fact."

We shake hands again. Then I put a new sheet of paper into the typewriter, and type, Everything Is, Unless it is Not. I stare at the words on the paper. It's been wonderful to type on such a new platen. I think I'll treat the typewriter to a new one when I get back.

"Damn."

"That didn't work then," she says. There is distinct, satisfied amusement in her voice, and she sits down on the day-bed and crosses her legs and hugs her knees with both hands.

"Perhaps you'll have to stay, whether you like it or not."

I pull the paper out and put a fresh sheet in.

"Take me back," I say, as I type.

I'm not sure if I hear Lucinda shout something, or if that might be me.

I woke on the floor of my study and it was definitely my study. I was inconveniently naked again, my dress lying underneath me. When I peeled it away, there were tiny circular impressions left by the sequins. I also found my IUD, which made perfect sense, and which if I'd thought about it, would have freaked me out.

I was just glad I didn't have to get it removed medically. I had my own body back, and I clutched each tit with gratitude.

There was another note from Bertrand on the floor near the door. Though the wording was slightly different, nothing had changed in essence.

The door was locked from the inside, and there was no annoying old woman, cultural icon of the 20th century, sitting on my day-bed, now reassuringly tatty and lumpy. I threw the IUD into the wastepaper basket along with Bertrand's second note and pulled the dress over my head, feeling vaguely hysterical. Why hadn't I asked her which important fact? Or perhaps I had. I checked my desk for the papers I'd typed and they weren't there. In the typewriter there was a piece of paper bearing the legend <u>Everything Is, Unless it is Not</u>.

I searched every drawer and file for any newly typed papers at all, but there was nothing.

I glanced up at the wall where the old woman's yellowing portrait had hung. The frame, now larger, contained a different photo, now of Coco Chanel. Weirded out by the change, I took it down to face the skirting board. I needed a drink, I needed breakfast, I needed to go to the toilet. I needed to find my phone.

The broken glass and palm fronds in the en suite had been swept into a heap in the corner and I left them there. The rest of the house was looking relatively unscathed, considering everything. Scooping up a few empties, I found my phone tucked into a corner on the bookshelf. Over breakfast I looked up Lucinda Peake, and was unsurprised - relieved - to find her. I wrote down the details, scant as they were, for later, though there was nothing about Lucinda having had children. Nothing out there at all.

I turned my phone off and for a while I sat and stared out the window.

The atmosphere of the Reading Room at the British Library was peacefully urgent. With the noise of fluttering laptop keys and the ruffling of paper all around me, I sat with my hands either side of Leslie Red by Lucinda Peake, on the table in front of me. But there's only so long you can sit with an impossible book without opening it.

I guessed what she would have done and I was right. She had taken the pages I'd typed last night, and constructed a surrealist novel around those couple of thousand words. She had embellished the en suite scene, and she had exaggerated certain aspects of my borrowed anatomy. And I think she pretty much fancied my tits off, figuratively speaking. She had done quite well, I supposed, to imagine the future on what little I'd provided. I was left thinking that she could have done more with it, that her legacy could have been so much more than this, and that really, I ought to go back and give her a few more pointers. Not to mention a few more print runs.(3)

Physical Pleasure for the Modern Woman no longer existed and that was great news. But an entire person - her child - and their entire artistic and cultural contribution to history had been wiped out. But if she no longer existed, and never had, why could I still recall her so vividly? And the question of why Lucinda's daughter did not exist began to bug me. Should she in fact, also have been my child? The thought was actually insane, and I found myself going away from the library toward a pub.

I should have got a room and binged on an epic Netflix series while replying to the

---

3. There were just three known copies remaining and this was the only one available to the public, as long as you could get to London, had a permanent UK address, could prove it, and be bothered to register for a reader's pass.

various messages I was getting from all and sundry about the open studio night and Bertrand. By 7pm I'd had a skinful, and was crawling through my contacts for someone, anyone, who hadn't been at the house last night. If I hadn't been so plastered I would have remembered why I hadn't invited Neil Scarlett. But anyhow, when needs must.

"Wake up," I prodded Neil. "Here."
    He sat up, drank the coffee, and listened to me with his eyes half-shut. I don't know why I was so determined that he should believe me. There were better people.
    "Didn't we agree last night that you were probably tripping?"
    "Yes. Time-tripping."
    "Look. Bertrand is definitely a dick, and I always said so. But you are starting to do my head in. You never shut up about this Lucy woman all night. You know how off-putting that is?" He reached for his phone and fiddled with it. "I have to go," he said.
    "Film it. Film me, in my study. Now. Let's do it."
    Neil threw off the covers and got out of bed. He pulled on his clothes the way he does when he's been caught cheating.
    "Get a grip and just do yourself a favor," he said, and was out of the room before I could reply.
    I followed him onto the landing and up the stairs to the top floor. He was taking them three at a time, and when I reached the study door, he was already sitting at my desk, already putting a new sheet of paper into my typewriter. I was out of breath and aching but that was nothing to do with the stairs.
    "What was it you typed?" he said. "Everything is, unless it is not? Stupid. Doesn't mean anything."
    "There should be two sheets. Could you just—"

"Shut. The. Fuck. Up."

He jabbed the keys inexpertly, his shoulders hunched, his body crowding the machine. The carriage crept along one painful stroke at a time, and I waited, wondering what I could say to convince him.

And it was just the merest blink of an eye. That's all. Like a silver shadow passing through the place where he'd been. I looked at the chair and his shirt slid off onto the rug; his trousers hung on, suspended by one leg. Some small objects clattered into the type basket. My heart thudded so fucking hard everything in the room throbbed.

If he was gone, did that mean no one would miss him, or would I be accused of murder?

I waited all day.

At 3 a.m. I heard the sound of the Underwood in my dreams. I bolted up to my study, but he wasn't there. Eventually his phone died and the barrage of messages from the girlfriend he'd kept quiet about stopped. In the morning I checked my contacts for the nth time and yes, he still existed. Or, would do. I am quite possibly fucked as hell, I thought.

Lucinda Peake's novel, Leslie Red, was so much improved that it had never been out of print. In Foyles, on Charing Cross Road, I opened the back flap of a nice hardback copy and scanned the biography.

"Internationally renowned author of the seminal feminist work, Everything is, Unless it is Not,... Began her writing career in 1942 as a war correspondent ... spent most of her life after WW2 with her life partner, fashion photographer Scarlett Neil (d.1987). Celebrated, loved, admired..."

I didn't want to read any more. The bastard took my place. The bastard took my Lucinda. I kneeled on the floor of the bookshop next to

the shelves of her life's work and the tears
fell onto the rough carpet.
    A shop assistant offered a tissue, and
asked if they could help. It felt like great
service at just the right moment, but I knew
they'd been trained to clear emotional clutter
promptly.
    "Thank you." I blew my nose thoroughly
and stood up. "As a matter of fact, yes."
    I bought a copy of <u>Everything Is</u>, to get me
started, and a copy of everything else to be
delivered. It crippled my finances but fuck it,
I had a lot of reading to do before I could
get to work.

Underwood 5, 1909

TIME KEYS
(You <u>Can</u> Go Home Again)

Marni Scofidio

Second-hand,
restored as new,
each daedal
machine
is ready to
use.

What can
we type?
How long's
a ribbon?

Recipes,
seed lists,
lust letters,
diaries,
garden labels,
housekeeping,
poetry,
pros & cons,
jewelry,
H.G. Wells-type
portaling,
air mail
journeying---

Cairo, Rome,
Montmartre,
Queens;
Shetland,
Cymru,
Kirribilli.

Stripped &
cleaned &
tightened,
we travel
back in time:

Fleet Hermes
makes it
'57, when my
birthday came
first time.

for Julie & Philip Chapman

Silver-Reed Silverette II

Treasureland

Ewan Matheson

After graduating from the university with a degree in computer science, I landed a much coveted programming job for a big video game studio in Glasgow. It was an intoxicating atmosphere, making worlds come alive with code. But the hours were horrendous, with our team often putting in seven-day work weeks for several weeks leading to launch. It left little time for myself, family and friends. Even when I had the time, I was too burned out to notice the world. Sensing my demise, my sister insisted I go on a date with one of her office mates.

It was going swimmingly, we'd hooked up at one of those after-work get-togethers. For the first time in forever my old self shined through. The university lad who could tip the pints, belt out a song and laugh at the absurdity. When my date grabbed my hand and whispered in my ear, I took that as a good sign we were headed for a more intimate setting.

We snagged a taxi to her flat on the east end, her body pressed against mine. I looked out the window at the mist that often seeps in at night off the River Clyde, the wetness dewing up against the glass. She had her phone out checking her feeds and I was too inebriated and happy to care for anything but the bliss of what might lie ahead. Suddenly, she shrieked something about how could I have posted such a rude thing? She told the driver to stop and ordered me to get out. After my pleas fell on deaf ears, I found myself on the curb watching the taxi speed off.

I couldn't blame her, for in all the hustle of the night, an office mate had gotten hold of my phone and posted a juvenile picture, along with something about shagging into the night. I wanted to text her what had actually happened, but the chances of her believing that feeble excuse seemed close to nil.

For a moment I felt sorry for myself, one moment looking forward to her warm embrace, the next shrugging my fleece collar around my neck. I decided a walk would clear my head. For a long stretch it was mostly darkened store fronts, vacant flats and scrub lots. Ahead, however, was a beacon of light.

It was a retro resale shop stuffed to the rafters with the discarded debris of people's lives, organized in the window display to make it seem as if it mattered. But one item stood out: a green typewriter. Its bulbous curves was unlike anything I thought a typewriter should look like. The name on it read, Hermes 3000, like it had beamed down from the future. But the future was now and nobody used typewriters. However, there was something about the familiar keyboard layout that spoke to me.

A little bell tinkled as I entered and was met with long-dead cigarette smoke and whatever else expired from all the stuff. A small balding man with grey hair, a neat tweed suit and grey wool tie appeared from the back, sweeping aside a curtain as he came to the counter.

"Evening, laddie," he said with an easy grin.

"That typewriter in the window, mind if I have a look?"

"Absolutely," he said and in several nimble steps had it on the counter.

I had written millions of lines of code and saw the video games that came to life in all the dimensions of reality, what sort of life could emerge from such a machine?

The shop owner rummaged under the counter and came up with a blank piece of paper, then rolled it into the typewriter. I stabbed a few keys in quick succession, but they got stuck together. The shop owner gave a kindly smile, unjammed them and came around the counter and stood next to me.

In a patient tone, he said, "Treat her like a musical instrument. You've got to feel the rhythm. Every note in its place." He tapped out a line. "Now you give it a go. Whatever thoughts pop into your mind. Feel the music, listen to your voice."

I closed my eyes. Between the lingering beer buzz and the exhaustion of the night, I let my fingers drop on the keyboard. I took a deep breath, let it out, opened my eyes with a soft gaze, then began typing in what felt like a hypnotic state whatever came to mind. For the next few minutes I typed line after line, striking the return lever whenever the bell dinged. I wasn't aware of what I was writing, but the more I typed, the easier it flowed. It felt like a water tap slowly opening, until finally it gushed in a torrent of words and sentences.

Then the strangest sensation tingled my finger tips, along with images and words that didn't seem my own. It felt like I was possessed with a spirit, speaking to me, yet they were also my own thoughts. What had this typewriter unlocked? I closed my eyes and continued to type, and that's when the images came of some other time and place. I would've said it was like watching a movie, but somehow I sensed I was in the picture. What sort of game had this typewriter conjured? It came to a sudden end when the paper flipped out of the roller. I snapped out of my reverie, feeling happy, exhausted and needing to see more of whatever had been in my mind.

The shop owner unrolled the paper and scanned what I'd written. "It's been a long time since I've read anything that good. You a writer?"

I gave a weak chuckle. "Hardly. But I did minor in literature at the university. Mainly to please my mum, she teaches the stuff."

"Perhaps it should have been your major, lad."

"Where's the money in that? Speaking of which, how much you want for it?"

"Let's see now," he said, rubbing his chin. "How much cash you got on ya?"

Before I could complain about his opening gambit, he pointed to a sign that read: CASH ONLY.

I desperately wanted that typewriter. More importantly, a little voice told me I needed it. "Can you hold it for me? I'll find the closest teller machine."

The shop owner grimaced. "Afraid not. Plus, I close in ten minutes."

An overwhelming sadness dropped my shoulders, like I had glimpsed another world, only to have it snatched away. I had never desired an object like this; all the things in my life were temporary, discarded when they became obsolete or stopped working. They never seemed possessed of life like this typewriter and in turn it seemed to possess me.

In my long moment of despair, perhaps the shop owner looked upon me with pity. He grinned and said, "I'll tell you what. You've got talent, lad. I'll let you have it tonight, no charge. In return, whatever you write with this typewriter, I get ten-percent if you're published."

I thought the offer over. There was a slim to nil chance of ever getting published, especially with a typewriter. "Ten-percent?" I said.

"I might be foolish, but it's up to you."

I'm sure I must've looked like a grinning dafty, as I thrust out my hand and shook his. "You have a deal."

The shop owner took what I'd written. "Mind if I keep this?"

"Might be the only thing you ever get out of me," I said.

The shop owner unscrewed the cap of a fountain pen and handed it to me. "How about it?"

"You want me to autograph it?"

"It's just a little something I need."

I was more than happy to indulge him his little game if it meant taking home that typewriter.

After explaining a bit more about the typewriter—it was a Hermes 3000, made in Switzerland in 1958—he grabbed the lid and as he was snapping it on, I noticed some writing on the inside. It looked like a name. I told him to stop as I flipped it over for a closer look. Painted in neat black letters, it read:

>AIBNE ROY
>21 E MARKET ST
>GLASGOW

I mulled the name for a moment; it sounded vaguely familiar. Then I remembered. "That's weird," I said. "We read him in one of my lit classes. This was his typewriter?"

The shop owner shrugged. "Never heard of him."

"Not many have," I said. "Wrote <u>Treasureland</u>. Our professor supposedly knew him, made us read it. Just some crazy nineteen-sixties psychedelic romp through time. Sort of a modern counterpoint to Robert Louis Stevenson's _Treasure Island_. After it was published Roy disappeared. Never heard from again. In his mid-twenties at the time."

"My, that's quite a tale," the shop owner said. "Seems you got quite a bargain there."

"Hardly. Just an unknown bloke from nowhere wrote a novel nobody ever heard of, never to be heard again."

The shop owner smiled. "Perhaps you'll change that story."

His statement made me think. "Change his story?"

"Aye, what I meant to say, perhaps it'll be your turn to change the story. It's your typewriter now. It's your turn to write that famous novel and become rich. That's what I'm banking on."

I wasn't sure what I wanted out of that typewriter, it didn't seem writing a novel was in there. I just felt its draw as something that needed more exploring. I was too tired to argue.

After an Uber ride to my flat, I cleared off a space on my desk for the typewriter, made a pot of tea, extracted paper from the laser printer and sat at my new machine. It seemed ludicrous that it was anything more than what it was: a device that imprinted letters on paper using ink. For a few minutes I stared at it, thinking it was a shop owner's parlor trick, to hypnotize the customer into believing they were buying into magic. What if it wasn't a trick? What if it was real? What would I unleash if I began typing and it really was some sort of typewriter time machine?

I typed slowly at first, then like a dream I was floating over an urban landscape, the familiar outlines of Glasgow came into view, the cathedral, the bridges, except the newer glass and steel buildings were gone.

The more I typed, the typewriter sounds faded, until finally like a feather falling to Earth, I settled on the ground, standing on the sidewalk in front of a row of two-story flats on a busy morning street. I looked around in a panic. People approached from both directions; their eyes seemed to pass through me like I wasn't there. Hadn't they just seen me float down from the sky? The cars, clothes and buildings suggested I was somewhere in the 1950s or 1960s.

Had the typewriter somehow hypnotized me into believing I had traveled to the past? What had I been writing before I was transported to this time? It involved something about my father. The Glasgow of this time was a much grimier version, the glare of the sun through a sooty sky, the smells and the traffic sounds were louder and more present. In this neighborhood people were out and about, mothers pushed prams, children played on the sidewalk and a cluster of shops lined one side of the street. It was bursting with the buzz of life.

I must've stood for several minutes taking it all in when a woman shouting interrupted my observations. I turned to her robust voice and standing on a front stoop of a row house was what looked like my grandmother, a younger version, erect of posture, a head of brown hair, full figured in a floral print dress with an apron around her waist. She called again; this time I heard her yell, "Charlie!" A young boy ran past me in knicker shorts and an argyle vest. I'd never paid attention to old photographs of my father, but this boy of around eight must've been him. He ran up the stairs two at a time, shot past my grandmother and into the house. She smiled, wiped her hands on her apron and went inside.

When I was about that age, I remembered driving down this street, while my father had pointed out the house he'd grown up in. His father passed away when I was two, while grandmother had moved in with her younger sister in Dumfries. I didn't know it at the time, but as I stood on the street now in this scene of 1960, I remembered my father sobbing for a bit. It all came back, as I asked him if everything was okay. He gave me a tousle of the hair and assured me it was.

I didn't know exactly how this typewriter time machine worked as I went up the stairs to my grandparents' house, but I figured the polite thing to do was knock. When I went to rap my knuckles, my hand passed through the door. Of course, it made sense, I was there like Ebenezer Scrooge, but without the ghost of Christmas past by my side. Like Scrooge, I felt I was here for a reason, I needed to witness something. I took a deep breath and walked through the door.

I found them in a room off the back. A workbench stood along one wall and on it were several half-exposed radio chassis with tubes and wires hanging out. Facing the window was a table with what surely was a shortwave radio, where my father and grandfather sat. My grandfather flipped a switch on the radio and it hummed to life. A speaker crackled with static. The way my father looked up to my grandfather, the two of them together, huddled close, ready to make contact with another far-off voice, seemed full of togetherness, the two of them launching into a radio journey.

My grandfather turned a large dial in the center of the radio; mixed with the static were voices, music and other odd tones. The spectrum was filled with transmissions, not like the time my father had shown me when I was his age now--the radio held little life except for a couple BBC broadcasts. My grandfather slowed his tuning and with fine back-and-forth movements settled on a clear frequency where a man's voice in a foreign accent said, "This is radio Nederland, the Dutch world broadcasting system. . ." For the next several minutes my grandfather and father listened to this faraway voice with rapt attention. Much of it was headline news, followed by reports from former Dutch colonies.

If I were to get these reports in the internet age, they'd hold little interest, but the intimacy and urgency of these voices compelled me to listen, the same way it did for my father and grandfather. They spent the next couple hours listening to broadcasts. My grandmother floated in a couple times to refill cups of tea, hovering for a moment to listen.

As I watched them, I realized this was much like the internet, except with these voices going out over the airwaves, live--never to be captured, stored and ready for consumption at any time. To connect with these broadcasts was to feel connected to the world in a way the World Wide Web lacked.

For the next several nights, I repeated these trips to my father's childhood and his radio days. When they weren't listening, my grandfather taught my father how to solder electronic parts, replace tubes and clean old radios. My father delivered these repaired and renovated radios to people in the neighborhood. I wouldn't call them customers, as no money ever seemed to pass hands. Perhaps they performed it as some sort of community service. My father took great pride in dropping off these radios and helping people set them up. He always gave them a final wipe down before he left. They were just ordinary radios, but in that day even at the dawn of television, they were still part of everyone's lives.

While these trips to my father's past were illuminating, I began to wonder if I could tap into someone else's past. Beyond just thinking about my father, I didn't have much control over where or when I went. By this time, my curiosity grew concerning the typewriter's original owner: Aibne Roy. Did it have the same capability then as it did now? Were his travels in Treasureland informed by these trips through time? Beyond what was in his novel, little was known about Aibne Roy. I was determined to find out more.

I rolled a fresh sheet of paper into the typewriter. For a long moment I sat and wondered about Roy, where he lived, what he looked like and the discussion in class about his novel. As I typed the flashes of the past began, but this time I saw a different landscape of Glasgow.

The people, cars and vibe of the place suggested the same early 1960s of my father's radio days. I went to the nearest intersection and found the street name. I was on Roy's street. I hustled down the block looking for house numbers, until I settled on his address. It was a five-story apartment flat. I went up the steps and found the occupant list on the buzzer panel. There it was: Roy. He lived in 2B. When I neared his door, I heard the muted sounds of a typewriter. My typewriter! Even in my ghost-like state I felt my heart race and my perspiration rise. I listened for a few moments, feeling if I stepped through the door, he might know I was there. Or would I find him in the same trance like myself, transported to some faraway place in space and time?

He lived in a spartan affair, not much more than a studio, with a combined kitchen and living area and off to the side an open bedroom and a single bed.

Roy sat at the kitchen table, his back to me, hunched over a typewriter. I went around to face Roy. He typed at a brisk pace, like someone was dictating to him. He looked about my age, mid-to-late twenties. On one side of the typewriter sat a stack of blank paper, while the other was filled with pages filled with type. When he was done with a page, he snapped to attention, snatched a fresh sheet of paper and began typing again. Suddenly, he stopped midway through the page like an alarm went off and looked off to the wall clock. It read three o'clock. He put the half-finished page on the typed stack, snapped the lid on the typewriter and stood.

He was a shortish man in brown chino pants and a tan button-down shirt. He wore the expression of a slight grin, as if he'd just gotten away with something. He put on a kettle to boil, then sat with his cup of tea at the sofa staring out the window doing absolutely nothing. He sat this way for a few minutes, each sip measured at regular intervals. What was going through his mind? I grew impatient at the nothingness, for what I was discovering about the man seemed rather uneventful. Then, as if another internal alarm went off, he stood suddenly, downed the last of the tea and rinsed his cup. The clock now read precisely three-fifteen. For the next few minutes he made a simple meal of potatoes, carrots and sausage. By four o'clock he had finished and had the plate washed and dried. He went about all this with ease and a smile. After a change of clothes and a trip to the wash closet, he stuffed his manuscript and several pencils in a leather shoulder bag and was out the door at four-fifteen.

I followed him on the street, where he kept a brisk pace, like he had an appointment to keep. We must've walked for thirty minutes, until finally he slowed in front of a movie theater with art deco columns and its name blazoned in neon: The Palace. In removable block letters, the marquee read <u>Village of the Damned</u>. Roy strode past the ticket counter and went inside. He nodded to a young woman at the concession counter, then went down a back hall, dropped off his coat in a staff canteen, punched his time card, then continued to the end of the hall where he opened a side door.

The room was dark and when my eyes adjusted I saw the projection equipment and a square porthole in the wall, the light shining through. There was an old, grey man sitting at a chair next to the projector. He nodded to Roy, then got up and left. Roy peered through the projection port; it looked like the credits were rolling. When the movie ended, he slid the dimmer switch, then went about checking the projector, unloading the film, finding another film can from the shelf, and loaded the projector. So that was Roy's job. He was a projectionist.

After setting up the projector, he joined the young woman at the concession counter and they chatted while they made popcorn. He cleaned the counter and stocked new candy. Soon a couple moviegoers appeared and he sold them popcorn and drinks. More customers came in and Roy and the young woman were busy bagging popcorn and working the cash registers. After the rush died down, Roy went to the projection room. He dimmed the lights and started the projector. After a couple trailers, the movie started. Roy watched through the projection port for a few minutes, then settled into a chair with a small desk in the corner.

It was semi-dark in the room and the loud, rhythmic chugging of the projector reminded me of the soothing sounds of a train. He turned on a small table lamp with a dim bulb and got his manuscript from his shoulder bag and started making notes and corrections. He'd brought a thermos of tea, poured some into its cup top and for the next hour and half settled into his manuscript. His only interruption was switching projectors about half-way with the second reel.

Between the magic of his typewriter and the uninterrupted time for revisions, Roy seemed to have the perfect writer's schedule. He was gainfully employed in a job that allowed him time to hone his craft. Between the showtime schedule and doing double-duty at the concession counter, he got away from his writing for much-needed forced breaks.

He repeated this schedule for three showings that night, with the last one ending at eleven p.m. Afterwards, he cleaned the bathrooms, vacuumed the lobby and locked up after his co-workers. He went to the projection room, started the film and went into the auditorium. It was a grand room, with a barrel-vaulted ceiling, columns along the side walls, deco plasterwork on the ceiling and red velvet curtains that swept aside to reveal the screen. He settled into the centermost seat and I sat next to him. Together we watched <u>Village of the Damned</u>, a terrifying story of mutant children gone astray in a small English village. I can't say I enjoyed the movie, but sitting next to him, alone in that empty theater, I felt a kinship. Whatever pressing matters of the day dissolved into the night of these imaginary worlds.

I visited Roy a few times and each day was much the same when viewed from the outside, but during this time his manuscript grew and evolved. He wasn't a total recluse. Besides the movie house job, on his off days he walked the streets, went to the library, talked with the librarian and other people who came and went. But every day, he got up at the same time, made a pot of tea and wrote.

Between my visits with Roy and my father, I travelled to see others in Glasgow of that time. And like a spectral spectator, these stories and lives informed my own novel. The allure of my tech-fueled life began to lose its hold. But still nagging me was what happened to Roy. With limited control over where or when I went, I couldn't fast forward to the end. If you've read Roy's novel, you'll know he had a far wider range than I. How much of it was real or imagined, I could never tell. Whatever it was, it was an arduous journey. Between the notes and drafts, he must've re-typed his manuscript three times. He was an assiduous editor, refining and bringing into focus his story with each draft.

The more I followed Roy, the more I changed my habits and schedule to match his. Every jump back in time moved me further along in his story and mine. It was going along too well and soon I feared the end. I knew the end. He got his novel published, then poof, nobody knew what happened to him. While he was a somewhat obscure writer, there grew a cult-like following in the years after his disappearance. They religiously sifted through his life, looking for clues to his whereabouts. Over time it turned into a game, a <u>Where's Waldo</u> of sorts, but without a trail to follow, much of it turned to speculation. Public records of the time were spotty; besides birth and death certificates, it was easy to fall off the grid, unlike today, where every movement is recorded, tracked and logged.

As my jumps came closer to the end of his novel, I was anxious to finally solve this riddle, but also feared its end might've meant his demise. The River Clyde's bottom held many lost souls. Then without warning, the typewriter no longer transported me back in time. I grew despondent, having had this power, then lost it. After several failed attempts, I finally gave up and focussed on finishing my novel. This, after all, was perhaps the purpose of the typewriter. I quit my soul-sucking job, writing code for virtual worlds of limited imagination. Instead, like my grandfather and father, I tuned into the frequencies of the real world. Like Roy, I relieved myself of all that was unnecessary and committed my life to writing.

With the publication of my novel, I dedicated it to my father and grandfather and with special thanks to Aibne Roy. Unlike Roy, I did not disappear, and it appears to be doing quite well, with translations into several languages and the movie rights sold.

I returned to that resale shop with check in hand to honor our agreement. I also brought the typewriter, the Hermes 3000. The same bell tinkled as I entered. I was eager and anxious to greet the man. To show him the check, to show him what I had accomplished, to return to where this story began. But I also knew that by honoring our agreement, I was going to change his life, like it had changed mine. It had been almost two years and if he didn't recognize me, then surely the typewriter. I lugged it on the counter and moments later he appeared, wearing that easy grin and his fine tweed coat and tie.

He seemed to recognize me as he said, "You're back." Then he frowned at the typewriter sitting on the counter. "Did it stop working?"

I chuckled. "Yes and no. It did its job. I'm here to return it, along with a little something for you. Ten percent, as I recall."

I pulled the check from my coat pocket and put it on the counter.

"My, that's quite a sum," he said with a huge grin.

"May I have your pen?"

He found the same pen with which I signed that first typed page and handed it to me. I signed the check; then, in the space that read "pay to the order of," I wrote: Aibne Roy.

I had many questions for Roy, as I'm sure do you, but that's his story to tell, not mine. In the meantime, if you find yourself in a resale shop and come across a typewriter, it might not hold the same magic as did Aibne Roy's, but in it holds a magic for your own journey.

Royal HH

White Out

Charles W. Ogg

I was poking around the attic when I found it.

I had just retired, my wife had died several years before, and it was time to move out of the big, empty house into a little apartment.

I lifted the case up, felt how solid it was, lugged it down the narrow stairs and set it down next to my oak desk. Removing it from the case and placing it on the desktop, I admired its curves. Big, blue, shiny, and metallic. I pulled a piece of paper from the printer feed, stuck it in and rolled the platen. The typewriter keys still shone, barely used. I touched them tentatively, then pushed harder.

Tap, tap, tap.

I watched in fascination as the crisp, dark letters appeared on the paper, affixed permanently. At first I was amazed the ancient ribbon worked at all. Then the act of typing pulled me back in time, back to the days when the archaic machine played a big role in my life. It was the early seventies. I was in college, an undergraduate yet to make the important decisions shaping my life. I hadn't committed to graduate school. I hadn't made my big splash. My insights into "errorless learning" had yet to rocket my career as a psychologist.

I had been so thankful in the eighties, computers "saving the day." No longer did I have to find a student friend, a female of course, who would type up my very rough drafts. I was sooo slow. Some people hunted and pecked, I searched and destroyed. My favorite "assistant" was Sheila, who actually edited as she typed. But Marie would do, passing along every little mistake in the original, subject only to White Out. I chuckled, wondering if White Out was still a thing. I Googled and discovered the correctional fluid was actually trademarked as "Wite-Out." It would always have an "h" in my mind.

I typed random sentences, feeling a strange rush as they appeared. I couldn't remember the last time I'd felt this way. My therapist kept pushing antidepressants, but I resisted. I was hoping retirement would change things. I was tired of passive students taking notes, pretending not to be bored, pretending to listen, rarely questioning or challenging what I said. I was tired of the "better" students watching my every move, waiting for pearls of wisdom to drop from my lips, when in fact I had come to question the very foundations of what I professed.

What was this thrill I felt? I couldn't stop typing, even though the keys jammed with my growing excitement. Words poured out like they hadn't for years, a joy! I was used to agonizing over every single word in academic papers, though I knew they would have little impact, like feathers dropped in a well.

I closed my eyes as I typed, pounding the keys instinctively. I recalled being back in college, working for the school newspaper. My friend Ed, the news editor, had talked me into being a reporter, though I kept telling him I wanted to study psychology. His enthusiasm was infectious. One day stood out, back in 1973, if I remembered right. We sat in that cramped, stuffy little office filled with piles of paper, a tiny black-and-white TV tuned into the Watergate hearings. Ed cheered on "Senator Sam." He yelled at the screen, "Nail that asshole! Nixon's so damned corrupt." He danced around the office when the president resigned, delirious. "Who'd have thunk it, my friend?" he said gleefully.

"Woodward and Bernstein of the Post made it happen. Reporters!"

At Ed's urging, I started covering student protests. While the administration branded participants as troublemakers, I got to know some of the leaders for who they were. Amy, for example, didn't just march around the quad, corralling fifty-some students as they chanted slogans and waved handmade signs. She also risked being interviewed by a reporter, hoping to get heard. By me.

We sat facing each other in the student union coffee shop, tape recorder perched on the table between us. Amy met my eyes and spoke in calm, measured tones. "Working students cannot afford the proposed tuition hike..." I glanced down, glad the record light was still on, finding her freckles, penetrating eyes, and fiery red hair distracting. It was my job to report fairly her ideals, goals and strategies, as well as getting the chancellor's perspective, he being part of what she called "the establishment."

Running into Amy soon after the story came out, I was invited to join her and her merry band of radicals to shoot pool. Afterward, we crowded into the booth at the "Dirty O" for burgers and the most delicious fries in town. I can still see her chewing thoughtfully, swallowing, then asking me pointedly, "Wouldn't you rather change the world?" I sipped my beer, pondered the question and thought I just might--if it meant seeing her again. But her sparkling eyes were drawn to another.

It all seemed so freaking clear to me.

Then it happened.

I sat at a different, ugly black typewriter. I glanced up nervously at the round analog clock in front of me, high on the wall. The big hand pointed to the nine. Fifteen minutes to midnight. Standing behind me, looking over my shoulder, was my old buddy Ed, a man I hadn't seen in many years.

A voice in my head urged me on. "Midnight is the deadline; the copy must be submitted by then. Triple spaced, three copies with two carbons." I remembered how, under such pressure, it all flowed together. I had done my best writing when every keystroke had to be just right.

"What the fuck?!" I yelled and jumped up from the typewriter.

Ed looked at me, concerned, and I stared back. He was just like I remembered: tall, thin, ponytail snaking down past his shoulders. Short, well-trimmed beard. So much intelligence it seemed to bleed from his eyes. I ran from the room, dashed into the nearby bathroom, and was relieved to see I was alone. I stared into the mirror. Holy fuck! I was young again. Reddish, curly beard and long, dirty brown hair. Jeans and plaid shirt. How was this possible?

I thought hard. I had two sets of memories! On the one hand, I was still a sixty-five-year-old man with medium-length, white, "old man hair" sticking out every which way. Someone who increasingly felt cheated by life. On the other hand, I was a twenty-two-year-old boy who thought he was a man; a junior in college excited about grad school, who also enjoyed making a few bucks reporting for the school paper. With only ten minutes left to get a story hammered out! The student protest. Amy's interview. I rushed back and, with a shot of adrenaline, pounded that sucker out. Even the third copy was legible.

Over the next year, I continued to report on issues important to students at my university. The tuition rose and the protests intensified, yet I spent more time working on papers for psychology classes, intent on advancing my career. This time, I'd do even better: publish as a junior.

Ed graduated at the end of the year and then started an "alternative" publication, the <u>Steel City Free Press</u>. Aiming to serve the university and its old Rust Belt city, he somehow scraped together the needed funds. Midway through my senior year, sales of the Free Press took off.

I continued reporting for the school paper. I loved the thrill of tapping into the zeitgeist, capturing political and social ferment. Save the earth. Women's lib. Black is beautiful. Yet the old man lingered on in my head, warning me, "It'll soon fade, filed under 'the sixties' and forgotten."

"But," I would argue back, "I get to report on actual people. Get to know who they are. It feels so much more rewarding than what you did--experiment on rats, pigeons, and undergraduates."

Then one day the typewriter arrived, big and blue, carried in by Ed. Landing on the little desk in my dorm room, it looked magnificent. My fingers drawn to its keys, I barely heard Ed's impassioned plea. "You must join my team, I want you to be our news editor. Together, we'll cover the city as it should be done. Righteously."

I grinned back at Ed, trying not to listen to another voice, the creaky one in my head. "Reporting as an occupation is doomed," the old man insisted. "Most newspapers will die." What made him easier to ignore was the weight of his weary memories; it seemed the life of an academic wasn't so rosy, either.

So, I made the big decision, graduate school could wait! I wanted to put Ed's marvelous typewriter to work printing the truth. I wanted to believe him when he said, "It will make us free." I wanted to share Ed's zeal. "We are on a mission." I told the old man, "You go back to whatever nightmare you came from. I'm going to be a reporter, for real."

Several years after joining Ed's paper, I struck gold through tedious, hard work, uncovering a major scandal. Corporate malfeasace of the worst kind, a factory releasing dangerous chemicals into a nearby river, followed by a cover-up. I even won the Peachtree Journalism Award, forcing me to invest in a tie for the ceremony. I was riding high.

By the end of the seventies, the social movements that once propelled us had indeed faded. Ed's paper survived by morphing from a scrappy rag to a more respectable, edgy newspaper, The Real Deal Journal. In 1985, it too died. I landed a job with the local daily, owned by a big chain, and was forced to cover political campaigns like horse races. It was rarely about the issues.

The old man's memories dimmed, his reality becoming increasingly dreamlike.

I married sweet but driven Rose, a co-worker and crack reporter. We had two kids, fraternal twins Jean and Derrick, and purchased a good-sized house in the burbs overlooking the city. As they grew into teenagers, I thought Rose and I did well, settling into a solid groove. I was happy to cook and watch the kids while she chased sources. After the kids went off to colleges at oposite ends of the country, I learned the truth. Rose sat me down and said she'd had enough, frustrated with my lack of ambition. She was moving to D.C., having snagged a job at the Washington Post! She'd made it to the show.

Rose stalked the corridors of power, bought an expensive townhouse, and at least in my imagination, fought off wealthy suitors. I continued my well-worn beat at city hall, had painful blind dates thanks to well-meaning co-workers, and puttered around the empty house.

I no longer heard the voice of the old man, convinced I'd imagined him.

My paper crashed and died, another casualty of the internet, and I was out of a job. I blogged, practically living on Twitter and Reddit. I stayed on the cutting edge by harvesting stories as they broke. Instead of a twenty-four-hour news cycle, the global news churn demanded a steady stream of barely-digested fragments. I worked my ass off writing them up, only to see Google pay peanuts for advertising and let others post my stories without compensation. I tried to comfort myself by saying that at least now I could speak truth to power. But, in a time when social media and even the president spewed disinformation, such stories no longer seemed to stick--even when Rose wrote them for the venerable <u>Post</u>. I grew sick of staring at screens, big and little. I even longed for the "good old days" of being paid to suck up to local pols, meeting face-to-face over martini lunches.

 Finally, having worked too many damned hours, my back gave out. I went on early Social Security and scraped by with meager savings. Deciding it was time to sell the house and get something smaller, I found it a formidable undertaking. The family had accumulated a ridiculous amount of stuff.

 One afternoon, poking through the attic trying to figure out what I could save, throw away or sell, I found it. The ancient typewriter given to me by Ed. How much was it worth? Lifting up the case, I appreciated its solidity. I lugged it down the narrow stairs into my office and set it onto the desktop. Opening it up, I admired the blue machine's metal curves. After sliding a piece of paper into the platen, I started typing.

 Tap, tap, tap.

 I began to feel a strange thrill as words tumbled onto the page, the letters curiously dark and crisp, though it had been many years since the ribbon was last used. Weird, I thought, stopping to stare. Frozen in place, fixed in indelible ink, the words seemed magical.

 I recalled hunching over a different typewriter, the one I'd used to write the rough draft for the paper that got me so excited about psychology, about "errorless learning." I remembered the joy I'd felt, giving the rough draft to Sheila, back in the days when I planned to go to grad school and become a college professor. I delighted in asking fundamental questions about humanity. "Who are we?" "What makes us tick?" I imagined that, by applying the principles of science, I could solve the fundamental riddles about who we are as a species.

And then, suddenly I was in my college dorm room, sitting at that very typewriter.

Tap, tap, tap. I was painfully slow.

I jumped up, ran to my little dorm bathroom and studied myself in the mirror.

Young again!

Corona Sterling circa 1935

The Spider

Richard Polt

You need an old thing and a paired quark.

The particle's safely confined, they tell me, inside my belt buckle, entangled by quantum magic with its twin, currently whipping around the double star Beta Trianguli Australis at 99.99% the speed of light.

The thing lies on my lap as I sit cross-legged in the musty office of a decrepit parking garage in Manhattan, tapping out the words, line after line, bracing for it to be so:

Today is July 26, 2001.
Today is July 26, 2001.

September 12 would have been our second wedding anniversary, though we'd been together since junior year of college. I thought I couldn't adore you any more than I already did, but as that second year of marriage filled out, I sensed your singularity more and more intensely. You'd be reading the Sunday paper, slumping on the couch, your chestnut hair disheveled, and I'd feel the miracle in every cell of my body: This woman is a unique event, never to be repeated. Her presence in my life is a unique event, never to be repeated.

You push your hair out of your dark eyes and catch me looking. A teasing smile steals across your face. "What?"

"You."

Ashley Patel was sitting, her back stiff, at the kitchen table in my Queens condo. She'd barely started to explain Stitch when I said I'd stop 9/11.

"Will, I appreciate that—of course we know about Melissa, and I'm terribly sorry—but we can't afford to send you back just 40 years."

"Can't afford to? Why the fuck not?"

"Look, as far as we can tell, we can't stitch people into a time before they existed. Otherwise we'd be assassinating Hitler and Stalin, or boosting the electric car industry in 1900. Nobody's old enough to get back there. So people like you are really valuable—"

"Like me? Broken-down relics, you mean?"

She pursed her lips tighter. "No, Will. Smart, fit operatives with decades of experience. We know you've been itching to get back in the game since you retired from Homeland. Stitch is your chance. But we can't waste you on 2001—we need you to go back farther. You're going to stop Three Mile Island."

"What the hell is that?"

"Nuclear power accident, 1979. You were almost five years old. If it hadn't happened, we calculate there'd have been enough growth in the nuclear industry to slow climate change to the point where the Antarctic ice shelves could have been saved. A stitch in time, and so on. All due respect, this is much more significant, in the big picture, than 9/11. And we've got other agents lined up to take care of that."

"Screw that. It's 9/11 or nothing. You will not find anyone more motivated for this mission." I jabbed at my wedding band, side by side with the Delta Tau Delta ring that had resided on my middle finger since Dad's aneurysm in 2012.

Two stubborn hours later, I had the mission I wanted.

Patel sighed. "You'll need an object made back then, ideally one that's been near you most of the time."

"I can find one. How did you figure all this out?"

"Controlled experiments. Mice. Getting them in the quark field, stitching them back by one day. Trial and error. We printed collars for them the day before the stitch, and they helped."

"Hey—so what happens to _you_?"

"What do you mean?"

"Let's say I stop 9/11. And I will. The rest of world history gets changed, Homeland maybe never gets created. Maybe Stitch never happens. Where does our world go, our 2041?"

Patel looked only slightly embarrassed. "We generally subscribe to the Lewis theory of possible worlds, with the Rayo modifications."

"Meaning?"

"When you stitch into the past, you create a new branch, and when you're ripped out—in your experience, that should be about 14 hours later—you arrive in the future of that branch. That is, the belt is ripped out into that future, along with whoever's wearing it and whatever else is in its field. You've generated a parallel future, hopefully a better one."

"So—did you ever again see those mice that you sent back into the past with their cute little collars?"

"The ones that actually disappeared ... no."

"In this world, then, 9/11 and climate change and covid38 are still going to be facts?"

"That is the theory."

"So what's the point?"

"The point is to create a much better reality for someone. For billions of someones. For an entire timeline, with all its organisms, for all the future. And if ..."

"What?"

"If the Park theory is right, and there's only one timeline, then if you change the past—" She frowned. "I'll never have existed. Not in this form. And if that happens, I'll never know it. There couldn't be any more painless way to vanish. Look, if even a few Stitch agents succeed, the world is going to be incalculably better. It's a sacrifice worth making."

Today is July 26, 2001.
Today—and the belt takes over.
the room's contours reveal their contours / they've slid past each other without changing position / cochlear mirages echoed in light / things will absorb the invisible radiances that they would have emitted / lungs were flooded with what might become alien exhaling / guts will have shifted to accommodate guts / and I'd been retching painfully while the incomparable presence of a bygone present beats down on me like the sun

I've arrived.

Sounds of men and machinery outside the metal door, though Homeland was sure this garage was empty in 2001.

I pull out a tissue and wipe the spattered vomit off my deep-blue period suit as best I can. My stomach is still cramping. But my mission is crystal clear. Today, Mohammed Atta checks into the Kings Inn Hotel in Wayne, New Jersey. I have about 14 hours to make sure he will never check out. A handful of well-honed messages in Arabic, combined with images of Atta's body, will derail the whole plot and sow fear and confusion in the organization.

I stand up straight and open the door. In my pockets are a camera and a revolver—both vintage, just to be safe. In my wallet, plastic credit cards linked to documented accounts, and a wad of antique currency. In a nylon case over my left shoulder, the thing I've been typing on, the thing that's followed me, migrating from closet to closet, for 40 years: your bulbous, teal, 2001 Apple iBook.

For 40 years, you've watched every move I make with your dark, unaging eyes, waiting for me to avenge you. I am never alone, and I've never fulfilled your silent demand. Just behind me, just above me, you watch with your teasing smile, reconstituted from the blood and ashes of a sunny September day, forever.

As soon as I could, I joined the spiders who wove the systems. We felt every twitch and spasm, overheard every utterance, ran for a kill when the threads sang. We caged the gnats and moths, grilled them, tormented them. We shot the prime fly between the eyes, dumped his corpse in the deep, did our justice. And still you waited for redemption, transcendence, salvation.

New evils, new flies in the trap. Vast surges of data, keen new algorithms to filter it. New enemies, foreign and domestic, left and right. New skyscrapers rising from the pit. But none of it redeemed. Nobody saved.

You are my widow. I'm the dead spider, incapable of life, while you can never disappear. The world in its brutality and fanaticism is the thinnest, tautest membrane behind which you watch me stumble on, a zombie predator killing the newest spawn of the imperishable race of murderers, snuffing out one insect only to have another two creep in.

For you, Melissa, I'll risk the world. I'll risk destroying the future, strangling it in its crib, reversing its countless lives and denying them even the possibility of death. Never to have been, let that be their fate, if only you can be rescued from the ultimate hopelessness: the prison of the eternally irredeemable.

In the garage, two long-haired young guys are leaning into the engine of an immense, angular car with its hood up. One of them gives me a glance and snorts with amusement. An electric wail keens from a radio. I act like I've got business here, because I do. I stride out through a side door into an alley that vents onto Second Avenue.

It's cloudy, and cooler than I expected. Then the scent strikes me. Ingredients I can barely name: rancid hot dogs, patchouli, smog. A sweaty, grimy undertone that feels all wrong.

The garish suits with wide lapels and ties. The sideburns. The hoops through women's earlobes. Groaning buses. This is not how I remember the turn of the century.

A kiosk is on the corner, overflowing with magazines, candy, cigarettes, newspapers on paper. The New York Times bears the date: Tuesday, October 2, 1973.

"Ya gonna buy that?"

I fish out a dollar bill and get back 85 cents in coins.

Mets Win East Title, Start Playoff Saturday ... Egypt Hires U.S. Concern to Construct Oil Pipeline ... Mrs. Meir to Go to Vienna For Talks on Soviet Jews. So there is still a Soviet Union. No doubt about it: I've overshot my mark.

How is this possible? Patel said you can't go back before you were born. And I was born on June 22, 1974. Shows you how much they know.

Suddenly I think to look south, far south and slightly west. And there they are: the Towers, restored, looming through the beige air. Fresh, new, and fragile—and now there is nothing I can do to save them. Mohammed Atta is four years old and living in Egypt. Bin Laden is a teenager in Saudi Arabia. Melissa won't be born until next year—just two months before me.

I thump down onto a graffiti-encrusted bench at a bus stop. I can't think straight. Patel was wrong about everything. Bits of our talk replay in my mind.

"Look, as far as we can tell, we can't stitch people into a time before they existed. Otherwise we'd be assassinating Hitler and Stalin. ... You'll need an object made back then."

A homeless man is shouting apocalypse at passersby. I cough and stare at the huge yellow taxis on the avenue. My trigger finger keeps clenching pointlessly.

On my left middle finger is the Delta Tau Delta ring. Which Dad got in college. From which he graduated in 1971.

Then that's the thing that got me back this far—not the iBook.

But why October 2, 1973? That's almost ... nine months before I was born.

"A time before they existed," she said. And now I get it. Mom and Dad must have had fun last night.

So Patel's theories hold, at least in part. But I may get ripped out soon. How much power does one fraternity ring have to keep me back in the past, anyway? And how the hell do I keep something from happening 28 years from now?

To get on the subway, I just need a quarter and a dime. I take in the exhalations from the tunnels, the echoing shrieks of the rails, the vandalized seats, the shut-down faces of the other passengers. Could I stand to take off the belt and let it disappear without me? Living in this world for 28 more years, intervening, holding on until the crisis arrives? Not likely—I'd have to make it to age 95. I'd hardly be a "smart, fit operative" then. More likely a corpse. And I'd never find out if I'd saved you.

The train moans and squeals southward until I reach the Wall Street station. People down here are well-dressed. I was beginning to think that wasn't possible in the early '70s. I make my way towards the World Trade Center, and finally reach the Towers.

I'd forgotten just how awe-inspiring they are. They gleam, clean and sleek, in the sunlight. Both tourists and locals crane their necks. I take a minute to sit by a fountain. I lean back onto the chilled granite. My eyes follow the soaring columns into the atmosphere, and I feel that I'm falling into the sky.

But time is short. I take an elevator to the observation deck, where I take in the dizzying view of a decrepit, dirty New York that's missing the most spectacular landmarks from my own day.

When I get back down, I ask a moustached guard, "Could I speak to the head of security?"

"What seems to be the problem, sir?"

"It's really something I need to speak to security about."

"I _am_ security, sir." He eyes my oddly-cut suit and hair, and the flat bag over my shoulder. "What is the problem?"

"It's ... I was just wondering if there could be an issue, with buildings this high ... if you worry about planes possibly flying into the buildings?"

The guard rolls his eyes. "There's someone every week. No, sir, you can relax, there's something called Air. Traffic. Control. Airplanes can't just fly anywhere, they've got designated airspaces, and none of 'em come close to the Towers. Don't worry about it, sir."

"But--what if someone hijacks an airplane and ignores air traffic control, and flies it into the Towers on purpose?"

The guard sighs. "Hijackers take planes to Havana. They don't fly them into buildings. They're not suicides."

"Could you just convey my concerns to security--I mean to higher levels?"

"Absolutely, sir. Will do. You have a good day now." He produces what's supposed to look like a reassuring smile.

I pace around the Towers until the same guard spots me and gives me a sharp look. Then I walk north, my mind racing but failing to grasp anything substantial. My technical expertise is all digital; it depends on a network that's barely imaginable in this world. My operational expertise is still valid—but who's my target? There's got to be a soft spot, a pressure point that can be activated to have effects 28 years from now. But how to find it?

I'm both agitated and depressed as I pass by Midtown Office Machines. An illuminated plastic sign reads: Authorized Remington Rand dealer. The window display features a variety of clumsy-looking devices with rows of keys, miscellaneous levers, and electrical cords.

A bell rings as I push the door open. I'm the only customer in the shop. The owner, a tired-looking Mediterranean with an orange necktie, looks up from a magazine.

"Good afternoon, sir, welcome. Come right in. How can I help you today?"

"Hey. I need to type a letter. Could I rent a typewriter from you?"

"You don't own a typewriter? You definitely need one, sir. Everybody oughta have a typewriter. Look, right here I've got a fantastic new Remington 711 electric. It's got all the office typewriter functions in a new, compact package. This baby's got contoured keys, touch selector, fully automatic tabulator. Normally $249.50, but today only, it's $225."

"Very nice. Thanks. I'm not looking to buy, though. I just need—"

"OK, a little too much, I understand. Here we've got two beautiful Remington Ten Forties. Blue or white. Portable, light, modern, plastic body. Just $86.50, sir. Tote one of those around with you instead of—whatever that is over your shoulder."

"Look, I just want to rent. But I need a really high-quality typewriter. This letter has got to look good. Professional. Neat."

"I know, I know. Yeah, OK, I got a Selectric for you. Everyone wants the damn things. Putting us out of business. I been a Remington man since 1952 and never seen such a bad market. Anyway, yeah. I got a two-year-old IBM in the back that you can rent for ... how long you want it?"

"Two hours should do it ... let's say three hours to be safe."

"I close in two hours. All right ... how about ten bucks an hour. That makes twenty bucks." He looks like he's ready to bargain, but I nod my head. His eyebrows go up a notch, but he heads straight to the rear of the shop, returning with a massive, boxy, brown thing that he places carefully down on the counter and plugs into a wall outlet. "Ya gotta use it here, no taking it away."

"Of course. No problem." I take out my wallet and hand him a twenty. "I'll need a few pieces of paper."

"Yeah, yeah." He brings over some sheets. "Go to it."

I vaguely remember typewriters. I set the iBook in its case down on the counter and inspect the contraption. First I try to feed a sheet into the front of the roller thing, then I realize it has to go in the back. I find the power switch.

The shop owner is looking down at the cash register, glancing at me, pacing. He walks back to a corner where a big phone is attached to the wall, and dials a number—the thing has an actual, round dial—then mutters into the handset, hand cupped over his mouth.

I can't be distracted by him. This letter matters more than everything, and it has to look competent and sane. For a while I'm confused by the "Return" key. I try typing "Melissa" over and over until I can do it without an error.

Then I load a fresh sheet. I peck out the characters very slowly, understanding that they can't be deleted, thinking about every word in advance.

October 3, 1973

To: Federal Bureau of Investigation
Washington, DC

I need to warn you about an upcoming terrorist attack that will kill thousands of Americans unless you stop it. I implore you to keep this letter in a safe place and note whether my predictions come true.

Next year, Nixon will resign. Vice President Ford will take his place. In 1976, Jimmy Carter will be elected president. In 1980 and 1984, Ronald Reagan. In 1988, George H. W. Bush. The Berlin Wall will fall in 1989. In 1992 and 1996, Bill Clinton will be elected. In 2000, after a Supreme Court decision, George W. Bush will defeat Al Gore.

On September 11, 2001

"So what's this all about?" An overweight, freckled policeman has just come into the shop. He surveys the place, sizes me up, waits for an answer from the owner.

The owner keeps his eyes right on me. He doesn't say anything, but hands some money to the cop.

"The hell?" says the cop. "Looks lopsided. Off center. Big fat picture of Jackson. What's the idea?"

"Look at the date!" hisses the owner.

"Series two thousand and one? Ya gotta be kiddin' me."

"This guy walks in here and tries to cheat me! With this play money! Tries to cheat *me*!" He's getting high-pitched.

"Sir," says the cop to me, "is it a fact that you tried to pay with this--piece of paper?"

"Ah, no, of course, I--"

"Where did you get this?"

"I--can't be sure."

"You're comin' with me, sir. Passing counterfeit money is a crime."

I think of shooting Officer Freckles and running for it, but he's just doing his job. And as I hesitate, he moves with surprising skill to get my hands behind my back and cuffs me, then searches my pockets. Before long, he's found a gun and camera that won't be made for a few decades, and a wallet full of more funny money.

As he marches me out of Midtown Office Machines, I glance at the nylon case lying on the counter and remember you hunched over a glowing screen at midnight, working on a spreadsheet that you'd brought home from the office on the 85th floor of the North Tower.

I think curses as I sweat in the back of the cop car.

When they book me, I fall deeper into the hole. I've got a driver's license—my name is Harold A. Jones—but it's manufactured to 2001 standards. More bizarre counterfeiting, as far as they can see.

They bring me to a holding cell on the second floor of the police station. As Freckles opens the cell door, another cop cautiously removes my handcuffs and says, "All right, take off your shoes and your belt."

"Is that really necessary, officer?"

"Take off yer shoes and belt!"

"OK." I crouch down gingerly as if to untie my right shoe, then bolt for the exit. The cops react immediately, but it sounds as if they crash into each other. There's swearing and shouting, and heavy feet stamping behind me. I leap down the staircase, shove open the door, and race for an alley next to the station. My knees are on fire. My whole body is cramping. Someone's right behind me. I'm panting, my heart pounding.

and the alley reaches out into itself / light will turn back into its own weight / concrete had become the weakness of its duration / my veins would be bloated with the finitude of the abyss

Retching, gasping, I lurch back into the autumn of 2041.

I've survived. And I've failed.

Pigeons startle and strut. The alley is devoid of anyone who could pity or despise me. I catch my breath and limp slowly out to the avenue, where crowds shift and hurry. There's a scent of kelp and steel—the Manhattan Seawall. There's a haze in my mind and in the air. As I look south, it clears just enough to reveal a faint, gray monolith.

No: two of them. Floating side by side, hovering over the svelte spires of this city, impossible twin sentinels.

There is a lightness in my head—a space that I had forgotten was possible—and then a shocking wave of solitude, as if, in the midst of these brightly-dressed pedestrians, I've entered a room where only I can fit.

Finally, I understand: she's not watching anymore. Her dark eyes aren't on me. She's not my widow anymore ... and I'm no widower.

I've saved you.

Or have I?

I stumble toward downtown, my eyes trained on the Towers. I bump into people who mutter at me. The men wear slick black caps and black-framed spectacles; the women, big cat's-eye glasses. Cars look squat and colorful. They all seem to be self-drivers.

There's a huge, glass-walled retail store on a corner. A pair of interlocked R's hovers over the name "Rem-Rand." People inside hunch over glowing, tilted bowls.

"Welcome to The Rem-Rand Store!" This girl in feline glasses could be my grandkid. She squints at me as her lenses sparkle. "My bad, looks like I'm having some trouble pulling up your Randtag at the moment, but if you can just flip your sig, we'll get you racked up."

"Randtag? Nope, don't have one."

"Oh? Well, uh, let's—"

"That's OK. I'll just wander around and let you know if I need any help."

"Yes, sir." She looks baffled.

Wall screens call the glowing bowl a RemDish 22. People are manipulating their Dishes with hand gestures, or typing on keyboards with thick green keys in front of the bowls. When I approach a bowl, the RR logo pops up in midair. I extend my finger, and the R's blossom into a bouquet of unfamiliar icons. I point at a book labeled <u>Encyclopedia Americana</u>, then type "Rem-Rand" on the keyboard.

Remington Arms Company of Ilion, New York ... Sholes and Glidden Type Writer of 1874 ... merged with Rand Kardex Corporation in 1927 ... leading manufacturer of typewriters, computers, and other business machines ... acquired by Sperry Corporation in 1955 ... A surprise breakthrough by Sperry Rand engineers in 1974 leapfrogged over rival companies, creating a radically compact and powerful microchip. In 1976, the company introduced a mass-market portable computer, the Rem-Rand Microvac. The "Vac," with its revolutionary touch pad, flat screen, and graphic file management system, was adopted by both businesses and individuals. Throughout the 1980s, Rem-Rand (as the company was now known) continued to produce ever more powerful and affordable devices, which were increasingly linked through the Randnet network. The implementation of Randnet in post-Soviet Russia in 1992 and post-Communist China in 1996 solidified Rem-Rand's global dominance. Rem-Rand systems became pervasive in law enforcement and security; protests against the company's ties to authoritarian governments gained little traction, especially since Rem-Rand technology proved essential in identifying and dismantling several terrorist networks in the late 1990s. After Rem-Rand acquired IBM in 2003, its devices matured into indispensable tools for education, creativity, and journalism. ... By the 2030s, RemSpecs and the RemDish had become ubiquitous personal equipment ....

I'm sweating and my ears are ringing as I locate something like a search engine and type your name into it.
Hundreds of photos and facts float in front of the Dish. There's no mistaking you in the few early portraits. You still went to Sarah Lawrence, still graduated in 1996. And there you are maturing, turning 40, 50, 60 ... looking more tired and heavy, but still yourself.
An address in Cos Cob, Connecticut. A warning: "Any use of public information to interfere with private activities is prohibited and will be recorded permanently in your Randtag." I memorize the address and walk out under the suspicious cat eyes of the greeter.

The train is full of commuters playing with little bowls that they cup in their palms. Another snatch of conversation with Ashley Patel comes back to me.
"So there's the two theories," I said over my kitchen table. "Creating a branching possible world, and rewriting the one and only actual world."
"Right. But we're pretty sure that branching is how it works."
"Couldn't you have made sure by testing this with your mice? You have an empty box on Monday. On Tuesday, you put a mouse in the box and send it back one

day. If you never see that mouse again, it created a branch--maybe. But if it went back and changed your own world, you'd now remember that a mouse appeared in that box a day ago."

Patel nodded. "And not just that: say the mouse was already in the box on Monday, and on Tuesday you stitched it back to Monday. Then on Monday it would have overlapped with itself. There would have been two of the same, identical mouse. One would just be a day older than the other."

"So then what if you decided, after seeing the two mice on Monday, not to send any mouse back on Tuesday?"

"Now you're seeing some of the paradoxes that the single-world theory involves."

"So you never ended up with two mice?"

"We did not. That's one reason we favor the Lewis-Rayo theory, though it's impossible to be 100% sure, because of the metaparadoxes of self-knowledge identified by Chao in a 2039 article. By the way, within the new branch, you'd again get two of the same mouse. Let's say you stitch the mouse back from Tuesday to Monday and create a new branch. On Monday, at the creation of that branch, the mouse shows up in the lab where it itself, or rather its duplicate in this branch, is living. A few minutes later, the mouse is ripped out to Tuesday on that branch, where its duplicate still lives. So you've got two mice--unless, of course, you decide to stitch one of them back again."

"My head's starting to swim. Good thing Homeland has people like you to figure this out. So--what's my weapon?"

"Next stop, Cos Cob," says a degendered voice. The train pulls in smoothly. My pulse speeds up.

An interactive map at the station shows me that Melissa's address is just a short walk away. It's a modest place by local standards--just a well-kept, white clapboard house on a corner, with a neat, fenced lawn and a gate. I walk around the corner, hoping I don't look too conspicuous in my 2001 suit with flecks of puke and spots of the grime of 1973. The evening is darkening, so maybe I can fade into the shadows.

Someone in the backyard. I pull back behind a tree and peer. This gray-headed, dumpy woman doesn't look familiar. She's pruning a bush, wearing yellow gardening gloves. She pushes a lock of hair out of her face with her wrist.

And now, I see you. I see you through my watering eyes. You live. You are present. A unique event, never to be repeated.

For several minutes, as the daylight fades, I watch. Then I pull myself together. There is nothing to do now but the obvious: walk up to the fence, look you in the eye, and reintroduce myself.

I am about to, but around the corner, a green single-passenger cab pulls to the curb, and a man gets out. I stay behind the tree and watch him walk toward the gate. He's maybe in his sixties, tall enough, clean cut, neatly dressed, in the usual black cap and glasses. A civilian's loose, unguarded stride. Before he's through the gate, Melissa has come around from the yard. They hug. They kiss. They laugh. He turns in my direction and, just before I hide, I know who he is.

The front door opens and shuts. Through a window, I can see them chatting, and she gives him a teasing smile. Then they move on into another room.

I stand there, by the tree, outside the clapboard house, until a half moon appears and crickets are chirping. The couple doesn't appear again in the glowing windows. I stand in solitude, unwatched, a spider watching, and I wish you many more years of happiness, and I wish them to myself.

Royal FP, Patrician Elite type
Olympia SG1, Congress type
Rheinmetall portable, italic type
IBM Selectric I, Letter Gothic type
Remington 17, elite type

Muscle Memory

Rachel Schnellinger-Bailey

My aunt learnt to type in a time when offices had glass ceilings and girls needed something to do between the end of school and the start of marriage. She enrolled in a typing class, with rows upon rows of colored keys and instructions for high wrists and straight backs. She passed, top of her class, and won the machine she'd learnt on as a prize; a Scheidegger-branded beast in grey. She took it home on the Tube and displayed it proudly on the kitchen table. I learnt all this from my mother; my aunt can't even read anymore.

The illness came for her like it was late for another appointment. Swift and unemotional, dementia rushed through the person we knew with a fury, leaving her like a child, bedwetting and afraid of the dark. She doesn't know us anymore, with the illness wrapping her in a blanket, suppressing the fire within.

There is not much of her former life - a house painted magnolia to rent out and a few boxes in my attic. But every now and then I take a keepsake to the place that feels like purgatory and see if it coaxes a smile or a cloud of confusion. Anything. I would take anything. But it seems most things in her life are permanently on the tip of her tongue, just out of reach.

One day I brought in a soft toy, a simple teddy, well-worn with love. My aunt was sat in the high-back chair in the corner, absently looking out of the window. A week or so later when I returned, she was cradling the teddy in her arms, swaying for comfort. She called it her baby, remembered my cousin's name for a fleeting second, beaming with love for her newborn who is thirty-nine and on the wrong side of the world.

Her room doesn't help the situation. It smells of mass-catered food and twice-weekly bed baths. All the pictures on the shelf are of people she doesn't know. I'm the "nice chap" who visits but never comes back, despite the fact I'm in there at least once a week.

I have tried to make it more comfortable, but the usual fixes don't apply here. And so I try to jog her out of her loneliness and fear with the odd familiar object, a cup of tea, a friendly smile.

I had never intended to take the typewriter in there, but an impending move meant sorting through her things and mine, before placing anything excess in the car for a trip to the charity shop. On a whim I took it in, placed it on the adjustable table and then wheeled the setup over her bed.

And nothing at first. Nothing. No change there. Then, clear as day she said "what am I s'posed to do with that?" and then a pause as long as hope, until she continued, "it's got no paper."

We solved the problem with some blank sheets from the nurses' station printer. Over the next hour I watched her vertebrae uncurl, her wrists rise, fingers fumbling keys.

I watched her, stealing glances of another time. Wage packets paid in cash in half-sized envelopes, the look on her father's face when she said she'd got a job in the City, the clatter of keys and the clouds of cigarette smoke, the year she bought all her Christmas presents at Harrods and had them delivered to her home, the companionship of the other office girls, the comradery of the company, polyester blouses and mass-produced tights.

Her fingers started slowly, but the tempo increased, muscle memory and unfamiliar dexterity, striking softly and efficiently.

And then, after a while her hands stopped and she looked at her wrist, paper-thin skin and liver spots.

"Oh, is that the time already?" she said to no one in particular, "best be off or I'll be late for my tea."

"Yes," I said "time really is flying."

Triumph Gabriele 20

Retrograde Crossing

Erich J. Noack

Amy completed the transaction and turned away from the split-flap timetable with her head down, pulling up the lapels of her coat as she made her way toward the platform. It was mid-morning, and the train station was awash in people -- a mass of families heading to the countryside for holiday and students returning home from university, all mixed with an already overwhelming number of everyday commuters. She pushed her way through them, trying hard not to show her haste.

The train to Lancaster was southbound, departing from Platform 8, forcing Amy to use the narrow connecting tunnel beneath the tracks. The din of human voices in the humid, confined space was sharp in her ears. A child screamed and Amy winced at the echoing screech that grew as the sound bounded off the concrete walls.

At the opposite end of the tunnel, flights of stairs on either side led upward to the platforms. They were wet with spring rain, the surface glistening with moisture at the foot of each flight. She found the entrance to Platform 8 without much trouble and took the stairs two at a time. An earthy smell hit her at the top, the wind driving a constant mist that dove under the awnings and wove itself between the waiting passengers.

The crowd was sparser on the platform. Trench-coated travelers huddled together in groups around their luggage while sharply dressed businessmen angled their umbrellas against the weather. Amy made her way forward to an empty bench -- still cautious to take a wide berth around the clumps of people -- and sat down. Further down the platform, a policeman and his partner paced back and forth benignly. Their high-visibility, neon yellow jackets stood in bright contrast to the gray sky, the clear plastic protectors on their checkered hats were dotted with droplets. Amy watched as they moved from group to group, closing the gap between themselves and her bench. She turned away, pulling a lock of auburn hair from behind her ear to hide her face.

As the policemen neared, her heartbeat quickened. To be recognized this close to freedom would mean all she had gone through would be a waste. And escaping Carlisle was just the first step in a larger plan to leave Britain entirely. "See it. Say it. Sorted." The blue-bordered posters throughout the station taunted her.

Amy crossed her legs and pretended to examine her fingernails as the two men approached. She had striking features, a classic beauty for which her mother resented her. To hope for the two men to completely ignore an attractive woman sitting alone on the platform would go against everything she knew to be true about men.

"Ma'am," the taller of the two said in greeting as they shuffled up to the bench. Amy looked up, half-smiled in acknowledgement, then looked down again.

The heavy black boots paused in front of her. "And where are you headed, if you don't mind me asking?"

Amy could feel his eyes on her. She cringed at the thought of his gaze, knowing that in his mind he was building a picture of her body beneath her coat. Inside her, a sense of hatred toward this man grew in a heady warmth. She gripped the ink pen in her pocket, instinctively poised to defend herself.

"Penrith," she answered in a quiet voice. "I've got family there. We're spending the holiday in the Lake District."

"Not a lot of luggage for a holiday to the lakes," the man pressed. "And catching the Royal Scot midway through its historic run?"

"I'm not much of a train enthusiast," Amy shot back. "It simply made sense with my schedule."

The policeman threw up his hands in conciliation. "Alright, alright. I meant no harm. It's our job to ask questions, you know." He tilted his head and lifted his cap with a finger, attempting to get a closer look at her.

"Have a safe journey."

The two policemen turned away, the tall one muttering to his partner. Amy exhaled and looked up the tracks toward a column of smoke in the distance, rising just above the trees.

Ruth heard the train before she saw it. It made a low chugging accompanied by a sort of wheezing as it approached the station. Then came a high-pitched whistle that drowned out the sound of the engine. Long and sustained, the piercing cry hung for a moment in the air before fading, finally succumbing to the noise of the engine once again.

The train appeared from behind the trees, making a final turn as it slowed to meet the platform. The black paint at the front of the engine shone with rain, the golden lettering "L.M.S." at the side coming into view as it neared. Ruth knew there was time to see the train close up during its stopover in Carlisle, but she loved the thrill of watching a train pull into a station and felt the sight would do her some good.

There was a gust of hot air as the engine came past her vantage point at the end of the platform. Steam and coal dust combined to surround her in a damp cloud. She reached up to steady her hat against the artificial wind, coat and dress flapping around her legs, hair whipping about her shoulders. The cars streamed by, rows of windows slowing gradually before coming to a whining halt. One final, massive whoosh and the procession was complete.

Ruth blinked the soot clear from her eyes, smiling for the first time since she learned of her brother's death two weeks before. Now, after a seemingly endless barrage of phone calls and letters, she was heading to London to meet with his attorney and settle his will. But here, on the eve of a journey -- despite the pain she'd felt over the last few days -- she found herself looking forward to the trip ahead. It was a chance to start again, and in her heart she knew Randall would want her to feel happy and eager.

She bent down, lifted her luggage, and, joyous with a newfound sense of purpose, started back down the platform, moving through the throng of arriving passengers. Each face was a friend and even the gray of the day couldn't dampen her spirit. The conductor, an older man in a vest with a white moustache, saw her coming. He reached out to check her ticket, then gestured further up the train to her car.

Ruth made it to the steps, grabbed the rail, then turned to take one last look at the Carlisle station. The town had been her home for most of her life, but without a reason to come back, she might never see it again.

The passengers were dispersing, on their way to connections or waiting taxicabs, and the platform was now nearly empty in the lull during the stopover. She glanced north, toward the end of the train, where two bobbies stood speaking to a woman. To the south, next to the engine, some of the crew stood in a huddle, smoking cigarettes. Ruth smiled again and entered the train.

The Royal Scot hissed beside the platform. Crew members moved back and forth, double checking valves, brake lines, and connections. Amy watched the men with a passive disinterest. A group further up the platform near the engine threw back their heads in momentary, muffled laughter before returning to their cigarettes.

Amy pulled a map from her purse and opened it on her lap, leaning over it to block the mist. A red line traversed the illustrated landscape from north to south, Carlisle to Lancaster, Lancaster to Liverpool, Liverpool to Birmingham, Birmingham to London. From Heathrow she would fly to Frankfurt, but from there her plan became less concrete. A cousin on her father's side used to live in Germany, but that was years ago. Her passport could get her over the border into Poland, but she had fewer connections there and her Polish was even weaker than her German.

A whistle blew, high and shrill. The crew threw down their cigarettes, stamped them into the pavement, and turned back to enter the train. Amy folded the map, stuffing it into the bottom of her purse before rising. She pulled out her phone to check her ticket, noted the car and compartment, then crossed the distance to the train and stepped up into the car without looking back.

The wood paneling along the corridor, the deep red carpet on the floors, the brass latches on the windows

— everything looked exquisite to Ruth. She ran her slender fingers along the wall, counting the doors to find her compartment.

The handle was cool in the soft palm of her hand. She pushed it down and slid back the door, revealing a small room with a window framed by padded seats upholstered in a deep green plaid, overhung with metal luggage racks. In the space between the top of the seats and racks hung small black-and-white pictures and an oval mirror.

Ruth stepped in and slid the door shut behind her. The noise of the station could still be heard through the single-paned window, and the room smelled clean, a mixture of fresh linens and polished leather. She set down her bags and removed her coat, hanging it on a hook below one of the luggage racks. Then she smoothed her dress and took her seat to await departure.

Everything smelled old to Amy, from the distasteful red carpet to the hideous plaid cushions on the seats in her compartment. There was a musty tang of hot vinyl that filled the confined space, reminding her of an old Georgia farmhouse and the backseat of some teenaged boy's car. She shook away the grimy feeling the memory gave her and removed her coat.

The tall windows looking out into the hall revealed passengers moving past one another on their way to their own compartments. Amy felt exposed. She crossed the room and pulled the shades down to block their view.

Another whistle blew, more distant sounding now, and the remaining people on the platform finished their goodbyes, hoisted their bags, and rushed to the doors. The train lurched and started forward. Amy sat down and reached into her purse for her journal, then settled in, preparing to ignore whoever joined her in the compartment for the four-hour trip to London.

The movement of the train jolted Ruth awake as it pulled away from the station. She rubbed her eyes and looked out the window at the still clouded sky and the platform. The station moved past in slow motion.

To her surprise, she was still the only occupant of her compartment. Out in the hall, a few stray passengers continued to mill about, but none stopped to enter. Ruth leaned forward and stretched her arms out in front of her, fighting off the groggy feeling from her quick nap. The world outside was moving faster now, stone walls and slate-roofed houses going by in a steady rhythm. Streaks of rain on the window began to curve, transitioning from vertical to horizontal as the train picked up speed.

Ruth stood and looked at herself in the oval mirror. You've got your mother's eyes, her father used to say, bright and deep blue, just like the Irish Sea. She smiled, revealing slightly gapped teeth from behind full red lips as she thought of Randall's response to this: And her father's flat arse!

She removed her hat to inspect the state of her dark red hair, repositioning a few kirby grips here and there to smooth down the places mussed by the weather. From her purse she produced a compact which she used to touch up her high cheeks and forehead and -- having completed this task and reassessed herself in the mirror -- headed to the dining car for a cup of coffee and a snack.

Just outside of Carlisle the train passed over the M6, then turned to snake its way south between the River Petteril and the dual carriageway. Amy looked up from her journal to see the saturated greens of rolling hills crisscrossed by dark lines of low stone walls, dotted every so often by a lone, spindly tree. She uncrossed her legs and returned the journal to her bag, then became aware that she was still alone in her compartment.

Standing up, Amy crossed to the door and lifted the shades. The hallway was devoid of people, the windows on the opposite side of the car presenting her with a near duplicate image of the view from her compartment window.

She turned back to the compartment, lips pursed, brow furrowed as she considered the situation. Without thinking, she removed the hair tie from her wrist and pulled the wavy strands away from her face into a low ponytail. Through some dumb luck, she'd managed to reserve the compartment to herself. An amused grin came to her lips. As impossible as it seemed, these new circumstances offered some obvious benefits and saved her the trouble of having to carry on pointless small talk with a nosy roommate. Satisfied with this turn of events, Amy gathered her purse and coat, opened the door, and stepped out into the hallway.

The train swayed lazily as she made her way through the cars. She noted the other compartments held two or more people, adding further satisfaction that hers was entirely her own. Annoyingly, every so often she would meet a fellow passenger head-on in the hallway, forcing one portly man to back up until he could find a space wide enough to let her pass.

Once in the dining car, Amy slid into a booth and ordered a double whiskey from an aloof, sandy-haired waiter. While she waited for the drink to come, she scanned the other passengers in the car. A young couple sat, to Amy's disgust, on the same side of a booth ahead of her, holding hands and speaking in low voices to one another. In the far corner, an old woman and her terrier occupied a small cocktail table. A middle-aged woman sat alone in another booth on the opposite side of the car, staring pensively out the window, her hands laced around a steaming mug of coffee.

Nearly every stool at the bar in the center of the dining car was occupied. The bartender -- a muscular 30-something with facial hair that appeared to be drawn on with black permanent marker -- moved back and forth, taking orders, making drinks, smiling at a passing comment from the more persistent diners. Amy watched him, noting with admiration his indifference, his affected interest in a story a group of old men were telling at a deafening volume. In a single motion he filled a tumbler with ice, poured a dark liquid over it, then held up his hand to motion for the sandy-haired waiter.

The bartender leaned in when the waiter took the tray. They spoke for a moment as Amy watched, then she saw the waiter nod toward her. The bartender looked in the direction the waiter indicated and made eye contact with Amy, who smiled coyly and blinked

slowly at the man's hideous beard. He turned back to
the waiter, spoke for a moment more, then went back
to his work.

The sandy-haired waiter approached her booth and
set the glass down on a waiting cocktail napkin.

"It's on the house," he said. He pointed over his
shoulder with his thumb. "From the bartender."

"Oh, how nice of him." Amy flashed her green eyes
at the waiter and picked up the drink with her long,
thin fingers. The waiter blushed, paused for a moment
as if he wanted to say more, then shook his head and
returned to his tables.

Amy took a sip, pleased with herself. She'd used
her body for far more -- and, frankly, far less --
than a free drink. She again pulled the journal from
her purse. Flipping to the next open page, she began
to sketch the scene: the booths and stools, the people,
the waiter and the bartender. Alone with her thoughts,
isolated at her table, Amy drew her surroundings in
high-contrast blacks and whites, displaying in
gruesome detail the dichotomy she saw between herself
and the rest of the world.

"Alright, Billy?"

Amy was shaken from her trance by a familiar voice,
deep and commanding. She lifted her eyes toward the
sound. The two policemen from the platform at the
Carlisle station had just entered the far end of the
dining car.

"Please come to my London office as soon as
possible to discuss your brother's considerable estate
... "

Ruth watched the landscape flash by from a window
in the dining car. The words of the letter from
Randall's attorney stuck with her: "considerable
estate." She knew her brother was a respected
criminal barrister, that he never married and kept
mostly to himself. Somehow, though, she never
considered he might be a highly successful, single,
respected criminal barrister -- certainly not one with
an estate worthy of being referred to as "considerable."

The mug of coffee in front of her steamed pleasantly,
smelling impossibly of both chocolate and potting soil.
She felt the warmth of the porcelain beneath her hands,

rotated the cup, and sighed heavily. The dining car was filled with holidaymakers, laughing and talking, exuding a kind of familial cheer for which Ruth longed. It had been far too many months since she last spoke to Randall and now she never would get another chance. She felt guilty for her initial excitement for the trip, for using his death as an opportunity to finally leave Carlisle. She blinked back tears, putting a final bite of shortbread cookie in her mouth.

A thin waiter suddenly appeared. "Can I bring you anything else, miss?"

Ruth wiped her eyes and swallowed. "Thank you, but I'm alright. I'm just about to go back to my compartment."

The waiter smiled faintly and walked away. Ruth removed some money from her clutch and placed it on the table, then rose from the booth and left the dining car.

The tall policeman was emphatically slapping a passenger on the back and introducing himself to the others surrounding a high-top table. Amy watched, wide-eyed and breathless, as his partner stuck his hands in his pockets and surveyed the room. She slid lower down into the booth and began packing her journal away.

In her mind, the presence of these two men on the train meant only one thing: they had recognized her in the station and were onto her. Plans change, she reminded herself -- this wasn't the first time and certainly wouldn't be the last. The dining car was too crowded to try anything drastic -- she needed to move, get back to the relative safety of her compartment and think through her options.

Amy shouldered her purse and tucked her coat under her arm, all the while watching the movements of the two men. The smaller one now held a full glass of beer in his hand and was looking for a way to insert himself into the boisterous conversation the taller one was carrying on with his new acquaintances. Seeing this distraction as her chance, Amy slid out of the booth and backed toward the door, turning away from the room only when she reached the threshold.

She gasped for air when the door came to behind her. Through the porthole, she was relieved to see the mood of the two men was unchanged by her exit.

Getting on the train had been a mistake -- she could see that now. Options for escape were few. The policemen likely knew her compartment number and would be watching it for the remainder of the trip. That meant jumping the train at Penrith or Oxenholme would be nearly impossible. Amy stopped dead, her brain spinning, hit by an unsettling realization: no wonder she was the only occupant of her compartment.

Further up the hallway, the fat man she had passed on her way to the dining car was coming back, again barreling down upon her. Heated with frustration and anxiety, Amy sped up as she approached him with a mind to either force him to move or walk right over him. The man looked at her, saw the blaze in her eyes, and attempted to flatten his frame against the wall, leaving a small gap between his belly and the far wall.

Amy refused to slow as she reached him. She turned sideways, put her arms up, and forced her way into the gap. "Excuse me ..." the man was saying, but the sound was far off, like a bad phone connection. She looked up to spit an insult back at the impudent, stupid man, but instead she lost her footing and hit the thickly carpeted floor with a heavy thud.

"Oh! Oh dear, you've had a fall. Are you hurt?"

Amy moaned, rolled over, and cursed the fat man. A woman was kneeling beside her, wearing an overly worried look.

"Here, take my hand," the woman said, helping Amy to her feet. "Come, my compartment is right here, you can sort yourself out in there."

Too dazed to resist, Amy allowed herself to be led to the compartment. The woman sat Amy down, then shut the door before lowering the shades. Amy was leaning over, elbows on her knees, head in her hands. She knew the fall wasn't bad, yet she was hit with a sudden headache and a vague nausea.

"I'm Ruth," said the woman. "Shall I go for a glass of water and a wet washcloth?"

Amy held up her hand. "No, no, I'm fine, really. It's very good of you to help me." She looked up at Ruth and forced herself to smile, pushing away the pain behind her eyes. "I'm Charlotte," she said, putting out her hand.

Ruth grasped Amy's waiting hand and smiled back apologetically. "Lovely to meet you, Charlotte. Are you sure there's nothing I can get for you?"

"Yes, I'm fine, really," Amy replied. "Just need a moment to get my bearings. I'm so embarrassed."

Ruth sat across from Amy and folded her hands around her knees. "Oh, no, please, it could happen to anyone. These fast trains are none too stable."

Amy feigned a smile again at this naive woman and glanced at her surroundings. This compartment was nicer than her own, smelled of paint and shellac as though it had been recently refitted. The carpet and upholstery were vibrant, the wood glossy and new. On the rack above Ruth was a single, old-fashioned brown leather suitcase. On the floor beside Ruth's feet rested a smaller, worn black case.

"Headed all the way to London?"

Amy realized she was drifting. She looked up and resumed the part of Charlotte. "No, getting off at Oxenholme to visit family. You?" As much as she didn't care, she didn't quite feel well enough to walk the rest of the way to her own compartment.

"Yes, all the way. My brother, you see, he passed away recently, and I've got to go handle his will."

"Oh, terrible business, I'm so sorry." A pantomime, that's what this was, and Amy was annoyed with pretending. Ruth's conversation bored her. She needed to concentrate, and this woman was getting in her way.

"Thank you -- that means a lot," Ruth returned. "You see, I've just received a letter and -- oh, oh no, Charlotte, you're bleeding!"

Amy reached her hand up to her hairline and felt the warm, slippery fluid on her fingertips.

"Now I must insist I fetch you a washcloth," Ruth was saying as she rose from her seat. "Please, lie down, I'll be right back." The compartment door closed behind her.

Alone, Amy's mind played catch up, remembering the policemen and her predicament. She got up, crossed the compartment and pulled down Ruth's suitcase from the rack. Inside she found various pieces of a strange wardrobe to match the woman's dated clothing, down to garters and stockings and slips. She shook her head, repacked the case, replaced it, and moved on to the smaller one on the floor.

She found it far heavier than she expected when she lifted it up onto the seat. The single latch was not locked and the lid lifted with ease, revealing papers, envelopes, and a shiny black typewriter with round white keys.

"What the hell?" Amy spoke out loud.

Movement in the hall made Amy jump. She closed the case and returned it to the floor, sitting back in her seat just as Ruth opened the compartment door.

"You're not lying down," Ruth exclaimed, plopping down next to Amy and dabbing her forehead with the warm washcloth. "There, now sit back and relax. Hold this on your cut. We'll have you all cleaned up before we reach Penrith if I have anything to say about it."

Amy snatched the cloth and Ruth resumed her upright position on the adjacent bench. She tried to avoid eye contact, tried to will herself to find a solution. For now, though, she felt safe enough to take her time thinking -- the policemen would have no way of knowing she was in this compartment.

"You were saying something about your brother ... " Amy hoped a slight prod at discussion would distract Ruth and fill the silence that was growing in the compartment.

"Oh, yes, well, as I was saying, I received a letter a few weeks back from his attorney. He sent his condolences then launched into some legal mumbo jumbo -- I won't bore you with the details -- suffice to say I, being my brother's only surviving relative -- he never married -- was named executor of his will. And here I am, a lone girl on her way to London." She smiled awkwardly.

Amy gave a reassuring, encouraging look back. She was now listening intently.

"Surely your mother or father would be named in his will? Unless ... " Amy let her voice trail off and looked at the floor.

"Sadly," Ruth replied, "they died a long time ago."

"Oh, Ruth, I'm so sorry."

"Please, don't be." Ruth's face was soft in the midday sun that was just poking through the clouds. She rubbed her hands together, shook her head, then straightened up and beamed at Amy. "One must endure these sorts of things, right? Anyway, I'm starting anew -- a grand adventure."

Amy nodded in agreement but didn't hear. She was scrutinizing Ruth's hair and eyes, the shape of her face, her figure. It wasn't exactly like looking in a mirror, but the similarities were undeniable. Amy now saw a path, a way to get off this godforsaken train. A way to disappear for good.

"Do you have a picture of your brother? I'd love to see it."

Ruth's eyes lit up. "Of Randall? Of course!"

She stood and turned to face her suitcase, putting her back to Amy. "I've got one in here somewhere from our holiday back in ... "

Seeing her chance, Amy rose and lifted the typewriter case from the floor, swinging it backhand in an upward arc into the side of Ruth's head. There was a sickening thunk. The case sprung open, releasing papers and machine out onto the carpet, the typewriter's bell sounding on impact. Ruth's body went limp and collapsed in a pile on the floor.

The bell's ringing faded away to the sounds of the train. Amy stood there, her heart beating in time with the clicking of the rails. A stream of blood ran from Ruth's left ear, forming the beginnings of a pool at her shoulders. No sounds came from the hall or nearby compartments.

It only took a moment for Amy to locate the attorney's letter in Ruth's coat pocket as she scrambled to find evidence that would support her plan. This letter was her ticket into the attorney's office, a boarding pass directly into Ruth's identity, Randall's estate, and a new life. It would mean betting the attorney had never met Ruth before, but that was a risk she was willing to take.

The letter was typewritten on fine stationery, the attorney's letterhead emblazoning the upper portion of the page. Amy scanned the lines, the words "considerable estate" jumping out at her. Then she saw it.

In the upper left above the salutations, the date: 25 July 1939.

Then the letter was a fake? Had Ruth been deep in a game, a role-playing act into which Amy had somehow been sucked? Confused, she shoved the envelope into her coat pocket and began searching the compartment for any reassurance her plan might still be viable.

The train began to slow, making its approach to Penrith Station. She was running out of time. Deep in Ruth's opposite pocket she found a scrap of paper, a train ticket. It was printed on sturdy cream-colored cardstock, the black text stamped over in red with a date: Mon. 14 Aug. 39. Further evidence of this woman's ridiculous obsession with props.

The car and compartment number were listed on the ticket's reverse.

"Impossible."

Amy rushed to the hall. On the door below the window, printed in pristine gold lettering, was Amy's compartment number, matching the information on Ruth's ticket.

Back in the compartment, Amy looked around desperately for an explanation. A square of paper protruding from Ruth's clenched fist caught her eye. She knelt and pulled a now crumpled photograph from the still-warm fingers. It was black and white, the glossy kind with a white border. Ruth's smiling face stared back at her, a lanky man at her side, similarly bright-eyed and innocent. A lake and mountains filled the backdrop.

On the back, in pencil, someone had written "Windermere, Summer 1935."

Panic tightened in a noose around Amy's throat. Out the window the station was coming into view. Men in dark suits and fedoras and women in knee-length dresses slid by. A woman in furs was being helped out of a narrow-wheeled, high-fendered car on a side street. A bobby in a pointed helmet and dark uniform with bright, silver buttons moved between the waiting passengers, idly swinging his billy club.

Amy leaned heavily against the window frame, her head down. She swallowed the bile rising in her throat, shook off the odious feeling in her gut, and squeezed the photograph into a tight ball. Plans change.

Then she took the suitcase down from the rack and began putting on Ruth's spare clothes.

Olympia SG-1, 1961

Ghosting

Denise Terriah

The pane of glass pushed free of the frame with surprisingly little effort. It shattered when it hit the floor, causing Sarah to duck back into the bushes. She waited for someone to yell, "stop thief!" like she was in a cartoon, but nobody seemed to notice. This would probably have been easier at night, but it was safer during the day.

After an appropriate length of silence Sarah tried to stand, but was forced back into the bush to untangle her blond ponytail. It had grabbed some branches as if it had the good sense not to go breaking into an abandoned house, unlike Sarah herself.

This wasn't just any abandoned house, and Sarah had a good reason to be here. As she stood, she adjusted her jacket that declared her credentials. Sarah was the newest member of MPRC, the Midwest Paranormal Research Club.

Admittedly, this wasn't a sanctioned investigation, they weren't supposed to trespass. But that didn't matter, Sarah had already convinced herself that these were extenuating circumstances. The house she was violating was the white whale of haunted houses in the area. It was supposed to be haunted by the ghost of a young woman who'd been murdered here in the nineteen seventies. Her body was never found, but it was a well-known local legend.

The house was owned by Mr. Seamon, who had just retired from his position as a coach at the local high school. The MPRC had approached him many times, over the years, to get permission to enter the abandoned structure. He'd always refused. Now it was scheduled to be bulldozed to an empty lot. This investigation was now or never. She had to do this. Sarah squared her shoulders.

The window latch was easy to reach through the missing window pane, and the paint gluing the window shut turned out to be less determined than Sarah. With one last backwards glance, Sarah slipped through the window.

Dust motes floated in the dim light, and the air smelled like mildew. Sarah found herself standing in a small living room where the wall-to-wall orange carpet sagged menacingly in the room's center. The ceiling had long since fallen in, and was scattered in chunks across the floor. Daylight drew a jagged shape on the carpet. When Sarah looked up, she could see the sky through a hole in the roof surrounded by drooping shingles. No wonder the floor was rotten.

Sarah tested each step as she moved further into the room. Who knew how far the rot might have spread? She was going to have to be careful, she'd hate to get stuck haunting a dump like this.

Sarah swung her backpack to the floor. It should have been full of high-tech gear, like a proper ghost hunter's pack, but she couldn't afford those things yet. She'd spent all her money on her jacket. Sarah pulled the zipper tab and was glad she was alone. She'd never even been on an investigation before. It was bad enough feeling like a loser on the message boards without having someone around to see how basic her tools were. All she had was a digital recorder and a flashlight which she put in her pocket. It was still full daylight outside; the flashlight was for emergencies only. Shining a light around in an empty house was a good way to get arrested. Lastly, she pulled her cell phone out of her pocket, turned it off, and dropped it into the bag. She'd heard it could cause interference when communicating with ghosts.

A quick look around the space made it clear that the rest of the house was in better shape than the living room. That's why she'd chosen to start exploring during the day; wandering around a dilapidated heap was too dangerous in the dark. Obviously, she might have to stay until nightfall, that was part of the nature of ghost hunting. Sarah skirted the sagging floor and crept towards the kitchen.

Cabinet doors hung crookedly from rusted hinges, and empty spaces outlined where a stove and refrigerator might have been. Mouse droppings were scattered across the countertops and cracked linoleum.

"Hello?" Sarah called softly to the empty kitchen. "I'd like to make contact with the spirit of this place. I'm friendly, and I hope that you are too."

Sarah stood perfectly still, holding out the recorder. She didn't want the rustle of her clothes, or her breathing, to obscure any answer she might receive. She wanted to do this right.

"I don't mean you any harm. I just came to find out what happened to you," Sarah continued, barely above a whisper as she slipped back into the living room. Sarah crept around the outer edge of the room and moved down the hallway towards what were probably the bedrooms. The groaning of the floor under the moldy carpet was the only reply.

"Hello? I just want to talk," Sarah called as she opened the door of the closet, in the bedroom, at the end of the hall. The space was lit by daylight from a hole high up on the wall.

A rustling noise made her stomach clench just a moment before a shape hit her face, scrabbling and sharp. She'd hit the creature hard against the wall and was running down the hall before she ever registered the rasping squawking of the crow. It was probably still trying to get its bearings where it had landed on the bedroom floor.

Sarah stood panting in the living room as she looked back down the hallway that led to the bedroom, where the bird was still making a ruckus.

"Some ghost hunter I am." Sarah looked at her empty hands as she pulled them back from her face. "Seriously?" Her digital recorder was probably what the bird was still making a fuss over in the other room. "Now I have to fight a bird for my stuff? You could have warned me about the bird," Sarah told the room. If there was a ghost here, it was probably having a laugh at her expense.

Sarah turned and started across the room to see if there was anything around to fight a crow with. As she did, her mind screamed a warning, but it was too late.

The floor bucked under Sarah's feet as boards snapped and she fell towards the sagging carpet. She held her arms out to catch herself, but instead of landing, she and the moldy carpet tumbled onward together.

Sarah's back hit the ground first. She attempted to breathe, but the wind had been knocked out of her. She lay making little barking attempts at inhaling punctuated by shallow coughs.

She managed to gasp a deeper breath as little black dots swam in her vision like an army of flies. She fought the embrace of the damp orange carpet but couldn't turn over. The ground beneath her was uneven, and the movement made her head ache and her stomach roll.

Sarah closed her eyes as another wave of nausea hit, and the adrenalin of panic warmed her veins. She was in an abandoned house. If nobody found her, she could die down here. What if she couldn't get up?

Sarah's eyes darted around the room. It was dark. The only thing she could see clearly was a decade of dust rolling through the air above her like a low-lying cloud. When she shifted to see behind her, she froze.

In the closest corner of the basement stood a figure--a young woman. Only vaguely more upsetting than the sudden appearance of the figure was that she was transparent. Sarah could plainly see a rolled-up rug behind the young woman. Not around her, through her.

"Help me."

The words were like a dim echo of a memory. Even after staring at the figure Sarah couldn't decide if she'd actually heard or imagined the words.

Sarah struggled to sit up, but clutched her head and curled into the fetal position to try to ward off the nausea and pain. "How can I help you when I can't even sit up?" Sarah mumbled from her position on the floor.

"Help me."

The voice was closer and clearer this time. Sarah lifted her head and found herself looking up at the apparition who stood over her. She could plainly see that the young woman looked out of place. Her clothes were all wrong for her age. She wore a blouse with a knotted bow at the neckline, and a knee-length skirt. Her hair was curly and just long enough to brush her shoulders.

"Who are you?" Sarah asked breathlessly. This had to be a ghost. She wasn't just imagining this, was she? She'd hit her head pretty hard, but this had to be a real ghost.

The ghost watched her, but said nothing.

"I have so many questions. Why are you here? What happened? What's it like being a ghost? Can you leave this place, or are you stuck here?" Sarah winced, holding her head, which was throbbing now, and continued. "How did you die? Is that a rude question? I'm sorry, I don't know afterlife etiquette."

The ghost continued to say nothing, it simply stood above her looking like a dim figment of her imagination.

"Are you real?" Sarah asked as she eased back down clutching her forehead and clenched her eyes tightly closed. The movement was agonizing.

When she opened her eyes, the ghost was mere inches from her face.

"Hey!" Was all Sarah managed before a cold darkness flowed over her. "What are you doing?" Sarah shrieked trying to push the insubstantial mass away from her. There was nothing to push, it was already gone, and she was alone.

She scrambled to her feet; the reeking orange carpet was gone. Her head no longer ached, and there was a light on at the other side of the basement. There was no hole above her head. This couldn't be the same basement at all. This one was just musty. The last one had been evil smelling, like mold, rot, and maybe worse.

"Hello!" Sarah called to the room in general.

"Please, let me go! Please, please, I won't tell anyone," a voice sobbed from the other end of the room. A wall of cardboard boxes and rusty junk hid that half of the room from view.

"Are you okay?" Sarah called.

The woman continued crying but didn't answer.

"I'm here! I'm coming!" Sarah assured the woman as she looked for a way through the junk wall.

"My Mom will keep looking for me until she finds me! They'll catch you!" the young woman yelled. The end of the sentence was punctuated by the rattling of a heavy chain.

That stopped Sarah in her tracks. What on earth was going on? "Hey girl, are you okay?" Sarah asked gently.

The sobbing continued, but the girl didn't answer.

"Hold on, I'm coming." Sarah spoke softly. "I'm going to have to move some of this, and I'll be right there."

Sarah reached for the top box on the stack in front of her and swayed on her feet when her hands passed through it.

"What the--?" Sarah stared at her hands. They had the same translucent quality as the ghost she'd so recently seen in the other basement. "No, no, no, no, no!" Sarah shook her hands as if she could make them solid by getting the translucence off them. "This can't be happening." She couldn't be dead, could she? Maybe her neck broke and she had rotted in the nasty basement of that abandoned house. But, if that were true, why was she here instead of there? Why this basement?

The sobbing continued from the other end of the room. The young woman clearly needed help. No amount of Sarah's feeling sorry for herself would do either of them any good. Sarah took a deep breath; why shouldn't ghosts help people?

After a couple of experimental shoves proved that Sarah couldn't interact with the boxes, she chose to walk through them. She'd expected it to at least tingle, but she didn't feel a thing.

On the other side of the junk wall, a young brunette huddled on the ground. A thick metal loop was sticking out of the concrete floor near her. One end of a heavy chain was connected to the loop, the other end was connected to a shackle on the young woman's ankle.

Sarah's mind rebelled at the horror of finding a young woman shackled to a floor, but something else was nagging at her about the scene. The vintage hair, the blouse, the skirt. This was the apparition that had been in the other basement, but the young woman on this floor wasn't a ghost. Tears ran down the young woman's bruised face while she let out messy gasping sobs. Another bruise was visible around the shackle at her ankle, just above her torn sock and dirty tennis shoe.

"Miss?" Sarah moved forward, kneeling in front of the young woman, who didn't look up. Sarah continued anyway. "Can you hear me?"

The young woman didn't respond to Sarah, but her head snapped up when a trap door was flung open at the top of the stairs. Sarah hadn't noticed it, or the stairs, until the light flooded down from above.

The young woman scrambled backwards, pulling the chain taunt, as a heavyset man stomped down the stairs. He had a buzz cut, a thick, dark mustache, and small, cold eyes. He was wearing a mustard-yellow, button-up shirt tucked into brown slacks. His outfit was as dated as the shackled woman's. Sarah couldn't exactly place the era, but it definitely had a seventies polyester ugly feel to it. Was she in the seventies? Wasn't that when the girl in the ghost story was supposed to have died?

The man lumbered over to where the loop stuck out of the floor and grabbed the end of the chain, pulling the girl across the concrete. The metal cuff bit into her leg, drawing blood.

"Don't touch her, you monster!" Sarah yelled, flailing wildly at the man, who didn't react at all to her presence. She gasped as he bent down and gripped the young woman by the throat. Sarah tried to peel his fingers away, but couldn't

touch him. Surely if she was really a ghost, she
should be able to scare him. It seemed unfair to
have to just stand here and watch.
 The man pulled the young woman's face towards
him, forcing a small gagging sound out of her.
 "If you don't quit your noise, I'll cut your
throat and pull out your voice box," he whispered
menacingly into her ear.
 The woman hiccupped into a sniffly silence.
 The brute took a deep breath and let the
young woman go with a shiver. He stood up and
smoothed his shirt over his chest. "I'm going to
enjoy watching you bleed out, you little tease."
 The young woman's eyes were so wide they
showed the white all the way around the pupil as
the man laughed.
 "Did you think I was going to let you go?
After the way you've behaved?" He turned away
chuckling to himself as he climbed the stairs
just as heavily as he'd come down them.
 "I'm going to die," the young woman whispered,
beginning to rock slowly.
 Sarah didn't know what to say. If she really
was in the past, then yes, the young woman was
going to die.
 The shackled woman was still rocking and
whispering when Sarah knelt down in front of her
again. "I'm going to need you to pull yourself
together. I think you sent me here, to the past,
to help you. I can't imagine why I'd be here
otherwise."
 The rocking continued.
 "If we look around, maybe we can find a way
to get you out of here." Sarah smiled
encouragingly and leaned forward to hug the
young woman. The young woman passed right
through her multiple times. The rocking stopped,
and she hugged herself shivering.
 "I'm not really helping, am I?" Sarah leaned
back. "Come on. Let's look around and see if we
can find some way for you to escape."
 Sarah watched the young woman, who was
sitting still, staring at nothing.
 "Don't worry, I've got this." Sarah assured
her.

The plan turned out easier imagined than accomplished; Sarah couldn't actually interact with her surroundings. There were no windows that Sarah could find. What might have been windows at one time were bricked over. The metal ring, chain, and shackle seemed heavy, and solid. What were they supposed to do?

"It would really help if I knew why you sent me to your time," Sarah muttered. She sat down and tried to lean against a stack of boxes, but passed through them instead. "That was unsettling." Sarah sat up dusting off her ghostly clothes, which seemed silly. If she couldn't touch a box, it only stood to reason, she couldn't touch dirt either. She leaned forward, putting her head down on her knees.

The rattling of the chain caught Sarah's attention as the young woman took a box off the top of the nearest stack. She opened the box underneath it, dropping a pile of dirty fabric hastily out of the way. She was clearly after something. It was a suitcase, no bigger than an overnight bag. She set it gently on the floor and opened it to reveal a grey typewriter.

Sarah knelt next to the young woman who had lifted the machine out of its case, revealing some scratch paper underneath.

"Do you think you could throw this at him? It looks really heavy." Sarah leaned in to look closer at the machine and its intricate parts. "Maybe you can make a weapon out of something here?"

The young woman was holding up a piece of paper with some writing scribbled on the back of it.

Sarah rubbed the bridge of her invisible nose. "Are you planning on giving him a vicious paper cut?"

The young woman ignored her, not that Sarah expected anything else from someone who couldn't see her.

Instead of tearing the machine apart, the young woman rubbed the ribbon between her fingers, making a black mark which she looked at thoughtfully.

"That was fun. Let's get back to trying to get you out of here! This is no time to write a strongly worded letter of complaint!" Sarah was nearly shouting in her exasperation.

The young woman slid the paper behind the platen, and turned the knob until it poked out on the front side.

"How is that going to help!" Sarah shouted at the young woman.

The young woman began typing slowly, looking up at the trap door at the top of the stairs--waiting. One type slug hit the paper every few seconds. It was agony watching her type.

March 1979

My name is Mary Kate Parks. I am 15 years old, and I am probably dead. I hope I'm not, but I thought it was important for someone to know what happened to me. Please, if you get this note, tell my mom that I love her and I'm sorry.

I was kidnapped by Coach Matt Seamon, who just started at the high school this year. I was walking home in the rain, and he stopped to offer me a ride.

I don't remember what happened in the car, but I woke up with a chain on my ankle in this basement. I don't know where I am, and I don't know how long I've been here. I guess it's been about a week because he's fed me 7 times. I don't want Mom to know what he's done to me, it would break her heart, so I'm not going to write it here.

He said he's going to kill me.

Please tell my momma that I prayed for Jesus's forgiveness for the things I've done and all the things that have happened here. I'm no longer afraid to meet him in heaven. Tell momma I love her, and I'll see her there one day.

Mary turned the knob, advancing the paper out of the machine. She clutched it to her chest as her shoulders shuddered, and tears streamed down her face. Then, she began folding the tear-stained paper gently with shaking hands.

Sarah stood in shock over Mary's shoulder. She had actually gone back in time. She was standing here in the year nineteen seventy-nine. Could ghosts time travel? Did this happen to all ghosts?

Sarah got up to pace while Mary cried. No wonder Mr. Seamon wouldn't let the MPRC in. He didn't need an investigation to know who the ghost was. He'd been the one who killed her. A chill ran up Sarah's spine. He'd worked at the high school for nearly forty years. Was Mary his only victim? Was she even his first? How could people overlook a monster for so long?

Sarah watched mutely as the fifteen-year-old girl smoothed the paper and fed it behind the platen again. She advanced the knob until the accordion-folded paper had just disappeared from view. Then, she returned the typewriter to its case, and carefully put everything away.

Sarah wouldn't have known the boxes had been disturbed if she hadn't just watched Mary do it.

Mary sat down and took several deep breaths before she steepled her hands and bowed her head. "Our Father who art in Heaven, hallowed be thy name..." Her prayer trailed off as she sniffled and hiccupped fresh tears. "Please Jesus, help my mom be comforted. Please let them arrest Coach Seamon. But mostly, Jesus, please let this be over with. I can't take any more." Mary didn't raise her head when she'd finished her prayer, she just dropped her hands to the floor and stared off into space.

"I'm not here to save you, am I?" Sarah sobbed, sitting unnoticed next to Mary. "I can't stop something that's already happened."

Sarah placed her hand over Mary's. She couldn't touch her, but her hand passed through and occupied the same space, which was the best she could do.

Mary looked briefly at her hand, but continued her silent crying.

"I'm not going to leave you alone," Sarah whispered, trying to brush the young woman's hair out of her eyes. When her hand passed through it, a couple of strands moved as if towards a balloon that had been rubbed on the carpet. It was all Sarah could manage. "I'm sure it will all be over soon."

Sarah sat in silence for hours with Mary before the man came back down the stairs. Mary didn't move when he approached, but Sarah threw herself at him howling. She did everything she could to stop the beast, but she couldn't even make him blink. When Sarah knew she couldn't stop him she decided that she should at least bear witness, for Mary's sake, so she wouldn't be alone. She wanted to, she tried, but she couldn't. She turned away and covered her ghostly ears, humming to herself to drown out Mary's cries until they fell silent.

When someone tapped Sarah on the shoulder, she couldn't stop herself from screaming.

"My name's Mary." The ghost who had tapped her on the shoulder waved.

"Sarah," she answered dumbfounded, "I'm Sarah. Are you dead?"

"I think so." Mary shrugged.

It should have been obvious. Mary was as transparent as the first time Sarah had seen her in the other basement. Sarah's eyes widened as she caught sight of Mary's body.

Mary grabbed her arm quickly, and turned them both away. "I'd rather you don't see that."

Sarah nodded, shaken.

Mary closed her eyes and smiled, swaying slightly, as if she was listening to far-off music. When she opened her eyes, she looked at Sarah. "It's time for you to go back now."

"Go back?"

Mary shrugged. "Forward actually."

"Why was I here?"

"For the evidence."

Mary grabbed Sarah's hand, and gave it a squeeze. Sarah coughed deeply. She was lying on a pile of rubble. From where she lay, she could see through the hole in the floor above her, all the way through the hole in the roof, to a darkening sky.

Her head no longer hurt, so Sarah sat up experimentally and squinted around in the darkness. The dust had settled, and now the shapes in the gloom were more familiar. This was the same basement. Piles of boxes, in various states of decay, stood in the familiar junk wall between Sarah and the other end of the room.

Sarah patted her pockets; the flashlight was thankfully still there. With the aid of her light, Sarah crawled across the rotted cardboard and debris until she reached the space where Mary had been. There was no sign of Mary's ghost in the basement with her. Was Mary ever actually here, or did she knock herself out and have some sort of crazy nightmare?

If it was real, then Sarah was here for the evidence: Mary's note. Watching Mary write the note felt like a lifetime ago. She had to find the typewriter. If it was really here, maybe she did actually go back in time.

The typewriter would be in the second box down on the far side of this space. Thankfully, the boxes here had fared better than the boxes on the other side of the room because the roof in this section seemed pretty solid. Here they were just curly, instead of outright rotting.

Sarah hurried forward, stubbed her toe, and fell sprawling onto the floor. She curled up, clutching her foot, as an unintended string of profanities left her mouth. When she turned to see what she'd fallen over, she could see a broken piece of concrete jutting up. It was right where the ring Mary had been tethered to had been. This couldn't just be a coincidence—could it? What other reason would there be for the floor to be broken in this exact spot?

Sarah stood and dusted off her pants. She was more certain than ever that she was going to find that typewriter. Sarah knocked the first box off the pile and shone her light into what remained of the second. Beneath the rotting fabric was a hard, black case. It was the right size. Sarah lifted the case from the box with her heart pounding. She set it on the floor and opened the lid.

Inside was the smooth, grey Smith-Corona typewriter she had seen Mary write her goodbye letter on. Her hands trembled as she fought the urge to turn the knob to see if the letter was inside. She'd watched enough crime shows to know they could probably get important evidence off this machine, so it was best not to touch the actual typewriter.

Sarah closed the lid and carried the machine up the creaking stairs. At the top she struggled with the trap door. When she finally worked it loose, she found the kitchen linoleum had been put down over the door. No wonder she hadn't noticed it when she first arrived. The linoleum was old enough that it broke and dropped away with less effort than Sarah had expected.

She made her way back through the house, set the typewriter by the door, and retrieved the phone from her backpack.

Telling the dispatcher that she'd found a crime scene wasn't as effective as telling him that she was breaking and entering. He informed her the police would be there soon, and to stay where she was. Sarah unlocked the door, and sat on the front steps to wait. Even the MPRC was going to have a hard time believing this story.

Brother Charger 11, 1970
Smith-Corona Galaxie II, 1965

Unquiet Writers

Matt Wixey

All typewriters, whatever their appearance, are solely designed for one thing, and in that thing they are mercilessly and ruthlessly functional - precise, inanimate, and sane. No component is superfluous or unnecessary to this objective. Time after time, typebars slap, levers extend and retract, gears click; all for the single-minded purpose of imprinting ink into the fibers of paper. That is all there is, and nothing more.

But when Michael Parratt saw the typewriter through the grubby window of the charity shop on George Lane, its bulbous frame seemed to defy this wisdom. Something about its aged form, the way it stood, suggested a machine greater than the sum of its parts. It had stories to tell. Had known things, seen things. Previous owners had, perhaps, left their own imprint upon it.

<u>Part of it,</u> he thought, peering into the shop's dingy interior, <u>part of it is romance, surely.</u> Being raised on a diet of digital devices could make one revere anything even vaguely antiquated. Hindsight is 20/20, the saying goes, but rose-tinted glasses can improve one's vision so much more.

Parratt stepped back and looked up. He didn't find himself on George Lane often, but had taken the route on a whim, on his way back from work. He couldn't recall seeing the shop before. It nestled like an ugly flower between a row of clean new buildings, slouching low-slung as though gripping the concrete for dear life, shrinking from the sky. On the yellowing window, a flyer had been stuck by some passer-by, a small patch of clean white against the grime, like enamel scraped from a decaying tooth.

And there, some way back, was the typewriter, alone on a shelf as though it had claimed the space for its own. Dark green and gleaming dully. Even from here, Parratt could see some corrosion, but the paintwork looked good, and something in him longed to touch it, to roll paper in and hear the machine speak the way it was meant to. He wanted that imagined sensation, so alien to one used only to flimsy computer keyboards, of thudding into keytops and hearing typeheads snap like machine-guns. To see words appear as if fired directly from the brain, smashing straight into paper. A good display piece, yes; an icebreaker, absolutely; but perhaps, somewhere within him, there was poetry, a play, a novel. A creativity which begged to be unlocked, constrained until now by the artificiality of the digital. <u>If I am to write something</u>, he thought, <u>I should use a machine made to write.</u>

   He pushed open the door. A bell rang out flatly above his head. Parratt did not habitually visit charity shops, but he associated them with secondhand bookstores, which he loved dearly. Both seemed to him to share a cheerful, cozy sort of shabbiness, sagging comfortably from the years. The staff were devoted curators of things once loved, the goods on the shelves tangible evidence of a better side of humanity. <u>Here, you can have this, I hope you enjoy it as much as I did.</u>

   Yet this shop seemed entirely indifferent to its own disrepair, and to the objects on its shelves. There was a sterile air about it, suggesting the shop cared nothing for the history of its contents.

   Putting these outlandish thoughts aside, Parratt approached the typewriter. Yes, heavy rust on the chrome fittings, and inside the segment. But up close, it was even more appealing than from the outside. No collector would have called it beautiful; no person unfamiliar with typewriters would have gasped in awe at the sight. It was bulging, bulky. The ribbon cover was a sudden, almost indecent hump that put him in mind of a beluga whale's head.

   But to Parratt - who had only ever used a computer, although he dimly remembered word-processor-typewriter hybrids displayed in stores when he was very young - it was a miracle in lush, military green. The chrome legend "Remington" glinted on the front, and below, in white: "Quiet-Riter."

   He reached out a hand and caressed the body. Cold metal, colder than he had anticipated. Gingerly, he hooked a finger into the paddle of the carriage lever, and gave it an experimental pull. As though stretching itself wearily after a long rest, the carriage groaned and grumbled and moved reluctantly across. Parratt grinned in delight.

There was no price tag. Turning to the till, he saw an old man, who had been observing him vacantly from across the shop.

"Excuse me," Parratt said. "The typewriter. How much?"

The old man's eyes slid past Parratt to the Remington, and back to Parratt, and back again, back and forth in little hard saccades.

"Ten," he said at last.

Parratt fumbled out his wallet and fished for a crumpled note. The old man snatched it from him.

"Bag?" he said.

Parratt had already turned back to the machine. "It comes with a case."

"Should have charged you more."

Parratt ignored this, and checked that the typewriter was secure inside its tattered brown box. A thought occurred to him.

"Do you know anything about the provenance?" he said.

"Don't think it's French," the old man said.

Parratt was nonplussed for a moment, and then laughed.

"No - not Provence. I mean, do you know anything about its history?"

"Take it to a museum," the old man said. "I just put the things on the shelves."

And with that, he shuffled to the other side of the shop, where he became absorbed in rearranging a stack of old jigsaw puzzles.

Parratt watched him, shrugged, and shut the case, noting with satisfaction the muted click as it latched shut. As he lifted the whole thing down from the shelf, the bell above the door gave its joyless cry, and a scrawny, bedraggled woman Parratt had never seen before threw herself into the shop, breathing heavily.

"That's mine."

"Excuse me?" Parratt said.

The woman came closer, staring at the case in Parratt's hand.

"The typewriter. I want it."

"I'm sorry, I've just bought it."

"Double what you paid. No, triple."

Parratt saw that the old man had turned away from his wobbling tower of jigsaws and was watching this exchange with bleary fascination.

"It's not for sale. Sorry."

"I have another just like it. At home. It's yours."

"So why do you want this one?"

The woman took another step forward. There were now only inches between them. Her gaze remained fixed on the case - at no point had she even looked at Parratt - but he noted with some discomfort that her eyes were small and black and without reason, like those of a shark which smelled blood.

"You don't understand. How long I've been looking."

"Please excuse me." Parratt made to walk around her.

"Let me just see it, then."

Before Parratt could respond, she had grabbed the handle and twisted it out of his hand with a strength he found it hard to believe could exist within her slight frame. He cried out, reached to take it back, but she held up a hand, and for some reason the gesture stopped him dead.

The woman inhaled, almost in awe, and set the case down. She flicked the latch open and with practiced skill moved the carriage to one side, flipped up the lumpish ribbon cover, and gazed, entranced, at something by the left spool.

"It is," she breathed. "It really is."

Parratt's curiosity got the better of him, and he knelt down to see. It was a serial number, stamped into the metal.

"EQR155900," she said. "Yes. And let me -"

She tipped the case up to better see the front. The Remington logo flashed prettily in the shop's weak light. Something he had missed; letters stenciled in white on the frame, below the spacebar. He caught a glimpse of the first few letters, "MX-", before the woman set the case down - rather carelessly, he thought - and at last looked him in the eye.

"Name your price."

"It's not for sale," Parratt said firmly.

"Are you a collector?" the old man said. "Is it valuable?"

"Sentimental value," the woman said, her eyes never leaving Parratt's face. "How much did you sell it for?"

"Ten," the old man said, in the same flat tone with

which he had quoted the price before. Parratt had a fortunately brief impulse to laugh.

The woman recoiled and gave a forced, twisted sort of smile. "Ten. You have no -" and she stopped herself short.

"Worth more, is it?"

"I'll give you a hundred."

Perhaps it was how rudely the elation at his purchase had been curtailed, but Parratt felt a fierce and peculiar anger choke him. This typewriter, this one, the one he had found - it was his, and his alone. <u>There are many typewriters</u>, his mind hissed, <u>but this one is mine.</u>

"Now look," he said. "It was for sale, so I bought it. He can't sell it to you, and I don't want to."

"Two hundred," the woman said quickly. "Each." She thrust a hand into her pocket and produced a fistful of notes. Some spilled out and whispered to the floor. She held the money out to Parratt, not bothering to count it.

Parratt felt that sick urge to laugh again; it was like the woman was begging in reverse. He fought it down and shook his head.

"I'm leaving." He picked up the case.

"A thousand."

"No!"

The woman howled - howled loud and long, like an animal, wholly inhuman. The two men looked at her in astonishment. The noise broke into whining sobs, and Parratt, rather disturbed, made for the door.

In an instant she was upon him. She pressed her body tight against his, her face flushed and warped obscenely.

"You don't want money, then. So. Take this."

Parratt detached himself from her with a grimace. "What the hell's the matter with you?"

He yanked the door open, the bell clanging bleakly. The woman followed him into the street.

"It's not for you," she said, the words falling out of her mouth. "You won't understand it."

She grabbed his arm and pressed a damp scrap of paper against his palm. A telephone number was scrawled on it, smudged and blurred.

"I can wait. I've waited before. Call me when you've had enough."

Parratt stuffed the paper in his pocket and strode off, his pulse pounding. He didn't look back until he was at the end of George Lane. When he did, he saw a small, forlorn figure outside the distant charity shop, standing perfectly still, watching him.

The Quiet-Riter, despite its rust, was not in bad condition, and remarkably clean. The next morning, Parratt consulted several websites, made notes, and eventually fetched a bottle of mineral spirits from under his kitchen sink. Gently, he wiped the typebars and segment down with a rag, smiling as the heavy brown smears faded to orange and then nothing. He used metal polish on the chrome lever and the paper bail, and cleaned the body with a soft cloth. Pinching the ribbon between his fingers resulted in a faint smudge; there was still life in it. The temptation to type something, then and there, overwhelmed him.

He contemplated the machine fondly. The paintwork really was excellent; he hadn't found a single blemish. And the stenciling the woman had found stood out, bright and clear. MX-327A. A military designation, perhaps. The dark olive green body would back that up.

He traced the keytops with his fingers. They were thick, chunky. Oh, there was history here; he could almost hear it chattering and vibrating at his touch. Who had used this machine? What had they typed on it?

Eagerly, he grabbed a sheet of paper from his printer and rolled it in, creasing it several times as he struggled with the unfamiliar process. At last, crooked and dirty from several aborted attempts, the sheet sat snugly over the platen. Parratt stared at it, feeling the same terror and exhilaration so many have felt, facing that same blank page: <u>what do I write? What if I can't?</u>

From somewhere deep in his memory, he dredged up a sentence, something he recalled had been traditionally used to test typewriters. He typed the first few words, and

He thought, later, that the transition — if that was what it was — had been instant. There was no swirling fog, no blackness, no vista of stars and galaxies. He was simply at his kitchen table one moment, and somewhere else the next, and the somewhere was nowhere he knew.

The air was thick with heat and the drone of insects. Almost immediately, sweat stung his skin and rolled down his forehead. He felt something land on his arm, saw a mosquito squatting, feeding. He slapped at it mechanically, smearing blood and broken wings.

He blinked. He was in a large canvas tent, the same color as his Quiet-Riter.

Distantly he heard helicopters, and shouting, but louder, unbearably loud, was the sound of typing. In the tent were rows of flimsy folding desks, perhaps twenty in all, and at each one was a man wearing clothes that same dull green, typing frantically on a typewriter. All were facing away; Parratt could only see the backs of their heads. With a start of recognition, he saw that each machine was a dark green Quiet-Riter, with white stenciling on the front of the frame. The noise was incredible: the rattle of keys, the ding of bells and rasp of returns.

Curious, Parratt stared at the paper rolled into the nearest Quiet-Riter.

OPERATION WHEELER ACTION REPORT ON ENEMY CASUA

Nobody seemed to have noticed him. He saw an open flap in the tent and crept towards it, poking his head through into the open air. The roar of the typing faded slightly. He saw sunshine, and trees, and soldiers with guns. A small group of them stood some twenty feet away.

Parratt had very little experience of soldiers, but a voice in his head told him that something was very wrong with these. They wore brimmed bush hats instead of helmets, and they were unkempt and dirty, with long hair and scraggly beards. Occasionally, one of them would shift from foot to foot. They moved lazily, almost sleepily. Parratt heard one of them say something – an American accent, he thought – and the others laughed with a barking, desperate, unhinged sort of hilarity. He had never heard anything so terrifying in his entire life.

He risked another glance back at the typists. They were focused entirely on their work.

A voice shouted from outside. Parratt's breath caught in his lungs. He peeped out of the tent again. One of the soldiers was strolling over, yelling something back to the others. If he looked at the tent he would see Parratt, couldn't _not_ see Parratt, and

Parratt, without quite knowing why, understood that he should not be seen, that he should not look this soldier in the eyes.

But the soldier didn't see him, not yet. Now he was looking to one side. His profile was drawn, sallow, his head too big for a thin neck, around which was draped a string necklace. Dark, misshapen lumps of flat stone dangled from it at irregular intervals, bumping together as the soldier moved. Something about this struck Parratt as odd, but in his fear it would not resolve itself.

The soldier was now less than ten feet away. Parratt, heart hammering, stole to the very rear of the tent and stood with his back to the canvas wall, trying to make himself as still and small as possible.

The soldier entered and turned right, towards the typists. He approached a desk and bent down to say something. The typist, a young man no older than eighteen, stopped writing and shrank away.

Parratt shuffled towards the opening. He had to get out; if the soldier had not seen him upon entering, he certainly would when leaving.

And then the typing stopped.

The silence was absolute. Even the distant helicopters had gone. The soldier stiffened, began to turn. As though following his lead, every one of the typists started to turn in their seats.

Parratt closed his eyes and waited for the sound of boots striding towards him.

When he came to, he was at his kitchen table, the Quiet-Riter in front of him. Foggily, he saw that he had, at some point, completed the test sentence. He passed a hand over his face, the heat and the dread still with him. He must have fallen asleep. A dream, although he couldn't remember ever having a dream so vivid. Shaking, he reached to roll the paper out of the machine, and stopped.

On his forearm was the bloody mess of a dead mosquito.

"But you must have _some_ idea where it came from!"

"Like I said. People leave things outside the shop. I just put a price on them."

"Well, did you see who left it?"

"Nope."

Parratt shifted the phone to his other ear. The

Quiet-Riter crouched in front of him. Faintly, he heard the dismal little bell of the shop door over the line.

"You've got CCTV, haven't you?"

A dry, creaking laugh. "Even if I did, I wouldn't use it. Who'd steal from a charity shop?"

Parratt reached out to the typewriter. Stopped himself.

"You said I should take it to a museum. Which one? Who'd know about something like this?"

"That woman. The one who wanted to buy it off you. Sounded like she knew what she was talking about."

Parratt gripped the phone tight. "She'll try to take it."

"Sounds like your problem," the old man said. "Not mine." He hung up.

The Quiet-Riter, stubby and thickset, regarded Parratt calmly.

"What are you?" he whispered to it. Suddenly, he knew he had to type on it again. But this time – this time he'd be prepared. He stood up and snatched a butcher knife from the magnetic runner over the sideboard. It came free with a delicate chime.

The soldiers were American; perhaps they wouldn't try to hurt him. But he remembered that panicky, eager laughter, more like screaming than anything else, and the heft of the big knife made him feel a lot safer.

He slid paper into the typewriter and jerked it down in dull clicks. When a small strip of white appeared above the paper bail, Parratt slammed the carriage home, clutched the knife in one hand, and with the other pecked out his test sentence.

Once again, he did not finish. Once again, he was no longer at his kitchen table. But this time there was no tent, no heat, no insects. No typists. No soldiers. Only blackness, a vast and unfathomable darkness which stretched away into the distance. He had the distinct feeling that he was in a vacuum, an absence. A meaningless space.

He scanned the empty horizon. There was no wind, no weather. It was neither hot, nor cold. The ground beneath his feet was neither soft, nor hard. These things simply were.

He picked a heading at random and walked. His footsteps made no sound. The weight of the knife, which seemed to have survived the journey intact, was comforting in his hand. He looked up, half-expecting, hoping, to see a ceiling, or stars, but there was not. Only that immense and endless black, rolling upwards and onwards forever.

And then, quite suddenly, there was something in front of him, as though it had always been there. It was the soldier with the necklace.

He was facing away, bending forward slightly. To the side, also with his back to Parratt, was a single typist at a desk, pounding away at a Quiet-Riter. There was no sound.

Parratt clutched the knife, and stepped forward uncertainly. For the first time, he heard something. A baby. It cooed and babbled and gurgled.

The soldier with the necklace cooed in reply. Slowly, still facing forward, he reached back an arm to Parratt.

"Hand me that, would you?"

Parratt froze.

"Aw, c'mon. I just wanna borrow it."

The typist snatched the paper from his typewriter, threw the carriage, fed a new sheet in, all in one fluid movement.

Parratt screwed up his courage. "What...what are you going to do with it?" he said. His voice shivered in the gloom.

The soldier said nothing.

The baby mewled, then began to cry. Parratt could not see it; perhaps it was in front of the soldier. The cry rose to a piercing shriek. The soldier did not react. The typist wrote furiously, fingers flying over the thick green keytops.

Parratt came closer, close enough that he could have touched the soldier, had he wanted to. He did not want to. The soldier's uniform was stained and torn. There were patches of dirt and old blood on his skin.

The soldier reached his arm back again, moving it from side to side. Parratt watched in horror as a hand found the knife, pinched the blade, and plucked it from his suddenly powerless grip.

The baby cried louder, the noise sharp and unpleasant. The soldier brought the knife forward, out of sight. Parratt felt a fury and a sadness he could not explain.

The baby's crying intensified, was deafening, and then stopped, abruptly, mid-scream.

There was silence once more.

The soldier was still for a moment, and then reached back and proffered the knife. Parratt realized he didn't want to touch it.

"I'll keep it, then," the soldier said, still facing away. "I'll use it. Hey, have I shown you my necklace?"

The necklace. Parratt understood what had struck him as odd about it. He'd assumed the things hanging from it were stones. But as the soldier had walked, they had hit each other, and hadn't clicked or rattled, the way hard things should.

They had never made a sound.

Parratt, remembering long-ago documentaries with grainy color footage, thought he knew what the objects on the necklace might be.

"You wanna see it?" the soldier said. He straightened, began to turn his head. "You wanna see it? You wanna see it?"

Parratt screamed.

When he opened his eyes again, he was still screaming, sitting at his kitchen table. In a burst of terror, he picked up the Quiet-Riter, and with the paper still in it - the test sentence once again completed - he threw it into its case, not even checking to see if it sat properly upon its catches. He crashed the lid closed, picked the case up, flung open his front door, and ran towards George Lane.

He returned home half an hour later, and took a moment to stand in the hallway and let out a long breath. The old man had been only too pleased to take the machine back, and had returned Parratt's money with a grin of barely-disguised glee. He'd also paid extra for the scrap of paper with the woman's telephone number on it. He would make a killing, Parratt supposed, and the woman would get what she wanted, but he didn't envy either of them.

He put a hand in his pocket, felt the reassuring crackle of paper money, and turned the light on. He would get his laptop out, and fully embrace the digital age of which he was suddenly relieved to be a part. <u>Typewriters</u>, he thought, <u>are not worth the trouble. Plenty of people write novels on laptops.</u>

He walked into his kitchen.

The Quiet-Riter was sitting on the table.

It sat there as it had sat before. Still and waiting, hunched and green.

Parratt stared at it. His lips stretched into a wide and savage grin of fear.

He groped in his pocket and pulled out the money.

There was none. Only the same dirty scrap of paper the woman had pressed into his hand yesterday.

He ran upstairs, tripped, recovered, stumbled into his bedroom and slammed the door behind him. He thought about how ridiculous it would be to lock it, and then did it anyway.

With trembling fingers he dialed the charity shop.

"George Lane —"

"It's me. Me. Bought the typewriter yesterday. Was — was I in your shop just now?"

A beat of surprised silence.

"Is this a joke?"

"Yes or no, damnit!"

"I haven't seen you since yesterday."

Parratt gazed, unseeing, at the blank white wood of the bedroom door. Behind it, downstairs, seemingly so perfectly inanimate and sane, the typewriter sat serenely.

"Problem with the typewriter?" the old man was saying. "Want to return it?"

"I — I'm not sure if I can."

"That woman's here. She'd take it off your hands. But hurry up, if you're coming. Shop's closing."

"She's there with you?"

"Came yesterday too, after you left. Just standing here. Like she's waiting."

Parratt thought. "Can I speak to her?"

"Do I sound like a switchboard?"

"Please."

A pause. "If she buys it, I want a cut. Something for the shop and something for me. Not fair if you buy cheap and make a profit. It's a charity."

"Fine," Parratt said through clenched teeth. "Fine, just put her on!"

There was a rattle as the phone was set down. Muffled voices, footsteps, and the woman, calmer now, almost amused.

"I said it wasn't for you."

Very faintly, as though from deep within a dream, Parratt heard the sound of typing from downstairs.

"I want it out of my house," he said. "Will you take it?"

"That depends," the woman said.

"On what? What the hell is going on with that thing?"

The woman sighed. The sound was thin and somehow rusty.

"Who is he?" Parratt pressed. "The soldier?"

"It's not important."

Parratt exhaled unsteadily. "You'd better tell me exactly what's going on, because I'm seeing things and hearing things and I've had enough, OK, I've <u>fucking had enough!</u> Will you take it, or do I have to throw the fucking thing off a bridge?"

"That won't help you." A brief pause. "Has he seen you yet? Looked at you?"

"What? Who? The soldier? No. No, I don't think so. He's always facing away."

"Then it's not too late. I'll take it. But listen. This is important. Don't type another word on it. Not a single word."

"I wasn't planning to."

"Bring it, then. Come now."

"But what is it? What does it <u>mean?</u>"

"I can't explain."

Parratt sagged, exhausted. "Please," he whispered. "Please just try."

Another dusty sigh. "Did you know that marine biologists used to keep dolphins in concrete tanks? And then they stopped. Because after a few weeks in captivity, every dolphin began to behave oddly. Unstable. Violent. Erratic. Not just once. Every dolphin, every time."

From downstairs, Parratt thought he could hear the line bell ringing, over and over again. Something shifting in a chair in the kitchen.

"The scientists thought it might be just the result of captivity. It can do odd things to any animal. But the dolphins kept in outdoor pools were fine. It was only the ones in concrete tanks. The scientists tested everything they could think of: food, disease, the handlers. But the fact remained - only dolphins in concrete tanks were affected. And eventually, someone figured out why."

"Why?"

"Dolphins communicate using ultrasound," the woman said. "And ultrasound bounces off concrete. It echoes. In a concrete tank, with several dolphins, all of their voices were endlessly bouncing back and forth, repeating continuously. Their own speech drove them insane."

"My...my typewriter is —"

"It's not <u>your</u> typewriter. It's the US Army's. And that, perhaps, is the problem." The woman let out a shaky laugh. "Would it be any wonder if a machine used in an insane time, to write insane things, absorbing the sound of insane words being typed, day after day, were to have some imprint, gain some ability to echo those —"

"<u>You're</u> insane," Parratt said. "You're mad. You're saying I have a haunted typewriter?"

"I'm not saying that Sam Ybarra's ghost is going to —"

"Who?"

The woman was silent, as though she knew she had said too much. After a while, she cleared her throat, and said:

"I'll wait here for you."

"Wait, what —"

But there was only the flat hum of a dial tone.

Parratt set the phone down and gingerly opened the door. He listened hard. Nothing. He crept downstairs, sweating heavily.

The typewriter sat as it had always sat. Parratt picked up the dark green form and placed it in its case. One of the catches refused to spring home, so he pushed down hard on the body, and as he did his finger slipped and struck the N key.

There was a single snap, paced and precise, and then only the Quiet-Riter remained.

qwertyuiopasdfghjklzxcvbnm
QWERTYUIOPASDFGHJKLZXCVBNM
23456789
"/@_&'()¼:%.?,.½;
EQRI55900

This rather fanciful story — not without a certain crude charm — was relayed to me by the auctioneers, but despite their insistence that this lurid tale added value to the item,

I was more swayed by the color (dark green, quite unusual) and by the military mark on the frame: MX-327/A.

Indeed, whilst it may be a coincidence, it does appear that a Pvt Sam Ybarra served in the 327th Infantry. The "A", I suppose, may stand for Airborne. Ybarra's crimes are also a documented historical matter.

Other aspects of the story are more problematic, however. No charity shop has ever existed on that particular George Lane, nor is there any record of a Michael Parratt having lived nearby.

And yet, I wonder. I wonder if a woman will try and buy the machine from me. I wonder if I might see Ybarra or those others with their necklaces of ears, deep in the throes of their descents. I wonder if Parratt is in that tent, one typist amongst many, locked in time, typing endlessly on a Quiet-Riter words of chaos and madness. I wonder.

But facts are facts. I've been typing on this machine for some time now, with nothing untoward to report. At least I've shown that it still works. Not a bad typer, actually.

And just to round it off, I'll finish with the traditional test.

Now is the time for

Hermes 2000
Remington Quiet-Riter

The Conservator from the Future

Philip L. Simpson

From his illegal campsite atop a ridge crest, Trevor observed the volcano as he did first thing each morning. The mountain's conical peak thrust upward some 5,000 feet to catch the first light of dawn. The green forest canopy at its base remained cloaked in shadow. The morning sky was clear of the jetting steam and ash clouds that had commanded the world's attention over the past few months. Even so, the north stone face bulged outward from the magma seething within.

He felt like packing up his tent and gear, hiking down to his Jeep Cherokee, and kicking up dust on the rutted road to get away. Why, he was not entirely sure. Over the past few months driving back and forth between Seattle and the mountain to cover the story for his magazine, he had gotten a pretty good feel for the eruptions and earthquake swarms. The ground underneath his feet was quiet this morning. But so was the forest. Though dawn was gradually filtering through the pines and Douglas firs, no birdsong accompanied it. The air stood inert, time itself suspended.

His Casio digital wristwatch read 7:04 a.m.

He walked to his orange tent to retrieve his leather case and a zippered cloth portfolio from inside the tent flap. Then he sat on his camp chair behind the folding utility table that served as his writing station. He carefully lifted his manual typewriter, a 1918 Corona 3, from the case. He unfolded the carriage back from the keyboard and placed the machine on the tabletop. From his portfolio, he took a clean white sheet of paper and wound it into the typewriter.

Trevor had been gifted the Corona 3 by his mother, who had inherited it from her father, the summer before he left home for college. "This kind of typewriter was Hemingway's favorite," she said as if bequeathing a boon to him. "He was a journalist too. It will bring you luck." The Corona 3 had seen him through college, so maybe it really did bring him luck as his mother had wished. He had long since stopped writing freehand.

Before he could start typing, he heard the distant sound of a car engine. Rising to his feet, he saw a green Ford station wagon bouncing and jostling up the abandoned logging road to the east, laboring toward him. Given that he had breached several police barricades to get here, he was relieved to see the car wasn't any kind of law enforcement vehicle.

The car pulled to a stop beside his jeep at the end of the road, slightly below the elevation of his camp. Trevor raised his right hand in welcome. A woman with a bob cut of thin brown hair turning gray hobbled out of the car and returned his wave. She appeared to be in her mid to late 50s, stocky of build and favoring her right leg. She wore a blue waist-length coat in the morning chill.

"Good morning," he called to her.

She did not reply. Her lips pressed tightly together as if containing some internal pressure as strong, in its own way, as that within the mountain four miles away.

"Do I know you?" he asked.

"No. But I know you, Trevor Landon."

"So, a fan club of one. You've gone to a lot of trouble to find me all the way out here."

"You have no idea." She smiled for the first time.

"And you are?"

"Mary Irene Montgomery."

"How may I help you, Mary Irene Montgomery?"

"First, you could invite me into your campsite. We need to talk. It's time-sensitive." She scoffed as if at some private joke but said nothing more.

"Okay," he said. Though puzzled, he sensed no threat from her. In fact, she somehow looked familiar, though he couldn't place from where or when. He walked down to assist her, as she clearly had a bad leg or knee that gave her what his dad would have called a "hitch in your get-a-long."

She was much shorter than he. Her head came up to his neck. He offered his left arm to her. She encircled her fingers, once long and graceful but now bent and swollen with arthritis, around the crook of his elbow.

They walked into his camp. "How did you know I was here?" he asked.

"It wasn't difficult," she said, without facing him. "The magazine article was pretty clear about it."

"What article? There are two people who know I'm here. One of them is my editor in Seattle. The other one is the guy in town who told me about this old logging road."

Instead of answering him, she asked, "What time is it?"

Sighing, he turned his wrist so she could see the watch face. "It's 7:20."

"Is your watch accurate?"

"Yes, pretty sure."

She fell silent. Then she looked up at him. Her blue eyes shifted to green. "We don't have much time," she said. "I have a lot to tell you and barely an hour to do it. And I know you're not going to believe me right away."

He was not sure exactly what kind of situation he now found himself in. But he felt no threat from her. He was at ease with her for no reason he could explain.

She looked here and there about the camp site, taking it in: the tent, the propane cook stove, the writing station.

"You've made yourself at home," she said. "Only a few miles from an active volcano."

"My per diem is lousy. I can't afford better lodging."

"Uh huh. Why are you really here? You know it's illegal."

"To get closer to the volcano. Because it's there, to coin a phrase. Make the story better."

Shaking her head, she fixed her eyes on the typewriter.

"May I?" she asked, gesturing toward the Corona.

He shrugged. She nodded her gratitude and limped in her dogged way to the table. He walked beside her ready to assist. Bracing herself against the table, she lowered herself into his camp chair. She spent a long moment looking at the Corona typewriter. When she placed her swollen fingers on the keys, she closed her eyes.

"This will not make any sense to you yet," she said, opening her eyes. "But I know this typewriter very well. May I type something?"

"Yes, if you tell me one thing first."

She smiled her enigmatic smile. "Okay."

"You know this kind of typewriter? Or you know <u>this</u> one?"

"<u>This</u> one."

"How is that possible? It's been in my family for two generations and I don't know you."

"You said you would ask one thing. That's two."

She turned from him and typed, with practiced fingers however swollen. For a minute or so, the air atop the ridge moved only with the sharp reports of the keys striking the paper snug against the platen beneath it. Then she stopped to read what she had typed. Satisfied, she wound the paper up out of the feed.

"Do you mind if I place this in your notebook?" she asked. She folded the paper in half.

<u>Play along</u>, he thought. Aloud, he said, "Not at all."

"I know you're humoring me, Trevor Landon. I'm asking you to trust me and hear me out."

"First thing, Mary Irene Montgomery, is we've got to stop using each other's full names. So please, call me Trevor, or Mr. Landon if you want to be formal, and we'll see if we can start trust from there."

She grinned. "Trevor it is."

"Then, Mary Irene, let's talk about why you're here and why you broke a few laws yourself to find me."

"Fair enough." She tucked the typed paper into the portfolio and straightened back up to face him. "No, I've never met you. But I heard a lot about you."

"So, we know someone in common."

"Yes, I think that's fair to say."

"Who?"

"Please. Let me do this my way. I've rehearsed so many times the best way to explain this to you." She breathed in deeply. "I'm going to tell you something about your future that no one else in this entire world knows."

Her blue-green eyes never left him. "At 8:32 this morning, May 18th, 1980, an earthquake will collapse the north face of the mountain. Seconds later, a gigantic lateral explosion equal to about 25 megatons of TNT will destroy everything around the volcano within an eight-mile circle. Damage all the way out to 20 miles. An ash cloud will cover the entire Pacific Northwest. Dozens of people will die."

She paused briefly. "I can't save them all. But I think I can save one."

Trevor, staring back at her, asked, "Who?"

She simply raised her eyebrows. The expression reminded him of someone somewhere. And nowhere. Just. . . elsewhere and elsewhen.

"You're saying I'm going to die here if that volcano erupts. Excuse me, we're going to die here."

"Yes, that's what happens in this here and now," she said. Her voice trembled.

"But you think you can save me anyway."

"Yes. I don't know for sure. But, I think, yes."

"How could you possibly know any of this?"

She didn't answer. The dawn light grew brighter, the sky bluer. And still the birds did not sing and the air did not move.

"Don't tell me. You're psychic. You know, it's no great trick to predict that mountain's going to blow sky-high. But you've certainly put yourself out there by picking the exact day and time, I'll give you that."

"No. I know it from history."

"You're trying to say--wait a minute."

Her eyebrows arched again. Patient expectancy.

"From." He held his palms parallel to each other

and then pointed his hands toward her to emphasize each word. "The. Future."

She smiled, the look of a satisfied teacher who has guided her pupil to a breakthrough.

"Mary Irene," he said. "You seem sincere enough and you clearly went to a lot of trouble to do an end run around around a police blockade to find me. But you really can't expect me to believe this. Can you?"

"All this will become clear, I swear to you."

"Fine. But you better hurry. Because"--he looked at his watch--"it's pushing on to 7:40. Less than an hour to Doomsday."

"Doomsday is coming. But not today." She looked off toward the great stone peak. "In 2035, the world cracks wide open down to the mantle, from Montana to Mexico. Tectonic stress, pressure. It fractures the entire continent, from sea to dying sea. It makes this volcano look like a child's firecracker. The scientists call it a Large Igneous Province and the start of a new geologic era. I call it the Mouth of Hell. The atmosphere all over the world is full of ash and smoke that blocks out the sun. It's always cold. Civilization starts to fall apart. It's long. Painful." She squeezed her eyes shut. "Violent."

"That's some story, Mary Irene," Trevor finally said. "And it makes me wonder, if it's true, why you'd want to bother saving me. Or anyone. If it's all going to end anyway."

"Because in spite of it all, we have hope." She paused. "Do you know the word conservator?

"Conservator. Like a museum curator?"

"Not quite. But close enough to get the idea. Your typewriter over there. I don't expect that's what's in your work office."

"No, not exactly. A personal computer and printer, along with an IBM Selectric."

"Hmm. Would it surprise you if I told you that just a few years from now, computers and practically every other electronic device you can think of will be connected through a global system of computer networks? The Internet? It's one of humanity's most incredible technological achievements. And it all comes to an end overnight when the earth splits open."

"Well, I'm impressed with the science fiction. I always loved H.G. Wells. But how does any of this make you a, what did you call it, a conservator?"

"I'm one of many. It's a union, or maybe guild is a better word. We find and restore pre-crash typewriters, just like your Corona 3. We build the communication infrastructure that keeps the words flowing and the world moving after the Internet is gone. The words are community. Commerce. Civilization. Life."

"So you're a conservator. From the future."

"Yes."

"So, conservator, how did you get here?"

She gave a rueful grin. "I died."

Crossing his arms, he said, "So now you're a time-traveling ghost."

"No. I'm as alive as you are."

He exhaled and spun in a circle, like a dog shaking water from his fur. "Look," he said. "You have to know how this sounds."

"Believe me, I know. I've had a lot of time, more than you know, to figure out how this all works. I don't claim to have it all figured out. But close enough.

"One Saturday morning in May 2070, I was in my study restoring a beautiful 1950s Royal Futura. And then, before I really knew what was happening, the earth erupted outside the house. I don't remember much about it. A flash of red light outside the window. Heat. Searing pain that I swear I could feel in every atom. I felt my body evaporating, swirling like smoke in a twister. I never even heard the sound. But I'm sure they did for many miles all around.

"It happens, sometimes. The Mouth of Hell is always hungry. It eats the Earth bite by bite from underneath. Entire towns, on stable ground far away from the wasteland. Just swallowed up or blown into the sky, without warning. Instant volcanoes. That's what happened to my house. Gone, like that. And me with it. That **should have been it**." She locked eyes with him again. "Except it wasn't."

"I was suddenly sprawled flat on my back on a city sidewalk, dressed in the work clothes I was wearing when the Mouth of Hell swallowed me." She giggled. "I guess I was lucky I wasn't in the bathtub when I died.

"But I felt alive, not dead. But I had no idea where I was, or how I got there. It was a small town. I later found out it was south of Kansas City. No one noticed I suddenly appeared there like a magic trick. I knew straight away I wasn't anywhere in the world I came from. The sky was blue and clean, like it is today. I could actually breathe the air. People were dressed in nice new clothes bought right from the store. There were cars everywhere, more than I'd **ever seen** ever. I walked around, trying to get my bearings. The newspaper I found on a park bench told me what I'd already started to figure. The date was Saturday, May 10, 1980.

"Somehow, that volcano tore the universe itself. A tear that's still open. Or a dimensional door. Whatever happened, I won some kind of cosmic once-in-a-millennium lottery that day. It's taken me many more lifetimes to figure this out. Because I haven't done this just once.

"After that first day, when time moved forward for me again, I died homeless on the streets a few months later. Hypothermia. I had no street smarts here, yet. Then it all started up again. Back to May 10, 1980. And it just kept happening."

"Like a record skipping."

"I suppose so. So many times I've lost count. I survived a few days on some loops. Several more decades on others. I've died a hundred different ways, some naturally and some...well, not. And every time that time reset, no one else in the world knew it had happened. At least not consciously. Only me. I remember every damn time. It all began in May 2070 and looped back to May 1980. And it just keeps looping, one concentric circle inside one and outside another. I **think this could** go on forever, quite literally." She clenched her arthritic fingers. "Except I think I know now how to stop it.

"I'm tired of immortality, Trevor. I was meant to die in 2070. What wasn't meant to happen was to fall into some kind of, I don't know, time trap I can't escape from. And every time it loops, it kills someone who didn't die the same way in the time I came from."

"You think I die here today. Because of you."

"Yes." Her voice was heavy. "I didn't know about you for many loops. Then, one day I was waiting to see a doctor about this damned arthritis. I saw your photo on the cover of a magazine on the chair next to me. I opened up the magazine and read an article about you. You didn't write it. Your editor Lori did, about a year after you died in the eruption. It was her eulogy for her colleague. Your body was never found. But you talked to her on the radio when the volcano erupted. She heard you die. Except I know you don't die this way. My coming here killed you as surely as if I'd shot you with a gun. Over and over again every time I looped."

She sighed. "Of course, I don't cause this volcano to erupt or those others to die. But funny thing about the universe. It's a poem. But not free verse. Everything has a meter. And it rhymes. I died when a volcano exploded under my house. I wasn't supposed to come back in time. But I did, and that's when you died in this eruption. Why, I don't know for sure. But I do know it's a couplet across time. Now, it's time to rewrite the couplet."

"So, we get out of here now?"

She winced and massaged her right knee. "No," she said hoarsely. "Even if we left right now in those cars, there's no time to get out of here down that road. All of this for miles around is going to be blown away."

"Then what was the point of this?" He

pointed toward the mountain. "If you're telling the truth, we'll both die here."

"Look," she said. "I've tried many times to stop you from coming to this mountain. I've tried to get to your office. Your home. Calls and letters never go through. I try to go there, something always happens to stop me. Bad luck. Car wreck. Once I even got shot. You're supposed to reach this mountain. I can't change that. But this is the first time I've ever been able to even see you, let alone talk to you."

"Which means what?"

"Which means the universe is trying to repair itself. Not in any kind of conscious way. More like a self-correcting machine trying to turn time back to what was before I began messing it all up. It threw me back as close to you as it could at the same time you were reporting from an active volcano. Except that somehow killed you when you hadn't been killed before by making you stay a day longer than you did before. But now I think that was so we could meet here to fix everything back."

"How does both of us getting killed fix anything?"

"If I'm right, I'll die for good in this eruption, like the one in 2070. Full circle. Closed loop. It's as close to the way I was supposed to die as I can manage. Time will go back to what it's supposed to be and you won't remember any of this because there'll be nothing to remember. You'll leave the mountain when you're supposed to and you'll go on to live your life. Now that's a good rhyme to rewrite the couplet."

He paced. "How can you possibly know that will work?"

"I don't, for sure. But it feels right. If I'm wrong, then I'll try something else the next turn of the wheel. I just know I can't stand you dying this way when it's because I'm here where I don't belong."

Her shoulders sagged. She looked spent.

He looked from the mountain to her. Then at his watch. "Well," he said. "It's about ten minutes away if it happens like you say it does. Nothing to do but wait, I guess."

He sat on the ground in a meditation posture to her right. Together they watched the summit of the mountain. Its granite slopes were still streaked with seams of snow even after the weeks of steam vents and earth tremors.

Mary Irene said, "I'm going to tell you something about yourself that I can't imagine anyone other than your mother and father know about. I doubt you even remember it at all. But I'll bet you will in a minute." She placed her hands on her knees and turned to face him.

"When you were two or three, you and your mom and dad lived in a house in Ironton, Illinois," she said. "Am I right?"

He nodded.

She said, "There was a railroad that went past town about a hundred yards from your house. When the trains went by in the middle of the night and shook the house, you would get scared, run into your mom and dad's bedroom, and jump into bed between them. You would cry, 'Mommy, Daddy. Monsters, monsters.' You were so little and so scared, but you knew nothing bad could happen to you with your mommy and daddy there." Her voice caught and she lowered her head.

He thought, <u>Damn, I do remember that. The trains roared like monsters and the house shook like it was an earthquake. Or at least that's what it sounded and felt like to a terrified little boy.</u>

"How do you know that?" he asked.

"I heard that story from my mom. But she never told anyone outside her family."

It suddenly came to him. "We're related."

"Yes." She released a shuddery breath. "You're my grandfather. My mom's dad."

He scrutized her features anew. She <u>did</u> look like his mother. That's what he had sensed about her earlier. The same jawline.

And that eye color that changed with the light like the sea.

"Who is your grandmother?" he asked. He didn't know how else to phrase it.

"Lori," Mary Irene said. "Your editor."

He had no words. He had never told another person how he felt about his boss.

"After you leave here on May 17th, yesterday, you'll see the eruption from a safe distance," Mary Irene said. "You'll then realize how little time one human life really is compared to geological time. You'll write that in your journal, the same one I'll read years later. At the same time as you meet your article deadline, you confess your love to Lori. She doesn't know what to do or say. After all, Trevor, she <u>is</u> your boss." Mary Irene smiled. "So you quit and get a job at a Seattle newspaper. The two of you start dating. You get married in 1984. Three years later, you have a daughter you name after your mother, Irene. Your daughter, my mother. I was born in 2015."

"Do we--you and me--know each other then?"

She shook her head. "No," she whispered. "I know you're going to ask, and because the only reason I'm telling you any of this is because you won't remember it, I'll tell you. You died in 2014, the year before I was born. It was quick. You didn't suffer. But you lived long enough to see your daughter marry a wonderful man. His name was Michael and you liked him very much." She laughed. "In spite of that, she married him anyway."

They fell silent and gazed at the mountain. The crisp air remained as breathless as it had been since dawn.

"I don't really know what to make of any of this," he said. "But I can say, I'm going to sit here with you and just see what happens at 8:32." He turned his Casio to her. "Which is two minutes from now."

"It's something I've always wanted to do," she said. "Meet Grandpa. Sit down with him. Talk." She smiled, almost shyly. "You're everything I expected."

"I assume that's good, right?"

She laughed. "Yes. Very good."

"So. What's my daughter like?"

"She reminds me of you. Calm. Quiet. She hears me out even if she doesn't believe me." She winked at him. "Never raises her voice. Good with words. She gave me that typewriter you're using. She loved you very much and wanted to be like you. I can hear it when she talks about you." Her voice trembled again. "It's going to break her heart when I die."

"You said it to me yourself. In spite of it all, we have hope."

She smiled and held her hand out to him. He took it. Her swollen fingers curled around his.

Then the earth lurched beneath them. "Earthquake," Trevor said. The trees around the campsite and off toward the mountain swayed. A rumble, faint at first, grew louder. Mary Irene's chair rocked from side to side. Both Trevor and Mary Irene planted their feet against the ground to steady themselves, as if they were sitting in a rowboat suddenly caught up in a series of deepening swells. He looked at his watch. 8:32. And finally he believed everything she had told him was true. She was his granddaughter.

"Mary Irene," he said. She looked back at him and saw in his eyes that he finally believed her as the earth convulsed under them and between them and around them all the way to the thousands of feet of mountain peak dominating the horizon. Tears streamed down her face. "Grandpa," she said. "I'm so sorry. We don't have much more time. Just a few more seconds and it will be over. This won't have happened to you. Everything will be set right again. I feel it."

Behind them, the table legs buckled and the typewriter fell to the ground with a thud that was nearly lost in the subterranean rumbling. He lurched to his feet as best he could. Mary Irene tried, but her bad knee prevented her. He pulled her up to him. She threw her right arm around his shoulder and leaned into him.

She let out a single sob as she dug her face deep into his chest.

He kissed the top of her head. "I'm glad we met, granddaughter."

"That note I typed," she said, her voice muffled into his shirt. "Please find it after if it's still there and do what it says. Please."

At that moment, as he looked away from her to the mountain, he saw the bulge in the north face of the mountain suddenly give way. The peak collapsed inward, as if the entire mountain had deflated. The north mountainside shattered instantly and thundered down to the green forest and lake below it. He could not comprehend the scale of what he was seeing. Almost simultaneously, air hit the suddenly exposed magma behind the landslide. Rock and pumice and ash and gases and molten rock exploded laterally in an enormous, boiling cloud that filled the entire sky. The superheated cloud raced to the landslide and consumed it and the forest and made their combined mass its own and roared at 400 miles per hour right toward Trevor and Mary Irene locked in their shivering embrace standing atop the ridge four scant miles away.

A childlike terror buckled him down to her and he shut his eyes tight. "Monsters," he cried to Mary Irene. He did not know he said that.

"Grandpa, I love--"

The pyroclastic cloud swept over the ridge and continued for another 15 miles. Geologists would later determine that everything within that direct blast zone, a circle of eight miles around the volcano, had been utterly obliterated. As if it had never existed at all.

On the Saturday morning of May 17th, 1980, as Trevor Landon sat down at his camp writing station to type his daily journal, he found a folded piece of paper in his portfolio that he had not noticed before. Curious, he pulled it free and opened it up. He could tell right away from the typeface that his Corona 3 had been used to type the note on the page. He read: <u>Trevor. Please tell Lori you're coming home now. It's the most important thing you'll ever do. It's not safe here. Time is short. Love, a friend.</u>

"That's weird," he said aloud. He did not remember typing this. But who else could have? He considered this for a few minutes, not quite sure what to do. Then he finally went to his radio to tell Lori he was leaving the mountain. It was time to come home.

✽✽✽✽✽✽✽✽✽✽✽✽✽✽✽✽✽✽✽✽✽✽✽✽✽✽✽✽✽✽✽✽✽✽✽✽
To my mother, Alice Irene Adams Simpson (1940-2020)

Royal KHY (rebuilt in 1939)

Contributors

DEDÉ ASSI, besides collecting and loving typewriters, recycles and creates steampunk art.

BRANDON BLEDSOE is a photographer, a stay-at-home parent, and a collector of hobbies. He enjoys letter writing, making zines, and quilting.

CLARA CHOW is a writer from Singapore. Her works include Dream Storeys (Ethos) and Modern Myths (Math Paper Press).

SHELLEY K. DAVENPORT lives in Pittsburgh, Pennsylvania. She writes stories when quarantine, cats, and children allow.

E.R. DELAFIELD lives in Central PA with her spoiled labrador retriever. Her first love was a green Smith Corona, which she stole from her mother.

FREDERIC S. DURBIN's latest novel, A GREEN AND ANCIENT LIGHT, received honors from PUBLISHERS WEEKLY and the American Library Association and won the Realm Award.

MATHILDA-ANNE FLORENCE is a Canadian Boreal Artist and Writer. She is a street poet along with Walter, her '29 Remington Portable 2. Three Gardenias is her first official publication.

DANIEL GEWERTZ is a writing teacher who covered Boston music, theater & movies for 30 years. He's been served tea by Jeremy Irons, sipped soda with Liberace, philosophized with Leonard Cohen & been photographed by Aretha Franklin.

N.E. GLENN writes for periodicals, advertising and PR, has been a test driver and instructor chef, and like Carole, is not a fan of time travel.

ALBERT GOLDBARTH's fingers have never touched a computer/laptop/tablet keyboard, and yet he thinks of himself as a regular kinda guy. His poetry has twice received the National Book Critics Circle Award.

MARTYN V. HALM, debauched poet and suspense fiction author of the Amsterdam Assassin Series, calls his turquoise 1957 Royal FP his partner in crime.

CHAD ALLEN HARRISON is an attorney by day, fantasy/sci-fi author by night. He, his wife, and their two kids live in Las Vegas, NV. chadallenharrison.com

MARTHA LEA aka Cloudy Type is author of The Specimen. She lives in the UK and has dreamt of time-travel since 1978. She loves the sea.

EWAN MATHESON chucked a promising career in the make-believe world of technology, for something more tangible and meaningful.

ANDREW V. MCFEATERS teaches literature and writing at University of New Mexico - Gallup, where he keeps the desert stars awake as he types into night.

BILL MEISSNER is the author of eight books, including The Mapmaker's Dream (poetry, Finishing Line Press) and a novel, Spirits in the Grass. He owns 21 lovely typing machines.

VINNY NEGRON is an American writer and typewriter enthusiast from the Northeast. Visit him on Instagram @soulpowertypewriters.

ERICH J. NOACK, lover of all things analog, lives in Kansas City with his wife and two cats, who are not analog. This is his second published piece of fiction.

CHARLES W. OGG is a retired professor, taught Sociology of News, reported for The Pitt News, and digs his Corona Sterling.

JOEY PATRICKT is a multiple media, digital/copy art artist in Oakland, Ca. He has been creating since 1972 on canvas, on paper, on stage, in the mail, on radio & TV. joeypatrickt.wordpress.com

MARK PETERSEN is a street poet, a storyteller, a collector of ancient or unusual things, a puddle splasher, and a seeker of magic portals.

RICHARD POLT is the author of The Typewriter Revolution, The Emergency of Being, and Time and Trauma. Yes, he has a melodramatic streak.

HANNAH RICKE
artist, writer
feet on the ground
head in the clouds

RACHEL SCHNELLINGER-BAILEY is a British writer, based in Switzerland.

MARNI SCOFIDIO is a US ex-pat, Welsh mountain-dweller, wicked stepmom. Debut novel is Knucklebones (PS Publishing).

PHILIP L. SIMPSON is a provost at Eastern Florida State College. He is a published writer of books, chapters in edited collections, journal articles, and short fiction.

DENISE TERRIAH is the author of the novel As It Ends and several published short stories. She writes on a typewriter whenever possible.

ARMANDO WARNER is a writer and restorer for "Californication Typewriter", Mexico. He has written 2 novels & 2 poetry collections.

MATT WIXEY is a cyber security researcher, PhD student, and playwright from London. He enjoys writing horror and sci-fi, and collecting (unhaunted) typewriters.

Manufactured by Amazon.ca
Bolton, ON